LIGHTNING STRIKES

STORM SERIES
BOOK 3

MELODY LOOMIS

Cover Design by
Vania Rheault via Canva.com

Title Font 1: Quicksand
Title Font 2: Brittany by Creative Fabrica
Author Font: Bebas Neue

Pictures purchased and used
with permission at depositphotos.com
Couple Photo ID: 128056506, @oneinchpunch
Lightning Photo ID: 4555353, @andrejs83

A NOTE TO THE READER

Content Warning: While there are no graphic scenes, this book has brief mentions of childhood abuse (all forms, including CSA), suicide, depression, workplace harassment, an assault on a female, death by drug overdose, and death of a parent. If you are sensitive to any of these topics, please read with care.

1

A sheet of rain pelted Elmer Sullivan's windshield as he passed a closed citrus stand. A homemade sign advertised it as "The Sunshine State's Best Oranges."

"Sunshine State my ass," Sullivan muttered. He had been here for two days, and he'd seen nothing but gray skies. Though of course, that was the whole point. Late May into June was when Florida's thunderstorm season began, and Sullivan was here for it. If only this damn rain would let up, maybe he wouldn't be late for his new job.

He turned up his music and felt the familiar jonesing for a smoke. He reached into the center console for his pack of Marlboro, found nothing, and remembered he smoked the last one yesterday. Fortunately, he had his emergency pack in the glove compartment.

Sullivan kept his eyes on the road as he fished around for the cigarettes. He grabbed the open pack and shook one out with his right hand with his left hand on the wheel. Once the cigarette was in his mouth, he felt around for his lighter in the cup holder. It was somewhere around here. Finally, he found it, and just as he was prepared to light up, a red Honda sedan pulled out in front of him.

Cigarette forgotten, Sullivan slammed on the brakes. He couldn't stop in time, and the front of the Honda collided with the passenger side of his Jeep Cherokee.

Well, *fuck*. This day was off to a fantastic start.

Sullivan eased his vehicle to the side of the road. Through the blur of rain, he tried to see how much damage the other car sustained, but he couldn't quite get a good view. Groaning, he pulled the hood of his raincoat over his head and stepped outside to survey the damage.

With his shoes splashing into several puddles on the grass, Sullivan walked around his vehicle. The impact of the collision had left a dent on the passenger door and a decent scrape in the paint. Sullivan knew little about car values, but his Cherokee had plenty of miles on it. He'd spent the past decade chasing tornadoes all over the central Plains, and it had been along for every ride. Even if the damage didn't look all that bad, this accident was likely to total it. *Shit.*

He turned his attention to the Honda, which had more substantial damage. The hood was crumpled, and the bumper had been torn off. It was definitely totaled, and certainly not driveable.

Standing in front of the vehicle was a woman in a red poncho. He knew it was a woman because her hood had fallen off, and the rain had soaked her long, dark hair. But at the moment, she seemed more upset about her car than her hair. She waved her fists in the air and literally stomped her foot as a string of angry Spanish curse words flew out of her mouth. Sullivan stifled a laugh. He was known to lose his temper, but he'd never seen a grown woman stomp before. She must not be hurt if she could move like that.

"Well, better get this over with," he said to himself, then slowly walked over to her. His introverted nature made talking to people difficult. Unfortunately, a conversation couldn't be avoided. At least she was attractive, so it wouldn't be all bad.

The woman glanced his way as Sullivan moved closer. Her eyes were dark, and she looked mad enough to hit someone. Sullivan racked his brain to remember his high school Spanish class. "Uh, *habla inglés*?"

"Yes," she said, a little short.

"Okay, I wasn't sure." He didn't know much Spanish, but he knew all the curse words, and she had spoken almost all of them. He looked at her vehicle. "You won't be able to drive that."

"I'm aware. I'll get it towed to my brother-in-law's body shop."

Like a faucet turning off, the rain stopped, and the woman looked up at the sky. "*Now* the rain stops."

Sullivan took the hood off his head, as it was harder to see with it on, then reached for her fallen bumper. "I'll move this out of the road for you."

"*Gracias.*"

Sullivan liked the way her voice had a lilt to it, but he couldn't think about a pretty woman right now. He had a busy day, and a car accident was not in his plan. He placed the damaged bumper onto the shoulder. "Look, I have somewhere I have to be. You want to just exchange information? I don't see any reason to call the cops."

The woman nodded. "Agreed. Who do you have insurance with?"

"The one with the lizard commercials."

"Okay, let me snap a photo of your insurance card, and I'll call Geico and file a claim for you."

Something about what she said didn't make sense. "Wait a minute. Did you say you'll call *my* insurance company?"

"Yes."

Sullivan chuckled, though not that he found anything

funny. Was she serious? "Lady, I'm afraid you have that backwards. Unless you also have a policy with Geico, you need to call *your* insurance company. You were the one at fault."

Her eyes widened. "You think this accident was my fault?"

"I was just going along my merry way until you pulled out in front of me," Sullivan said in an irritated tone.

"No, you were speeding! This road here has a limit of thirty-five, and you had to be going at least forty-five, way too fast for the rainy conditions."

Sullivan pointed to the stop sign. "You see that sign over there? That means you're supposed to yield."

"How could I see you when you were driving without your lights on? You're supposed to have those on when it's raining. Florida law."

"Did you even look both ways when you were turning?"

"Of course, and you wouldn't have hit me had you been going slower." She glared at him.

Sullivan reached for the phone in his pocket. He should have known she'd be argumentative. She had been yelling at her wrecked car. "Well, I guess we're at an impasse. I'll call the police after all. We'll let them sort this out."

"Yes, you do that. And tell them how fast you were going!"

Sullivan muttered a curse as he walked back to his damaged Jeep. He was definitely going to be late now. At least Professor Torres was cool. He'd understand. Sullivan would be sure to text him after he called the cops.

When he got off the phone with the 911 operator, he watched the woman from his mirror. Her rear end stuck out as she bent down to examine the damage. Sullivan cursed himself for checking out her ass.

A light rain started again, and the woman got back into her vehicle. Sullivan reached for his cigarette. Might as well get in his smoke while he waited for the cops.

Isabel Torres Fuentes balled up the citation in her hand. The cop found her at fault for failure to yield, even though that jerk had clearly been speeding and driving without his headlights on. Now, she had a wrecked car, and her insurance was sure to go up. When it rained, it poured. Isabel hit the steering wheel with the flat of her palm, then regretted losing her temper. All that accomplished was making her hand hurt.

A car engine roared to life, and the dark-haired guy in the Jeep took off. Isabel glared in his direction. If they had met under friendlier terms, she would have struck up a conversation about the weather gadgets attached to his roof. He had Kansas plates, so she guessed he was one of those storm chasers. But what was he doing here in Florida?

Shit. Did he know her *tío?* If he had anything to do with the meteorology department at the university, she'd run into him again. She really hoped he wasn't Tío Fernando's former student who was starting today. No, he couldn't be. Isabel was pretty sure that guy was from Texas.

Isabel uncrumpled the paperwork the officer gave her. In addition to the citation was a driver exchange form, which she would need for her insurance claim. His name was Elmer Sullivan, and Isabel smiled. *Elmer?* What kind of old-fashioned name was that? He should be called Mr. Grumpy Ass. He looked like he never smiled.

A horn beeped. Isabel glanced in her rearview mirror and saw her mother's white Toyota. She gathered her purse, along with her soaked poncho, and got out.

The back door of the sedan opened, and her six-year-old son Miguel ran out. "*¡Mamá!* Your car!" His small hand ran across the crushed exterior.

"I know, *nene*, it looks bad."

"*¡Mija!* Thank God you're not hurt!" Carlita, her mother, hurried over to her. "You're not hurt, are you?"

She had a feeling her neck would bother her later, but there was no need to worry her mother over that. "I'm fine. It's my car that's in bad shape. I've already got Ricardo's tow truck guy on the way."

"Tío Ricardo can fix it!" Miguel said.

Isabel eyed the bumper on the ground. The car was old, and she was almost certain it was totaled. And just when she finally paid the damn loan off. "I'm not sure it can be fixed, *nene.* I'll probably need a new one."

"You can borrow my car, *mija,*" Carlita said. "I don't need it today."

"*Gracias, Mamá.*" Isabel looked at her watch. "I was supposed to be at work forty-five minutes ago, but this tow truck is taking forever."

"Fernando won't mind if you're late," Carlita said.

"I know. I already texted him, and he said to take my time. But his former student is coming on board for the lightning video project. I should be there."

Carlita frowned. "You're going to get struck by lightning if you're not careful, *mija.* I really wish you could find a less dangerous line of work. Why can't you see if another news station is hiring?"

"*Mamá,* don't worry. The cameras are inside the truck. I'll be fine."

"I know you, Isabel. You're just like your father, always taking unnecessary risks. You be careful if you get out of that vehicle. No picture or video of a lightning strike is worth your life. I'm glad this job of yours is only for three months."

"I'll be careful, *Mamá,*" Isabel said.

The tow truck finally arrived, and after her beat up Honda was hauled away, Isabel went back to the house to drop off her mother and Miguel. They lived on the same property, though

Isabel and Miguel stayed in the detached garage apartment. Her mother only charged her half the rent of a regular apartment in town, and she was nearby to take care of Miguel when she was at work.

Miguel came to the driver's side window. "When will you be home, *Mamá?*"

"I'll try to be back before dark. Be good, and let Abuela give you your insulin injection, okay? No arguments."

"*Sí, Mamá.*"

"Please be safe, *mija*," Carlita said.

"I'll drive more carefully this time. At least it's not pouring rain right now." Though hopefully, the rain would pick back up later. She needed a good thunderstorm to lift her mood and get this day back on track.

SULLIVAN'S WRECKED Jeep rolled into the parking lot. His GPS told him he was at the right place. Professor Torres said it would be a nondescript office building next to a field with a tall tower. This was it.

Inside, there was no one at the front desk. Sullivan peered down the hall and saw a room with the door open. "Professor Torres? Are you back there?"

A man with graying hair emerged from the office. "Sullivan, you made it. Have a hard time finding the place?"

"No, but I'm sorry I'm late."

"Hey, it's okay. You can't help that you were in an accident. Must be the morning for that. My niece had a wreck with someone too. That rain caused a lot of headaches. Well, are you ready to see the LIV?"

"Hell yes."

Torres grabbed a key from the wall hook and headed to the door.

At the edge of the parking lot sat a white box truck. Sullivan had seen it when he pulled in, but hadn't realized this was the LIV. He'd been used to his buddy Ryder's tornado chasing vehicle, so the ordinary truck seemed like a letdown.

"I know what you're thinking," Torres said. "It doesn't look like much from the outside. The inside is where it stands out."

Torres unlatched the rear door and lifted it up. "Here she is. The Lightning Intercept Vehicle."

Sullivan heaved himself up to get a closer look inside. There were computer monitors, a spider's nest of cords, and camera equipment everywhere. Above his head, the truck had been outfitted with a dome skylight. Sullivan spotted a camera mounted in the middle of it.

"This the camera?" Sullivan asked.

"Yep, that's her," Torres replied. "High-speed, high-resolution. Expensive as hell. It rotates 360 degrees. You don't even have to leave the comfort of the truck to use it."

Torres indicated the front, where a section of the truck had been removed so that the operator could literally walk from the driver's seat to the computer.

"There's a few more cameras mounted to the dash," Torres continued, "but this is the main one. You can see what the camera sees from the monitors."

For the next fifteen minutes, Torres gave Sullivan a crash course at how to use the camera equipment. The goal was to get lightning on video so it could be played back in slow motion to study it.

"You did a hell of a job with the LIV," Sullivan said.

"Oh, it wasn't just me. An entire group of people at the university got this project off the ground. I'm glad you wanted to be a part of this."

Sullivan sat in the driver's seat with the door open as he got a feel for it. "When you offered, I couldn't say no. Hours out in the field chasing thunderstorms. Who could refuse that?"

"If you'd like to take the LIV out for a test drive before the afternoon storms fire up, feel free. Isabel is used to driving it already. One of you can drive while the other monitors the radar."

Sullivan's eyebrow twitched. "I thought I'd be working alone."

"No, my niece will join you. I didn't tell you that? Chasing storms is a lot easier with two sets of eyes. She's a hell of a meteorologist. In fact, I think that's her now."

A white Toyota pulled into a nearby parking space. Sullivan looked at the driver and recognized the dark-haired woman.

The woman he'd had an accident with just an hour ago.

Well, *fuck.*

2

It was bad enough that he'd have a partner, but did it have to be *her?* He'd seen her name on the driver exchange form, but didn't give a second thought to the fact that her surname was Torres. He figured that was a common name around here. But of course, she had to be related to the professor.

She emerged from the car and shielded her eyes from the sun. Now that the rain had stopped, the humidity was so thick it felt hard to breathe. Yes, it had to be the humidity. It wasn't that she was so attractive that she took his breath away. Without that red poncho, he could see the curves of her hips and the fullness of her chest. Why did she have to look like *that?*

Torres waved her over. "Isabel, come meet Sullivan. I was just showing him the LIV."

Sullivan put his lusty thoughts aside and remembered he was annoyed. Here he was, thinking that he'd be out on the road by himself, but he'd been wrong. She was going to ruin his solitude by tagging along. He hopped down from the truck and headed over to where Isabel stood. "You," he said, his eyes locking with hers.

"And you," she said, her tone accusatory.

Torres looked from Isabel to Sullivan. "You two already met?"

Isabel glared at Sullivan. "*Sí,* Tío. He's the guy who was speeding and hit my car."

"Because you failed to yield," Sullivan said, shooting eye daggers right back at her. "That's what the officer cited you for."

"But you were going too fast and didn't have your lights on!"

"Doesn't matter. You were the one with the stop sign."

Torres stepped in between them. "Whoa, okay, let's calm down. Look, it was an accident. They happen. But we've got a job to do. Let's put aside this hostility, because you two will have to work together. Can you both do that?"

His tone reminded Sullivan of a father gently scolding his children, though not that Sullivan would know what that was like. The only father figure he had growing up was Dick. Dick wouldn't have had a talk with him like some television dad. Dick would have beaten him with his fist.

"*Sí,* Tío," Isabel said.

Torres looked at him. "Sullivan?"

Sullivan nodded. "Right, we got a job to do."

The frown faded from Torres's face. "*Excelente.* Now, let's show Sullivan the rest of the facility."

ISABEL FELT a headache coming on as she followed Tío Fernando and Mr. Grumpy Ass inside. This day was going from bad to worse. She already didn't like the guy, and now she had to work with him for three months.

Three long months.

Despite her annoyance with her new coworker, she had no plans to quit. Tío Fernando had given her this opportunity when she had to leave her job at the station, and she needed the money. She'd just have to try to get along with him.

"Can I see some footage from the LIV's cameras?" Sullivan asked.

"Of course. It's on my laptop. I'll be right back."

Fernando disappeared down the hallway, leaving Isabel alone with Sullivan.

"Did you call your insurance company yet?" Sullivan asked.

His tone suggested he'd be pissed if she hadn't. Isabel was in no mood for it. "Of course. They'll be in touch, so keep your pants on. I can't believe you're Tío Fernando's favorite student. You must be really good at what you do, because otherwise, you're not a very likable person."

"I thought I was going to be working alone. I didn't know Torres was going to let his niece tag along."

"I'm not tagging along. I'm here to do a job, same as you."

"I just don't think it requires two people to take a video."

Isabel got into his face, determined to not let him belittle her purpose here. "If that's how you really feel, there's the door." She pointed behind her and hoped he would walk. There was a hint of cigarette smoke on his clothes, and she was already tired of smelling it. Yet another thing to not like about him.

To Isabel's relief, Fernando came back into the room. "Okay, I've got the footage cued up."

He placed his laptop on the counter and played the video Isabel had taken two nights ago. She'd driven an hour away just to get it, but it had been a beautiful storm with frequent cloud to ground lightning. The clip showed a lightning stroke in slow motion.

"Look at that return stroke," Fernando said.

Sullivan replayed the clip. "That's amazing. You take that?"

"No, that was all Isabel." Fernando placed his arm around

her shoulder. "Isabel is a great photographer. She gets that from her father."

Sullivan looked at Isabel with his resting grump face. He almost looked disappointed.

Fernando pulled up the weather site on his computer. "We should check out the forecast for today."

"Already did," Isabel said. "Some thunderstorms will develop near Ocala today."

"Great. After lunch, you two can hit the road. Well, Sully, how about that grand tour now? I could show you the tower."

"Lead the way," Sullivan said, following him out the back door.

Isabel opted not to join them. She didn't need to spend any more time with Mr. Grumpy. And to think at first, she thought he might be a nice guy. He did move her bumper out of the road, but then got an attitude when she suggested the accident was his fault. She didn't care what the officer said. Maybe she had failed to yield, but he was still partially at fault.

Isabel looked up from her phone when Fernando came back, and was relieved Sullivan wasn't with him. "Where's Mr. Grumpy?"

"Isabel," Fernando warned.

She sighed. "I'm sorry, Tío, but why did you choose him? You have hundreds of former students you could have picked."

Fernando walked to the window and stared out into the parking lot. "Because, *princesa*, he's one of the best damn students I've ever had. And I knew no one else, except maybe you, appreciated a good lightning storm like I do."

Isabel followed Fernando's gaze out the window. Sullivan stood in the parking lot puffing away on a cigarette. She narrowed her eyes as he exhaled a cloud of smoke.

"Just try to get along with him, okay? You got off to a rocky start, but he's a good meteorologist. And more importantly, I trust him to be alone with you. Unlike that Mateo guy. You'll be safe with him, *princesa.*"

Her uncle smiled at her, and she smiled back, touched that he had taken that into consideration. "Thank you, Tío." She wasn't looking forward to working with this guy, but hell, she'd take him over Mateo any day.

Fernando reached for his laptop. "I wish I could be out there in the LIV with you, but I've got too much work with these summer courses. Not to mention I still need to get ready for next semester."

"You should retire. You work too hard."

"Why? I love what I do."

"I know, but if you leave your teaching position, maybe I could take your place."

Fernando laughed. "You'd be wonderful at it, *princesa.*"

The door opened and Sullivan came back in. He brought with him the stench of cigarettes, and Isabel tried not to gag.

Sullivan caught her staring at him. "What?"

"Haven't you heard that smoking kills you?"

He just grunted, then headed for the break room.

After lunch, Sullivan headed outside for another smoke. There wasn't much to do until the storms fired up. The tour Torres gave him of the lightning research facility was mildly entertaining. He was intrigued by the tower in which Torres ran lightning experiments, but today wasn't the best day for that. Another time, for sure.

About midway through his cigarette, his phone rang. Sullivan groaned as he dug his cell out of his pocket. He hated talking to anyone on the phone, but he supposed he'd make an exception for the one friend he had.

"How's the Sunshine State?" Ryder asked when Sullivan answered.

"The humidity is already pissing me off." Sullivan took a drag of his cigarette.

"I told you it would! I can't believe you took a job in Florida. And right at the height of tornado season. What are you going to chase in Florida?"

"Florida has tornadoes."

"Sure, those weak little waterspouts that come on shore, huh?"

Sullivan knew Ryder was just ribbing him, but it pissed him off all the same. He knew how to get him to shut up. "I saw you missed that EF3 outside of Tulsa over the weekend. That was practically in your backyard."

Ryder sighed on the other end. "Yeah. I'm still pissed about that. I thought the storm in Texas would be better. Kit tried to tell me, but I wouldn't listen."

Sullivan shook the ash off his cigarette. "How is Kit? Must be tiring for her to deal with both you and a baby. And she still has time to publish a paper on the fluctuating velocity of a tornado."

"I don't know how she does it, Sully. I told you she was a better meteorologist than me."

"She kicks your ass every time." Sullivan cracked a smile and took another drag.

"Are you smoking?" Ryder asked.

"Don't give me another lecture about quitting, not unless you're ready to give up beef jerky and Mountain Dew. Those are bad for you too."

"Fine. So, tell me about the job. You ride around in that lightning vehicle yet? What does Professor Torres call it?"

Sullivan glanced at the vehicle in question and shook the ashes from his cigarette. "The LIV—Lightning Intercept Vehicle. And no, we haven't gone out yet. Waiting for the storms to fire up." Sullivan took a final puff of his cigarette.

"Wait a sec—we? Is Torres going with you? I thought you said you'd be on the road by yourself."

Sullivan tossed the cigarette on the pavement and snuffed it out with his shoe. "Yeah, I thought so too, but Torres insisted his niece ride with me."

"Niece, huh?" Ryder said, his voice indicating he was intrigued by this development. "Is she attractive?"

She was gorgeous. If he'd met her under any other circumstance, he'd like to take her to bed. But Isabel was feisty, and it was obvious they wouldn't get along.

"Well?" Ryder asked when Sullivan didn't respond.

"She's Torres's niece."

"You didn't answer my question."

Sullivan sighed. "Yes, she's attractive."

"Oh, so you have to be on the road for hours with a pretty woman. That must be such a hardship for you."

"We already don't get along."

"You don't get along with anyone."

Sullivan just grunted.

Isabel stepped outside and headed for the LIV. "Are you coming, or are you going to talk on the phone all day?"

"Sully?"

Distracted by Isabel, Sullivan realized he didn't hear Ryder's question. "Sorry, I got to go. Time for us to hit the road. I'll talk to you later."

"All right. Enjoy those waterspouts!" Ryder laughed before ending the call.

Isabel was already climbing into the driver's seat. No way in hell was he letting her drive. He knew from experience that she caused accidents.

"I'll drive," he said, staring her down.

Isabel didn't move. "Oh, hell no. I'm driving. You go too fast."

"You don't pay attention and pull out in front of people," he snapped.

"I've been driving the LIV for weeks. I know what I'm doing."

Sullivan dug a quarter out of his pocket. "Let's flip for it."

"Fine. I call heads."

Sullivan tossed the quarter in the air, grabbed it, and placed it on the back of his hand. He grinned. "It's tails. I'm driving."

Isabel glared at him, but she moved out of the seat. Sullivan took his place behind the wheel and buckled up. It was going to be a wild ride.

For the first twenty minutes, the drive was silent, save for Sullivan's irritating country music, which Isabel had told him to turn down twice already. It made her head pound.

When Tío Fernando joined her, the drive was enjoyable. They'd listen to the Spanish music station, and he'd entertain her with stories of her father when they were kids. The present company, however, was anything but pleasant. He never smiled and didn't talk much, preferring to answer her questions in grunts and facial expressions.

She stared out the window and let her mind wander. She hadn't given a thought to dinner tonight, and Miguel's insulin was running low. She'd have to make a pharmacy run soon. She tried to get her mind off her troubles and focus on the fun stuff, like the dark clouds that were developing. It definitely looked like it would be a lightning producer.

A flickering sound pulled her out of her thoughts. She snapped her head around to see Sullivan lighting up a cigarette.

"Hey! You can't smoke in the LIV!"

He took a puff and blew the smoke out the window, but Isabel caught a whiff of it anyway. "Put that out!"

He muttered a curse and tossed it out the window.

"You know, most people would have the courtesy to ask if they could smoke before lighting up."

"I didn't even realize I was doing it."

The smell of nicotine still lingered, and Isabel turned the air conditioner on full blast to get some air circulating. "You should have realized you can't smoke inside here. This isn't your own personal vehicle. It belongs to the university. Do you know how expensive all this equipment is?"

"I got the message. Loud and clear. Don't make such a big fucking deal about it. I just did that out of habit, okay?"

"A filthy habit," Isabel muttered.

"I guess Little Miss Perfect doesn't have any of those, huh?"

She was about to make a retort when Sullivan took the exit. "Why did you get off the interstate?"

"I'm going to stop at this gas station up ahead."

"We don't need gas. It's nearly a full tank."

Sullivan stopped at the intersection. "I know, but I need a smoke, so we're stopping."

Isabel rolled her eyes. "Oh, by all means then, let's stop work so you can go have your damn cigarette. *Que te folle un pez.*" It wasn't every day that she wished someone to be fucked by a fish, but she felt like saying it today.

Sullivan glared at her. "What did you say to me?"

Isabel smirked. "Wouldn't you like to know?"

SULLIVAN FELT BETTER after his smoke and got back behind the wheel. Some Spanish song was playing on the radio, and he narrowed his eyes at Isabel. "You changed the station."

"Yeah. I got tired of hearing that song about the cowboy drowning his sorrows in beer."

Sullivan turned the dial back to his station. "I'm not driving for an hour listening to music I can't understand."

"Well I don't want to listen to some whining guy with a guitar." Isabel switched the station again.

"Okay, new rule. The one who's driving gets control of the radio. When it's your turn, you can listen to all the Spanish music you want. Deal?"

Isabel sighed. "I guess that's fair, but I get to drive on the way home."

He turned the dial back to the country station. "Anything popping up on the radar?" He hated to ask. If he had it his way, he'd be on his own and would have the radar all to himself.

"Nothing yet, but the models indicate some storms will be south of Ocala in about forty-five minutes. It'll be a shame if we miss them because you had to take a ten-minute smoke break."

"It was five minutes tops," Sullivan snapped.

From the passenger seat, Isabel gave him an icy stare before turning her attention back to the radar. He didn't know why she made such a big deal about stopping for a few minutes. Though she was right about one thing. They had better get a move on. The storms would develop soon, and they still had miles to go.

Just south of the Ocala city limits, a few cells popped up. They parked outside a shopping center to determine their next course of action.

Sullivan leaned over the console to get a better look at the computer. "The north cell looks good."

"Yeah, but the south cell looks better."

"I'm the one driving. I'm the one who makes the decisions."

Isabel crossed her arms. "Excuse me, but what part of partnership do you not understand? We're supposed to be working together."

He didn't feel like arguing again. "I guess there's only one way to solve this problem."

"Yeah, you move back to Kansas."

Sullivan reached into his pocket for his quarter. "I was going to suggest we flip for it."

"Fine. Heads we go south, tails we go north."

"Shouldn't it be the other way around?"

Isabel gave him an annoyed look. "Just flip the damn quarter."

He flipped it and cursed when it landed on heads.

Isabel looked practically giddy. "Looks like we're going south."

Sullivan grumbled to himself as he put the LIV into drive. "You better be right about this storm."

"I am. I've lived in Florida for most of my life. I know these storms like the back of my hand."

He wanted to know why she thought going south was a better option, but that would imply that he actually wanted to talk to her. And he didn't. So instead, he silently fumed about not getting his way while he headed south.

When they arrived at the target location, Sullivan parked the LIV where they had a good view of the storm clouds in the distance. A beautiful bolt of lightning streaked across the gray sky. Sullivan would never admit it, but Isabel had been right about the south cell. The north one petered out, while the southern one grew stronger.

Isabel hurried to the back of the vehicle. "Let's get this on video before it's over."

Sullivan watched as Isabel sprang into action. Even though Torres had shown him all the features of the LIV, Isabel was clearly the expert. In no time at all, she had all cameras poised in position to capture the storm. Sullivan barely had to lift a finger, which was actually kind of nice. Not that he would admit that either.

Sullivan grabbed his own personal camera and pressed record. He made a mental note to clean the windshield later. A bird had shat on it earlier, and it didn't completely wipe off with the wipers, thus ruining his view of the lightning show.

Isabel headed back to the passenger seat and reached for her own camera. She then pulled out a tripod from under the seat and opened the door.

"What the hell are you doing?" Sullivan said.

"What does it look like? I'm going to set my camera up."

They were far enough from the storm to not have any rain, but lightning still posed a risk. It was a risk Sullivan took sometimes when he chased tornadoes, but he knew when to back off. "That lightning is intense. You should stay in the vehicle."

"I'll only be a second," she said, and closed the door behind her.

He watched as she set up the recorder on her tripod. Not only did she piss him off, but she was stubborn as hell.

There was a loud rumble of thunder as Isabel got back inside the LIV. The storm was getting closer.

"You have all these cameras on the truck. Why do you need one outside too?"

"That isn't for the LIV. It's for Miguel, my son. He likes it when I do the time-lapse videos. He calls them my movies."

He wanted to be annoyed with her, but the fact that she was a mother made it hard to hate her now. It was obvious from the tone of voice that she cared about her son.

Isabel caught his eye. "Why are you staring at me like that?"

Sullivan shook his head. "No reason. Just didn't realize you had a kid."

"Miguel is the best thing that ever happened to me. He's six, almost seven."

"You're married?" As soon as he asked, he noticed there was no ring on her finger. The only jewelry she wore was a silver cross necklace.

"No," Isabel answered. "Miguel's father took off the moment he found out I was pregnant. Said he wasn't able to be a father. I didn't know where he was until my cousin Eddie tracked him down in Puerto Rico."

"What happened then?"

Her chin trembled. "Nothing," she said, her voice cracking. "He died of a drug overdose. They found him in his hotel room. Lorenzo struggled with addiction for a long time. And now, Miguel will never know his father."

She dabbed the corner of her eye with a tissue, and Sullivan felt like a jerk for making her cry. "I'm sorry. I know that must be hard for your little boy. I never met mine either. Left before I was born too." He felt a twinge in his chest as he thought of how it felt growing up without a father. He'd been jealous that other boys had their dads around, but that wasn't in the cards for him. Even before he was born, people wanted nothing to do with him.

A crack of thunder turned their focus to the oncoming storm, a welcomed relief from the heavy conversation. A dazzling lightning show was happening about five miles from where they were, and it was a sight to see. They watched the storms shift west to east for a half hour.

"It happens so fast," Isabel said. "It's amazing all the detail you can see when it's on video in slow motion."

Sullivan always enjoyed a good lightning show. It always made him think of his little sister, Emmy. He wondered if storms were happening where she was, and if so, did she remember what he told her?

You don't need to be scared. That loud boom is just a positive charge meeting a negative charge, and it makes a pretty flash. It's like a firecracker in the sky.

Isabel got out of the truck, interrupting his thoughts. She hurried to get her camera gear inside. Seconds after she was back in the vehicle, it poured rain. "Whew, I got in just in time!"

Isabel said with a laugh. "Now, get out of my seat. It's my turn to drive. We got our lightning, and I'm ready to go home."

It was just after six o'clock when Isabel made it home. Her sister's car was in the driveway, so Isabel headed for her mother's house. She still didn't know what to do for dinner, but she had a hunch that her mother would happily fix her and Miguel a plate.

"Hi, *Mamá!*" Miguel shouted from his friend's front yard.

Isabel waved at him. "Hi, *nene!* We'll eat dinner at Abuela's. Come inside soon, okay?"

She entered the house and found her mother and her sister, Paulina, at the counter preparing a meal. "Perfect, I'm starving." Isabel headed straight for the freezer and took out the ice pack. Her neck was killing her.

Carlita turned around. "Headache, *mija?*"

"My neck hurts."

"*Mamá* told me about your car accident this morning," Paulina said. "Ricardo said he'll look at your car tomorrow."

Isabel molded the ice pack around the back of her neck and sat in the living room recliner. "Thanks."

"Can I get you anything, *mija?*" Carlita asked.

"Just a plate for me and Miguel would be great."

"I'm staying too," Paulina said. "Ricardo took the kids out for pizza."

Isabel sighed. She'd love to go out for pizza, but with Miguel's diabetes, pizza was tricky.

Carlita came into the living room with a glass of water. "Drink this. You've been on the road for hours and are probably dehydrated."

Isabel took the glass, wondering how her mother knew she was thirsty, and took a grateful sip.

Paulina placed four plates on the table. "Did Tío Fernando's student start today?"

"Yes, and I don't like him. It was such a bad day. Not only did I wreck my car this morning, but the guy I had an accident with is the same guy I have to work with."

Paulina flinched. "Oof. Talk about bad luck."

"What's wrong with him?" Carlita asked, resuming her work in the kitchen.

"He never smiles. He argues with me. He smokes. We had to stop like three times so he could have a cigarette break."

Carlita smiled. "Your father used to smoke. It was when we first met."

Isabel raised an eyebrow. "I never knew that."

"That's because I told him I wouldn't marry him unless he quit. He never picked up a cigarette again after that." Carlita laughed.

The screen door slammed, and a sweaty Miguel ran in. "*¡Mamá!* Juan got a puppy! Can we get one too?"

"No, *nene*, no pets right now. We'll talk about it next year." She could barely afford his medication. There was no way she could take on the additional expense of a pet.

Miguel looked disappointed, but seemed to understand. "Okay. Well, can I go with Juan and his parents to take it to the vet?"

Isabel smiled. "I'll talk to Juan's mother. Now go wash the puppy smell off your hands. We'll eat dinner soon."

Miguel ran to the bathroom, and Carlita laughed. "He's been over there playing with that dog all day."

Isabel smiled. "At least he didn't miss me while I was at work."

~

Sullivan's Airbnb rental wasn't much to brag about. It had a musty smell that greeted him every time he came home, and the "home gym" consisted of only a treadmill and hand weights. But the place was furnished, and it was easier than getting an apartment for three months. At least it was only temporary.

He was glad to be done with everything for the day. Relieved to be alone was more like it. Sullivan could only handle people in small increments, and then he had to be at home by himself to decompress and recharge his battery.

He had a voicemail from Isabel's insurance company and decided to call them tomorrow. Of all the people to have an accident with, he hated it had been Torres's niece. And now, he had to work with her. Which in all honesty, hadn't been that horrible, except for maybe her music on the drive home. Still, he would have preferred to operate the LIV by himself.

After eating a frozen meal in front of the television, he reached for his laptop. He pulled up his old Facebook account, the one Ryder forced him to make, and searched again for the Emmy Sullivan who lived in Clearwater, Florida.

Everyone thought Sullivan took this job because he needed a change. And part of that was true. Though he enjoyed being a meteorologist, he hated his job at the airlines. More specifically, it was the people he couldn't stand. His supervisor, the fucker, wrote in his evaluation that he needed to work on getting along with others. Made it sound like a first grader's report card.

But the real reason he accepted Professor Torres's offer was the possibility that Emmy was here. He couldn't explain why he felt the urge to locate his sister after all these years. Maybe it was the fact that he was getting older and felt more alone than ever. Sure, he pushed people away because he enjoyed his solitude, but she was the only family he had left. And as Ryder often reminded him, smoking was going to send him to an early grave. If he were to die tomorrow, he'd regret not knowing what became of her.

The couple who took her in, the Johnsons, were no longer alive. Sullivan came across their obituaries a few months ago. James Johnson had died three years ago of some sort of illness that put him in hospice care. His wife died a year later, killed in a car accident, according to a news article. There was no mention of Emmy in the obituaries or any other children they may have had. Did Emmy have foster or adopted siblings she was close to? Or was she entirely on her own in the world now?

One thing he knew for certain was that somehow, she ended up in Florida. He hoped she was still in Clearwater. And maybe Professor Torres offering him this opportunity was the universe's way of reconnecting him with his sister.

Emmy's profile loaded, and Sullivan clicked on it. Even though he hadn't seen her since she was five, he knew it was her. Emmy always had a dimple in her cheek when she smiled, and a mole above her lip. The birth date confirmed it. This was his sister, and she had grown into a beautiful young woman. Hard to believe this was the little girl he once knew.

Nothing had changed on Emmy's Facebook page since the last time he visited the site. There were only two pictures. The first was of her and two other girls holding fruity cocktails at some restaurant. Above the photo, Emmy posted, "The Pelican's Roost is serving *us* tonight! A waitress needs a night off once in a while!" He couldn't believe she was of drinking age already, but yeah, she would be twenty-five now.

The second post was a smiling Emmy with heavy eye makeup. The picture was taken at a club. Sullivan only knew that because he had googled the sign above her head. He couldn't imagine his baby sister old enough to dance at a club, and he hoped the sleazy college boys there weren't taking advantage of her.

She looked happy, and that was the important thing. Of

course, the pictures were from a year ago. Who knew if Emmy was still in Clearwater? And was she still as happy as she was in the photographs?

Sullivan hovered over the Friend Request button. It was stupid to consider it. For one, she clearly didn't update her Facebook anymore. And two, the last thing he wanted to do was to bring back terrible memories for her. If she remembered him at all. A part of him hoped she didn't. Life in that trailer had been a hellhole, and he'd accept Emmy forgetting him if it meant she'd forgotten everything else as well.

He closed Facebook without submitting the request. It was for the best that he left it alone.

3

"Sorry, Isabel, but it's totaled."

Isabel waved her fists like Miguel sometimes did when he didn't get his way. "No, Ricardo, that's not the right answer. Can't you just repair it and say it's not totaled? I don't care if it looks beat up."

"I'm afraid that's not how it works. I wish I had better news for you."

Isabel sighed and ran her hand along the crumpled hood. "I know. I just don't want another car payment. I finally paid off the loan for this one. And with Miguel's medical bills and now mine." Isabel rubbed her neck. "Paulina suggested I see her chiropractor. Dr. Gomez squeezed me in this morning."

"I know a guy who could get you a good deal on a used car. Want his number?"

"Sure. I guess I better look soon."

She followed him into the office where Ricardo went to his desk. He scribbled something on a sticky note and handed it to her. "His name is Carlos. You tell him I gave you his number and he'll help you find something. And try not to stress about it. The Honda you were driving was an older model. But now, you get to have a car with all the safety features. Won't that make you feel better when you drive around with Miguel?"

Ricardo made a good point, and Isabel reminded herself to think of the positive. "You're absolutely right. I needed an upgrade anyway. I guess I should get my personal things out."

"I'll clear out the car for you and box it up. You need to get that neck taken care of. Do you need a ride?"

"Oh, I can walk. It's only a few blocks. And Paulina is picking me up after my appointment to take me to work. I know you're busy."

Ricardo reached for his keys. "Really, Isabel, it's no problem. Let me save you the walk. It's already hot and steamy out there. I'll have Diego hold down the fort for a few minutes."

"Okay. *Gracias*, Ricardo."

Ricardo spoke briefly to Diego, then Isabel followed Ricardo out to his car. She climbed into the passenger seat, then cursed when she moved her neck wrong and felt a sharp pain.

"Are you sure you should work today?" Ricardo asked as he started the car.

"I will not give Mr. Grumpy the satisfaction of me not showing up. I'm going to go to work and do my job, and if he doesn't like it, he can move his ass back to Kansas."

Ricardo chuckled. "Paulina told me the guy you're working with is the guy you got into an accident with."

"Yeah, of all the rotten luck."

Ricardo made the turn toward Dr. Gomez's chiropractic office. "It's only a temporary job, right?"

"For three months."

"It'll go by fast."

The problem was, she didn't want these three months to fly by. She was doing what she loved, and she was getting paid for it. At the end of this gig, what the hell was she going to do to pay the bills?

SULLIVAN ARRIVED at the Lightning Institute before Isabel, which he was grateful for. He sat at the front desk and reviewed the videos from yesterday.

Torres came out of his office. He had a fast food biscuit in his hand, and the smell of the sausage made Sullivan's stomach growl. He'd only had coffee and a cigarette for his breakfast.

"You two got some great footage yesterday."

"Yeah, we did all right," Sullivan said, though he had done nothing but drive. Isabel had taken over the cameras.

Sullivan replayed part of the video, slowed down, while Torres watched over his shoulder. The leaders of the lightning bolt branched downward in a zigzag pattern until one met a charge from the ground, resulting in a connection. The bright lightning bolt looked to be motionless when slowed down, though in actuality, the whole thing had happened in less than a second.

"Beautiful," Torres said.

"The models show some thunderstorms developing south today."

"Yeah, I saw that. You'll probably find the most action somewhere between Fort Myers and Naples. You and Isabel will have a long drive today."

Usually, Sullivan would make a sarcastic comment, like how much he was looking forward to being on the road with her. But given that Isabel was the professor's niece, and that Torres was the reason for his new job, he figured he'd keep his mouth shut.

A crumb from Torres's biscuit fell on the desk, and Torres hastily wiped it away. "Sorry."

"Where'd you get that from?" Sullivan often skipped breakfast, but a biscuit right now seemed like a good idea.

"There's a few fast food places nearby. Just turn left on the main road and you'll find them. I think they're still serving breakfast for about twenty more minutes if you want one."

A phone rang in Torres's office, and he excused himself to answer it. Just as Sullivan was contemplating a food run, Isabel stormed through the front door.

"Well, thanks to you, my car is totaled," she said instead of hello.

"Thanks to me? No, Izzy, you were the one who pulled out and hit my car. The police officer ticketed *you*."

"He should have cited you for speeding. And don't call me Izzy. I hate when people call me Izzy."

Sullivan made a mental note to call her Izzy every damn chance he had. He stood and grabbed his keys. "Going to get something to eat. Be back in a few."

"Good. It'll be nice not to smell your smoky clothes."

He flipped her the bird as he left, but Isabel wasn't looking, which took the fun out of the gesture.

An hour later, they were driving south with Isabel behind the wheel. Sullivan's eyebrow twitched as Isabel's Spanish music played. She had paired her phone to the bluetooth speaker, and now, the same lyrics were on repeat. It was irritating as hell. But it had been Sullivan's rule: the driver ruled the sound system. He'd just have to deal with it.

The good thing about riding shotgun was that he had control of the radar. That meant that he told Isabel where the storms would be, and hopefully, he'd make the call about where they would chase today.

The bad thing about not driving was the fact that he had to depend on Isabel to stop, and he really needed a cigarette right now. He looked at the GPS and figured out where the next gas station was. "Take this next exit and stop at the Exxon. I need a smoke break."

"No."

"Excuse me?"

"Oh, I'm sorry. We don't have time for you to ruin your lungs. We have a developing thunderstorm to chase."

"Pull the fuck over, Izzy."

Isabel glanced at him. "No. We'll stop when we get closer. You can wait, *Elmer.*"

"Don't call me Elmer," he snapped. "Only one person is allowed to call me by my first name, and you're not her."

"If you call me Izzy, I'm going to call you Elmer."

Sullivan grunted. "Next time you need to stop for a bathroom break and I'm behind the wheel, I'm going to keep on driving."

"Fine. I'll just not drink anything so I won't have to go."

Sullivan clenched his jaw.

FORTY-FIVE MINUTES LATER, Isabel gave in and found a gas station. Try as she might, she couldn't hold her bladder indefinitely. She'd only held off on stopping sooner to piss him off. Though now, he was pissing *her* off. The longer he waited for his cigarette, the grouchier he became. He snapped at her twice for not passing a slow vehicle, but Isabel couldn't afford another accident. She didn't want to admit that it still hurt a little to turn her neck, and the Advil she'd taken for the pain had already worn off.

The moment she pulled into a parking space, Sullivan reached for his pack of cigarettes and hopped out of the LIV. Isabel made her way to the bathroom, relieved to have a break from him.

When she returned, Sullivan was nowhere in sight. She hadn't seen him inside the convenience store, and he wasn't anywhere outside she could see. She looked at her watch, then at the radar. Where the hell was he? They needed to hit the road soon before they missed their chance at catching the storm.

Nearly fifteen minutes later, Sullivan came from around the building. It was almost as if he was deliberately taking his time. No rushing at all, just a slow walk. He sat in the passenger seat with no apology for taking so long.

"Where have you been?" Isabel asked. "Does it really take you fifteen minutes to smoke a cigarette?"

Sullivan glared at her. "If you must know, I had to take a shit. Must have been that biscuit messing with my stomach."

"Well now, we might miss the storm."

"Then quit wasting time complaining and drive already."

Sullivan muttered another curse, but Isabel ignored it and backed the LIV out of the space.

By the time they reached Naples, the thunderstorms had indeed fizzled out, leaving only a thick air of humidity behind.

"Are you happy now?" Isabel complained. "If you hadn't had to take a smoke break, we would have been here on time."

"You're blaming me? What about you? There were senior citizens driving faster than you on the interstate."

"Excuse me for driving safely!"

Sullivan scoffed. "You really want to go there? Driving safely? Who caused that accident yesterday morning?"

Isabel unbuckled her seatbelt. "Then why don't you drive, *Elmer?* My neck is killing me anyway."

"I'd be glad to, *Izzy*. Maybe we'll get home by dinnertime at least."

Isabel settled into the passenger seat while Sullivan got behind the wheel. It had only been two days with this infuriating man, and it had been the longest two days of her life.

4

Isabel held the syringe in her hand. "Miguel, don't fight me on this."

Tears streamed down the boy's face as he crouched behind the couch. "No! I want to do it later."

Isabel sighed. She knew it was unpleasant for the child, but what choice did she have? Her lousy insurance wouldn't pay for an insulin pump. And buying one without insurance wasn't an option—unless she had an extra $6000 lying around.

"*Nene*, you need your insulin or you'll get very sick. You don't want to end up in the hospital like last time, do you?"

Miguel reluctantly sat on the couch.

"I promise this will be quick." Isabel cleaned his upper arm with an alcohol wipe. In her other hand, she held the syringe. A few moments later, it was done, and Miguel's tears were already dry.

"See, that wasn't so bad, *nene*. You're all done. Now go grab your bag to take to Abuela's. I've got a lot to do today."

There was a low chance of thunderstorms today, which meant it was the perfect day for running errands. The first item on her to-do list was a stop at her insurance office, where she had a check waiting for her. She hoped it would be enough for a down payment on a car, but the price of everything had gone up these days. She'd probably have to dip into her savings.

Next was car shopping. She'd lost the sticky note Ricardo had given her of his car dealer friend, but she didn't want to bother him about it. Her brother-in-law was awfully busy with running the body shop and helping her sister raise three boys. And anyway, the Jeep dealership was right down the road. It wouldn't hurt to look.

Isabel looked at the clock and hurried to gather her things. As she took her phone off the charger, she noticed a text notification. Immediately, she felt a tightness in her chest. *Mateo.*

Mateo: Isabel, can we talk? Por favor, cariño.

"No, we can't talk." Isabel swiped the notification away. She thought she was done with him. And calling her *cariño?* She was no one's darling. Certainly never his.

Miguel ran into the living room with his bag on his shoulders, pulling her attention away from her phone. "I'm ready!"

Isabel tossed the phone into her purse and put on a smile. "Great. *¡Vamos!*"

Later at the dealership, she walked around the maze of new models. It was probably stupid of her to even look here. She already knew a used car was in her future. No way could she afford anything recent. But it was nice to browse and dream a little.

At the front of the lot was a two-door Jeep Wrangler with a shiny crimson exterior and hardtop. Though Isabel preferred the soft top version, it was still nice. She could easily ask Ricardo to install a soft top on it, and then it would be perfect for the beach.

Her hand ran along the door as she peered inside. What if this was hers? She imagined riding up and down the highway with the top off—a hint of salt in the air and the wind whipping her face. Miguel would be in the back, singing right along with her to some song on the radio. Absolute bliss.

She closed her eyes, lost in the daydream. But instead of smelling the salty sea air, there was the stench of cigarette smoke. Isabel opened her eyes and saw Sullivan's figure in the vehicle's reflection.

"I'm taking it for a test drive," he said in his usual gruff tone, his voice probably ruined from years of smoking.

Isabel groaned and turned to face him. Even on her day off, she couldn't avoid him. "You."

"I saw it first. The sales associate is getting the key. Need a new set of wheels, thanks to you. Insurance adjuster said mine was totaled."

Isabel looked longingly at the red Jeep. A glance at the price sticker told her it was out of her budget, just as she knew it would. "It's too expensive anyway for me. Must be nice to afford something new."

She stomped off, wanting to get away from Sullivan. He smelled like a damn ashtray, and the last person she wanted to see on her day off was him.

Isabel headed straight to her mother's car and got in. She didn't want to be here if Sullivan was here. And there were other places she could shop for a car.

As she started up the Toyota, her phone beeped with another message. She hoped it wouldn't be Mateo again, and breathed a sigh of relief when she saw Ricardo's name.

Ricardo: Good news. Got a loaner vehicle for you until you find something else.

Seconds later, another text from Ricardo came through.

Ricardo: Did you call Carlos?

Well, time to fess up. Isabel typed out her reply.

Isabel: Thanks for the loaner! And no, I haven't called Carlos. I lost his number. Sorry!

Ricardo: No problem. If you'd like, Paulina and I can go with you to help you find something.

Isabel considered his offer. She really didn't want to go car shopping on her own, and having Ricardo, who knew about cars, would make this process so much easier. Mind made up, Isabel went home.

After dinner that night, Ricardo pulled into the driveway with a beat up Ford Focus. Paulina, with the kids, followed in their SUV. As Miguel played with his cousins, Ricardo dropped the keys into her palm. "Here you go, Isabel. It's seen better days, but it'll get you around."

The car was blue and heavily rusted. Isabel thought her wrecked Honda looked better than this clunker, but she wasn't about to look a gift horse in the mouth. "*Gracias*, Ricardo. That's very nice of you. Where did it come from?"

"Diego fixed it up. It's one of his father's old cars, but he never uses it."

Her mother opened the driver's side door and peered inside. "Is it going to break down?"

Isabel smiled. She was glad her mother had the guts to ask.

Ricardo gave them both a hesitant expression. "I wouldn't take it for a road trip, but it'll get you across town. You want to try it out?"

"I'm sure it's fine," Isabel said. "Is there anything I need to know about it?"

"The A/C is busted, but the windows roll down easily."

Paulina slapped her husband on the arm. "Ricardo! You never told me the air conditioner didn't work."

Ricardo held up his hands. "I'm sorry, but I figured she would only need it for a couple of days."

"It's fine," Isabel said.

Carlita cleared her throat. "Paulina, come help me with dinner. Isabel, drive that car before Ricardo leaves to make sure it'll run again."

Her mother and sister left to go inside, and Isabel looked at the car. "I guess she's right. I'll take it for a quick spin."

"When do you want to go shopping for a new car?"

Isabel sighed. "I'll let you know. I should probably wait until after my next paycheck. This clunker will have to do for now."

"Don't call it that," Ricardo said. "Call it by its name. Rusty."

Isabel laughed.

For the second day in a row, the skies were less than cooperative, and the Sunshine State was living up to its name. With no thunderstorms to chase, Sullivan drove to Clearwater. He needed to start somewhere in his search for Emmy, and her old place of employment was as good of a place as any.

The new Jeep was a smooth drive. Not only was it updated with more bells and whistles than his last vehicle, but it was roomier. Cleaner too, with that new car smell every time he opened the door. That had been one reason he opted not to smoke inside it. He paid a lot of money for this vehicle, and if he ever sold it, the value would be severely diminished if it smelled like cigarettes. But it was hard. He missed driving with his left arm out the window, holding a Marlboro and blowing smoke anywhere he pleased.

The other reason for not smoking was that he had considered quitting. Or at least, smoking less. If Isabel was going to drive for over an hour and not stop to let him smoke, he was going to have to train his body to get used to going longer without. Sometimes, he wished he'd never started. But then, if he didn't smoke, what would he do on his work breaks? At least it was something to do, and it made him feel good, if only for a moment. Sullivan didn't have a lot of things to look forward to, but he enjoyed a good nicotine fix.

A Google search informed him that the Pelican's Roost was out of business, but he drove to the address anyway. It was now called Captain Jack's. Probably a lot of the same people worked there. Either the place had a new name, or new owners.

The smell of fish hit him the moment he walked inside. It was just after eleven, early for lunch, and there were only a few customers. A blond girl who looked like she was in her twenties greeted him at the door. "Hi, dine in or takeout?"

"Actually, I'm not here to eat. I was looking for a girl who might work here. Or used to work here. Back when this place was called The Pelican's Roost." Sullivan took out his phone and showed the hostess his sister's photo. "Do you know this girl?"

The blond examined his screen, then shook her head. "No, sorry, but I've only worked here a few weeks. You should ask Michael. He's been here longer."

"Okay, where's Michael?"

The girl pointed to the kitchen where a man was working. "Back there. Hey, Michael, can you come here for a sec?"

Michael came over momentarily, and Sullivan showed him Emmy's picture.

"I can't say for sure," Michael said. "I started here just before the new owners took over and changed the name. I didn't know all the wait staff. We get a lot of college students that come here for summer jobs, and then quit in the fall when it's time to go back to school. Maybe she was one of them."

Sullivan considered the possibility. Maybe Emmy had gone back to Texas. Perhaps she'd only been in Florida for the summer. If so, he was chasing his tail and getting nowhere. Sullivan pulled up the second picture on his phone, the one with Emmy and her two friends. "What about the other women? Do you know any of them?"

Michael shook his head at Sullivan's phone. "No, sorry."

"Is there anyone who's been here longer than you?"

"Afraid not."

Sullivan sighed and put his phone away. "Well, thanks for your help anyway."

He tried the dance club next, which was just across the street, but the place wasn't open yet. He'd have to come back later. At least he knew where it was now.

Sullivan walked back to his Jeep. A drive with the windows down would clear his head. Perhaps a walk on the beach would do him some good too. Maybe he'd get some new ideas if he could breathe in a little salt air.

He needed to brush up on all those new social media apps. Maybe she didn't use Facebook anymore because that wasn't considered "cool" by the younger crowd. The Gen Z kids were on SnapChat and Instagram and that other one. What was it called? TikTok? Sullivan didn't like any of them. The only thing social media was good for was posting storm videos. He wasn't about to be social with anyone.

The other possibility, and this was a big one, was that she'd gotten married. He'd google-searched the hell out of "Emmy Sullivan," but if she had changed her name, how would he ever find her?

Or maybe the Johnsons had adopted her and changed her last name to Johnson. Just because she went by Emmy Sullivan on Facebook didn't mean that was her legal name anymore. Unfortunately, Johnson was a more popular surname, and looking for Emmy in a sea of Johnsons was like looking for a needle in a haystack.

The thought of hiring a private investigator crossed his

mind. If he couldn't get anywhere with the club, he might do that.

~

WITH THE SUN shining and no chance of rain in the forecast, Isabel had another day off from work. Rain would return in the forecast tomorrow, and since Miguel had been begging to go to the beach, it was the perfect day for it.

She sat in her beach chair with her big sunglasses, which Miguel said made her look like a bug, and watched as he played at the water's edge. Living near the ocean had its perks. It was mostly free entertainment, save for the cost of sunscreen and the parking meter.

The problem, of course, was always the struggle to leave. If Miguel had his way, he'd stay at the beach all day. But it was getting late, and Isabel only had a half hour left on the parking meter.

"Can't we stay longer?" Miguel begged when Isabel began to pack up their gear. "Five more minutes."

"I'm sorry, *nene*, but it's time to go. Now grab your shoes and rinse off your feet."

She kept an eye on Miguel as he used the shower at the public access. She hurried to stuff her folded chair in its bag and slung it over her shoulder. The sooner she could get Miguel home, the better. She needed to keep him on a regular eating schedule.

As they walked down the boardwalk to the parking lot, Miguel pulled her hand as they passed the ice cream stand. "*Mamá*, can we get ice cream? Please?"

She looked into Miguel's pleading brown eyes and found it hard to say no. "*Nene*, ice cream isn't good for you."

"Please? Just a little won't hurt."

Isabel considered it. "How about we see if they have a no sugar option, and if they do, I'll let you have a small bowl."

"Yeah!"

The way Miguel lit up, she hoped and prayed there was a no sugar option. Or at least a low sugar version. She had Miguel's emergency insulin pen if necessary.

At the stand, Isabel scanned the menu. The very last item was the non-sugar option, and Isabel thanked God there was something on the menu Miguel could have.

When it was her turn to order, Isabel stepped up to the register. Next to her, Miguel peered over the counter and tapped the edge. "I'll have a small bowl of the no sugar salted caramel, please."

"That'll be $6.20," replied the man behind the register.

Isabel thought that price was a tad outrageous for a tiny scoop of ice cream, but this ice cream stand catered to tourists, and of course, they jacked up their prices. She opened her wallet for a ten dollar bill, but only found a five. Panic set in. She thought for sure she had more money than five dollars.

The man behind the booth had his palm up, ready to accept the cash. Miguel kept tapping on the counter.

"Ice cream, ice cream, ice cream!" Miguel said impatiently.

Isabel smiled at the cashier. "Just a second. I'm sure I have it."

She searched the zippered pouch on the wallet for the remaining dollar and twenty cents, but only came up with two quarters and a penny. She looked in the main compartment again, hoping a few extra bills were hiding behind her insurance card. No luck. And of course, her credit card was locked in the car. She didn't like to carry that to the beach and have someone steal it.

"Miss, do you have it or not?"

Isabel sighed. "No. It looks like I'm a little short."

"*Mamá*, you don't have it?"

Isabel looked at Miguel's disappointed eyes. "I'm sorry, *nene*. I don't have enough money. No ice cream this time."

A twenty dollar bill appeared on the counter. "I'll pay for it."

Isabel turned, and her mouth fell open. It was Sullivan.

If the ice cream had been for herself, she would have politely refused. But since it was for her child, she couldn't say no, especially when Miguel's eyes lit up as the man scooped ice cream into a bowl.

"Thank you," Isabel said weakly. "That was unexpected."

Sullivan just shrugged. "Hate to see a kid not get ice cream." He turned his attention to the cashier. "Can I get a small cone of chocolate? And something for the lady."

Isabel shook her head. "You don't have to get me anything."

"It's just ice cream. Don't you want some?"

She did, but these days, she often went without the things she wanted. It seemed impolite to refuse though, so she nodded. "Okay, I'll have the same. I'll pay you back tomorrow."

Sullivan shook his head. "Not necessary. So, this must be your kid."

"*Sí.* Miguel, this is Mr. Sullivan. He works with me and Tío Fernando. Can you tell him thank you for the ice cream?"

Miguel gave Sullivan a big toothy grin. "*Gracias.*"

Sullivan nodded. "*De nada.*" He looked at Isabel. "I know a little Spanish. I grew up in Texas."

"I like your shirt," Miguel said, pointing to the tornado shirt Sullivan wore. "You like tornadoes?"

"Yeah, and I've seen a lot of them. Used to ride around in Kansas and look for them."

Miguel squinted at the shirt. "*I'd rather be chasing tornadoes,*" he read slowly, pronouncing each syllable.

"A buddy bought this shirt for me. But between you and me, I like lightning way better. I'd rather be chasing that."

"We like lightning too. We always watch the thunderstorms when they come at night."

"Yeah, it can be quite a show to watch, especially when it's dark."

Isabel was speechless as she watched this exchange between her son and this man she continued to call Mr. Grumpy. He wasn't acting like a jerk, and it was surprising to see him actually be nice and carry on a conversation. Maybe he was one of those people who got along better with kids than adults.

The man slid Miguel's bowl of ice cream forward, and Miguel happily accepted it.

"*Nene*, why don't you sit at that picnic table over there and eat your ice cream?"

When Miguel was out of earshot, Isabel turned to Sullivan. "Why did you do that?"

"Two chocolate cones," said the man, handing them each a cone.

"Do what?" Sullivan asked, taking a lick of his.

"Buy us ice cream. I know you don't like me."

"Like I said, I hate to see a kid not get ice cream. How's yours?"

Isabel hadn't even tasted it, too stunned at Sullivan's demeanor. She licked the ice cream and nodded. "It's good."

Isabel walked to the table where Miguel sat. He had nearly devoured his bowl, and Isabel handed him a napkin.

Sullivan took the seat across from them, further surprising Isabel. It was shocking enough that he bought them ice cream, but he was sitting with them too?

"Do you make lightning videos like Mamá?" Miguel asked him.

Sullivan took out his phone, pulled up the photo app, and handed it to him. "These are some of them. I take better pictures and videos with my other camera, but sometimes, you only have your phone with you."

"Cool," Miguel said, playing one video.

Isabel hurried to finish her cone. She didn't care if she got a brain freeze. She was ready for this awkward situation to be over. "*Nene*, let's hurry and finish up." Isabel glanced at Sullivan. "Our time at the parking meter is about to expire."

Miguel, with a mouthful of ice cream, held up the phone. "This one is cool. Where did you take that?"

"Kansas," Sullivan said. "A bad thunderstorm came at night, and I hurried to get my phone to record."

"The lightning is so bright that it makes the night look like day," Miguel said.

Isabel snuck a look at the phone, not wanting to admit to Sullivan that she found his video entertaining.

"We'll have some storm action tomorrow," Sullivan said.

Isabel realized he was talking to her. "Two sunny days in a row with no thunderstorms is kind of rare around here." She took a bite of her cone.

"You have, uh..." Sullivan pointed to the corner of his mouth.

"Oh. *Gracias.*" Isabel grabbed a napkin and wiped her lip. She felt hot with embarrassment, though she couldn't figure out why. Maybe it was because it made her feel like a child who was a messy eater.

They finished their ice cream, and Isabel quickly gathered the balled up napkins and Miguel's spoon and bowl. "Well, I better get going. I think I have three minutes left on that meter."

Sullivan rose. "Yeah, I should go too."

"Thanks for the ice cream. *Nene*, give Mr. Sullivan back his phone."

Miguel handed it back with a smile. "I like your storm videos."

Sullivan walked with them to the parking lot, and Isabel felt confused over the whole situation. What just happened? Was this the same man who grated on her nerves at work? From her experiences with Sullivan, he was always so gruff. But just now, he had a moment of humanity. Maybe he liked kids. That was encouraging. He had a heart somewhere inside of him.

He walked toward the same section of parking lot she was in, and Isabel realized he was going to see the rusted Ford. It didn't even have a working remote, so she had to manually unlock it.

"You bought that?" Sullivan asked. She could tell by the look on his face that he was horrified.

"No, it's just a loaner from my brother-in-law until I find something. Did you buy that Wrangler you were looking at?"

Sullivan nodded to the left, and Isabel saw the shiny red vehicle parked directly behind her.

"Sorry I beat you to it," he said, and from the look on his face, she thought he actually meant it.

Isabel shrugged. "It's okay. I couldn't have afforded it anyway. I don't know why I looked at new vehicles. Well, I'll see you tomorrow."

Sullivan nodded.

"Bye, Mr. Sullivan!" Miguel waved.

"See ya, kid."

Isabel got behind the wheel and prayed the car would start. The situation with the ice cream had been awkward enough, and it would be beyond embarrassing to have this car fail her, especially when Sullivan had bought the car she had her eyes on.

Fortunately, the old Ford cranked up. Isabel backed out of the space, being extra careful to not hit any cars, especially Sullivan's. The last thing she needed was another accident with him. As she drove away, she saw him leaning against the back of the Jeep, smoking. Well, at least he wasn't ruining the new car smell with his cigarette.

"I like Mr. Sullivan," Miguel said. "It was nice that he bought us ice cream."

"Yeah. He's... full of surprises."

SULLIVAN TOSSED the cigarette and got into his car. He wasn't usually the type of person who got ice cream on a whim, but after his walk on the beach, ice cream sounded good. When he saw Isabel in line, he almost turned around and walked away before she noticed him. That was the moment she said she didn't have the money, and Sullivan would have felt like a jerk if he had done nothing. Even if Isabel annoyed him, he wasn't about to let a kid go without ice cream.

He remembered a time when he had to scrounge together a few cents to buy Emmy a popsicle from the ice cream truck. And when he didn't have it, he'd steal it from his stepfather's wallet. He'd gotten beat up a few times for that, but it had been worth it to put a smile on his sister's face.

Maybe he had Isabel pegged wrong. She was a hardworking mother, and she was having a terrible week. He'd made it worse yesterday by rubbing the Jeep in her face, and she drove that piece of shit car. He wondered if it was really a loaner, or if that was all she could afford. If he owned that car, he'd tell people it was a loaner too.

He started up the engine and turned up the music. He needed to focus on something else other than Isabel.

5

Isabel glanced at Sullivan in the passenger seat. His gaze was focused on the laptop. Thunderstorms were firing up in northern Florida today. They had waited all day for them to percolate, and by the dinner hour, the radar was lit up with green, yellow, and red. Severe weather was expected to last into the evening, which Isabel was excited about. Nighttime lightning was spectacular. She loved how it would illuminate everything in the pitch black sky.

From the safety of the LIV, Isabel set up the cameras to record, then returned to her seat to watch the show. Usually, Sullivan had his personal camera out to film, but instead, he just stared out the windshield. He'd been quiet the whole drive, though that wasn't unusual. But the fact that he hadn't complained about her music or driving at all made her wonder if something was bothering him.

The truck was quiet, save for the sound of the roaring thunder outside. The silence was deafening, and Isabel felt it strange that they had barely said a word to each other. She understood Sullivan didn't like to talk. Maybe she needed to start the conversation.

"It's beautiful tonight," she started.

Sullivan didn't respond.

Isabel decided to try again. "Hey, I just wanted to thank you again for the ice cream. That made Miguel's day. I'll pay you back for it. I don't have any cash on me at the moment."

"I don't want your money."

His tone of voice suggested that he was either pissed, or annoyed. But why, she couldn't understand. She hadn't asked him to buy ice cream. Isabel let it go. Yesterday, she thought she'd seen a hint of a smile when he talked to Miguel, but today, he was his usual grouchy self.

Isabel cleared her throat. "I don't let Miguel have sweet treats too often. He's diabetic, so I have to watch his diet. Fortunately, the stand had a sugar-free option, so at least he could get something. It's so hard when his cousins want to go out for pizza or have birthday cake. It's difficult to explain to a six-year-old why he can't eat that, you know?"

Sullivan nodded. "It's like trying to explain to a child why she can't have a Snickers bar because of her peanut allergy."

Something in his voice told Isabel he was speaking from personal experience. "Who are you talking about?"

"No one," he said.

Isabel didn't believe him. Did he have a little girl? He never mentioned a daughter. Maybe something awful had happened, and if so, Isabel couldn't blame him for not wanting to talk about it. The only thing she knew about his past was that he was from Texas, went to A&M University, and was an aviation meteorologist. And that information came from Tío Fernando.

Isabel wondered how she could find out without directly asking him. "Tío Fernando told me you used to work for the airlines. What was that like?"

A loud crack of thunder shook the vehicle, and Sullivan looked at her with a cold stare. "I'd really like it if we could just not talk right now. Okay?"

Isabel nodded, deciding his mood met the stormy conditions outside. So much for finding out anything about his past.

She wondered what he was hiding.

AFTER THE STORMS FIZZLED OUT, Sullivan took the wheel and drove them home. Isabel slept, which Sullivan was grateful for. She'd been chatty, and Sullivan knew she was eager to pry into his history. He shouldn't have said anything about Emmy's allergy, because now Isabel had questions. And Sullivan preferred to keep the past in the past.

He nudged her awake when he pulled into the Lightning Institute's parking lot. Isabel blinked a few times, and Sullivan had a vision of a sleepy Isabel in bed. When he was tired, his lower anatomy did the thinking. But there was no way he was going to entertain thoughts of taking Isabel to bed, even if she was sexy. She still irritated him sometimes.

"What time is it?" Isabel asked, yawning.

"After midnight."

Isabel groaned. "I'm sure Miguel has been asleep for hours now. I hate when I miss tucking him in."

"Your boyfriend watching him?" Sullivan didn't know why that popped out of his mouth, but apparently, his subconscious wanted to know if she was available.

"Boyfriend? Uh, no, I don't have one of those. My mother watches him when I'm at work. I live in her garage apartment, so that makes it easy for Miguel to stay with her. Speaking of which, I have to get home and go to bed."

I'd like to take you to bed, Sullivan thought, then groaned. He needed to get out of his vehicle. He needed a smoke. Yeah, a smoke would be good right about now. It would at least get his mind off this woman.

On Monday, Isabel sat in the driver's seat of the LIV and looked at her watch. Sullivan was late, but had texted he was on the way. A part of Isabel wanted to leave his ass behind, but she didn't want another scolding from Tío Fernando about not getting along with him.

When he finally pulled into the parking lot, fifteen minutes later, Isabel rolled the window down. Sullivan got out of the Jeep and leisurely made his way to the LIV, further pissing her off. Didn't he know they needed to be on the road by now?

"Where the hell have you been?" Isabel snapped.

"I need a cigarette and I'm out," he said, not answering her question. "And move. It's my turn to drive. You drove to the storms yesterday. Remember?"

Isabel moved to the passenger seat and steeled herself for a few hours on the road with him. He appeared to be extra grouchy this afternoon, judging from the scowl on his face. His craving for a smoke wasn't making the situation better.

He drove them to a gas station, even though the tank was full, and went inside the convenience store. He'd probably stand outside and smoke it, which would further prolong their storm chase. As she waited, she watched the radar and saw the red blooming on her screen.

When he finally made it back to the vehicle, Isabel turned the laptop screen so that he could see. "We're missing this action."

"Why don't you relax already? There'll be plenty of storms rolling off the coast today. Chances are high we'll see some lightning."

While that was true, Isabel was still pissed. It was as if he wasn't taking this seriously at all. "So why were you running late?"

"I was just late, okay?" He turned on the radio, and that was the end of the conversation.

Isabel reached into her bag and pulled out her noise canceling headphones. If she had to be on the road with Mr. Grumpy for hours, she didn't want to hear him—or his music.

A DRIVER on the highway cut off Sullivan. He honked the horn, flipped off the driver of the Dodge Ram, and let out a few choice expletives.

Next to him, Isabel took off her headphones. "You should have slowed down to let him merge."

"The motherfucker sped up in front of me." Sullivan reached for his pack of Marlboro, remembered he couldn't smoke in the vehicle, and cursed as he put it back.

"But you should slow it down when cars are merging into the lane. Or move over to let them in."

Sullivan glared at her. "You need to stop being a backseat driver."

"What's got you in such a pissy mood today? More pissy than normal, I mean."

Sullivan kept his eyes on the road and chose not to answer. He realized this morning that it was the fifth of June—the shittiest day of the year. Every year when this day came up on the calendar, it brought back bad memories of life in the trailer. In his mind, he could still see that smirk on Dick's face, daring Sullivan to pull the trigger. So yeah, he was in a pissy mood.

"Okay, fine, don't tell me," Isabel said. "Hard to believe you're the same guy who just the other day had ice cream and a pleasant conversation with my son."

Sullivan glanced in her direction. "Put your headphones back on, Izzy. I don't feel like talking."

"Fine, I don't want to talk to you when you're like this anyway, *Elmer*."

Isabel put the headphones back on, and Sullivan was relieved he didn't have to make conversation anymore.

Thunderstorms were rolling off the gulf coast this afternoon, so they stuck close to the beach and monitored the radar. He parked the LIV in view of the ocean where gray storm clouds gathered.

"Look at these idiots," Sullivan said. "A thunderstorm is coming, and they're on the beach."

Isabel grabbed her camera. "I'm going to join them." Moments later, she was out the door.

Sullivan cursed under his breath. Despite the storm clouds, he had seen little lightning with this one. But it was still a sight to see with the darkening sky. He reached for his own camera and stepped outside.

Ahead of him, the wind picked up Isabel's dark hair. She struggled to hold it back while holding her camera, and Sullivan cracked a smile. He thought her wind-whipped hair looked sexy, and he once again reminded a certain part of his anatomy to behave. Yes, she was gorgeous, but she irritated him to no end. And she hated him too. There was no chance of anything physical happening between them.

He caught a whiff of the salty sea air, and the waves crashed onto the shore, knocking one man on his ass.

"Not a good day to be out in the water," Isabel said when Sullivan caught up to her.

Sullivan nodded toward one man riding a wave to the shore. "Don't tell that to the surfers."

Isabel aimed her camera over the ocean. "Look at that sky."

Sullivan turned his own recorder on. The storm clouds looked ominous. As he studied them further, he thought he saw a hint of rotation. "A waterspout is about to form," he said. "Just watch."

"Why do you think I wanted to be out here filming?" was Isabel's response.

After a few minutes of observation, a finger-like cloud lowered from the sky. The wind picked up the water, and the waterspout was born.

A crowd formed on the beach to watch, and for once, Sullivan missed being out in an open field chasing tornadoes. Kansas wasn't crowded with all these damn tourists.

The waterspout grew in size but didn't appear to be moving. Sullivan knew from experience what that meant—it was coming at them.

"It's coming onshore!" Sullivan yelled. "Come on!"

He turned to run, but quickly realized Isabel hadn't followed him. Did she not realize how dangerous this situation could be?

"Izzy, come on!" When she still didn't move, Sullivan yanked her arm and pulled her with him.

"It's so beautiful," Isabel said, running with her camera still aimed at the waterspout.

"You can get a better shot later! That thing is coming toward us and we need to take cover!"

Maybe it was the urgency in his voice, but to Sullivan's relief, Isabel put her camera down and hurried after him.

The closest place for them to take shelter was behind a sand dune near the beach access. For a few moments, they were safe. Isabel resumed her filming, and Sullivan wasn't about to be the only one without a good video. He turned his camera back to the action.

The waterspout roared onshore, kicking up beach chairs and sending a pop-up canopy tent flying. People screamed as they took cover. The wind kicked sand up, getting it into his eyes and mouth. He spit it out and pushed Isabel to the ground. "Get down!"

A plastic trash can barreled toward them, and Sullivan

threw himself over Isabel and braced for impact. The can hit his leg before the wind carried it away. More debris was flying, as was more sand, and he remained over Isabel until the wind finally died down. Thankfully, waterspouts on land usually died out pretty quickly.

He realized he was still over her. She smelled like sweat and ocean air, and Sullivan couldn't understand why that appealed to him. Isabel wiggled, and he hastily moved off her.

"Sorry," he said. "I wasn't sure you realized how serious that was."

Isabel stared at him, wide-eyed. "I've never seen one of those come onshore before. I think I got most of it on camera. That was wild!"

"Yeah, and if a beach chair or umbrella had hit us just right, we could be dead."

Her smile faded, as if she was realizing the gravity of the situation. "You're right. I guess I was caught up in the excitement. Thank you for shielding me. You didn't have to do that."

He *did* have to do that. No way was he letting her son lose her and be without both parents. And yeah, he didn't want her to get hurt either. "I just didn't want you to get hit by any debris. I didn't hurt you, did I? When I pushed you down?"

Isabel stood and dusted the sand off her shorts. "I'm fine. Are you okay?"

His leg was probably bruised from the trash barrel, but he wouldn't mention that. "I'm fine." He coughed then, feeling gritty sand making his way down his throat. "Let's go."

They headed back to the LIV, and when they got inside, Sullivan did a quick radar check. There were a few more storms popping up, but he didn't feel like chasing anymore today. After the adrenaline rush, Sullivan felt drained. The experience brought back another childhood memory. His mother and her boyfriend of the month, both passed out drunk, during a tornado warning. Sullivan alone had to grab his infant sister and run out of the trailer before the twister hit. Fortunately, the storm missed their home, but he still remembered Emmy's cries as they took shelter in the ditch.

"Why don't we just go home?" Sullivan said.

Isabel nodded. "Yeah, that was enough excitement for one day. I'm exhausted."

Sullivan put the LIV into drive and pulled out of the parking lot. Enough excitement indeed.

6

There was a smile on Isabel's face as she drove home. Although they didn't find any good lightning, the waterspout coming onto shore made up for it. She was eager to look at her video.

Her neck bothered her, an aggravation from the accident. Craning her neck to see the waterspout while Sullivan held her down to the ground also didn't help matters, though Isabel didn't blame him. It was nice that he was concerned for her safety. He didn't strike her as the protective type, but she supposed she'd been wrong. It kind of turned her on.

Wait, where the hell had *that* thought come from? No, she was not turned on by Mr. Grumpy. Okay, sure, he looked good with his perpetual five o'clock shadow and his thick, dark hair. And he was good with her son, but perhaps that was his only redeeming quality. But no, she was not attracted to him. He was a total curmudgeon who reminded Isabel of her *abuelo* in Puerto Rico, always yelling at the kids for running across his lawn. That would be Sullivan in forty years. And anyway, he smoked, a habit Isabel would absolutely not tolerate in a partner.

Isabel passed the pharmacy, then groaned when she remembered she had to stop there. She made a U-turn up ahead and pulled into the parking lot.

The line at the pharmacy counter was long, which of course, it would be. It was a Monday after normal work hours, and everyone was picking up their prescription. Isabel stood behind a coughing man and an elderly woman having a lengthy conversation with the pharmacist. She tapped her foot. All she wanted to do was to go home and be with Miguel.

When it was finally Isabel's turn, the pharmacist looked annoyed that she had another customer to assist. "Picking up?" she asked in a bored tone of voice.

"Yes, for my son, Miguel Torres."

The woman clicked around on her computer. "Date of birth?"

"June seventeenth."

The pharmacist stepped away and came back moments later with a bag. "That'll be $385.34."

Isabel's jaw dropped. "I'm sorry, what? That can't be right. My health insurance is supposed to cover that."

"I'm afraid it doesn't cover this type of insulin."

Isabel pounded the counter with her first. "What? How can insurance not cover it? It's insulin! He needs it to *live!*" She was well aware she was making a scene at the counter and had an audience, but she didn't care. This was her little boy's health, and this was outrageous.

"Your plan doesn't cover this insulin. You'll have to either get your doctor to prescribe one that is covered, or have them give the insurance company a prior authorization."

"Where's Mr. Rodriguez?" Isabel demanded. This pharmacist seemed unsympathetic, but Mr. Rodriguez was her regular pharmacist and a family friend. He would help Isabel solve the problem, or at least be kind about the situation. Sometimes, he'd give her discounts, but this lady didn't appear to have a caring bone in her body.

"He's on vacation."

"Mr. Rodriguez told me insulin would be covered under this insurance plan."

"It probably was, but insurance companies drop coverage for certain drugs all the time. Or maybe you're not on the correct plan. Look, ma'am, I've got a long line of customers. Do you want to buy the insulin or not?"

"You could be nicer about the situation," Isabel snapped as she dug out her credit card. "Do you have a little boy who almost died because of undetected diabetes?"

"I'm sorry, ma'am, but I don't make the rules." Her tone suggested she was more annoyed than sorry.

The pharmacist gave her the insulin, and Isabel stormed out of the store. It was too late to call the doctor or insurance company. That would be something she'd have to deal with tomorrow.

THE DOG from next door barked when Sullivan got out of his car. He ignored his neighbor's greeting and made a beeline for the front door, slamming it behind him. He hadn't meant to slam it, but he'd been in a hurry to shut the world out. He needed to be by himself.

He turned on the television for some noise and rooted around in the freezer for a frozen meal. As he waited for the microwave to cook his meatloaf, he occupied himself by reviewing his video. He'd actually got some decent footage of the waterspout coming onto shore.

As he ate dinner, he uploaded it to his YouTube channel. Ryder would have told him to sell it to the news outlets, but

Sullivan didn't want that kind of attention. He just wanted to post it and be done with it.

Later, when he was having his after dinner beer and cigarette, his phone rang. He grunted, not in the mood to talk, but pressed the green accept button on his phone anyway.

"What?" Sullivan answered.

"I see you found your little waterspout," Ryder said with a laugh.

Sullivan tapped his cigarette into his ashtray. "Little my ass. That thing picked up beach chairs and a canopy. Had to take shelter behind a sand dune."

"Okay, for waterspouts, I guess it was pretty decent. But you should have seen the beautiful stovepipe tornado in Texas yesterday."

"No need to brag. I saw your video."

"I know you miss Kansas. I bet Florida is so crowded with tourists you're dying for an open field."

Sullivan took a puff of his cigarette before saying anything. Ryder had him there—he missed the vastness of the Plains. But when he glanced at the picture of Emmy he kept on the end table, he remembered why he came here. "It's only a temporary job. And anyway, Florida is the lightning capital of the country. Almost daily storms here."

"Daily storms in Tornado Alley, too."

"Yeah, but lightning is more dangerous, more unpredictable than tornadoes."

"I suppose you're right. Well hey, I have two exciting things to tell you. First, Jim and I had a meeting with the execs at Adventure TV, and the show is happening next year."

"You're finally getting your own reality show. Bet it helps to have a famous meteorologist father-in-law."

Ryder laughed. "It sure does. It's really more of a docuseries, but yeah, it's happening. It'll only be nine episodes, but if they like it, maybe they'll want more. And with the second T-Rex vehicle nearing completion, I'm going to need another driver. Are you sure you don't want to be a part of this?"

Sullivan took a final drag of his cigarette and snuffed it out in the ashtray. "I told you already. I have no interest in being on television. Ask Austin. He'll do it. He's got a following on his YouTube anyway."

"All right, just thought I'd offer one more time. But if you change your mind, you can still be a part of the show."

"I'll keep that in mind. What's your second exciting news?"

"That would be that we're coming for a visit. Kit wants to see her sister and take the baby to the beach, so we'll be in Florida on Friday. We're renting an Airbnb in St. Pete, so you're welcome to come join us."

"Let's see, here at home by myself, or sharing a bathroom with three adults and a screaming baby in a beach house. That would be a hard no."

"You can have your own bathroom."

"The answer is still no."

"Well, can't say I didn't offer. I gotta run now. I'll see you on Friday."

"Later."

Sullivan ended the call. With the phone still in his hand, he pulled up the Instagram app he had downloaded earlier. He hadn't had time to play around with it yet, and honestly, he hated it already. All he wanted to do was search for a user, but the app was too damn confusing. Sullivan wanted to throw the phone across the room.

Once he found the search bar, he typed in his sister's name. A few Emmy Sullivans came up, but none of the profile pictures resembled her.

He then tried different variations of her name, such as her given name, Emmeline, or simply Em. Again, nothing came up in the results. And when he tried Emmy Johnson, that was a dead end too.

He thought at one point, a girl named Em Sullivan was her. She was from Texas, but there was no profile picture. Could it be her? The last time this Em Sullivan had posted something was around Halloween, and the feed was full of chocolate bars filled with peanuts. Unless Emmy had grown out of her allergy, he doubted this was her.

He closed the app and tossed the phone aside. Maybe today wasn't the best day to contact her anyway, considering it was the anniversary of when things changed forever. He reached for another cigarette and lit up.

STORMS WERE EXPECTED to fire up in the panhandle today, which meant at least a four-hour drive. Isabel arrived early at the Lightning Institute. At the desk, Sullivan was showing off some video to Tío Fernando. He wore a red faded shirt with the words *Weather Geek* on them. How did he look so good in an old t-shirt? No, she was not going there. She liked the shirt, that was all. So what if it was fitted and showed off the bulge of his muscles? That was what she was reacting to. She liked a strong man. But she definitely wasn't attracted to *him*.

"Hey, there she is," Fernando said as she walked in. "That was some waterspout footage."

Isabel smiled. "Not exactly lightning, but it was exciting all the same."

"I had to force her to take cover," Sullivan said.

Fernando laughed. "That's our Isabel. Always preoccupied with filming."

"And my video was way better than Sullivan's," she teased.

Fernando stood. "I'd love to see it later, *princesa*. I've got to get online now and teach a class. You two better get a move on. Aren't you driving up to Tallahassee?"

"*Sí.*"

"Have fun. Hope you get a good thunderstorm." Fernando headed back to his office.

Sullivan placed his pack of cigarettes in his pocket. "I could drive if you want me to."

Isabel grabbed the keys to the LIV. "Not a chance. It's my turn. You just want to be behind the wheel so you can stop for all your smoke breaks."

Sullivan grunted. "I'm going to the bathroom first."

"Smoke your cigarette now!" Isabel called after his retreating form. "It's a long drive to Tallahassee!"

The door to the bathroom slammed.

Isabel laughed to herself as she headed out the door. It was fun to annoy him, and she needed some entertainment today. Her day was already off to a bad start. When she called Miguel's doctor, she had to leave a message, and who knew when the nurse would return her call. And a call to the insurance company was even worse. Isabel was on hold for twenty minutes before hanging up. She'd have to call back later.

Outside, she tripped over the uneven pavement, but caught herself before she fell.

"Be careful, *cariño*. You don't want to fall and scratch that beautiful face."

Isabel froze at the sound of his husky voice. Slowly, she turned around. He was six feet from her, and had appeared seemingly out of nowhere. A whiff of his cologne hit her nose. He always wore too much of the sickening scent. "Mateo."

"Did you get my text message?"

"*Sí*. I was ignoring you the first time."

Mateo chuckled. "Oh, Isabel, don't be like that. Please, I want to talk to you."

"I have nothing to say to you," Isabel snapped. "And how did you find me here anyway?"

"Dan Forsyth at the university told me you were working with Fernando on his lightning research."

"Leave, Mateo. I'm busy, and there's nothing for us to talk about." Isabel marched toward the LIV, but Mateo was too fast and moved in front of her.

"Isabel, just hear me out. I'm sorry if I did anything to offend you or make you feel uncomfortable. You have to excuse me. I get a little carried away sometimes."

"Oh, is that what you call it? You got 'carried away?' You put *your hand* up my skirt! Did you really think that was an appropriate thing to do?"

"Isabel, I'm sorry. You're right—it was inappropriate of me."

"And the time you texted me a dick pic?"

"I told you, *cariño,* that picture was meant for someone else. Please come back to the station. The replacement we hired isn't working out. She doesn't have your camera presence, and the viewers agree."

"So fire her and look for someone else."

"But they want you. We need you, Isabel. You can have that raise, and I promise I won't do anything else to make you feel uneasy."

Isabel fought the urge to roll her eyes. Mateo was always full of promises. Like the time he made a sexual innuendo, or the time he kissed her unexpectedly. He always apologized and said he'd never do it again, but he did.

Isabel had enough of it, and of him. "Mateo, I want you to leave."

"Isabel, I know this job is only temporary. What will you do when it's over? What about your little boy?"

"You leave Miguel out of this. Now go."

"I'm not leaving until you at least agree to think about it."

A blur of faded red fabric moved into her line of vision. Sullivan was taller than Mateo, and suddenly, he was staring Mateo down.

"The lady said leave," Sullivan said, his voice deep and his eyes glaring. "Take a hike, *Rico Suave.*"

Mateo's eyes widened, and Isabel liked to think that maybe Mateo was scared of him. Sullivan looked like someone you didn't want on your bad side. Slowly, Mateo backed away and glanced in her direction. "Text me when you change your mind, *cariño*." Mateo got behind the wheel of his silver Mercedes and started it up. Moments later, it sped out of the parking lot.

"Ex of yours?" Sullivan asked.

"No," Isabel said, maybe a bit too quickly.

"Then who was he?"

Isabel chewed on her lip, not wanting to spill her life story to Sullivan in the middle of a parking lot. "He's the chief meteorologist at the station I used to work at. My former supervisor. He wants me to go back."

"It looked like a tense conversation to me."

"It was. Please don't tell Tío Fernando he was here." Isabel headed to the driver's side of the vehicle.

Sullivan placed his hand on the door, preventing her from opening it. "Why shouldn't I tell your uncle? Are you considering taking your old job back, or is that guy bad news?"

"I'm never going back to my old job, and I don't want to talk about it. Now move your hand. We've got to get going."

Sullivan moved away and walked around the truck. Isabel sighed in relief, grateful the questions had stopped.

WITH NOTHING on the radar yet, Sullivan had little to distract him from his thoughts. Isabel's reaction to her former supervisor bothered him. He suspected she was bothered by his visit too, because she'd been unusually quiet during the drive. She didn't pester him with questions or complain about him needing a smoke break. She didn't even sing along to her music, and after a while, turned the radio off.

Sullivan wanted to know what was wrong, but if Isabel didn't want to talk, he understood. He hated when people told him to "talk about his feelings." The last thing he wanted was to have a shrink tell him the many ways in which he was screwed up. He already knew.

A blue sign off the interstate informed them of some food options at the next exit, and Sullivan's stomach growled. For breakfast, he'd only had a cigarette and soda, and the cigarettes only curbed his appetite for so long. He needed to eat, and a cheeseburger sounded good right about now. "Can you take this next exit?"

Isabel glanced at Sullivan, but instead of an annoyed glare, her face was blank. "Another smoke break?"

"No, it's lunchtime. Aren't you hungry?"

"Not really, but I guess it's a good time to stop." Isabel took the exit. "Where to?"

"Anywhere I can get a burger. I don't care."

A few minutes later, Isabel pulled up to a Wendy's. Sullivan unbuckled his seatbelt. "What do you want?"

Isabel shook her head. "I'm not hungry."

"You need to eat something."

"I have snacks in my bag."

"Suit yourself," he said, then hopped out of the LIV. Sullivan suspected she would be hungry soon, especially once she smelled his food, so he decided to get her an order of fries. And what the hell, he'd get her one of those Frosty desserts too. He knew she liked a frozen treat.

The line to the register was long, and there was only one employee at the front, further pissing Sullivan off. The drive-thru hadn't been an option due to the truck's size, though the line was long there too. After an agonizing ten minutes, he made it out. No way was he eating inside. There were way too many people, and a screaming baby to boot.

As he rounded the corner of the LIV, he heard Isabel

talking on her phone. The door was open with her legs, tone and brown, dangling from the driver's seat. She hadn't noticed him yet. He would have taken a moment to admire those legs, but the worried tone in her voice squashed any feeling of desire.

"No, Paulina. I just want to forget it ever happened. If Mateo comes back around, I'll tell him not to bother me again or else I'll get a restraining order."

Sullivan's fist crumpled the top of the paper bag he was holding. He knew that Mateo guy was bad news. What the hell had he done to her?

"He took off when Sullivan scared him off. I guess he sensed he was bothering me." Isabel was quiet for a moment, then suddenly let out a hearty laugh. "Yeah, I guess Mr. Grumpy is good for something."

Sullivan would have been annoyed by the dig, but yeah, she was right. He was always in a foul mood. He was glad he'd been there when Mateo showed up. Obviously, this guy had hurt Isabel. He'd be sure to show him the door if he showed up again.

"Oh, Paulina, can I borrow a hundred dollars? I hate to ask, but there was a mishap with my insurance at the pharmacy last night. I had to pay for Miguel's insulin at full price. I'll pay you back. I just need enough to get some groceries for the week."

Sullivan caught a whiff of the greasy food and felt glad now that he'd bought her something to eat. Isabel had probably been lying when she said she wasn't hungry. She probably couldn't afford it. Sullivan imagined Isabel was the kind of mother who let herself go hungry just so her child could have a full belly. His own mother had never been so kind.

Figuring he'd heard enough of the conversation, and not wanting the food to get cold, Sullivan walked to the passenger side of the truck and opened the door.

Isabel glanced at him. "I have to go, Paulina. Back to work.

Gracias... Te amo." She ended the call and eyed the fast food bag. "That's a greasy bag."

Sullivan looked at the bag and saw the bottom of it stained with oil. "That means it's good." He placed the tray of Frosty desserts on the center console. "I got you some fries and a Frosty. I know you said you weren't hungry, but you have to eat."

"You didn't have to do that."

"Of course I had to. You can't go to Wendy's and not get a Frosty. And I don't want you stealing my fries."

He saw a hint of a smile on her face. "I guess I am getting a little hungry now. Thank you."

They ate their food in silence, save for the hum of the air conditioning and the Spanish music Isabel turned on. Sullivan wasn't about to complain about it. It sounded like she was having a hell of a day, so no need to deny her a little enjoyment.

"Are you sure you don't want me to drive?"

Isabel grinned. "So you can control the radio? No way."

"I just thought you had a lot on your mind and you'd like to be occupied with the radar. I overheard your phone conversation."

Isabel's smile fell. "You were eavesdropping on me?" Her eyes narrowed. "What did you hear?"

"Not much, but you want to tell me why the hell you would need a restraining order against your former boss?"

"No, I don't want to tell you, because it's none of your business."

"It is my business. We work together, and I want to know if this guy is going to come back and cause trouble. So how dangerous is he?"

"He's not going to come around with a gun if that's what you're worried about. I don't think he even owns a firearm. We need to get going if we want to make it to those afternoon thunderstorms on time." She gathered the trash. "Why don't you throw all this away?"

Sullivan took the greasy bag from her and went outside to toss it in the bin. He knew what Isabel was doing. She was changing the subject because she didn't want to talk about Mateo, and that was fine. Of course now, he had to know. You didn't get a restraining order against someone unless you had reason to fear for your safety, and Sullivan was determined to find out what he did.

7

Isabel was having a bad morning.

She'd gotten home late last night, and though she had been exhausted, she hadn't been able to sleep much. She had a nightmare that Mateo broke into her house. Sometimes, she wondered if he'd be brazen enough to do that. But no, he wouldn't with Miguel in the next room and her mother's house a stone's throw away. Would he? When she had more money, she'd buy a security camera. She didn't really think he was all that dangerous though. He was more like a Florida mosquito—relentless and annoying. All he needed was a good swat.

When she picked up Miguel from her mother's, it took ten minutes to get him to sit down for his morning injection. Then, he refused the eggs she had made for him, so she had to make something else. She ended up eating the eggs. With money tight the way it was, she couldn't let anything go to waste.

It was at this point that she realized she hadn't done laundry, so she had to throw on an old shirt. It was a size too small, and she didn't like the way her stomach stuck out when she wore it, but it was all she had that was clean to wear.

There was a chance of thunderstorms this afternoon close

to home, so Isabel waited until later to leave for work. Of course, as soon as she was ready to go, her lousy loaner car wouldn't start.

Isabel hit the steering wheel, then took a deep breath. This day needed to turn around, and fast.

"*Mija*, I'll call Ricardo!" her mother said from the porch. Using the Toyota today was not an option, as she knew her mother had an appointment later. She was stuck with Rusty.

Ten minutes later, Ricardo came by with jumper cables. "I'm sorry, Iz. I know this car is a piece of junk."

"Do you think jumper cables will fix it?"

Ricardo lifted the hood. "I guess we'll find out."

The car started, thankfully, and Isabel hoped she could make it to work with no further trouble from it.

At the Lightning Institute, Fernando and Sullivan were already sorting through the data from the past week. "Sorry I'm late. Ricardo had to jump start Rusty."

Fernando looked up. "*Princesa*, you need to get a better car. That loaner Ricardo gave you is on its last leg."

Isabel pulled up a chair to the desk. "I know, and I will. Just waiting for payday."

Sullivan stared at her but said nothing. She knew he still had questions about Mateo, and at the thought of answering them, she felt a queasiness in the pit of her stomach. She didn't like to talk about the past, and she had hoped that chapter of her life was over. But with Mateo showing up, it put a wrinkle in her plans.

"You two got some amazing footage," Fernando said, his attention on the laptop in front of him.

"Is that the Tallahassee video?"

Fernando nodded. "*Sí*. Look." He turned the computer around and showed the slow motion video to her. It was a beautiful lightning bolt against a dark gray sky. One of the more spectacular storms they'd gotten yet.

Fernando's office phone suddenly rang. "Excuse me," he apologized, then hurried down the hallway to answer it.

Isabel pushed the computer away and sighed.

"Are you okay?" Sullivan's gruff smoker voice asked.

Isabel massaged the spot between her eyes. "I have a headache, and I didn't sleep well last night. A lot of bad dreams."

"About him?"

Isabel looked up. How could he possibly know that? Was he reading her mind? "What makes you say that?"

"I figured that guy shook you up yesterday. He's probably on your mind."

Fernando whistled as he came back to the front room. "I've got to run to the university. Hope you get some thunderstorms later."

Once her uncle left, Isabel turned back to Sullivan. "You didn't say anything to Fernando about Mateo coming here, did you?"

"You asked me not to, so no, I didn't. You think he'll show up again?"

"I don't know. He might. But I didn't think I'd see him again until he came here yesterday."

"If he comes back again, I'll deal with him." He pushed his chair back and stood. "I'm going to get a smoke before we head out."

"Wait. Sullivan?"

He stopped and looked at her.

"I realized I didn't thank you for running off Mateo yesterday. *Gracias*."

Sullivan just shrugged, as if it hadn't been a big deal. "You asked him to leave, and I could tell he was being a jerk, so I told him to go."

He went out the door, leaving Isabel more confused than ever about this man. Sometimes he irritated her to no end. And there were other times, like now, when she thought he actually might have a heart.

~

Green was on the radar, but all Sullivan saw out the windshield was rain. He had parked the LIV next to the high school's baseball field, which would provide an unobstructed view of the sky if lightning were to produce. But so far, there was nothing.

The dark clouds moved closer, and raindrops hit the windshield. Sullivan turned the music off and listened to the sound of them hitting the roof of the truck. He thought of the rain app he had on his phone that helped him sleep sometimes. He hadn't used it in a while. Maybe it was time to start back.

He stole a glance at Isabel, who had been quiet the whole drive across town, other than to tell Sullivan this would be a good place to observe. She stared out the windshield with a worry line etched on her forehead. Sullivan felt a pang of sadness for her. Was she thinking about that creep Mateo? Or maybe she was concerned about her little boy. It wasn't right that she was struggling to pay for his insulin. Sullivan knew what it was like to be poor. Though he'd done pretty well in building up a savings account, he certainly hadn't come from wealth.

"He was harassing me at work," Isabel said, breaking the silence that had settled upon them. She didn't look at him, continuing to stare out the windshield and apparently lost in her thoughts.

Sullivan involuntarily gripped the steering wheel a little tighter. "I was afraid it was something like that."

"He wasn't like that in the beginning. When I started at the news station, he was kind and generous. He took me under his wing and showed me the ropes. It was my first meteorology job." She looked at Sullivan. "I sort of got a late start. I had to take a break from school when I got pregnant with Miguel."

Sullivan remained quiet, deciding to let Isabel tell him as much as she felt comfortable sharing.

"Everyone liked him, and all the women had a crush on him, myself included. But I wasn't about to entertain thoughts of dating him. He was my boss, you know?"

Sullivan nodded.

"At first, it was benign comments. He'd say my new haircut looked nice, or that I had a great presence on camera. But after a while, the compliments made me feel uncomfortable. It would be the tone of his voice, or the way he would stare at me, like he was undressing me with his eyes. One day, he cornered me in the back hallway where no one could hear, and he said I was beautiful. He wanted to go out with me, but I refused because it would be inappropriate. After that, things got much worse."

"He didn't..." Sullivan didn't finish the sentence, didn't want to think of going there, but Isabel picked up on what he was referring to.

"No, but it almost got to that point. My last day at work, I was working the evening shift. It was after midnight and we were still at the station. Everyone non-essential had gone home, but we were required to stay in case we had to break in for a tornado warning. We were having a lot of bad weather that night. He..." A sob escaped her throat.

"He *what?*" Sullivan demanded, then cursed himself for raising his voice. "What did he do to you?" he said in a softer tone.

"He called me into his office, and when he locked the door, he kissed me and put his hand up my skirt. I'm sure he would have done more, but I poked him in the eyes like Tío Fernando told me to do. After that, I got out of that room, grabbed my purse and keys from my desk, and ran outside. It was pouring rain and lightning, but I didn't care. He was calling for me as I got into my car, but I drove away and never looked back. I sent him an email the next day and told him I quit."

Now Sullivan wished he'd punched that asshole when he'd had the chance. "*Shit*, Izzy! Why isn't this douchebag in jail? Did you press charges?"

Isabel wiped her eyes with the back of her hand. "You don't understand what it's like. No one would have believed me. Everyone at the station loves him. The viewers love him. He's been there for fifteen years and I was there only nine months. I just let it go. But now, he's texting me and showing up, and I don't know what to do."

Sullivan took out his phone. "I tell you exactly what you're going to do. You're going to talk to the Pinellas County Sheriff's Department."

Isabel snatched the phone out of his hand. "No! You'll make things worse!"

"This guy assaulted and sexually harassed you for months. Are you going to just sit there and let him get away with it?"

"Look, I would love for Mateo to pay for what he did to me, but calling the police won't do anything. He comes from a family with a lot of money and lawyers on their payroll. All pressing charges would do is piss him off and make him want to retaliate. I would just like to leave it alone. If he bothers me again, I'll consider it, but please don't make this situation worse."

She stared at him as if she were waiting for him to promise her.

Sullivan sighed. "Fine, I won't call the authorities. For now, anyway. If he shows up again and bothers you, I can't make any promises."

Isabel handed him back his phone. "*Gracias.* Can we go now? Looks like this is just a rain shower."

"Yeah, might as well." Sullivan put the LIV into drive and

pulled out of the parking lot. He turned on his favorite country music station to drown out his thoughts, but a damn commercial was on. He turned it back off and thought of everything Isabel had told him. He couldn't explain or understand it, but the woman who once annoyed him was now his number one priority in keeping safe.

He had a hell of a lot to process here.

8

The smell of her mother's empanadas hit Isabel as she walked in the door. "*Mamá*, that smells delicious."

Carlita came out of the kitchen, but instead of a smile on her face, she looked upset. "*Mija*, why am I just hearing now that Mateo came to see you at work?"

Isabel sighed and threw her purse down. "I didn't want to worry you. I told Paulina not to say anything."

"Your sister is concerned about you." A timer dinged, and Carlita headed back to the kitchen.

Isabel followed her. "*Mamá*, I don't think Mateo will come back." Though she said that, she couldn't be sure.

Carlita took the pan of empanadas out of the oven. "The only way to be sure he never bothers you again is if he was behind bars."

Isabel busied herself with setting the table. She had already told her mother to expect them for dinner. She hadn't gone grocery shopping yet, and her funds were still lacking. "I told you. Pressing charges against him will do no good. If he goes to jail, he'll be right out."

"Thank God that meteorologist you work with scared him off."

Isabel thought of the crazed look in Sullivan's eyes when he told Mateo to take a hike, and it brought a smile to her face. "Yeah, I guess as much as he annoys me, I was glad he was there." Isabel cleared her throat. "Where's Miguel?"

"In his room playing with that video game again. I can't seem to tear him away from it."

Preferring to get away from her mother's questions and disapproving looks, Isabel peeked in on Miguel. His bedroom had once been theirs when she had to live with her mother. Being a single mother was much easier when she had help. When her mother's tenants moved out of the garage apartment, the timing had been perfect. Isabel had just gotten her first job at the station, and she could finally afford a place on her own.

But now, her savings were dwindling, and if she had to keep paying for Miguel's insulin at full price, she didn't know what she would do. She knew her mother wouldn't kick her out, but it would be unfair to stay there if she couldn't make rent. Maybe after Tío Fernando's lightning project was over, she would find something else.

Miguel was relaxed on the bed with the game console in his hands. He had borrowed it from Juan, who was grounded at the moment. If Juan couldn't play with it, Miguel asked if he could. Isabel smiled as she thought of how Miguel had a way of getting the things he wanted. She was sure he'd want one for his birthday coming up, only she didn't have an extra $300 lying around.

"*Hola, nene.*"

Miguel barely looked up.

"Miguel."

"I'm racing, Mamá."

Isabel sat on the edge of the bed and watched him play his game. He was playing some kind of strange character on a go-cart speeding through a maze that made her almost dizzy. She didn't have Miguel's full attention until the race was over.

"Did you find any lightning today, *Mamá?*"

She ran her hand through his hair. It was getting longer and needed a cut. "No, not today. Just some rain. Did you let Abuela give you your injection?"

"*Sí.*"

"Good." She kissed the top of head. "Go wash your hands and we'll eat soon."

At dinner, her mother didn't bother her about Mateo anymore. It wasn't the kind of conversation she could have with Miguel at the table. But before they left, Carlita pulled her aside.

"*Mija*, please be careful. If that man bothers you again, you call the police."

Isabel nodded, but was saved from further conversation by Miguel running back into the room.

Back at their apartment, Isabel closed and locked the door behind them. She still wasn't convinced that Mateo would actually come over here, but it didn't hurt to be cautious.

When Isabel checked the forecast the next day, she had a feeling it would be a repeat of yesterday–nothing but showers. Perhaps a pop-up thunderstorm would roll off the coast, but the odds were low.

Despite this, she went into work anyway. If nothing else, it would give her some time to look into another health insurance plan. She heard from the doctor this morning, who promised to send some paperwork to her insurance to get Miguel's insulin covered. Only now, the insurance company was saying they needed something else.

The door opened, and Sullivan walked in. He moved to the counter, and she caught a whiff of cigarette smoke.

"Are we heading out?" he asked.

Isabel shrugged. "I thought we'd wait and see if anything shows up on the radar first."

Sullivan nodded. "Good plan. No need to waste gas just for a rain shower." He looked at the desk where Isabel had all her insurance papers and forms spread out. "What's all this?"

"Just me trying to get Miguel's insulin paid for. I don't know why I have to jump through all these hoops just to get my son the medication he needs. For all the good things about this country, its healthcare is not one of them."

"Ain't that the truth." Sullivan came around the desk and sat in the chair beside her. "They charge me an arm and a leg for insurance because I'm a smoker."

"Maybe you should quit."

She thought a remark like that might get a rise out of Sullivan, but instead, he seemed more interested in what was on her computer screen. "Looking for health insurance?"

Isabel sighed as she turned back to the computer. "Maybe. If they're going to fight with me over insulin, I should drop them." She felt her eyes water and reached for a tissue. "Something in my eye," she said, not wanting to let on that she was about to cry.

"Look, I don't know how dire your financial situation is, but I'm guessing Miguel could qualify under Medicaid or something."

"I don't know about any of that. I'm probably not poor enough. You know how those government programs are."

"Nah, I'm sure you probably qualify for some sort of government assistance. My mother was the expert at that. When I was growing up, she applied for everything she could get. Food stamps, free lunch, WIC. Hell, she even applied for disability. She said if she wasn't getting any help from a man, she would have the government pay for it. And you're not getting child support from Miguel's father since he's deceased."

"No."

"See, there you go. You might as well apply for something. Got nothing to lose. The worst they can say is no."

Isabel played with the tissue in her hand, folding it up and smoothing it out. "I guess I never thought of that. Seems like you know a lot about it."

He shrugged. "I suppose."

"Will you help me apply for it?" She hated to ask, but this was not the time to be prideful. She had no clue about these things, and she had to do what she could to help Miguel.

Sullivan seemed surprised she would ask him that. "I don't know how much help I could be, but I could look at it with you. Maybe you could help me with something too."

"Anything." She hoped it was quitting smoking.

He reached into his pocket, but instead of pulling out his pack of cigarettes, he pulled out his phone. "Do you know anything about this Instagram app?"

It was not the question she thought he would ask, and she cracked a smile. "You want to learn how to use Instagram?"

"No, I hate this stupid app. But I need to find someone who knows how to use it."

"If you hate it so much, why do you have it on your phone?"

"Never mind." Sullivan put his phone back.

"No, wait, I could help you with it. I use it all the time." She pulled out her own phone and showed him her feed. "I use it to post my storm pictures."

"I need to know how you find someone on it."

"Oh, that's easy." She showed him the search function, but Sullivan shook his head.

"No, I know how to do that. But what if you search for their name and can't find them? Is there another way you can tell if they have an account?"

"If you can't find them, they're probably not on there, or they're using a different name. Do you have an email address? Who are you trying to find?"

"Never mind. It's not important." He stood abruptly, and Isabel saw the pack of cigarettes in his hand. "I'm going for a smoke, and then I'll help you with that insurance stuff."

"Didn't you just take a smoke break?"

"We're about to spend some time looking at applications for government assistance programs. Trust me, I need a smoke break. You might want to get a snack too."

Sullivan went out the door, and despite her annoyance of his smoking habit, she cracked a smile.

If someone had told Sullivan he'd enjoy spending the afternoon on a computer rather than out on the road chasing a storm, he wouldn't have believed them. Not that helping someone apply for Medicaid was exciting, but the present company made it bearable. That in itself was a shocker. Sure, she grated on his nerves when she asked him too many questions or complained about his smoking, but otherwise, he liked her. She smelled nice, probably a hell of a lot better than he did, and that lilt in her voice was pleasant to listen to.

"I feel so stupid," Isabel said. "I didn't realize I would qualify for any of this. No one ever told me. She turned her head, resting her chin on hand, and smiled at him. "Thank you for helping me with this."

Sullivan shrugged. "No problem."

"I guess we missed any storms that popped up."

Sullivan pulled up the radar on his phone. There were a few green specks here and there, but nothing worth bragging about. "Nah. Just a repeat of yesterday."

Isabel reached to turn off the computer. The shirt she was

wearing today had no sleeves, and Sullivan caught a glimpse of her bra. Sullivan turned away, not wanting his thoughts to go there again.

"I should go home to Miguel," Isabel said. "It's almost dinnertime."

"Yeah," Sullivan said, rolling the chair back.

She headed down the hall toward the bathroom, and Sullivan went outside for a smoke. The late afternoon sun was sweltering, and Sullivan moved to a spot of shade. As he smoked, he pulled up his phone and checked out the forecast. Tomorrow was a forty percent chance of rain. Sunday was seventy percent. Even better.

He snuffed the cigarette out when Isabel appeared. He hadn't quite finished it, but he didn't want to be the jerk blowing smoke in her face. She struggled with the lock for a moment, then finally got the key to turn.

"That lock is so tricky," she said to him. "I hope we have better luck tomorrow with the storms."

"We might, but Sunday's looking much better." He showed her his phone with the weather forecast still displayed.

Isabel squinted at his screen. "Seventy percent. I like those odds. Well, have a good night."

Sullivan's evening plans involved a frozen dinner and listening to his neighbor's loud music. That guy was playing it all the time. Not what he'd call a good night. But he nodded politely anyway. "You do the same."

He watched as she made her way to the rusty old Ford. Parked next to it was his shiny Jeep with the new car smell. It almost felt like he was rubbing his new car purchase in her face, but it wasn't as if he could help it. He had to get a new vehicle, and she had caused the accident. Though funny, he wasn't even mad about that anymore. He liked the Wrangler. He'd spent yesterday morning attaching all his weather gear to the roof. Now it was perfect for a beach day or a chase.

As Sullivan contemplated getting another cigarette or going home, Isabel tried to crank her car. The clunker sputtered several times, and Sullivan cursed. So much for another smoke. He walked over to the vehicle.

Isabel rolled the window down. "It won't start."

"I can see that."

"Maybe it just needs another jump."

Sullivan doubted that. The most likely possibility was that something else on it had died. "I don't have jumper cables with me."

Isabel sighed. "Okay. I guess I'll call someone to pick me up."

Sullivan felt his eyebrow twitch. He was tired, and he had almost reached his limit of social interaction for the day. But leaving her here would be an asshole thing to do. And anyway, he couldn't risk Isabel being here by herself if Mateo showed up. Being careful not to show his reluctance, he nodded toward his vehicle. "Come on. I'll give you a ride home."

"Really? You don't mind?"

"You don't live far, do you?" he said, not answering her question. He did sort of mind the slight inconvenience of it, but it wasn't as if he had anything waiting for him at home.

"No, it's less than ten minutes away."

He unlocked the Jeep and got behind the wheel. Isabel gathered her things and climbed inside.

"Wow," she said as she closed the door. "It smells like a new car in here and not like cigarette smoke."

Sullivan ignored the subtle dig at his smoking habit. "I figured if I ever sell this, no one will buy it if I smoke in it."

"And I see you already have all your weather gadgets set up on the roof," Isabel continued. "What do you use it for?"

"If I chase tornadoes."

"Here? Or in Tornado Alley?"

"Doesn't matter." Sullivan pulled out of the parking lot. "Where am I taking you?"

"Oh, take a right at the road and go straight for about two miles. I'll tell you when to turn."

Isabel's place was in the same direction as his own, and not too far away from his rental. He'd driven past this road several times on his way to the grocery store. When he pulled onto her street, Isabel instructed him to turn into the driveway.

The plan had been to drop her off and leave, but Sullivan could already tell that would not happen. Miguel and a woman, presumably Isabel's mother, came out to greet them.

Miguel ran to the driver's side and tapped on the glass. Sullivan rolled down the window.

"Hi, Mr. Sullivan!"

"Hey, kid."

Isabel was out of the vehicle. "That junk car wouldn't start again."

The older woman stepped closer and put her hands on Miguel's shoulders. "I'm Carlita, Isabel's mother. It's so nice of you to give Isabel a ride home. Are you hungry? Please stay for dinner!"

"Yeah, stay for dinner, Mr. Sullivan!" Miguel said.

He looked into the pleading child's eyes, then at the smiling older woman. A tenseness settled in the pit of his stomach. He always felt awkward at the table with others, never knowing when to make conversation. In fact, the last time he sat down for a meal with others was Ryder and Kit's wedding reception two years ago. How was he going to get out of this situation?

Sullivan rubbed his jaw. "I really shouldn't impose."

"You wouldn't be imposing!" the older woman insisted.

Miguel's small fingers grabbed hold of the edge of the window. "Stay, Mr. Sullivan! Abuela's making *chuletas fritas*. It's *muy bueno!*"

He glanced at Isabel, who cracked a smile. "Have you ever had it?"

Sullivan shook his head. "I don't even know what that is. Some kind of Puerto Rican dish or something?"

"It's fried pork chops," Isabel said. "You like pork?"

Sullivan did like pork, and his stomach growled just thinking about it. It sure beat his frozen dinner at home, and hell, he couldn't disappoint the kid. He was still giving him the puppy dog eyes. There was no way he could say no to a kid. "All right. I suppose I can stay for dinner. I love pork chops."

"Yay!" Miguel cheered. The child opened his car door for him, and Sullivan wondered what the hell he'd just gotten himself into.

ISABEL SHOULD HAVE KNOWN her mother would invite him to have dinner. Carlita always said it was rude to not offer someone a meal if they dropped by. Isabel figured Sullivan was the kind of person who avoided social occasions, so she was surprised he accepted the offer. She steeled herself for an awkward dinner.

"What's that on your car?" Miguel asked, pointing to Sullivan's weather gear.

"It's an anemometer," Sullivan said. "It measures the direction of the wind and its speed."

"And what's that?" Miguel pointed to something else.

"A barometer. It measures pressure."

"Dinner will be ready in five minutes," her mother said. "And Paulina and Ricardo will be here soon. We'll have a nice big family dinner together. Won't that be lovely?"

Isabel shot a glance at Sullivan. Was he bothered by the idea of strangers at a dinner table? If he was, he kept it to himself. He picked up Miguel to give him a closer look at his weather gadgets.

"I'll be inside," Isabel said to them. "Come in whenever you're ready."

Her mother held the door open, and Isabel followed her into the house. "Mamá, I wish you hadn't invited him for dinner."

Carlita shrugged. "Why not? He was nice enough to give you a ride home. It would be rude not to offer him a meal. Plus, I'd like to get to know the man you've been driving around Florida with."

"I know, but he's not very social."

The kitchen smelled overwhelmingly of pork, and Isabel saw the chops were on a plate, ready to be served. Her mother handed her a bowl of rice. "Put this on the table, *mija.* He seems social enough to me. And I see Miguel had taken a liking to him."

Isabel looked out the window, where Miguel was now showing Sullivan his myriad of water toys. "Yes, Miguel likes him." And it appeared the feeling was mutual. Sullivan practically lit up as he showed Miguel his weather gear. She wouldn't have pegged Sullivan as the type of person who would be good with children, but he continued to surprise her.

Her mother placed the beans on the table and leaned in closer. "He's attractive, *mija.*"

Isabel rolled her eyes. "Mamá, don't bother playing matchmaker. We work together. And you know my opinion on workplace romances."

Carlita smiled. "I'm just saying it's nice to find an attractive man who likes children."

The front door opened, and Sullivan walked in behind Miguel. Isabel couldn't tell if Sullivan was overwhelmed by the attention. If he was, he hid it well.

"I'd like to wash up beforehand," Sullivan said, looking at Isabel.

"Oh, down the hall. First door on your right."

Sullivan nodded and headed to the bathroom.

By the time Sullivan came out, her sister and Ricardo had arrived with their three boys, who were loud and boisterous. Sullivan seemed polite as introductions were made, but her gut told her he wanted to escape.

Isabel took the chair next to Sullivan. "You don't have to stay long," she whispered.

"Trying to get rid of me?" he whispered back.

Isabel spread her cloth napkin over her lap. "No, I just thought you might be overwhelmed by a big group of people."

Sullivan shrugged. "I'll stay. It's been a while since I've had a home-cooked meal. My stomach wants me to stay."

"My mother makes the best meals."

Paulina sat across from them at the table, and when Isabel caught her eye, she wondered how long her sister had been staring at them. "Isabel is an excellent cook too."

Isabel looked at Sullivan and shook her head. "I'm not that great in the kitchen."

"Don't sell yourself short, *hermanita*," Paulina said. "She made the pernil all by herself last Christmas."

Sullivan looked at Isabel. "What's pernil?"

"It's a slow-cooked Puerto Rican pork roast," Isabel said. "We eat a lot of pork around here," she added with a laugh.

Paulina passed him the platter, and Sullivan speared a chop to put onto his plate. "Well, it looks mighty delicious."

HE ONLY STAYED because he felt he had no other choice, and he didn't want to say no to the kid. To his surprise, he was having a good time. It felt like being at Ryder's house for Thanksgiving, with the conversation flowing and the occasional burst of laughter. He reminded himself that not everyone came from a dysfunctional family.

When he'd cleaned his plate, he was still hungry, but didn't want to be greedy and ask for seconds. Isabel's mother noticed right away and held up the pork platter. "Have some more!"

Sullivan nodded. "All right. Don't mind if I do. Everything is good."

Carlita smiled. "I bet this is your first authentic Puerto Rican family dinner."

"Yes, ma'am, I believe it is."

"Please, call me Carlita." Carlita continued to smile at him, and after a while, the wide grin of hers almost felt awkward. "You look so familiar to me," she eventually said.

Sullivan took a second helping of rice. "I guess I just have one of those faces."

Carlita shook her head. "No, that's not it. You look like someone." She frowned as if she were trying to figure out who it was. Her face then lit up. "I know who it is! You look like that man from the television show. The one with the plane that disappeared over the Bermuda Triangle, and they crashed onto this Caribbean island with dinosaurs. Oh, *mija*, what was the name of that show? I can't remember."

"*Bermuda Time Warp.*"

"*Bermuda Time Warp*! That's it! You look like Jase Holler from *Bermuda Time Warp!*"

Sullivan hadn't a clue about the show. "Never seen it."

Isabel grinned at him. "You do kind of look like him. No one ever told you that?"

Sullivan shook his head. "I suppose not. I don't watch much television except the Weather Channel."

As dinner wrapped up, Sullivan was ready to leave. As kind as Isabel's family had been, he was ready for some alone time. He thanked Carlita for dinner and promised Miguel he'd take him for a ride sometime to "test out his weather gadgets."

Isabel walked him to the door. "Well, thanks again for the ride home."

"I could pick you up tomorrow if you need a ride."

"Oh, I wouldn't want to inconvenience you. And Ricardo said he could get me another loaner vehicle."

"It's no inconvenience. Your house is on the way, and we're going to the same place."

"True. I just figured that you're stuck with me in a vehicle for hours. An extra fifteen minutes would be torture."

She had it wrong. Torture? It wasn't torture being around her. Unless the torture part was the way his body reacted when she was nearby. Throughout dinner, her arm kept bumping against his, and he liked it. What the hell was happening to him?

Sullivan grabbed his keys by the door. "I guess you're growing on me, Izzy. Have a good night."

"Goodnight," she said, and for once, didn't call him Elmer.

He walked out the door and inhaled the fresh evening air. He needed a smoke, and maybe a cold shower.

9

Sullivan quickly snuffed out his cigarette when he saw Ryder's truck. He got enough dirty looks from Isabel every time he smoked, and he didn't need it from his best friend either.

Ryder emerged from the vehicle and looked at him over his sunglasses. "Is that you, Sully? You look tan. Working at the beach must be such a drag."

"I thought you were bringing the T-Rex," Sullivan said. The T-Rex stood for Tornado Research Explorer, and it was Ryder's chase vehicle out in the field. "You mean you're actually taking a break from tornadoes?"

"What tornadoes am I going to chase here?" Ryder said, smiling. "Actually, the T-Rex is in the shop. It broke down and needed some work."

"You put enough miles on it."

Kit walked over holding Jake, the baby, and Sullivan couldn't believe it was the same kid. "Wow, your kid got bigger."

"Nine months already," Kit said. "You want to hold him?"

Sullivan shook his head. "He looks happy, and you'd probably want me to wash the nicotine off my hands anyway." That was just an excuse. Baby Jake reminded him too much of his own baby sister, right down to the chubby cheeks and pouty lips.

"Is Professor Torres here?" Ryder asked. "I'd like to say hello."

Sullivan nodded toward the door. "Inside."

Isabel was at the front desk on the computer. She looked up expectantly when she saw Sullivan had company.

"Isabel, these are some friends of mine. Ryder and his wife, Kit."

Isabel tilted her head. "You have friends?" She then gave him a teasing smile.

"I like her already," Ryder said, laughing.

Isabel's attention turned to the baby. "And who's this little guy?"

"This is Jake," Kit answered.

Isabel immediately came around the desk to get a closer look. "Oh, he's so cute!"

While the women got acquainted, Sullivan showed Ryder the latest lightning videos from the LIV's cameras.

"That's amazing to see it in that detail," Ryder said.

"You'll never look at lightning the same."

"I'll admit, it's beautiful, but I still think tornadoes are way better."

"I thought I heard voices," Torres said as he came out of his office. "Ryder, it's been a while. Good to see you."

The men shook hands and began to chat about the weather and their storm chasing adventures.

"Too bad the T-Rex broke down," Torres said. "I would love to ride in it."

Ryder sighed. "Yeah, I know. I'm disappointed about that too. Hopefully it'll be up and running soon. It's best to take a regular vehicle when we have the baby with us anyway. Speaking of vehicles, I'd love to get a look at the LIV."

"I'll do you one better," Sullivan said. "We're going to be up near Brooksville or Hernando Beach today. About an hour north. You want to ride with us?"

Ryder's eyes lit up with excitement. "Hell yes, I do." He then turned to his wife. "Can I?"

Kit laughed. "Sure, go have fun."

A half hour later, Sullivan started the LIV. It was hot and stuffy inside, and while he waited for the A/C to cool things down, he rolled the window down to let some of the hot air out.

The passenger door opened and Isabel stepped inside. The aroma of her coconut sunscreen lotion filled the cab. Damn, why did she always smell so good?

She made a little sigh as she fanned herself. "*Hace calor.*"

"Yeah, I know. I got the A/C going full blast."

Across the parking lot, he heard Kit and Ryder talking. They fussed over strapping the baby in his car seat, then seemed to take their time saying goodbye to each other with some very public displays of affection. Sullivan rolled his eyes. They acted like they wouldn't see each other for a week when it would only be a few hours.

Isabel pulled up the radar on the computer. "Is Ryder coming?"

Sullivan nodded his head toward Ryder's truck. "Yeah. Just waiting for the lovebirds to say goodbye."

Isabel leaned over the console to peer out his window, and Sullivan got another whiff of her coconut lotion. "I think they're cute together."

Sullivan grunted. He acted like their affection annoyed him, but he was more annoyed with himself. A deep and loving relationship came naturally for Ryder, but Sullivan never had it that easy. No woman ever said she loved him, and Sullivan didn't blame them. He knew he was screwed up.

Outside, Ryder still clung to his wife like he was about to ship out.

"Don't get struck by lightning," Kit said. "It's the number one weather killer."

"Wrong," Ryder said. "Extreme heat is the deadliest."

"Okay, so maybe lightning is number two. Just be safe."

"I'll stay in the truck."

Sullivan cleared his throat. "Ryder, are you coming today? We got storms to chase."

Ryder finally detached himself from his wife. "I'm coming."

Kit walked up to Sullivan's window. "You can stay with us if you want, Sully. There's an extra room at the beach house. Just bring your stuff when you drop off Ryder."

Sullivan shook his head. "No thanks, but you have fun."

"All right. Bring my husband back in one piece."

When Ryder finally got in the truck, Sullivan pointed to the back. "You'll have to sit with the camera equipment."

Isabel got up from the passenger seat. "No, I'll sit there. Ryder can have my seat."

"You don't mind?" Ryder asked.

"Not at all. You want to experience the LIV, right? You can be our co-pilot for today. Just monitor the radar, and I'll handle the cameras. Sullivan can do all the driving. You'll just have to endure his country music. The driver controls the radio."

"No way, man. Guests overrule drivers." Ryder took the passenger seat and promptly turned the dial. Once he landed on the alternative rock station, he turned the music up. "There, that's better."

Sullivan's eyebrow twitched, but at least Ryder's taste in music wasn't as grating as Isabel's. "All right, let's hit the road." Sullivan put the LIV into drive.

"Can't believe you turned down a free beach house," Isabel said. "I would have taken it."

"And with his own bathroom," Ryder said. "This house has four of them."

"I'd like to sleep tonight, and there's no sleeping with a crying baby," Sullivan said.

Ryder chuckled. "Well, that is true. I've never been so sleep-deprived in my life."

"You used to drive all night chasing tornadoes, and now you whine if you don't get a full eight hours of sleep. You must be getting old and can't handle long nights anymore. In fact, is that a gray hair?" Sullivan glanced at his friend and cracked a smile.

"Shut up, man," Ryder said with a laugh.

ISABEL LEANED FORWARD to get a glimpse of the radar. There was a tiny speck of green, which didn't look like much, but Isabel figured in time, it would fire up. "It's about to get started, boys."

"Should we go north?" Ryder asked.

"Nah, we should get east of it," Sullivan said. "That way, it'll come right to us. But first, we need gas."

Isabel nudged Ryder's arm. "He means he needs a cigarette."

Ryder laughed. "Yeah, I know that trick. Or he'll say he needs a quick bathroom break or a bite to eat, but then he'll stay out in the parking lot puffing away."

"Shut the fuck up," Sullivan said.

"Okay, Mr. Grumpy," Isabel mumbled.

Ryder turned his head to look back at Isabel. "In college, I used to call him Oscar. You know, for Oscar the Grouch?"

"That's a good one!"

"That's just how I talk to people!" Sullivan snapped as he made the sharp turn into the gas station.

Isabel tapped Ryder. "He really needs his cigarette," she whispered. "Badly."

"Oh yeah, he's niccin out," Ryder said.

Sullivan parked at the pump. "See, I pulled up to the pump. I really am getting gas."

"Whatever you say, man," Ryder said. "I'm going to run inside and grab a snack."

"Me too," Isabel said. "The only chance I get to use the bathroom is when he needs a smoke break."

When Isabel returned to the LIV, she found Ryder in the vehicle alone and Sullivan nowhere in sight.

"Is he smoking?"

Ryder pulled out a strip of beef jerky from his Jack Link's bag. "You called it. Said he'd be back in five."

Isabel returned to her seat. "It's so annoying. One time, he took so long that we completely missed the storm we were chasing."

"He's made me miss a tornado or two for the same reason."

"How long have you been Sullivan's friend?" Sullivan wasn't one to volunteer information, but maybe his best friend could clue her in on his past.

"We've known each other since college. We lived in the same dorm building and had a lot of the same classes together."

"Sullivan's kind of..." She didn't know how to word it.

"Difficult?"

Isabel smiled. "Yes. Sometimes."

Ryder cracked open his bottle of Mountain Dew. "Sullivan has a rough exterior, and a temper sometimes, but underneath it all, he's actually a good guy."

"Sometimes I see hints of that man, and other times, he seems like a grouch."

Ryder took a swig of his soda. "Yeah, that's Sully. Just know when he's being an ass, he had a hard life, and he probably doesn't mean to take it out on anyone."

"What happened to him?"

Ryder seemed to hesitate. "You should ask Sullivan. I don't feel like it's my story to tell."

Isabel nodded. "Understood. Can I ask you one question though?"

"Sure."

"If he's such an ass, why are you his friend?"

Ryder chuckled. "You know, I ask myself that very question. If Sully had it his way, he'd be a hermit. I sort of forced him to be my friend. Wouldn't take no for an answer, you know? Truth was, it was hard to make friends in college. It's so easy when you're young and your best friend is the kid across the street. You're friends because it's convenient. Once you're out on your own for the first time, it's hard. And Sully looked like he hadn't made any friends, so I came over and introduced myself. We've been friends since."

"That's nice. It is hard to make friends as an adult. I lost touch with all my girlfriends from high school. I mean, we like each other's Instagram posts, but that's about the extent of our contact these days."

"Sully and I probably would have lost touch too, but he got close to my family. Mine was kind of like a second family to him, you know?"

Isabel didn't know, but she tucked that information away.

"He was there for me when my dad died. It was a hard time, but Sully didn't expect me to put on a brave face or pretend to be strong. He let me feel what I needed to feel and was just there if I needed anything. So after that, he's like family to me."

The door opened, and Sullivan climbed in. "Told you it wouldn't take long."

"You were gone like, ten minutes," Isabel said.

"Fifteen counting the time it took him to pump gas," Ryder added.

"Do y'all want to chase some storms, or do you want to joke around and make fun of me?"

Ryder gave Sullivan a smile. "Just ribbing you, man. Of course we want to see some storms. And according to the radar, if we keep heading in this direction, we'll run right into it."

About twenty minutes later, yellow and red splotches bloomed on the radar. A look at the dark clouds ahead confirmed it—a thunderstorm had arrived.

"Wow, look at that gray sky," Ryder said.

Sullivan grunted in response.

Isabel looked through the windshield and saw a bolt of lightning. "We should get the LIV parked."

Sullivan found an empty business park and pulled into a space. There were a few trees, but otherwise, the view wasn't terrible.

While Sullivan showed Ryder how the cameras inside the LIV operated, Isabel hurried to get her personal camera into position. Outside, a cool breeze whipped her hair, and a rumble of thunder sounded in the distance.

From inside the LIV, she thought she heard Sullivan laugh. Isabel couldn't remember ever hearing him laugh, and it was weird to think that Sullivan actually had friends. Maybe there was more to him than she thought.

SULLIVAN STIFLED a yawn as he drove Ryder to his vacation rental that evening. They'd caught a pretty spectacular lightning show just outside of the Brooksville city limits, and Ryder begrudgingly admitted he enjoyed it.

"It wasn't quite a tornado," Ryder said. "But it was still beautiful."

"Now will you stop teasing me for chasing waterspouts?"

Ryder nodded. "Okay, I'll admit, it was pretty fun just chasing a regular ole thunderstorm. And I like Isabel. She seems nice."

Sullivan said nothing in response and hoped the conversation would steer away from Isabel.

Earlier when they arrived back at the Lightning Institute, Torres was still there, saving Sullivan from driving Isabel home. Inwardly, he had been relieved. He didn't want to be roped into another dinner with her family. Not that he hadn't enjoyed himself last night, but it was best not to make it a habit.

"You're quiet, which means either you're pissed about something, or you don't want to talk."

"Nothing to say."

"You two seemed to get along all right. You know, when she wasn't teasing you about your long smoke breaks."

"Yeah, I guess so." No way was Sullivan admitting he was attracted to her. He'd never hear the end of it. Especially when he'd made a point in the beginning to say how much he couldn't stand her.

"I don't know how she puts up with your miserable ass."

Sullivan stopped at the light and shot Ryder an annoyed look. "You want to get out and walk to your beach house?" He was only joking, of course, but sometimes, Ryder got on his nerves.

Ryder smiled. "Come on, I'm not telling you what you don't already know. When you were taking one of your smoke breaks, we got to talking. She was asking questions about you."

An alarm bell went off in Sullivan's head. "What did you tell her?" he asked, his tone sharp.

"Nothing, just that you're a good man underneath that perpetual scowl of yours."

"You didn't tell her about…?"

"No, man. I didn't tell her anything about your past. That's your business."

Sullivan relaxed his grip on the steering wheel. He should have known Ryder wouldn't betray him. If anyone would understand what he was going through, it would be him. "I haven't told you yet, but I think my sister is living in Florida. Maybe in Clearwater."

"You found Emmy?"

"Maybe. I don't know. She has a Facebook account, which gave me the Florida clue, but she hasn't updated it in over a year, and I don't know if she's still there. I thought if I took this summer job, I'd have a chance to see if it was true."

"Have you tried looking for her yet?"

He came up on another light and stopped behind a van. "I went to Clearwater last week and asked around at the place she used to work at, but no one there knew her. The restaurant changed ownership and staff, so it was a bust. I'll make another trip there tomorrow. There's a nightclub in one of her Facebook pictures that I've been meaning to check out. Maybe she still hangs out there."

The light changed, and Sullivan made a turn. "Where is this place?"

"I think it's up ahead. Number 202. Kit said it was on the right side. Just look for my truck."

The house came into view, and Sullivan pulled into the driveway. "Well, I guess this is your stop."

"Thanks for the ride and storm chase. I had fun. Not quite like a tornado chase, but it was a good substitute."

"Next time, we'll find a waterspout."

Ryder laughed, then his expression grew serious. "Hey, I hope you find your sister."

"Thanks. You enjoy your beach vacation with your family."

"You know, the offer still stands. If you change your mind this week and need to get away, we've got room at the house. St. Pete isn't that far from Poquito Beach. Or even if you just want to come for the day. Tomorrow should be nice."

Sullivan considered it. Maybe a beach day would do him some good. "All right, I'll come for a few hours."

Ryder got out and stood at the open door. "Okay, see you

tomorrow. And tell Isabel I enjoyed meeting her. You should be nice to her. I think she likes you for some strange reason."

The door closed, and Ryder headed toward the house, leaving Sullivan stunned. There was no way Izzy could like his sorry ass. She was beautiful and kind, and she hated his nicotine habit. Sure, they tolerated each other a lot better than when they first met, but there was no way she felt anything for him. At least, he didn't think she did.

But hell, he was definitely feeling some things for her. Even when she teased him, he kind of liked it.

10

"I can't believe you're in Florida for the summer and don't own a pair of swim trunks."

Sullivan cast a glance in Ryder's direction. "It ain't like I've been here that long." He grabbed whatever was his size, not caring much about the design as long as it didn't have something stupid on it, like smiley faces. "And I haven't needed swimwear in ages." Sullivan tried to remember the last time he'd been swimming. Probably at a hotel's pool during a multi-day storm chase.

Ryder picked up a pair of sunglasses and tried them on. "Have you even been to the beach yet? And not for work."

"Once for a walk." Sullivan selected a couple more pairs of swim shorts and headed to the register. He thought of the day he ran into Isabel and Miguel at the ice cream stand. It had been purely coincidental that he found them there, but he was glad now that he had the impulse to go see the ocean.

"Earth to Sully." Ryder waved his hand in front of his face.

"What?" he said, annoyed.

Ryder laughed. "Where were you right now?"

"I was thinking I need a smoke." He wasn't about to tell Ryder the real reason he was distracted.

"You better get that out of the way before we get to the house. There's no smoking there."

Sullivan gave Ryder a dirty look.

At the beach house, Sullivan opted for the quiet of the deck while Kit, the baby, and Kit's sister, Dawn, were at the beach. He'd take a dip later when it wasn't so crowded. Trips to see the ocean were few and far between when he was growing up, but watching the waves and smelling the salty air was relaxing.

The screen door opened, and Ryder came out with two beers. "Now we can really relax," he said.

Sullivan took the cold can, which felt good on a hot day like this, and cracked it open. "I could get used to this view."

"Stay as long as you like. If you stay for dinner, you can have tacos."

"Nah," Sullivan said. "I've got something to do tonight."

"Got something better to do? Something with Isabel?" Ryder wiggled his eyebrows, a gesture that annoyed the hell out of Sullivan. Ever since Ryder had gotten married, it seemed like Ryder kept pushing him to settle down. Sullivan was getting damn tired of it.

"No. I was going to check out that night club in Clearwater."

Ryder's expression turned serious. "Oh, right. I forgot about that. Have you thought about hiring a private investigator? Maybe they could help you find your sister."

Sullivan took a sip of his beer, letting the cold, fizzy liquid run down his throat. "I've considered it, but sometimes, I wonder if I should even bother. It's been twenty years since I've seen her. She's probably out there living a good life, and she doesn't need her ugly past showing up at her door."

"Sully, from what you've told me, your sister adored you. I don't think she would be upset to see you."

"But I'll remind her of everything she left behind, if she remembers it at all. Maybe I should just leave it alone."

In the distance, there was laughter. Kit and Dawn were struggling with their beach blanket as a breeze threatened to blow it away. On the wind was the sound of a baby squealing in delight.

"I don't know, Sully," Ryder said. "Spending time with my family makes me feel happy. When I'm having a shitty day, it makes all the bad stuff in the world a little more manageable. But you don't have any of that. Wouldn't it be nice to reconnect with the only family you have left?"

Sullivan felt a twinge in his chest, the same uncomfortable feeling he always had when he thought about how much his life was missing. Of course, he wanted that feeling of belonging to a family, but life wasn't always fair. You couldn't always get what you wanted. And as good of a friend as Ryder was, he wouldn't understand. Ryder didn't have the same childhood as he had.

"I think I'll take a smoke now," Sullivan said as he stood up. He needed some alone time, and smoking was sometimes the only way to get it.

Isabel fanned herself with her hand as she followed Paulina and Ricardo around the used auto lot. Car shopping was the last thing she wanted to do on a sweltering day like this, but she was determined to leave with a vehicle this afternoon. Her paycheck had finally hit the bank, and she could afford a small down payment. She just hoped Ricardo's friend gave her a good deal.

"Relax," Ricardo said. "Carlos is an honest man. He won't sell you anything that he wouldn't drive himself."

Given that Ricardo was in the car business himself, Isabel trusted his judgment.

"This one is nice," Paulina said, running her hand along the exterior of a white sedan.

"It's a Honda," Ricardo said. "And it's much newer than the one you were driving before."

Isabel took a closer look. She wished it were red or silver, but the white wasn't terrible looking. "Is it going to be noticeable every time I need to wash it?"

Ricardo smiled. "Just bring it to the shop. I'll give it a courtesy wash. There's Carlos now."

A young bearded man headed their way. "*Hola*, Ricardo, how's it going?"

"*Hola*, Carlos. My sister-in-law needs a car."

Carlos gave Isabel a big, flashy smile. "You came to the right place. Whatever you need, I'm sure I have. You like this Honda?"

Isabel peered inside. "I'm considering it."

"Hondas are a good and dependable car."

Isabel gave Carlos a smile. "And affordable?"

He smiled back at her. "I can give you a reasonable price. You want to take it for a spin?"

She nodded. "Please."

"I'll get the keys."

Ricardo followed Carlos back into the sales office, leaving Isabel and Paulina with the car.

Isabel walked around the Honda and checked the exterior. "It looks to be in good condition. I could see myself driving this. And I like that it has four doors. It'll be easier to get Miguel in and out."

"I enjoyed meeting Sullivan the other night," Paulina said, changing the subject.

"I was surprised he stayed for dinner."

"I don't know why you call him Mr. Grumpy. He seemed perfectly pleasant to me."

Isabel looked into the back seat and found it to be roomy. "You haven't seen him when he's craving a cigarette."

Paulina nudged her arm. "I thought he was quite attractive, too."

Isabel sighed. "Not you, too. I already heard this from Mamá."

"What? You don't find him attractive?"

Isabel felt her cheeks grow warm. Of course she thought he was attractive, but she wasn't about to admit that. "If he quit smoking, sure."

"You like him."

"I don't like him!"

Paulina laughed. "Yes you do, *hermanita*. You know how I know? Because I saw the way you looked at him when he talked to Miguel."

Isabel was saved from responding when Ricardo and Carlos returned.

"Got the keys for you," Carlos said, holding them up. "I think you'll love this car."

By the end of the afternoon, she signed the paperwork for the Honda and left the lot in it. She took the long way home and used the drive to clear her mind. She was in no hurry. Miguel was having a sleepover at Juan's, and her mother had gone to the movies.

She didn't like Sullivan, did she? She certainly didn't like him in the beginning, and he wasn't always easy to get along with. But he'd been patient with Miguel, perhaps more patient than he was with adults. She'd been blessed with an inquisitive child, and the dates she had brought home in the past always wanted to shoo him away. Sullivan, however, didn't seem to mind. And she knew Miguel liked him, otherwise he wouldn't have begged him to come to dinner again.

If anything made her attracted to a man, it was getting along with her son. And that was certainly something to think about.

As she pulled up to the house, she noticed a familiar silver Mercedes parked along the curb. Mateo stood against the door, casually smoking, and her breath hitched as her mind raced for what to do. She considered driving past him, but Mateo had already spotted her.

With shaking limbs, Isabel slowed her car and carefully backed into the driveway. Her new Honda had a nice rear camera, and backing up was essential right now. If she needed to get the hell out of here, she wanted to be able to drive right out. She already decided she was staying in the vehicle, and she was leaving it running.

Isabel rolled down the window as Mateo walked to the car. The cigarette was still in his hand, and a cloud of smoke wafted into her vehicle. Isabel coughed and waved it away. "Put that away!"

Mateo frowned, then tossed it on the ground. "Sorry, *cariño*. I forgot you hate the smell."

He didn't forget. He just didn't care.

"What are you doing here?" Isabel demanded. He'd only been to her house one time, but of course, he remembered her address. He'd offered to drive her home when her car was in the shop several months ago. Having no other option, she reluctantly accepted the ride. It had been an uncomfortable drive, made worse when he put his hand on her thigh and attempted to kiss her.

"I didn't want to bother you at work, and I knew you would ignore any phone calls or texts, so I thought I'd try you at home. Please, Isabel, I just want to talk to you."

"I'm not coming back to the station, so you can stop asking me."

"That's not what I came here to say, though I still wish you would change your mind. Can you get out of the car? Maybe we could go inside and talk. I could order us dinner."

Isabel gripped the steering wheel and held her foot on the brake, ready to let go and press on the gas at any moment. "I'm not getting out of this car until you leave. So say what you came here to say, then go."

Mateo rested his arms on her window. "I came here to apologize for my behavior."

"And what behavior are you apologizing for? Making me feel uncomfortable at work? Shoving your tongue down my throat when I didn't ask for it? Assaulting me?"

"*Cariño*, I didn't mean—"

"Don't '*cariño*' me. I'm not your darling! And I want you to go. *Adiós!*"

"Isabel, I'm truly sorry for it all. I know I came on too strong, and I'm working to become a better man. I should have never treated you that way. You're a beautiful and special woman, and I'm afraid I lost control. But it'll never happen again."

Isabel rolled her eyes. "You've told me this before, and you always lie."

"I mean it this time."

"Mateo, I want you to leave. Please don't make me get a restraining order against you."

Mateo flinched. "Do you really think I would hurt you?"

Isabel wanted to scream, but she didn't want to make a scene. "You tried to force yourself on me!" she hissed.

"*Cariño*, I wouldn't do anything you didn't want."

"Go, Mateo. Leave now, or I'll call the cops." Isabel held up her phone and pulled up the call screen.

Mateo held up his hands. "All right, I'll go. *Lo siento*. I never meant to hurt you, Isabel. If you change your mind, you'll always have a job at the station."

Isabel waited as Mateo walked back to his Mercedes. Once

he drove away, she released her death grip on the steering wheel.

With weak legs, Isabel slowly got out of her car and climbed the stairs to her apartment. She didn't have an appetite for dinner now, and she was glad Miguel was in good hands for the night. Juan's mother was a nurse, and she felt comfortable knowing that she would make sure Miguel got his insulin injections on time and would check his glucose levels. As much as she loved her son, it was nice to get a break from parenting duties for a while. Being a mother was hard, but being a single mother was much harder.

She looked in the mirror, and as the tears fell, her mascara ran. Isabel washed her face, showered, and put on her pajamas. But sleep, she knew, wasn't happening tonight. She was too wired after her encounter with Mateo.

She couldn't believe he came to her house. Thank God he left, but what if he came back? What if her nightmare came true, and Mateo was planning to return when she was sleeping?

Miguel had been begging for a dog, and maybe that wasn't a bad idea. Dogs were good for security. So were boyfriends. Too bad she didn't have one of those either.

Sullivan flashed through her mind. He'd done a pretty good job of scaring Mateo off. If Sullivan was here, then for sure, Mateo wouldn't bother her.

Isabel sank onto the couch and reached for her phone. She had Sullivan's number. Sullivan would probably want to know if Mateo was bothering her again. Maybe she should call him, and he could come over to make sure that Mateo wasn't still lurking down the street. That might make sleep a little easier tonight.

After several moments of hesitation, Isabel finally pressed the call button. It rang several times, then clicked over to a voicemail with a generic robot voice telling her to leave a message after the tone.

She immediately hung up. He probably didn't want to talk on the phone. He cursed every time his cell rang, and he told her before that the only call he ever answered was Ryder's.

Well, maybe it was for the best. She wouldn't have known what to say to him anyway.

SULLIVAN FELT out of place amongst the twenty-somethings waiting in line. He couldn't believe there was a crowd of people wanting to go to this place. He certainly didn't want to be here. At thirty-five, he was definitely too old for it, and the thumping music blaring from inside was already giving him a headache.

When he finally made it into the *Infinite Rave,* he took a moment to let his eyes adjust to the dim light and his ears to the loud bass. This was his idea of hell, but if someone here knew where his sister was, he had to try.

On the dance floor, scantily clad bodies gyrated to the music, and Sullivan didn't like the idea of his baby sister being out there. Was she even here? He searched the faces of every brunette, but no one matched Emmy's description.

He made his way to the bar where a group of girls lingered. One of them gave him an icy stare, and Sullivan wanted to tell the woman to calm down. He wasn't trying to hit on her.

"I'm looking for someone," he told her, showing her his phone.

"WHAT?" she shouted.

Fuck. The music was so loud that he'd have to shout. "I'M LOOKING FOR SOMEONE. DO YOU KNOW HER?"

She squinted at his phone, then shook her head.

Sullivan spent twenty minutes—that was all he could tolerate—showing Emmy's picture around. No one he spoke to knew her, and none of the faces at the club were hers.

He exited and breathed a sigh of relief to be out of there. That was his first and last time in a dance club.

A street bench was up ahead, and Sullivan sat down for a smoke break. He wasn't getting anywhere in the club. His throat was already sore from shouting, and it was hard to find anyone who would stay still long enough for him to show Emmy's picture.

A small group of young adults walked past him, and Sullivan looked to see where they were going. He followed them, hoping he didn't look like a stalker. They led him to the boardwalk, and Sullivan figured that was as good of a place as any to ask around. Yeah, people Emmy's age would probably hang out on the boardwalk.

"Excuse me," he said to the group. "I'm looking for my sister. Do you know this woman?"

They all looked at his phone and shook their heads. Sullivan thanked them, then walked around some more. Every person about Emmy's age, he showed them her picture. No one knew who she was, and finally, Sullivan gave up. Showing Emmy's picture to random people at the beach would not help him find her. It was a futile attempt, as they were probably all tourists. He might as well be searching for a lost pet.

He considered again the possibility of hiring a private investigator. Immediately after that thought, he wondered if he should just give up. He wanted to find her, but he didn't want to bring back bad memories for her. She was probably out here living her best life, and who was he to ruin that for her?

His phone was nearly dead by the time he made it back to his vehicle. As he hooked it up to the charger, he realized he'd missed a call earlier. He probably couldn't hear it ring over that damn music.

The call was from Isabel, giving Sullivan pause. Why would Isabel call him? She hadn't left a voicemail, nor had she texted. Maybe she called him by accident?

Sullivan, not one for calling people, sent out a quick text. If it was important, she'd text him back. Otherwise, he could talk to her at work.

ISABEL CHECKED to make sure her door was secure for the third time. She even pulled on all the windows to ensure they were locked, though she never opened them as the air conditioner was always running. Isabel turned off the light and stood guard at the window, ready to see if anyone was lurking outside.

A text notification sounded on her phone. Isabel looked at the screen, seeing a message from Sullivan.

> Sullivan: Saw I missed your call. Did you need to speak to me?

There was no way she was telling him now that Mateo had been over. It had been stupid to call Sullivan. What did she expect him to do? Come over here and guard her door? He'd probably badger her again about calling the sheriff, and she wasn't about to do that.

No, best not to tell him anything. It would only create unnecessary worry, and the situation was over now. She hoped, at least. But she had to tell him something. Isabel thought of a reply and typed it out.

> Isabel: Just wanted to tell you I got a new car, so I won't need a ride to work anymore.

Sullivan texted back moments later with a thumbs up emoji, and Isabel let out the breath she was holding, relieved that he didn't suspect she was lying.

She'd been about to put away her phone when she saw he was typing something else.

Sullivan: Sunday looks good for some severe storms in the afternoon. See you tomorrow?

Isabel smiled, glad to have the conversation shift to something else.

Isabel: I'll be there.

11

Isabel yawned as she peeked out the window the next morning, seeing no sign of Mateo. Maybe it was silly to think he'd be outside her house this early, though she hadn't expected he'd be waiting for her when she got home. What if he came back when Miguel or her mother was here?

A knot settled into the pit of her stomach. If her mother found out that Mateo had stopped by, Isabel was sure she would drag her to the Pinellas County Sheriff's Department to report his assault. But reporting Mateo would mean a media circus, and the last thing Isabel wanted was that kind of attention or scrutiny. She was sure people would accuse her of lying about what he did. Why couldn't Mateo just leave her alone?

Her phone dinged with a notification, distracting her from her thoughts. The text was from Elena, Juan's mom, letting her know Miguel was on the way home. Isabel needed to shake off her worry and put on a smile—fast.

A few moments later, Isabel heard Miguel's fast-paced footsteps on the stairs and his cheerful little boy voice. Isabel let Miguel in and waved to Elena across the street. "*¡Gracias!*" she called out.

Miguel, still in his pajamas, ran past her and threw his overnight bag on the couch. "You got a new car, Mamá!"

"Yes, I did! We'll go driving in it later. Did you have a good time, *nene?*"

"The best! Juan's dog slept next to me all night, and when I threw the tennis ball, he'd bring it back to me. Please, Mamá, can we get a dog too?"

Isabel sighed, knowing that even though a dog might make her feel safer, it was out of the question right now. "We'll talk about it later, *nene*. Now, let's do your injection, eat some breakfast, and get out of those pajamas. I have to go to work today, so you'll be spending the day with Abuela."

Miguel grimaced. "Does that mean I have to put on church clothes?"

"*Sí, nene.*" She knew her mother would give her grief for skipping church to work on a Sunday, but she would deal with that argument later.

"Aw," Miguel whined. "But I hate wearing church clothes."

"So you'll bring something else to wear after." She grabbed his bag from the couch. "Take this to your room and get what you need."

An envelope fell out of the side pocket as she handed it to him, and Isabel picked it up from the floor. "What's this?"

"It was in the mailbox," Miguel said as he went to his room.

Isabel thought it was strange that there was mail in the box. The postal worker had come before she went car shopping, and Isabel had emptied it out. Maybe a neighbor had placed it in her box. Sometimes she got their mail too.

As she turned the envelope over, she saw only her first name scribbled across the front in shaky letters. Only one person she knew had terrible handwriting like that. Her heart raced as she pulled out the glossy card from the unsealed envelope. On the front were several palm trees against an orange sky at sunset. An otherwise beautiful card if it weren't for the sender. Inside, there was a short message.

> *Lo siento, cariño. I didn't mean to upset you again.*
> *- Mateo*

Isabel pressed the foot pedal on the trash can and tossed the card in the bin. Moments later, she dug it back out and stuffed it in the junk drawer. If she ever had the courage to report Mateo to the authorities, it would be good to keep it for evidence.

A GUSTY WIND slammed rain into the windshield as Isabel swerved to stay in her lane. It was afternoon, and the Storm Prediction Center had put north central Florida under a slight risk for severe weather. There was even the possibility of a rotating storm. The National Weather Service had several counties under a tornado watch.

Isabel reached for the radio dial and turned off the music. She could barely hear it over the rain anyway, and she needed to concentrate. She didn't like driving when the rain was this intense, but with the threat of tornadoes, Sullivan wanted to man the radar for once. He was even wearing his tornado shirt today.

"I can't believe Ryder didn't want to join us with the threat of tornadoes," Isabel said, making conversation. "I thought that was his thing."

"Yeah, it is, but he said they were going to Orlando today and he couldn't get out of it. Makes no sense to take a child less than a year old to a theme park."

Isabel laughed. "It's probably more for the adults. Hope they don't get rained out."

"These storms are moving fast, so if they do, it won't last long."

Isabel eased on the brake at a light. They were driving through a populated part of town, and Isabel was eager to get out of this area and back on the highway. "If we could just get past this intense line of storms, we'd be able to get a good lightning show. Should I keep heading north?"

"No, pull over. I'm concerned about this cell. I'm looking at the velocity."

Isabel frowned. "Rotation?"

"Yeah, they'll probably issue a warning on it."

They hit a sheet of rain that brought visibility down to almost nothing, and Isabel managed to get the LIV safely to a grocery store's parking lot. As she put the vehicle into park, a loud rumble of thunder startled her. Rain pummeled the windshield.

"Let's just wait this out for a bit," Sullivan said.

The shrill sound of an emergency alert sent Isabel's heart racing. She grabbed her phone and read the message:

TORNADO WARNING

"Shit! Tornado!"

"We're fine where we are," Sullivan said. "It's north of us. That's why I didn't think we should go any further."

Isabel's limbs felt weak as she struggled to get her breathing back to normal. "How can you be so calm right now? I feel like my heart just jumped out of my chest when that alarm went off."

Sullivan shrugged. "I guess it doesn't faze me anymore. I've heard that emergency sound so many times, and I was expecting it. And Ryder said there are no tornadoes in Florida to chase."

"You should text him."

Sullivan reached for his phone. "I think I will."

Isabel couldn't help but be nosy and glanced at Sullivan's screen.

> Sullivan: Tornado warning in north Florida. Bet you wish you'd brought the T-Rex.

She thought she saw him grin, but it happened so fast that she wondered if she imagined it.

"How long is this warning going to go on?"

"Until two-thirty, unless it dies out before then."

She pulled up the radar app on her phone and saw the red polygon over the map. The storm was moving away from them, but still close enough for them to be in the warning zone.

Sullivan's phone dinged, and Isabel was shocked to hear him laugh. Maybe he only laughed when he talked to Ryder. "What's funny?"

He showed her his phone. "He sent me a middle finger emoji."

Her heart had finally slowed down, and she felt her anxiety lessen as the rain eased. Isabel was used to waterspouts, but it wasn't often that she was so close to a tornado on land. "What's the craziest twister you and Ryder ever chased?"

He was quiet for a moment as he considered her question. "I guess that would have to be the first one we drove into with the T-Rex. That was wild."

"Weren't you scared?"

"Nah. Been through way scarier things than that. It was nothing."

"Like what?"

Sullivan looked at her. "What do you mean?"

"What could be scarier than driving into a tornado?"

"People."

He didn't elaborate, and when Sullivan turned his attention back to the radar, Isabel realized that was all he was going to say.

The rain finally stopped, and just before two-thirty, the National Weather Service ended the warning. Sullivan and Isabel had a decision to make.

"If we go north, we'll run into some more storms, but that'll put us getting back late," Sullivan said. "What do you want to do?"

Isabel considered chasing more storms, or being at home with Miguel. "I don't want to get home late. It would be nice to eat dinner with Miguel."

"Then let's head home. There'll be more lightning this week."

Isabel put the LIV into drive. "Maybe not tomorrow. I heard sunshine was in the forecast."

At the gas station, Sullivan took over the wheel. Isabel was grateful for the chance to rest her eyes. She was tired and just wanted to go home and see Miguel. The adrenaline rush from the tornado scare had drained her energy.

As they pulled into the Lightning Institute's parking lot, she received a FaceTime call. Isabel saw Miguel's smiling face.

"Hi, *nene.*"

"Hi, Mamá. When are you coming home?"

"Soon. Mr. Sullivan and I just got back. I'll be home in about ten minutes."

"Hi, Mr. Sullivan!"

Isabel turned the phone so that Sullivan would be in the shot.

"Hey, kid."

"Did you and Mamá get a lot of lightning videos and pictures?"

Sullivan shook his head. "Not really, but we saw a lot of rain and almost got caught in a tornado."

"Were you scared?"

"Nah, but I think your mom was."

Isabel's jaw dropped. "I was not! It was only the phone alert that startled me. I wasn't scared of the storm."

"Okay," Sullivan said, though the look on his face told Isabel he didn't believe her.

Isabel turned the phone back to face her. "We were fine, *nene*. And you know what? Tomorrow it should be sunny. Might be a good beach day. What do you say?"

"Yes! Mr. Sullivan, you want to come too?"

Isabel bit her lower lip. She knew Miguel liked Sullivan, but she hadn't expected him to invite him to their beach trip. "*Nene*, I'm sure Mr. Sullivan is busy tomorrow."

"Are you busy, Mr. Sullivan?" Miguel asked. "Because if you're not, you could come to the beach with us. It's a lot of fun!"

Isabel tried to gauge Sullivan's reaction. "It's up to you," she whispered.

Sullivan shrugged. "I could be persuaded to go."

"Yay!" Miguel cheered.

"Okay, *nene*, let me go and I'll be home soon. *Te amo*."

"Love you too, Mamá."

Isabel ended the video call. She looked at Sullivan. "Sorry, I know it's kind of hard to say no to him."

"It's all right. I like the ocean. Do you want me to pick you up?"

Isabel was about to say yes, then changed her mind. "Actually, let me pick you up. Miguel always drags sand in, and you don't want to get your brand new Jeep all dirty. And anyway, he still has to sit on a booster seat. Just text me your address, and I'll pick you up at nine-thirty? Or is that too early?"

"That's fine."

Isabel nodded. "Great. It's a date." She regretted her choice of words and thought of correcting herself, but Sullivan was already getting out of the LIV.

"I like your new car," Sullivan said as they made their way to their vehicles.

"It's not flashy like that Jeep of yours, but it gets me around. And Carlos had it detailed, so even though it's used, it sort of looks new."

Sullivan peered into the backseat. "Ain't going to look like that tomorrow after the beach. You sure you don't want to take my vehicle?"

Isabel tossed her purse into the driver's seat. "I'm sure. It'll get dirty soon enough. Tends to happen when you have a kid. Well, see you tomorrow."

Sullivan gave her a nod, then Isabel closed the door. As she buckled her seatbelt, she watched him from her rearview mirror. He was lighting up a cigarette, even though he'd already smoked one about a half hour ago. She knew he couldn't resist a cigarette at the end of the chase day. It was really too bad. If it weren't for his filthy smoking habit, she might actually find him attractive. Because of course, she didn't find him attractive, no matter what her sister said.

12

Sullivan checked the clock and wondered if he had enough time to get a smoke in. Isabel was on the way. If it had been his choice, he would have picked her up. He didn't care about getting his vehicle sandy, and he would have volunteered to put Miguel's booster seat in the back. But Isabel insisted on driving, so Sullivan agreed.

But now he wanted a smoke, and it was almost nine-thirty. He shook a cigarette out, lit up, and closed his eyes as he inhaled.

Outside, a horn beeped. A text from Isabel followed.

Isabel: We're here.

Sullivan leaned his head back. So much for a smoke. He got in one more drag, stubbed it out into the ashtray, then headed out the door. He'd have to get his nicotine fix later.

Isabel's shiny Honda sat idling in the driveway. It was a smaller car, and his head nearly hit the roof, but he didn't complain. The interior smelled overwhelmingly of Isabel's coconut sunscreen, and Sullivan liked that.

"Hi, Mr. Sullivan!" Miguel said from the back.

"Hey, kid. Ready for the beach?"

Miguel held up his sand bucket. "*Sí.* Will you help me make a sandcastle?"

Sullivan never had much beach time as a kid, and therefore, had never perfected the art of sandcastle building. But he put on a smile and nodded. "Sure, we'll see if we can build a big one."

When they arrived, Sullivan paid the meter before Isabel got out her credit card.

"Just let me pay for it," he said. "You spent the gas picking me up and driving here."

Isabel smiled. "Okay, I suppose that's fair. Thank you."

Once they hauled their stuff to the beach, they found the place packed. Typical, Sullivan thought. All the damn tourists were out too. But at least there was one open space he could see. "Over there, by the pier," he said, pointing to the right.

"No, we can't swim by the pier." She leaned in closer. "Too many people are fishing on the pier, and sharks are attracted to the bait."

Sullivan nodded. "Right. I guess that makes sense."

"I grew up on the water, so I learned these things. Let's walk further down."

Miguel ran ahead and waved when he found a spot he liked.

Isabel looked at Sullivan and smiled. "I guess that'll do."

Miguel reached for the sand bucket in his bag. "Can I go now, Mamá?"

"*Sí*, but stay where I can see you, and don't go in water above your knees."

"I won't!" Miguel shouted as he took off toward the water.

Isabel laughed softly. "Good thing we already put on sunscreen. Remember when you were a kid, and all you wanted to do was get in the water, but you would have to wait first?"

Sullivan didn't, but he nodded anyway. "You need help with all this?" He indicated the beach chairs and umbrella he'd helped carry from the car. Isabel had brought everything to the beach. When Sullivan made a beach trip, he just brought himself.

Isabel pulled the blanket from her tote bag. "That would be great."

Sullivan set up the umbrella while Isabel spread the blanket on the sand. Once the chairs were placed in the shade, Sullivan sat in one. He breathed in the salty air and felt himself relax.

"Help yourself to some water if you want some," Isabel said, indicating the cooler she had brought. "I brought more than enough."

He felt thirsty, so he pulled out a cold bottle. "Thanks. You thought of everything."

"When you're a mom, you have to. I think I'll join Miguel. It's hot, and a dip sounds lovely."

She took off her shirt, revealing a red bikini top underneath, and Sullivan quickly averted his eyes before Isabel caught him staring.

"You coming?" Isabel asked. She pulled down her shorts and tossed them on the blanket. Her bikini bottoms were tiny, and the outline of her rear end was clearly visible.

Sullivan choked on his water.

"You okay?" Isabel looked at him with concern.

He coughed. "Fine. Just went down the wrong way." He coughed again. "You go ahead. I'll join you in a bit."

"Okay. Don't be too long. Miguel will want to build that sandcastle soon."

Isabel walked toward the water, and as she did, Sullivan couldn't help but notice her backside again. He did want to join them, but he needed a moment to himself.

And he needed a certain part of his anatomy to behave.

Isabel held Miguel's hand as they let the waves hit their ankles. The water was a little cold at first, but she soon got used to it and ventured out a little further. Miguel, who never thought the water felt cold, let go of her hand and sat in the surf. A wave rolled in and splashed his chest, and the boy laughed.

"You'll get sand in your swim trunks doing that," Sullivan said.

Isabel turned around. He wore a pair of blue swim shorts, and she tried not to stare at his bare chest. Who knew grouchy Sullivan worked out?

She must have been gawking at him, because Sullivan gave her a questioning look. "What? Do I have sunscreen on my face or something?"

Isabel shook her head, scrambling for an excuse. "Oh, no. I was just—you really do look like that guy from *Bermuda Time Warp*." Though in Isabel's opinion, Sullivan looked way better.

"I looked up the show online, and I don't see the resemblance between me and the lead actor."

"Well, there were a lot of scenes with him walking on the beach without a shirt on, and you reminded me of him." Isabel felt her cheeks grow hot. Why did she say *that*? She didn't want Sullivan to know she was staring at his abs.

When he turned slightly, Isabel caught sight of a tattoo on his shoulder and back. Finally, something else to focus on. "What's that?"

Sullivan turned around. "What's what?"

"Your tattoo."

"Oh, this?" Sullivan showed her his back shoulder. "Had it done a few years ago."

It was a tattoo of dark clouds and lightning bolts. Isabel wanted to touch it, but held back. "The detail is beautiful."

"It should be. The tattoo artist was booked out for a year. It was worth the wait."

"What made you get it? You love lightning that much?"

"It reminds me of someone."

Isabel wanted to ask who, but before she could, Miguel ran over and grabbed Sullivan's hand. "Come on, Mr. Sullivan! Let's go swimming!"

They played in the water for a while. Sullivan and Miguel splashed while Isabel simply tried to stay on her feet when the waves came in. When Isabel needed a break, Sullivan offered to stay in the water with Miguel.

"Are you sure?" Isabel said. "Don't you want to sit under the umbrella and relax for a while?"

"I'll relax when I'm ready," he said. "Go sit under the umbrella. I've got him."

Isabel crossed the hot sand to her beach chair. This was definitely a first. The last guy she'd brought to the beach seemed annoyed by Miguel's constant pestering. She didn't date that guy long.

Sullivan, on the other hand, played hard with him. She even heard Sullivan laugh a few times, which was a rarity for a man who never smiled.

Isabel watched them from the shade of the umbrella as they worked on building a sandcastle. When Sullivan placed the wet sand in the bucket and dumped it out, his creation crumbled.

Miguel laughed. "No, not like that. Let me show you."

Miguel took the bucket, filled it with wet sand, and overturned it to create a perfect bucket-shaped pile of sand. "Do it carefully. See?"

"Ahh, okay. I don't make a lot of sandcastles."

Isabel closed her eyes and listened to them carry on a conversation. She felt safe resting her eyes for a moment. Miguel was in good hands.

When Isabel took Miguel for a bathroom break, Sullivan took the opportunity to grab a smoke. Playing with Miguel had been a good distraction from his craving, but now, the need to smoke was urgent. He lit up his Marlboro and closed his eyes as he enjoyed the first inhalation. For the next few minutes, he could relax.

By the time he was extinguishing his butt in the sand, Miguel suddenly appeared. Sullivan looked up, but didn't see Isabel.

"Where's your mom?"

"She's slow." Miguel pointed behind him, where Isabel was casually walking toward the blanket. "Are you smoking?"

"I was."

"You shouldn't smoke. It's bad for you."

"Yeah, I know."

"You should quit smoking because it makes you sick."

"I agree," came Isabel's voice. She sat in her beach chair and waved her hand in the air. "And it stinks. I still smell it."

"Y'all are getting on my case, huh?" Sullivan wanted to be annoyed, but he knew they were right.

"Have you ever tried to quit?" Isabel asked him.

Sullivan shrugged. "A few times."

"Well, if you'd like to try quitting again, I could make this fun for you."

Sullivan looked at Isabel. She had a spark in her eye. "What are you suggesting, Izzy?"

"If you quit smoking, I'll let you have complete control of the radio in the LIV, even when it's my turn to drive. You can listen to all the country music you want, and I won't complain about it. And, as a bonus, I'll stop calling you Elmer."

"Elmer?" Miguel laughed. "Is that your first name, Mr. Sullivan?"

Sullivan winced. "Yeah. Ain't it awful?"

"Sounds like Elmer's glue."

"Yeah, which is why I go by my last name. You get teased when you have a name like Elmer. Elmer's glue. Elmer Fudd. I hate it. I was named after my grandpa. It's some old-timey name."

"So, are you going to take the bet?" Isabel asked. She took some strawberry scented lip balm and rolled it over her lips, and damn if Sullivan didn't imagine those lips on him.

He shook his head, trying to get thoughts of Isabel's pouting mouth out of his mind. "No, quitting is hard."

"Oh, too bad. I find smoking such a turnoff. And I think you might actually clean up nicely once the nicotine is out of your system. But if you want to keep on ruining your good looks, be my guest."

Sullivan tried not to smile, but felt the corner of his mouth turn upward anyway. He couldn't believe what he was hearing. "You think I look good?"

Isabel looked him up and down in a discerning manner. "You'd look better if you gave up the cigarettes. But I guess it's too hard for you to stop, which is too bad."

Sullivan couldn't explain why he wanted Isabel's approval. Usually, he didn't give two shits what anyone thought of him, but Isabel was different. And she thought he was attractive?

With a sigh, he gave in. "All right, Izzy, I'll take your bet. But if I can't do it, does this mean I'll have to endure hours of *Livin' La Vida Loca* or whatever it is you listen to?"

"If you cheat, then absolutely. And by the way, I haven't listened to Ricky Martin in forever. But I'll be happy to play that request just to annoy you."

Sullivan grunted. "I'm sure you would." He reached for his cigarettes and held them up. There were three left. "But look, the bet starts tomorrow. You've got to let me finish this last pack. Paid good money for these."

He caught Isabel rolling her eyes. "Fine, have your last few smokes. But tomorrow, if you show up smelling like an ashtray, I'll know you cheated."

He knew she was right. Damn.

THE NEXT DAY, Isabel knew Sullivan hadn't had his morning cigarette. For one, he was grouchier than all get out. His road rage was fierce, with every driver getting either cursed out, honked at, or flipped off. He'd even snapped at Isabel a few times when she was slow to read the radar. Isabel weighed which Sullivan was worse: cranky Sullivan without a cigarette, or regular grumpy Sullivan who smoked a pack a day. Well, she was glad not to smell it. And without the stench of cigarette smoke, she could actually smell the soap he'd used in his shower this morning. It was nice.

"Chill out," Isabel said. "You just have to give the radar time to load. We'll get to the storm."

"I'm stopping at the gas station."

Isabel's head snapped up. "Oh no, you're not buying cigarettes. I know you're craving one, but you'll get past it."

"I wasn't going to, but I need something."

Isabel didn't know what that "something" was, but she herself craved a big glass of wine. She couldn't wait to be home.

Inside the convenience store, Isabel stuck to Sullivan like glue, not trusting him to not buy cigarettes. At the register, he purchased a multi-pack of Big Red gum and a soda.

"See? I told you I wasn't going to buy them."

Isabel smiled. "I'm proud of you for not giving in. You must really hate my taste in music, huh?"

Sullivan had already ripped open the gum and shoved a stick into his mouth. "I just want to prove to you I can quit. You don't believe me, but I'll show you."

Isabel placed her own items on the counter. "Okay."

"You don't think I can do it?"

Isabel shrugged. "I know the first few days will be hard, but I'm sure it'll get easier." Not that she had ever had an addiction to cigarettes, but she knew habits were hard to break.

By the time they reached their storm destination, Sullivan had already gone through an entire pack of chewing gum.

Isabel picked up the foil wrappers that Sullivan had tossed to the floor. "You're going to rot your teeth out."

"I ain't smoking. Isn't that what you wanted?"

"At least it's not chewing tobacco," she said, then regretted it. She didn't want to give him any ideas. Her abuelo chewed tobacco, and it had always grossed her out.

They watched the lightning show, with Sullivan cracking his gum the whole time. Isabel flinched every time she heard the pop, but didn't complain anymore. She'd take the gum smacking over the stench of cigarette smoke.

HE'D MADE IT. One full day, minus the remaining hours until bedtime, without a cigarette.

It had been hell.

Not that he didn't want to quit smoking—on the contrary. He knew it wasn't good for him, but it wasn't like other people didn't make bad health decisions. Some people ate junk food all the time. Others drank too much. Sullivan didn't do any of that. Well, he wasn't perfect when it came to eating vegetables, and he only occasionally got drunk.

The point was that Sullivan had a bad habit, just like anyone else. But quitting was hard. He'd tried it a few times and only lasted a day or two. A lot of times, he wished he hadn't started at all. He still remembered that first cigarette he'd stolen from his mother's purse. He'd merely been curious, and only started because his stepdad told him not to. He wasn't ever going to listen to what that bastard had to say.

An older woman gave him a dirty look as he entered the pharmacy. He probably looked like he was about to murder someone. If he didn't get some nicotine in his system, he'd be tempted to. Heaven help anyone who pissed him off right now.

Five minutes later, he walked out with cinnamon-flavored nicotine gum, which he figured would help him a lot better than Big Red. At least this way, the cravings would calm down, and he could think straight.

In his car, he ripped open the package and popped one into his mouth. It wasn't half bad—he just hoped it actually worked. If not for himself, then definitely for Isabel.

13

Isabel looked up from the desk when Sullivan walked in the next day. He ignored her when she said good morning, and twenty minutes later, she heard him yelling at the vending machine. She wondered if he'd kept his promise not to smoke. Judging from his foul mood, she guessed he had.

She stood at the entrance to the break room and watched Sullivan shake the vending machine. It was notorious for taking money but not giving you anything. She looked behind the plexiglass and saw his snack hanging on the edge. "If you want the chips that bad, you can just buy another bag."

He glared at her. "I don't want to buy a second bag. I put in four quarters, and I want my damn Lays."

Isabel sauntered into the break room, inserted a dollar bill into the slot, then selected the button for the chips. Both bags fell, and Isabel reached for them. "There, Mr. Grumpy. Your barbeque chips."

Sullivan snatched one of the bags and stormed out of the room.

Isabel opened her chips and followed him. "Someone is

grouchy this morning. I guess this means you haven't had a morning cigarette."

He sat at the computer and pulled up the latest weather models.

"You haven't, right? I mean, I don't smell cigarette smoke, but I suppose you could have showered and used mouthwash."

He closed the laptop. "For your information, no. I haven't lit up since Monday night."

"Okay, just checking. Come find me if you feel like giving in and having a cigarette. I could distract you."

Isabel turned away and wanted to smack herself. *I could distract you.* Why the hell did she say *that?* And distract him by doing what? Talking to him about the weather? Arguing with him? Certainly not kissing him.

Except she sort of wanted to. His breath didn't smell like an ashtray now.

She sat down and ate a chip. Last night, she dreamed she and Sullivan were on the island from *Bermuda Time Warp*. They drove through the tropical forest in the LIV. Outside, a thunderstorm raged on, and a country ballad played on the radio as he kissed her. When she woke up, she could almost feel the stubble from his five o'clock shadow. She blamed Paulina for putting thoughts of liking Sullivan into her head.

"Sarasota to Cape Coral looks good," Sullivan said, startling her out of her thoughts. "Leave in ten minutes?"

Isabel nodded. "Fine."

Sullivan headed out the door. From the window, Isabel saw him standing in the middle of the parking lot. She wondered if he was trying to sneak a smoke break, but he just stood there.

She shrugged, then ate another chip.

~

SULLIVAN MONITORED the light green on the screen while Isabel drove. Because he hadn't smoked, Isabel let him control the music selection. It was, at least, some kind of distraction from his cigarette withdrawals, but he was going to need a lot more than that to get through this day.

"Anything on the radar?" Isabel asked. She turned on the blinker and slowly eased into the other lane, even though Sullivan couldn't see any cars behind them.

"You drive like a grandmother."

"Radar?" she asked, ignoring his comment.

"Just keep driving south. Something will pop up soon."

Twenty minutes later, the light green on the radar bloomed into splotches of yellow and red. They were usually fast pop-up storms, but fortunately, they had arrived just in time. Isabel parked the LIV near a school ball field for them to observe.

Sullivan occupied himself with the camera equipment and tried to ignore his craving for a cigarette. His body was jonesing for some nicotine, and bad. He wished he had an IV of it straight into his vein. He eyed the gas station across the street, and the urge to go in and buy a pack of Marlboro was strong. Anything to stop the shaky feeling taking over him.

"Don't even think about it."

Sullivan looked at Isabel. "What?"

"I know what you're thinking. That gas station is right over there, and they have exactly what you want right now."

Sullivan glared at her, hating that she could read his mind. Not being able to fight the urge for nicotine any longer, he reached into his pocket and pulled out his gum.

"That's not Big Red. Did you go through that entire package already?"

He didn't answer and popped the gum piece into his mouth. It wasn't as good as a cigarette, but it would have to do.

Isabel picked up the gum package. "This is nicotine gum."

"So? Is that not allowed? Because I'm using it to help me quit. I'm not smoking. Isn't that what you wanted?"

She placed the gum back into the console. "I'll allow it. Certainly smells nicer."

Sullivan looked at the gray skies and saw a lightning bolt connect to the ground. A loud crack of thunder immediately followed, and Sullivan relaxed. Weird how a fierce storm from Mother Nature could put his mind at ease.

Isabel moved to the back of the vehicle and came back moments later with her tripod and video camera. "I better get my time-lapse video for Miguel."

"You need to stay in the fucking vehicle," he snapped. "The storm is too close, and it's dangerous."

"Says the man who used to drive through tornadoes," Isabel countered, then stepped outside.

Sullivan supposed she had him there. He gave his gum a hard chew. The cinnamon flavor was already fading.

Outside, he heard Isabel curse in Spanish as a wind toppled over her tripod. That at least gave him a chuckle. Her hair whipped around her face as she struggled to get it upright. When she finally got her camera attached, a light sprinkle started.

"*¡Mierda!*" Isabel cursed.

Sullivan laughed again as Isabel came back inside with her camera and tripod. "It's sprinkling."

"Told you the storm was too close."

Isabel narrowed her eyes at him. "I could do without your smug attitude. Chew your damn gum."

Sullivan cracked a smile. Seeing Isabel pissed was at least entertainment. And as a bonus, it gave his mind something else to think about other than a cigarette.

~

ON THE WAY BACK HOME, Isabel let Sullivan take the wheel. She was tired of driving, and Sullivan did drive faster, so at least she would be home soon.

Her phone rang, and Isabel reached for it on the console. It was her mother. "Hi, Mamá."

"*Mija*, I have bad news. The magician you hired for Miguel's birthday party just canceled. He said he had a family emergency. He can give us a refund or we can reschedule."

"We'll take the refund. There's no point in rescheduling. His birthday is on Saturday."

"Should I find someone else? A clown or someone who dresses up like cartoon characters or something? We have to have some kind of entertainment."

"No, Mamá, don't bother. We'll have the bouncy house, and that should be enough." She was actually grateful the magician had canceled. This party was already getting expensive, and she could use the extra funds. "Look, let's just let it be a simple birthday party. Miguel will have fun with his cousins and friends, and we'll make sure everyone has something they can eat."

"I'm making those keto vanilla cupcakes for him and a regular cake for everyone else."

"That's perfect."

"Oh, Miguel wants to talk to you."

She heard the shuffle of the phone being passed to Miguel. "Hi, Mamá. When are you coming home?"

"Soon, *nene*."

"I don't have to have a magician for my party, but can Juan bring his dog?"

Isabel smiled. "Okay, but tell Juan to bring poop bags in case his puppy uses the bathroom in our yard."

Miguel laughed. "His dog poops *a lot!*"

Which was why she was glad they did *not* have a pet. But

she supposed at some point, she'd give in and let Miguel have one. Maybe for Christmas. Or sooner, if Mateo kept bothering her. She'd have to research breeds that made good family guard dogs and start saving up for one.

Isabel looked up and saw the Lightning Institute's parking lot come into view. "Oh, Mr. Sullivan and I just got back to work, so I'll be home in a few."

"Ask Mr. Sullivan to come to my birthday party."

Isabel wasn't so sure Sullivan would accept, but smiled. "I'll ask him. See you soon. *Te amo, nene.*"

"*Te amo.*"

Isabel ended the call and smiled at Sullivan.

"Ask me what?" He looked like he was already going to say no.

Isabel cleared her throat. "Miguel invited you to his birthday party on Saturday. My son really likes you." Not that she would admit it, but Isabel liked him too.

Sullivan hesitated. "I don't know. A birthday party with a bunch of screaming kids doesn't sound like the way I'd like to spend my Saturday."

"I get it. I do. Before I had kids, the last thing I wanted to do was to be around loud children. But adults will be there too, and the kids will play with each other. And also, there'll be alcohol. You like beer?"

The corner of Sullivan's mouth turned upward. "Well now, if there's going to be beer, I might be persuaded."

"Miguel really wants you to come."

Sullivan was quiet for a moment as he appeared to mull it over. "What time?"

"Around four. If you come any sooner, it might be a little crazy with Miguel's friends over. After that, it'll be just family. You can leave anytime, but if you stay, you could join us for dinner. So, you want to come?"

"I'd hate to disappoint the kid, and I won't turn down free alcohol. I'll be there."

"Miguel will be so excited." She was too, but kept it to herself.

ISABEL WATCHED as her mother flipped a quesadilla in a pan. She and Miguel had come over for breakfast as Isabel was low on groceries again. Her mother was a better cook anyway, and today's breakfast was egg and cheese quesadillas. Isabel would have been fine with a bowl of cereal, but since Miguel's diagnosis, they were trying out more diabetic-friendly options. Carlita had already made a few.

Isabel leaned closer to the plate. "It smells delicious."

"Mamá?" Miguel called out from the living room.

"Yes, *nene*?"

"Mr. Ramirez is here. I see his car outside."

Isabel froze. After the weekend incident, she'd been afraid Mateo would come back.

"What's he doing here?" Carlita demanded, abandoning the quesadilla and hurrying to the living room. Isabel followed.

Miguel pointed out the window. "He's at our house knocking on the door."

Isabel pushed the curtain back. Mateo was at the top of the stairs holding a box. He'd obviously rang the doorbell and was waiting for Isabel to answer. He didn't realize she wasn't at home.

"Are you going back to work at the TV station, Mamá?"

"No."

The screen door squeaked open, and Isabel snapped her head around to see her mother storming out the front door. Isabel hurried after her.

"Get off my property!" Carlita yelled.

Mateo turned around, the box still in hand. "I just came to bring Isabel her things."

Carlita held up her fist. "You leave that box, then you get the hell off my property! And you stop bothering my Isabel!"

Isabel's eyes widened. If anyone ever wondered who she got her fiery temper from, she was looking at her. Isabel placed her hand on her mother's arm. "Mamá, let me handle this."

Carlita frowned at her, seemingly reluctant to let Isabel get close to him, but she nodded.

Mateo came down the stairs and met Isabel in the driveway. "I didn't mean to cause any trouble, *cariño.*"

"Stop calling me that!" Isabel snapped.

"Right, sorry. I just thought I'd bring your personal belongings you left at the station. I guess it's obvious you don't want to return."

"Thank you for bringing my things back. You can go now."

Mateo glanced over Isabel's shoulder, then looked back at Isabel. "I'll leave. *Adiós.*" He walked back to his vehicle with his designer black leather shoes crunching on the gravel below.

Her mother muttered a curse under her breath, which Isabel hoped Miguel had not heard.

"He better not come back," Carlita said.

Miguel had the screen door cracked, and Isabel caught a whiff of something burning. "*Mamá, las quesadillas.*"

"Oh!" Carlita hurried back into the house.

Miguel gently tugged on her shirt. "Mamá, why did Abuela yell at Mr. Ramirez?"

Isabel hadn't told her son anything about Mateo, as there was no need to trouble him with adult matters. "*Nene*, Mr. Ramirez and I don't get along anymore. He didn't treat me kindly at work, and that's why we told him to leave."

Miguel frowned. "I thought Mr. Ramirez was a nice man. He showed me the green screen at the TV station."

"I know, and he was polite in the beginning, but I'm afraid

he's not a nice man at all. Come on, let's go help Abuela in the kitchen."

"Thanks to him, this quesadilla burned," Carlita complained as she threw the remains of the burnt one into the trash.

"At least the other ones are fine," Isabel said. "And I think we have enough now. Miguel, go have your breakfast before it gets cold."

Once Miguel was settled at the table, her mother motioned for her to come to the bedroom. Once there, Carlita closed the door.

"I didn't want Miguel to hear us talking, though I am sorry for losing my temper in front of him."

"It's okay."

"It's not okay. That's the second time that man has dropped by to see you. He could have mailed your things back or had it delivered by someone else."

Isabel bit her lip. "Actually, Mamá, that wasn't the second time I've seen him. He came by Saturday when you were gone."

Carlita's eyes bulged. "What? Why didn't you tell me?"

"I didn't want to worry you. He was waiting for me when I came home. I stayed in my car until he left."

"What did he want?"

"He said he came to apologize, but it's nothing I haven't heard before. I know he's not sincere."

"That's it, *mija*. You are going straight down to the Sheriff's tomorrow and you'll make a formal charge!"

"Mamá, no! He's a local celebrity. Everyone loves Mateo Ramirez the Weather Guy!"

"I certainly don't love him."

"It'll be a media circus if word gets out. I just want to move past this and forget it." Isabel looked at her watch. "I should get to work soon."

"You eat breakfast first, and then you go to work. It's sunny right now. No storms to chase."

Isabel sighed. So much for avoiding the conversation.

"*Mija,* I fear for your safety. This man needs to leave you alone. Please do something."

Carlita blocked the doorway, and Isabel knew she wouldn't allow her to leave until she agreed to go to the authorities. "If he comes back, I'll file a protective order. I promise. But I think that's the last time I'll see him. He just came to drop off my things. That's all."

Carlita huffed. "I hope and pray that's the last we'll see of him. You should be careful when you're out on your own. And you carry that mace I gave you."

Isabel nodded. "*Sí,* Mamá."

"¡Mamá!" Miguel called out from the kitchen. "I spilled water on the table!"

"Got to help Miguel," Isabel said, grateful for the distraction as she slipped past her mother.

SULLIVAN CURSED when he saw Isabel waiting for him at work. He was late, and Isabel was standing outside the LIV with her arms crossed. She looked pissed, and if he had to guess, it was because of him. Usually when she had that look on her face, she was mad at him for something.

She charged toward him as he stepped out of his Jeep. "You were supposed to be here a half hour ago. We're going to miss the storms."

Yep, she was pissed. "Relax, Izzy. Look up." He pointed to the sky. "See those gray storm clouds? Ain't like we got to drive too far today."

Isabel glared at him. "Look, I've had a bad morning, and I

have one nerve left. Don't step on it." She wrenched the LIV's passenger door open and climbed in.

The gum in his mouth had already lost its flavor, so Sullivan spit it out on the pavement. No point in chewing it once it was rubbery and tasteless.

"Oh, that's nice," Isabel said, looking down at him. "Spit it out so that someone will step it in later. Thanks for littering."

Sullivan grunted, picked up the wad of gum, then marched to the front of the building. He tossed it in the trash receptacle outside the door. "Happy now?"

"No," Isabel said. "I'd be happy if we were on the road chasing this developing thunderstorm."

Sullivan fought the urge to say something snarky. This day was already off to a shitty start.

Once he was settled behind the wheel, he fired up the LIV and maneuvered the vehicle out of the lot. He glanced at her, watching the computer with a scowl on her face. The damn thing was taking forever to boot up. "What's got a bug up your butt today?"

He heard Isabel sigh. "I'm sorry. It's just been one of those mornings. You know?"

"Yeah, I know. Having one of those days myself." Sullivan took notice of the dark clouds gathering, then made his turn toward them.

"Why were you late?" Isabel asked.

"Held up. Lunch hour rush." He left out the part where he'd stopped to buy more nicotine gum. Best not to give her another reason to complain. But his stash was getting low, and he wasn't about to run out of it on the road.

Twenty minutes later, at Isabel's suggestion, they parked at the vacant high school lot. School was out, so Sullivan had his choice of spaces. They watched the gray storm clouds moving east and hoped to catch an occasional lightning bolt.

"It's beautiful," Isabel said.

Sullivan grunted. It was day three of no cigarettes. He was niccin out for one so badly that he could barely concentrate on the beauty of the storm.

"I love parking at this school," Isabel said. "With all the ball fields, not many trees blocking our view, you know?"

Sullivan dug out the gum from his pocket. "You'd like the Plains then. Lots of open fields there." He popped a piece of gum out of the pocket and shoved it into his mouth.

"Yeah, but it's so far away from the beach. Should you be chewing another piece of that gum so soon? Isn't that dangerous?"

Leave it to Izzy to not let him chew his damn gum in peace. "I ain't going over the twenty-four piece limit," he said. "That's what the package says."

Isabel gave him a look like he should know better.

"You want me to go back to cigarettes? Because I will."

"Then you'll lose the bet, and I'll get control of the radio. *Livin' la vida loca,"* she sang with a shoulder shimmy.

Sullivan gave his gum a hard chew.

THE STORM PASSED, but another was poised to roll off the coast. Isabel figured it would be best to stay put, but Sullivan wanted to move.

"Just be patient," she told him.

"I can't be patient, Izzy. I need to move."

Sullivan tapped the gear shift repeatedly, to Isabel's annoyance. "Fine, let's go." Anything to stop his fidgeting. He was worse than Miguel.

Sullivan put the LIV into drive, and Isabel held on as Sullivan peeled out of the parking lot. "You don't have to go so fast," she complained, but Sullivan didn't slow down.

On the highway, rain pelted the windshield as they hit the storm. Thunder cracked above them.

"We'll get ahead of it and watch it come back in," Sullivan said.

Isabel didn't want to admit it, but perhaps Sullivan had been right to chase this cell. As it moved further inland, it intensified into bright yellow and red on the radar. They'd get some decent lightning strikes for sure.

"How's that little storm you wanted to wait for?" Sullivan asked.

"Petered out," she said.

She caught a rare grin from Sullivan. "Told you."

Isabel clenched her fists. She hated to be wrong, but at least it put Sullivan in a better mood.

They drove out of the rain and left the storm behind. Once at a good distance away, Sullivan brought the LIV to a stop. "Let's get this lightning on video."

The storm was coming at them, bringing with it dark clouds and frequent lightning. Isabel moved to get the camera rolling, but the screen was dark.

"Come on, *Izzy*."

"Hold your horses. The main camera is unresponsive."

"Fuck," Sullivan muttered.

"It's not the only camera, *Elmer,*" Isabel snapped. "Get the backup ones in position while I figure this one out."

Her phone rang at that moment, which was an inopportune time. Isabel ignored it. She turned the camera off, then on again, and was relieved to see the screen light up.

The phone rang again.

"Aren't you going to answer that?" Sullivan said. "That ringtone is driving me crazy."

Isabel sighed and reached for the phone. Her mother. "Hi, Mamá. I'm busy right now."

"*¡Mija!* They're taking Miguel to the hospital!"

Isabel's limbs went weak, the camera the last thing on her mind. "What? Hospital? What's wrong with him?"

"He was playing outside with Juan and passed out. We called the paramedics."

"Did you give him his emergency insulin?"

"*Sí*, but the paramedics thought a doctor should examine him. I have to go. I'm going to ride in the ambulance. They're taking him to County General Hospital."

"I'll meet you there."

She ended the connection and dropped the phone because her hands were shaking so badly. "Drive me to the hospital on Poquito Beach Road. *Now*." Isabel hurriedly got back into the passenger seat and buckled up. The storm be damned. This was more important.

Sullivan, no longer looking annoyed, seemed concerned. "What's wrong with Miguel?"

"His blood sugar must be too low. He fainted. It's a good thing we weren't hours away on the road somewhere."

Sullivan nodded. "Don't worry. I'll get you there as fast as I can."

Isabel felt the LIV accelerate. Sullivan was probably speeding, but for once, Isabel didn't care. Getting to Miguel was the priority.

She wondered what could have caused this episode. He'd probably gotten too hungry, and with the heat, it was likely he was dehydrated too. He hadn't eaten much of the quesadillas. She shouldn't have rushed off to work. She should have stayed longer and made sure Miguel ate properly. It was all her fault. Isabel began to sob.

"Hey, don't worry. I'm sure he'll be just fine. The doctors know what to do."

"This is all my fault."

"It's not your fault. He's a diabetic, and he's going to have episodes sometimes."

"But I should have made sure he ate more of his breakfast. He was so eager to get outside and play with Juan and his dog. He's probably been running around for hours and not realizing his symptoms."

"Stop blaming yourself. When was he diagnosed? It was recent, right?"

"Last year." Isabel wiped a tear rolling down her cheek.

"Then you're both still learning about this condition. Cut yourself some slack."

A short while later, the hospital came into view, and Isabel felt marginally better. Miguel was probably there by now. She hated to think of her little boy suffering, and there was nothing she could do for him except pray.

Isabel held on as Sullivan made a sharp turn at the light. He pulled up under the awning outside the emergency room, and Isabel held on again as the LIV screeched to a halt. "I'll find a parking space and meet you inside."

"You don't have to stay." Isabel grabbed her purse from the floorboard.

Sullivan reached for her arm, and Isabel met his eyes. "I want to, Izzy. Now go."

Isabel nodded, then hurried inside.

Her mother was waiting for her in the emergency room. "Oh, *mija*, they just took him back. It happened so fast!"

"How is he? Do you know?"

"He's fine, but weak. Oh, Isabel, this is my fault. He raced through lunch. He wanted to get back outside and play before it rained. I should have been watching him more carefully. But he and Juan were outside laughing and playing, and I thought nothing was wrong. And then, I heard Juan yelling for help."

"No, it's probably my fault. I should have made sure he ate more at breakfast."

Carlita looked over Isabel's shoulder. "Oh, there's the nurse now."

A woman in sea green scrubs approached them. "Ms. Torres?"

"*Sí.* How's Miguel?"

"He's doing much better. They're monitoring his glucose levels now. We're going to keep him for a little while to observe, and if he continues to improve, we'll discharge him tonight."

Isabel let out the breath she'd been holding. "Oh, *gracias a Dios*. Can I see him?"

"Of course. Follow me."

The nurse took them behind a set of double doors. Several curtained areas were lined up against the wall, and Miguel was in the first one. He looked so tiny in the large hospital bed, but he was awake, and he was smiling. All good signs.

Isabel rushed over to his side. "Miguel."

"Hi, Mamá."

She wrapped her arms around him. "*Nene*, what happened?"

The child shrugged. "I felt bad when we were playing."

"Did you let yourself get too hungry?"

He looked down and rubbed the sheet between his fingers. "*Sí.*"

"Oh, *nene*, remember that you can't let your blood sugar get too low, okay? If you start to feel bad, you let someone know."

"*Sí*, Mamá."

They sat with Miguel for a while, and Isabel felt relieved that Miguel was all right. This hadn't been their first time in the emergency room, but Isabel hoped it would be their last.

The curtain pulled back, and the nurse appeared with Sullivan.

"He said he was with you," the nurse said.

Isabel nodded. "*Sí*. Thank you."

The nurse left, and Sullivan stepped in. "Hey, little man. How are you feeling?"

"I got sick."

"I see that. I'm sure the doctors will have you feeling better in no time."

When the nurse came back to check on Miguel's vitals, Isabel stepped out of the cubicle and motioned for Sullivan to follow her. "Thanks for driving me here, but you don't have to stay. I know you probably want to get those afternoon storms coming off the coast."

"No, I'm right where I want to be. Do you need a ride home when they discharge Miguel?"

"That's nice of you to offer, but I don't think my mom and Miguel riding home in the LIV would be ideal."

Sullivan cracked a smile. "No, I suppose not."

"Thanks anyway. My mother has already called Paulina. She'll give us a ride. We'll probably be here for several hours, so really, don't feel obligated to stay. But I appreciate you getting me here so quickly. I'm sorry I ruined our chase."

"I'm not mad about that. You sure you don't want me to stay? I could get some lunch for you and your mother."

The offer surprised Isabel. If anything, she was certain Sullivan wanted to get out of here. She never met anyone who wanted to wait around in the emergency room. "That's kind of you, but I don't think either of us can eat right now."

"All right. Call if you need anything."

"*Gracias.*"

The nurse stepped out from behind the curtain. "Miguel is doing much better. I'll come check on him again in about an hour. Press the call button if you need me to come before then."

Isabel nodded. "Thank you."

"Well, I guess I should say goodbye to the little man," Sullivan said. He headed back into the cubicle.

"Can I go home now?" Miguel asked.

"Not yet, *nene*," Isabel said. "The doctors want to make sure you're feeling better. Mr. Sullivan is leaving now. Say goodbye to him."

Miguel looked up at Sullivan. "Are you still coming to my birthday party Saturday?"

"Wouldn't miss it. I'm going to buy you a present tomorrow."

"Yay!" Miguel cheered.

Sullivan said his goodbyes, and Isabel followed him to the door.

"I probably won't be at work tomorrow," she said. "I want to stay home and make sure Miguel takes it easy. So you'll finally get to ride around in the LIV without me. Don't cheat and smoke, okay? Because I'll smell it and know."

"I'm sure you would," Sullivan said in a flat tone.

"Thanks again for everything."

"No thanks necessary. That's your kid. I'd be worried too. I guess I'll see you at Miguel's party."

"It'll be outside unless it rains."

"Nah, it won't. Twenty percent chance. And if it does, nothing wrong with a little rain. That ain't the worst thing in the world to happen."

Isabel smiled. "No, I suppose not. See you Saturday."

Sullivan nodded, then went through the double doors that led back to the waiting area. Even though he didn't need to stay, it touched her he was willing to.

Back in the cubicle, Miguel laughed, which was a good sign. Maybe he was feeling better. "What's so funny?"

"Mamá, why did the nurse need a red crayon?"

Isabel shrugged. "I don't know."

"Because she needed to draw blood."

Isabel laughed softly and went to Miguel's side. "You must be feeling better if you're telling jokes. Where did you hear that one?"

"The man in the ambulance told it to me. When can I go home?"

"As soon as the doctor says so, but probably by tonight. And we'll take it easy tomorrow so that you'll be ready for your party."

"I'm so happy Mr. Sullivan is going to come."

On the other side of the bed, Isabel caught her mother smiling at her. "It was very kind that Mr. Sullivan offered to stay. I heard you talking through the curtain." Her mother was always nudging her to date again, and she had that matchmaking look in her eyes at the moment.

"*Sí*, it was. And I'm glad he's coming to the party too."

14

Friday afternoon, Sullivan took the LIV out on the road and headed to Sarasota where the storms were firing up today. It felt weird to be storm chasing without Izzy. He'd grown so used to her constant chatter that the quietness bothered him. He turned up the radio, even though it was on a commercial break, just for the sake of noise.

The LIV's tank was a quarter full, so Sullivan pulled into the lot of the nearest gas station. After filling up, he went inside to buy a soda and some snacks. Behind the counter, lined up neatly, were all the cigarettes he could buy.

He wanted one. Even though Isabel said she'd know if he cheated, he didn't think she would. If he smoked in the vehicle, sure. Isabel would smell it because she had a nose like a bloodhound. But if he smoked outside, she wouldn't know. And it wasn't as if he would wear the same clothes tomorrow. Plus, he'd be sure to use mouthwash.

One smoke wouldn't hurt.

When it was Sullivan's turn, he placed his items on the counter and pointed to the cigarettes. "Can I get a pack of Marlboro Red?" He dug out his credit card as the employee rang up his purchases.

Someone bumped him, and Sullivan looked down to see a little boy with black hair grabbing a package of cookies. A dark-haired woman reached for his hand.

"No snacks, *nene.*"

For a moment, Sullivan thought it was Miguel and Isabel. Hell, the woman even sounded like Isabel, with the same Spanish lilt to her voice and nickname for her kid.

"It's waiting on you," said the man behind the counter, pointing to the credit card machine, and Sullivan inserted his Visa.

Outside, the air was thick with humidity, and soon enough, those storms would pop up. Gray clouds were already forming, and Sullivan hurried to get a move on.

As he drove, he glanced at the plastic bag in the passenger seat. The Marlboro pack peeked out, and Sullivan was tempted to pull over to the side of the road and smoke one now. Or two. But there was no good place to stop. And anyway, he didn't have time for a break if he wanted to catch this thunderstorm.

Once he got off the highway, he found a place to park and set up the camera equipment. He thought it might be nice to lift the rear door and sit on the edge of the truck. He could watch the lightning show in the distance and take a smoke break. Smoking with the door open would be okay, right? He'd practically be outside, and surely the wind would carry the cigarette smell away from the vehicle.

He lifted the door, hopped up onto the platform, and tore the plastic off the package. He reached into his pocket for his lighter and came up empty.

"Fuck." It had been a habit to keep a lighter in his pocket, but since he'd quit smoking, he hadn't brought it. He could see it in his mind, on the edge of his kitchen counter.

Okay, so he didn't have his lighter, but maybe he had something else. Reaching for his wallet, he looked in the pocket until he found a matchbook hiding behind an old receipt. "I knew I kept this for a reason." Emergencies, that was why. And this was definitely an emergency.

He finished opening the cigarette package and shook one out. A gust of wind picked it up, rolling it off his lap and onto the ground. When he'd finally gotten another cigarette in his hand, he knocked down the matchbook.

"Shit," Sullivan muttered. It was like the universe was trying to stop him from having this good smoke.

A bolt of lightning lit up the sky, followed by a loud crack of thunder. The storm was getting closer, but maybe too close. Sullivan sighed. Knowing his shitty luck, he'd be struck by lightning. They'd find his body next to the LIV, holding a cigarette in his hand, and Isabel would know he had cheated. He didn't know why that bothered him so much.

No, he would not let Isabel or Mother Nature or anything else get in the way of his smoke. He grabbed the matchbook from the ground, took one out, and lit it up.

The cigarette was ready, but Sullivan couldn't bring himself to smoke it. He was on day four of no smoking, and that annoying voice in his head told him that if he smoked just this one, he'd be back to square one. The voice sounded a lot like Izzy.

Sullivan dropped the cigarette on the pavement and snuffed it out with his shoe. Day four of no smoking had been a bitch, but day one had been hell. And if he smoked, it'd be like when his mama was sober and fell off the wagon—back to day one. All the progress made—gone.

He didn't want to go there again.

With a sigh, he tossed the pack of Marlboro into the trash bin outside the McDonald's parking lot. He was not losing this bet to Izzy. She'd probably be able to tell just by looking at him that he cheated, and for some reason, he didn't want to disappoint her.

ISABEL STARED OUT THE WINDOW. Some light gray clouds were forming, but Isabel knew the real storm action today was happening further south. She imagined Sullivan out in the LIV driving alone, and she hoped his willpower not to smoke would be strong enough. She'd be sure to look for evidence the next time she was in the LIV. It would be like Sullivan to leave a cigarette wrapper behind.

"I have the balloons," her mother said as she walked into the apartment. Isabel hurried to help her carry them and placed them on the coffee table.

"They'll still be inflated by tomorrow, right?" Isabel asked.

"They better be," Carlita said. "I'm not getting any more."

Not working today turned out to be a good thing. Not only could she keep an eye on Miguel, but she could also get a head start on the party preparations. She peeked into his room. He was occupied with Juan's handheld game again. Juan, the sweet boy, had let Miguel borrow it while he was sick.

"I wish I could afford to buy him one of those," Isabel said.

Carlita placed the decorations on the table. "I wouldn't worry about that, *mija*. By the time we have enough money to buy him that, they'll be crazy about something else. Where are your scissors?" Carlita held a roll of curling ribbon. "We can use this to tie the party favor bags."

"They're in the junk drawer." Isabel reached for the bag of small toys she'd purchased at the dollar store. "I hope this will be enough."

"What's this?"

Isabel turned around. Her mother held the card from Mateo in her hand, and Isabel wanted to kick herself. She'd forgotten she'd placed it there.

"It's nothing, Mamá."

Carlita stared at Isabel with wide eyes. "Did he come here again? Tell me, *mija!*"

Isabel snatched the card from her. "That was from last weekend when he stopped by. He placed it in our mailbox."

"Why is it here?"

"I thought I'd hold on to it in case the police needed it."

Carlita's expression relaxed. "Did you decide to press charges?"

Isabel shoved the card into her purse. "I'll think about it, okay?" She grabbed the scissors from the drawer and shut it.

From the expression on her mother's face, she could tell it wasn't the answer she wanted to hear. "All right, *mija*, let's get these party bags ready. There will be a lot of children coming tomorrow."

Isabel nodded, glad her mother had dropped the subject.

SULLIVAN FELT out of place as he walked across the lawn to Isabel's house. He glanced at his watch and realized he had come too early. Isabel said four. But he was here now, and it would be awkward to turn around and go back to his car. There were a lot of people here, all speaking Spanish, and way more children than he thought there would be. Isabel made it sound like it was a small gathering of family, but it looked like Miguel had invited his entire class. They crowded around a blue and red bouncy house.

Among the dark-haired children, one turned around and smiled.

"Mr. Sullivan! You came!" Miguel ran toward him, then surprised him by throwing his arms around his waist. The last time a child hugged him, he'd been fifteen years old.

Sullivan felt unsure of what to do, so he gave the boy a pat on the back. "Happy birthday, kid. This is for you." He handed Miguel the wrapped birthday gift in his hand.

"Wow! What did you get me?"

"You'll have to open it to find out."

He undid the bow, but Isabel appeared and scooped the present out of his hand. Sullivan looked her over. She wore a short white dress, giving him a pleasant view of her long legs. He saw a hint of cleavage too and reminded his body to behave.

"*Nene*, you can open presents later," Isabel said. "For now, what do you say to Mr. Sullivan?"

"*¡Gracias!*"

Isabel ruffled his hair. "Now go play with your friends."

"Glad you could come to my party, Mr. Sullivan!" Miguel shouted as he ran back to the bouncy house.

"He looks like he's feeling good."

"*Sí*, he's doing much better. Thanks for this." Isabel hugged the gift to her chest. "What did you get him?"

"A drone. Is that all right?"

Isabel gave him a surprised look. "That's more than okay, and way more gift than I expected you to get. Aren't they kind of expensive?"

Sullivan shrugged. "It wasn't much. We saw some guy playing with one on the beach and he thought it was cool. It's one for kids, so it shouldn't be too complicated."

"You really didn't have to, but thank you. He'll love it. You want something to eat? Drink? We've got snacks in the back."

What he really wanted was a cigarette, but food could be a good distraction. "I could eat."

"Come on."

He followed Isabel to the backyard. The dress hugged her

backside just right, and when she turned around, he had to remind his body to behave again.

"Look who came," Isabel said.

Right away, Isabel's mother rushed over to him. She took his arm and led him to the refreshment table. "It's so nice of you to come! Sofia, doesn't he look like the guy from *Bermuda Time Warp*?"

"Just like him," replied a woman who looked about Carlita's age.

Carlita patted Sullivan on the arm. "That's my sister. Please, have something to eat!"

Sullivan looked at the spread before him. It had been a while since he'd had a pig in a blanket, and he popped one in his mouth.

He couldn't eat in peace though, because soon enough, Carlita, Sofia, and a few more women surrounded him. They were all fawning over him like he was a damn celebrity.

"You must be related to him," one of them said. "The resemblance is striking!"

"Are you sure you aren't him?" another teased and pinched his cheek.

He looked to Isabel for help, who mercifully took hold of his hand. Sullivan liked the feel of her soft hand against his calloused one. She pulled him away, her grip surprisingly strong. "I have to talk to Sullivan about a work thing. If you'll excuse us."

Isabel led him to some chairs near the fence and let go of his hand. "I don't really have a work thing to ask you. I just thought you might need some space away. My mother and her friends can be a little overwhelming."

It was funny how Isabel could sense that. He didn't enjoy crowds, though forced himself to be "social" at times like this. Isabel was respectful of his feelings. "Appreciate the save."

"Want a beer?"

"You don't think it's too early?"

"Of course not. It's a party. I'll be right back."

She was gone for a while, and Sullivan wondered what was taking her so long. He felt awkward sitting there by himself. Weird how this woman used to annoy him, but now, he enjoyed being around her.

"Sullivan, surprised to see you here."

Torres stood over him with a corn dog in hand, and Sullivan felt grateful for the familiar company. He hated parties because he had to make conversation with strangers, but at least he knew Torres. "Miguel invited me."

Torres took the seat next to him. "Hard to say no to that kid, isn't it? Isabel says her boy has taken a liking to you."

He shrugged. "I guess so, but I can't imagine why."

"How's the no smoking going?"

Sullivan groaned. "It would be better if you didn't mention that right now. I'm trying not to think about it."

Torres laughed. "Understood. It was hard for Miguel to quit too."

Sullivan looked at Torres, figuring the professor must have misspoken. "I'm sorry, Miguel?"

Torres chuckled. "Not that Miguel. My brother, Isabel's father, may he rest in peace." Torres made the cross symbol. "Carlita said she wouldn't marry him unless he quit, so he did. You should try the patch. Worked for him."

"I'll keep that in mind." He reached into his pocket for a piece of nicotine gum, but Isabel appeared with his beer. Alcohol would suffice.

"Tío, can I get you anything?" she asked.

Torres rose from the chair. "No, I'm good. You think the kids will let a grownup have a turn in the bouncy house?"

Isabel laughed. "Be careful you don't break a bone, old man."

Torres laughed, then headed to where the children played.

Isabel took the seat her uncle had vacated. "Are you wishing you hadn't come now?"

Sullivan took a swig of beer and thought about her question. "Didn't want to disappoint Miguel, but it is kind of noisy."

Right on cue, Miguel let out a loud squeal as two other boys chased him. A black barking dog followed.

"Miguel's friends will leave soon, and then it'll be just family. And Mamá is making a roast pig."

The corner of Sullivan's mouth turned upward. "Your family really does eat a lot of pork."

"It was Papá's favorite, so Mamá learned how to make every pork recipe in the cookbook."

She had a sadness in her eyes at the mention of her father, and until only a minute ago, he had been unaware that her father had died. He assumed Isabel's father was out of the picture, just like his old man. "Torres told me your father was also named Miguel."

Isabel smiled, her eyes still glistening with what looked like unshed tears. "*Sí.* I named Miguel after him. Papá passed when I was twelve."

"I'm sorry." The only parent Sullivan had known was his mother, and he hadn't grieved much when she died. She'd been a terrible mother, but Sullivan already knew Isabel's family differed greatly from his. "How did it happen? Was it unexpected?"

"A hurricane was coming, and we were under evacuation orders. Papá insisted on staying. He didn't think it would be that bad, and he wanted to get some pictures and videos of the storm. He was a photographer."

"But it sounds like you and the rest of your family evacuated."

Isabel nodded. "We did. Mamá had been through plenty of hurricanes in Puerto Rico, and she wasn't taking any chances. She and Papá argued about his refusal to go, but he assured her he would be fine. He urged us to leave, because he knew the power would go out and we would be miserable. But he wanted to stay. He said if the water got too close, he would use the sandbags to keep it at bay."

"But that wasn't enough."

Sullivan caught Isabel wiping the corner of her eye with her finger.

"No. The storm surge was very bad. Have you ever been through one?"

"A few, but where I lived in Texas, it was further inland, so the impact wasn't as severe."

"I've been through so many of them, I've lost count. Every time, they bring back terrible memories. Tío Fernando said I could move to Texas and stay with him if I wanted to. I even considered going to school at A & M to be one of his students. I was that tired of hurricanes. But I had Miguel, and I could never leave my mother or sister, so I stayed."

Sullivan's eyebrow twitched. He'd left his sister behind. He thought of how Emmy had cried, and how he told her he would see her again, knowing full well that he was lying to her. It had been for her own good, but it made him feel like the shittiest person in the world.

He stood up. "I'm going to go for a walk. I need a break from the noise." And to clear his head.

Isabel nodded. "You want some company?"

Sullivan shook his head.

"Okay," Isabel said. "Don't stay away too long. We'll be having dinner soon. Pork."

Isabel was trying to make him smile, but he wasn't in the mood. He slipped away with no one noticing.

When he made it to his car, he thought about getting in and taking off, but reconsidered. He couldn't just leave without saying goodbye, and Miguel probably expected him to stay for at least a slice of birthday cake.

He walked away from the vehicle and dug out some gum from his pocket. It relieved his craving for the moment, but nicotine could not make him forget the past.

ISABEL PEEKED into the bouncy house, expecting to find her *tío* out of breath, but she only saw Miguel and his cousins. "Did you wear Tío Fernando out?"

"He said he hurt his back and went inside for some ice," Miguel said.

Isabel shook her head. "I warned him."

"When will it be time for presents?"

"After we eat. Don't get too tired, okay? Remember to take breaks and drink water."

"I know, I know," Miguel said, as if he were tired of his mother reminding him.

Inside, Isabel found Fernando sitting on the couch with an ice pack behind him.

"I told you to be careful."

Fernando sighed. "I know. You abandon Sullivan out there?"

"He said he needed to go for a walk. It was a bit too loud for him."

"In that case, sit down. I need to have a talk with you." Fernando patted the seat next to him.

Isabel sat on the couch. "Am I in trouble? Because the last time you took that tone of voice with me, you told me to stay away from Miguel's father."

"Carlita told me that Mateo has been bothering you. Why am I just hearing about this now?"

She should have known her mother would talk to Fernando. "Because I knew you'd be upset."

"You're damn right I'm upset," Fernando said, his voice raised. "Isabel, do you know what your father would do if he were still alive? He would go to that news station right now and give Mateo the beating of his life for hurting his little girl. And since my brother is no longer with us, the duty of taking care of you falls to me. I'm going to have a talk with him." Fernando moved to stand, then winced and sat back down. "After my back heals."

"Tío, please don't cause any trouble. Mateo isn't worth it. I already told Mamá that if he comes back, I'll get a protective order."

"I really wish you would press charges. He *assaulted* you."

Isabel took a deep breath. "Tío, I've already told you that I don't want to make a scene. Why doesn't everyone just leave this alone? It's in the past, and I want to move forward and forget about it."

Fernando leaned in closer. "Because, *princesa*, we love you very much. Let me ask you this. If the same thing happened to your sister, would you be upset if she didn't report it?"

Isabel reached for the throw pillow and played with the frayed edges. "When you put it that way, yes, I'd be upset. If anyone hurt Paulina, I'd want them to pay."

"So you see why we won't let this go?"

"*Sí*, Tío," Isabel said, unable to look her uncle in the eye.

"I'm glad Sullivan is with you. He could take Mateo in a fight, don't you think?"

A small laugh escaped her lips. "Yes, I'm sure he could."

The back door squeaked open, and an excited Miguel ran inside. "Abuela says dinner is ready. And after that, I can open presents, right?"

"Yes, we'll eat, and then you can open all your gifts." Isabel stood, grateful for the subject change.

Fernando reached for her hand as she turned away. "Isabel, you be careful."

Isabel nodded, then followed Miguel outside.

By the time Sullivan returned from his walk, most of the kids had left. That was a relief. Isabel waved him over to get some food. Dinner was served casually with everyone balancing paper plates on their laps in the backyard, but the pork was delicious. Carlita smiled at Sullivan every time he went to the table to get a drink or seconds.

Fernando sidled up to him. "Sullivan, can I talk to you privately for a moment?"

Sullivan tossed a balled up napkin and dirty plate into the trash. "Something wrong?"

Fernando looked over at Isabel and Miguel. Isabel was laughing as Miguel struggled with tearing open a present. "It's Isabel. Keep an eye on her, will you? There's a guy that's been harassing her."

Sullivan involuntarily clenched his fists. "Yeah, I know about him. Told that ass to take a hike when he bothered Isabel at work."

"He's not getting the message. He was waiting for Isabel when she came home on Saturday. If he comes around again, I want you to let me know."

Sullivan nodded. "I will. I didn't mention him stopping by before because Isabel asked me not to say anything to you. I thought she had it handled. I didn't know this guy was still bothering her."

Miguel's shrill scream pierced Sullivan's ear, interrupting their conversation. When Miguel held up the drone Sullivan had bought him, his scowl faded. At least the kid was excited about his gift.

"I love it, Mr. Sullivan! *¡Gracias!*"

Sullivan nodded. "You're welcome, kid."

"Will you show me how it flies?" Miguel was already tearing open the box.

Sullivan gave Miguel a crash course on how it worked, then watched as Miguel spent about a half hour playing with it. He was glad the gift put a smile on the kid's face. It reminded him of the time he had saved up his lawn cutting money and bought Emmy a remote controlled car. She'd played with it for hours until Dick broke it in a drunken rage.

Isabel sauntered over and handed him a Budweiser. "Here, you're looking grumpy. Have more alcohol."

Sullivan cracked the can open. He wasn't an alcoholic like Dick had been, and for that, he was relieved. He didn't want to have anything in common with that bastard. "You just want me so drunk that I can't leave." Why he said that, he wasn't sure. It just flew out of his mouth. Why would Isabel want him here? Miguel was the one who invited him.

"Maybe I want you drunk so you can loosen up a bit," Isabel said, the corner of her lip turning upward.

As she walked away, Sullivan gently reached for her arm to hold her back. "Hey, your uncle told me that guy came to see you again. Are you sure you don't want to go to the authorities? If Torres is concerned about you, then I'm sure as hell concerned too."

The smile on her face fell. "Look, I appreciate everyone looking out for my safety, but there's nothing to worry about. He just dropped by the other day to bring the things I had left at the station."

"But your uncle—"

"Look, I don't want to talk about Mateo, okay? It's my son's birthday, and I just want to have a good time. Really, I've got the situation under control. Don't worry about it."

A smile returned to her face as she sauntered away. Isabel was avoiding the subject, a tactic he knew well. But if Isabel didn't want to talk about it, he would not force her.

After he finished his beer, Sullivan felt a delightful buzz, and instead of thinking about cigarettes and Emmy, he found his mind occupied with Isabel. As an introvert, he preferred being by himself, but he'd suffer through a social event if it meant he'd get to watch her dance. And boy, could she move. He was even getting used to her taste in music. He'd heard so many of these songs on the road that—damn it—he was actually starting to like it.

"Come on, Mr. Sullivan!" Miguel reached for his hand and pulled him out of his chair.

Sullivan shook his head. "Sorry, kid, I'm not much of a dancer."

Miguel ignored his protests and led him to the middle of the yard anyway. Once there, Sullivan didn't know what to do, so Miguel took hold of his hands and urged him to move. Sullivan moved his legs from side to side.

"Not like that!" Miguel said. "You got to move your whole body!"

"Let me show him," Isabel said.

Isabel stood in front of him and gyrated her hips. "Like this."

He made a half-hearted effort to bob his head to the beat, but there was no way Sullivan was moving like that. Though he didn't mind seeing Isabel move that way.

The music, which had been fast-paced, turned into something slower. He caught a whiff of her coconut lotion as she pressed her body against his. Sullivan had never slow-danced before, but Isabel knew what to do. She guided his left hand to the small of her back, then laced her fingers with his while placing her other hand on his shoulder. Against him, she felt warm and soft, making him think of inappropriate thoughts at a child's birthday party.

"Just move with me," she said.

Sullivan locked his eyes on her. He didn't know which was worse: making a fool of himself trying to dance to the fast-paced music, or having Isabel in his arms for the slower songs.

He was enjoying the latter.

"See?" Isabel said. "You can dance."

"As long as I don't step on your foot."

"You're doing fine."

When the music stopped, Isabel slipped out of his arms, and Sullivan was surprised that he felt disappointment.

"Let's have some cake now!" Carlita said, and everyone headed to the deck.

"You like vanilla?" Isabel asked. "Mama made Miguel a vanilla keto cake, which sounds disgusting, but it's actually pretty good."

"I'll try anything once," he said.

Dancing with Isabel hadn't been so bad. Maybe a keto cake would be good too.

IN THE KITCHEN, Isabel found her mother and sister cleaning up. "I was going to do that," she said.

Her mother waved her off. "We've got it, *mija*. Go back outside and enjoy yourself."

"No, there's a lot of cleanup to do. And having the party here was my idea." She picked up a dirty paper plate and headed for the trash can.

Paulina seized the plate. "Let us clean up, *hermanita*. We've got this. And anyway, Sullivan is out on the front porch." She nudged her. "Why don't you go talk to him?"

Behind Paulina, her mother grinned at Isabel. "We saw you two dancing."

Isabel felt her cheeks grow warm. "Miguel and I were just trying to encourage him to have a little fun."

"He was having fun, all right," Carlita said, nudging Paulina as if they were sharing an inside joke.

"We like him," Paulina said. "And he's so good with Miguel."

Her mother turned on the faucet and began rinsing off the cake pan. "You keep saying he's so unpleasant, but honestly, *mija*, I don't know what you're talking about. He seems perfectly pleasant to us."

Her mother and sister were always encouraging her to date, and if she stayed in the kitchen, she was going to get an earful. "I'll be outside if you need me."

"We won't," Carlita said. "Stay out as long as you'd like. We'll keep Miguel occupied."

They laughed as Isabel went out the door. The house felt stifling with the conversation and heat from the oven, but outside, a breeze was blowing. It was a clear night with a crescent moon and stars in the sky. When her eyes adjusted to the dim light, she saw Sullivan leaning against the railing.

Sullivan looked at her. "I wasn't sneaking a smoke if that's what you're thinking. I just wanted some fresh air. And it's quiet here."

Isabel moved to stand next to him. "I wasn't thinking you were. In fact, I'm very proud of you for going this many days without a cigarette."

"You were right. I should quit. Might be nice to spend my money on other things."

"Like expensive drones for little boys?"

He looked her in the eye. "I told you... it was nothing."

"It wasn't nothing. He really loves it. I think that's his favorite birthday gift."

Sullivan picked up his beer from the ledge of the porch rail. "I'm glad he likes it. I would have loved one of those when I was his age."

Isabel inched closer. "When we first met, I didn't like you. You smoked, you were always in a bad mood, you drove in the rain without your lights on."

Sullivan chuckled, which made Isabel smile. Getting a laugh from him was never easy.

"Despite all that, you're growing on me. You're a good man, Sullivan. Not many people would go out of their way to make a little boy happy. Miguel still talks about you buying ice cream for us."

"I did a good deed, but that doesn't make me a good man."

"What are you saying? You've had brushes with the law? That doesn't surprise me. You seem like the type of guy with a checkered past."

He took a drink of beer. "I mean it, Izzy. You shouldn't want anything to do with me."

"Tío Fernando trusts you."

"Your uncle doesn't know everything."

Sullivan talked little about his past, and Isabel wondered if the alcohol made conversation easier for him. If she wanted to ask questions, maybe now was the time. "Okay, Mr. Not a Good Guy, what did you do?"

Sullivan took another swig of beer, not answering.

"I know you're not a sex offender, because I check the registry religiously. So what was it? Theft? Bar fight? You didn't murder someone, did you?"

She'd said it in jest, but Sullivan didn't respond. She thought she saw his jaw clench, and the blood drained from her face. *Had he killed someone?* "Sullivan?"

"What if I did?" He turned to look at her, and his eyes were dark and piercing.

"I'm sure if you did, you had a good reason," she said, her voice trembling. She knew Sullivan had a temper, but she'd also seen the good side of him. Would he kill someone if it wasn't justified?

He moved to the porch steps and sat down. "It's a long story."

Isabel took the space next to him. "That's okay. I have time. And I want to know." She *needed* to know. Sure, Sullivan got angry at times, but how dangerous was he?

He took another swig from the beer bottle, then placed it on the step. "My dad wasn't around, but there was always a man at the house. Mama had a string of never-ending boyfriends. Eventually, she got pregnant by one of them, and my sister Emmy was born."

"You have a sister?" The news surprised her, as she assumed he was an only child. He never talked about any family other than his mother.

"Used to."

"Oh." Isabel hated that she had opened up what had to be a painful wound for him. "I'm sorry for your loss."

"No, she's not dead. At least, I don't think she is."

"Is she the one person you'll allow to call you Elmer?"

He nodded. "Emmy was the only one who did. Everyone else called me 'moron' or 'bastard' or 'good-for-nothing-son.'"

"So why did you say you 'used to' have a sister? Did you two have a falling out or something?"

"No, nothing like that. The foster care system separated us when she was five."

"Oh, that's terrible. You mean you haven't seen her since?"

He shook his head. "No. She might be in Clearwater. Or at least, she was last year. I found a Facebook profile for her. When this job opportunity came up, I thought maybe it would be my chance to find her."

"Finish your story."

"Emmy's father took off like mine. When he left, Mama was devastated. As soon as Emmy was born, she started drinking and doing drugs again. I had to take care of my sister when Mama wouldn't. I was the one who cleaned and prepared her bottles. I was the one who checked on her in the middle of the night. I'd come home from school, and I'd find Emmy crying with a dirty diaper and Mama passed out drunk in front of the television."

"How old were you?"

"Ten."

Isabel shook her head. "I don't understand. Why did it take Child Protective Services five years to take you two out of there?"

"Oh, they would occasionally. Some teacher or neighbor would get suspicious, make a call. Either Mama would lie her way out of it, or we'd get sent to a foster home for a while. But we always ended up back with her. The state's goal is to reunite the child with the parent. Mama would go to rehab and come back clean and sober, and the courts would think she was doing good again. So back we went. Then it would go downhill again."

"That must have been so awful. I can't imagine."

"Anyway, fast forward two years, she married Dick. His name was actually Richard, but he went by Dick, and behind his back, I called him a dick. He lived up to his name. When he had a few beers, he got angry."

Isabel had a feeling she knew where this story was going. "Did he hit you?"

"All the time. Anything would set him off. If you just looked at him wrong when he was in a bad mood, he'd come after you with his fist."

"Did he hit your sister too?"

"He slapped her only once that I know of, but no, mostly Emmy was spared. At first, I thought it was weird how he could be so mean to me, but he'd shower Emmy with candy and gifts. Sometimes, it seemed like he was capable of good, and I was glad that at least he was nice to her. But he wasn't. I should have known better."

A sinking feeling settled in the pit of her stomach. Now she definitely knew where the story was going. "Was he abusing her in another way?"

Sullivan was quiet for a moment, then nodded. "Yeah. I blame myself for not realizing it sooner. I'd catch him coming out of her bedroom in the middle of the night. He'd say she'd had a bad dream or something, and I believed him. But the day Emmy told me he'd been touching her, that was the last straw. Dick could hurt me all he wanted, but my sister was off-limits." He looked Isabel straight in the eye. "That night, I killed him."

15

Isabel exhaled in relief. Sure, he'd just admitted to murder, but it wasn't as if it weren't justified. If she'd been in Sullivan's shoes, she figured she'd do the same thing.

Sullivan stared off in the distance as if he were lost in thought. "He was in the detached garage where he kept that damn motorcycle of his. I confronted him, and of course, he denied it. He said I was trying to stir up trouble. We fought, but I was so angry, something inside me snapped. He had his 9mm on the table. He always cleaned it in the garage so Emmy wouldn't see it. I didn't even know if it was loaded, but I grabbed the gun and pulled the trigger. Shot him in the chest. I would have let him rot, but Mama heard the gun and came running out and called the ambulance. So there it is, the whole ugly truth. I killed a man. In cold blood. And I'd do it again. You still think I'm a good guy?"

"*Sí*. You were protecting your baby sister. If anyone hurt Miguel like that, I'd want to kill them too. Did you do time?"

Sullivan picked up the empty beer bottle and peeled the label off. "The cops who came to the scene hauled me off in their police cruiser. Emmy was standing on the porch in her pajamas, crying. I told her everything would be okay, but I didn't know that everything was about to change. They probably would have charged me with murder, but the detective working the case was familiar with Dick. He was always getting into bar fights. When I showed the detective the bruises on my body, he bought my story that it was self-defense." He looked at Isabel. "But it wasn't self-defense. I wanted to kill Dick. The gun was just a happy coincidence. Otherwise, I would have killed him with my bare hands. Killing him was the only way to put an end to what he was doing."

Isabel took a deep breath, letting all that sink in. "Wow, I can't imagine. So what happened after that?"

"Everything went to shit. Mama came to the police station and told me not to come home. She didn't want to believe me when I told her what Dick had been doing to Emmy. But I think on some level, she knew it was true. That night, she swallowed a bottle of sleeping pills and never woke up."

"*Dios mio.* What happened to you and your sister after that?"

"Emmy got sent to live with a foster family. I ended up staying with my science teacher, Mr. Gordon. He was the only adult in my life at that time who gave a shit about me. Eventually, the Johnson family expressed interest in adopting Emmy. He was a preacher. The wife was a homemaker. Just a good Christian family who could provide her with a loving home. I went to the social services building to say goodbye to her. She got into a car with them and waved at me from the back seat. That was the last time I saw her."

"Did they not let you come visit her? You were her brother. You were the only family she had left."

"The social worker told me that if Emmy was lucky, she'd forget everything that had happened. She was still young. I thought it'd be best to not contact her anymore. I was afraid that if she did forget what Dick had done, my presence would bring it all back. It's not that I wanted her to forget me, but I didn't want to give her any reminders of what happened in that hellhole. So, to answer your question—it was my choice not to see Emmy. And I haven't seen her in twenty years."

His voice cracked at the end, and Isabel sensed Sullivan was trying not to cry. Words seemed insufficient after hearing his story. Instead, she reached for his hand and squeezed it.

"Do you want to find your sister?"

He shrugged. "I don't know. I've gone to Clearwater twice, but I couldn't find anyone who knew her. Maybe it's for the best. She doesn't need her past coming back to haunt her. And then, there's the chance that she doesn't remember me. I don't want to mess up her life. But I have considered hiring a private investigator. I'm curious what she's like now."

"My cousin Eddie is a P.I. He's in Miami. I could call him if you'd like."

"I'll think about it."

Isabel yawned and looked at her watch. "*Dios mio*, look at the time. It's late. You probably need to get home." She stood and wiped the dirt off her dress.

Sullivan rose, his gait a little unsteady. "Can't. I'm drunk, if you didn't already figure that out." He looked at her. "I get real talkative when I drink."

Isabel laughed softly. "So I've noticed. You can stay as long as you need to. Or I have a pull-out sofa if you want to crash."

She turned to go back into the house, but Sullivan reached for her hand. "Wait. I haven't told that story to many people."

"I won't say anything."

"I really appreciate you listening... and not judging."

"I don't think you did anything wrong. Like I said, if I had been in your situation, I'd do the same thing."

He was still holding her hand, and Isabel felt something in the air shift. Sullivan was gazing at her, and her heart raced.

"Izzy? I mean, Isabel. Sorry. I know you hate it when I call you that."

"Actually, Izzy is kind of growing on me."

"Izzy, I just want to say..."

"Say what?"

Sullivan said nothing. Instead, he kissed her.

It had taken her by surprise, but Isabel wasn't complaining. In fact, she sort of liked it.

When he pulled away, Isabel smiled. "I like that your breath doesn't smell like cigarettes."

Sullivan chuckled. "No, it just smells like beer now."

"Well, yeah, but so does mine." Isabel grinned, and this time, she kissed him.

SULLIVAN CRACKED open an eye and realized it was morning. It was bright, which was odd, because he had blackout curtains which kept his room dark.

He spotted a crucifix on a beige wall, definitely not something he owned. He was on Isabel's couch. But how the hell had he ended up here?

As he moved to a sitting position, his head throbbed, and he winced at the pain. Memories of last night came rushing back to him. He'd drank too much, and they had talked. He'd told her everything, and for some reason, Isabel didn't think the worst of him.

And he'd kissed her. Probably the booze had been responsible for that, but he'd been wanting to anyway. And judging from the way Isabel was kissing him back, she had too.

And had they danced? No, he was probably imagining that. No way would Sullivan make a fool of himself like that.

But yes, they had most certainly kissed. She felt warm and

soft, and just the thought of her in that sexy little dress gave him a hard-on.

"Good morning."

Isabel stood about ten feet away. Sullivan quickly tossed the blanket over his jeans.

"Morning," he grumbled. He hated mornings. There was never anything good about them.

In her hand, she held a glass of water and a bottle of what he hoped were pain pills.

"You probably have a hangover. Thought you'd like some aspirin."

"Please."

She set the items on the coffee table, and Sullivan swallowed two of the white pills down with water. He tossed her a grateful look and handed her back the bottle.

"Better?"

"Getting there." He took another sip of water. His mouth felt parched, and he needed a toothbrush. "Do you remember what happened last night?"

"*Sí.*" she said. "Do *you?*"

"Some. I don't remember how I ended up on this couch."

"I offered to let you crash here. This folds out into a bed, but you insisted you could sleep on the couch as it was, so I brought you a blanket from the closet. When I came back, you were passed out."

The details were fuzzy, but Sullivan could remember it now. "Right. And I remembered we talked before that. You're not going to tell anybody, are you?"

"Like I told you last night, I won't share it with anyone."

He nodded, grateful for Isabel's silence. Not that the law would come after him, but people had a tendency to see you differently if they knew you had killed someone.

"You're welcome to stay for breakfast, but with that hangover you're nursing, you'll probably want to head on home. Miguel will be up soon, and he's always loud and full of energy first thing. If you want a quiet morning, now is your chance to escape."

Sullivan nodded. "Yeah, I think I will take off." He was already dressed, albeit in wrinkled clothes, but his shoes were off. He reached for them. "I'll just put these on, make a bathroom run, and then I'll be out of your hair. Sorry for the inconvenience."

"It was no trouble, really."

"All the same, thanks for letting my drunk ass crash on your couch."

"Sure. I'm just sorry it was so uncomfortable. And don't say it wasn't, because I've fallen asleep on this thing and woke up with a crick in my neck every time."

Sullivan's neck did hurt, but he kept quiet about the pain. He didn't want to seem ungrateful for the couch. "It's no problem. I slept in worse places."

He finished up in the bathroom, and after a hasty goodbye, made his exit. He walked to his Jeep, wearing yesterday's clothes, like he was doing the damn walk of shame.

Though if he were honest with himself, he wouldn't mind spending the night again.

~

On Sundays after church, Isabel's mother enjoyed a big family lunch. In the kitchen, Isabel and Paulina helped their mother cut tomatoes.

"*Hace calor!*" Carlita complained, fanning herself with her hand.

Isabel looked up from the cutting board. "Mamá, I told you to get that A/C unit checked out."

"And it's only going to get hotter," Paulina added.

Carlita opened the freezer and stuck her head inside. "I'm sure it's just the oven making things hot."

"The ice cream is going to melt," Isabel said, teasing her mother.

Carlita closed the freezer. "I'll adjust the thermostat and change into something more breathable."

She left the room, and Isabel and Paulina laughed.

Outside, Miguel shrieked, and Isabel peered out the window. She smiled as the children and Ricardo played with the drone. "You're going to have to buy Ricardo one now," Isabel said, making Paulina laugh.

Paulina gave the pot on the stove a stir. "I saw Sullivan playing with Miguel yesterday. He's really good with him."

Isabel placed the chopped tomatoes in a bowl and rinsed off the knife. Even if Sullivan claimed he didn't like being around a bunch of kids, he had Miguel and his cousins' full attention with the drone.

"Speaking of Sullivan," Paulina said, "Mamá said that this morning, Sullivan's Jeep was still parked along the curb." She elbowed Isabel. "What was that about?"

"Don't get the wrong idea. He just crashed on my couch because he had too much to drink."

Paulina smiled. "Okay, I believe you. But I will say... you two spent a long time out on the porch." Paulina wiggled her eyebrows.

"Yeah. So?"

"For a guy you claim to hate, you sure spent a lot of time with him."

"I don't hate him. At least, not anymore."

Paulina grinned. "I had a feeling you liked him at least a little. What did you talk about?"

Isabel wasn't about to tell her. "Just private stuff."

Her sister's smile grew bigger. "Private stuff?"

Isabel sighed. She might as well tell her. "Okay, we kissed."

Paulina squealed. "I knew it!"

Carlita came back into the room dressed in a tank top and shorts. "What did I miss?"

"Isabel and Sullivan kissed last night."

Isabel shot her sister a glare, but Paulina just smiled.

Now her mother was giving her a sly look. "I knew the two of you liked each other, *mija*. I saw his vehicle was still outside this morning."

"Okay, for the last time, nothing happened. He slept on the couch. He drank too much at the party."

"Too bad," Carlita muttered. "If I were thirty years younger, I'd be all over that Jase Holler look-a-like. I would, what do you young people say, *hit that?*"

"*¡Mamá!*" Isabel said, shocked.

Carlita shrugged. "What? You think just because I'm in my sixties that I don't find men attractive anymore? Of course, no one holds a candle to your father, but I still know a good-looking man when I see one, and that Sullivan is a cutie patootie."

Isabel couldn't help but laugh. She wouldn't use the words *cutie patootie*. She would say sexy, but she kept that thought to herself.

Next to her, Paulina took out the salad dressing from the pantry. "And it's been a while since Isabel's seen anyone. What happens now, *hermanita?* Are you going to date now?"

Isabel's smile fell. "I don't know. We didn't talk about it."

Paulina looked disappointed. "You didn't talk about it?"

"No. When it was over, he said he was too drunk to drive, and that he'd take me up on my offer to sleep on the pull-out sofa. When I came back into the living room with a blanket, he was already asleep."

Carlita reached into the oven and pulled the chicken out. "Did you talk this morning?"

"Not really. He had a headache, and I told him if he wanted a quiet morning, he had to leave before Miguel woke up."

"You should talk to him," Paulina said. "Get a feel for what he's thinking."

"Invite him over for dinner, *mija*," Carlita said. "Then he can spend some time with you and Miguel."

Isabel smiled. It wasn't a bad idea. "Okay, but maybe I'll wait a few days. He's probably had enough of the Torres family for one weekend."

SULLIVAN WOULD HAVE PREFERRED to spend the rest of the day nursing the pain in his head in his dark bedroom, but Ryder wanted to have lunch. It was his friend's last full day in Florida, and it'd be rude not to at least show up for one last get together.

The hostess led him to a booth by the window, and Sullivan winced at the sunlight pouring in. When the hostess left, he pulled the blind down.

"Wow, you got here before me," Ryder said, sitting down in the seat across from him. His arms were red with sunburn.

"You look like you got some sun."

"And you look like hell."

"I might have drank too much at Isabel's last night."

Ryder grinned. "You were at Isabel's?"

The waitress arrived with impeccable timing to hand out menus and take their drink orders. When she left, Ryder ignored the menu.

"What were you doing having drinks at Isabel's?"

Sullivan glanced at the menu. "Nothing. It was her kid's birthday and he invited me. Isabel said there would be alcohol for the adults, so I went."

Ryder finally opened his menu. "And I'm sure that was the

only reason, right? It wouldn't have anything to do with Isabel being an attractive woman, would it?"

He thought back to Isabel wearing that sexy white dress and her lips pressed against his. He closed the menu. "Cheeseburger looks good. What are you having?"

Ryder chuckled. "You're avoiding my question."

"Fine. I might have kissed her."

"Might have? You don't remember?"

"Okay, I definitely kissed her."

Ryder closed his menu. "I knew you liked her. I saw the way you two bickered and thought you'd be a good match."

"It was just a drunken kiss. Nothing more."

"Yeah, keep telling yourself that."

The waitress arrived shortly after to take their orders, and once the food came, Ryder did most of the talking. Fortunately, the conversation had shifted away from Isabel and on to more interesting things, like the weather. They joked that people talked about the weather when they had nothing else to talk about, but to them, it was always the main topic of interest.

Ryder dipped his fry into the small container of ketchup. "Where are you and Isabel taking the LIV tomorrow?"

"We'll determine that in the morning. I think it's going to be one of those days where the storms come off the gulf and go all the way to the east coast."

"Wish I could ride with you again, but we have to hit the road early. We'll stop by on our way out to say goodbye."

"Torres is still disappointed you didn't bring the T-Rex for him to have a look."

Ryder laughed and popped another fry into his mouth. "Next time, I promise."

After lunch, Ryder walked toward Sullivan's new vehicle. "I didn't really get a good look at it last weekend. This new model is nice." Ryder ran his hand along the crimson exterior.

"Yeah, it's all right."

Ryder pointed to the weather gear on top. "You look like you're ready to go chasing."

"When this stint with Torres is done, then yeah, I'll catch some storms."

"But you still don't want to drive the T-Rex for my documentary?"

"Not a chance."

Ryder poked his head into the vehicle. "It still smells like a new car."

"Yeah, because it is."

"No, I mean it doesn't smell like cigarette smoke."

"Quit on Tuesday."

Ryder turned around, his eyes wide. "Quit? You quit smoking?"

"Isabel doesn't like it."

Ryder let out a hearty laugh. "I can't believe this. I've been trying to get you to quit smoking for years, and all it takes is a pretty woman to ask you to stop, and you do it. Unbelievable."

"We made a bet that I would stop. She doesn't think I can do it, but I'm going to prove her wrong."

"Where was Isabel when we were in college? She could have saved your lungs all those years of suffering."

"Shut up," Sullivan said, but he wasn't really mad. He wished Isabel had been in his life sooner too.

WHEN ISABEL ARRIVED at work the next day, Sullivan was already there. Ever since Saturday night, their kiss had been on her mind. Would things be weird between them now?

She found Sullivan at the desk, his attention focused on the computer. He barely glanced at her.

"We can stick close to home and follow the storms east," he said.

No "good morning." No "how are you doing?" No smile, of course, but that wasn't unusual for Sullivan. It was almost as if nothing had happened between them. Maybe he'd been so drunk that he couldn't remember. Isabel didn't know if she should feel relieved or annoyed. "Great. We'll wait for them to fire up."

A horn outside honked. Isabel peeked out the window to see a blue truck pulled up at the curb. "I think your friends are here."

Fernando poked his head into the room. "Is that Ryder?"

"Yeah, they're leaving today." Sullivan got up from the desk and brushed past Isabel as he headed out the door. Isabel sighed, then followed him. She wanted to at least see that cute baby one more time.

Outside, the doors to the truck were open, and Isabel heard the baby crying. Isabel walked over to Kit. "Is he all right?"

Kit unhooked the baby from the car seat. "I think he needs to poop. He would as soon as we hit the road."

"Good thing we stopped," Ryder said. "Just came to say goodbye before we head back."

"You need to bring the T-Rex next time," Fernando said.

Ryder nodded. "I will. Promise."

The baby was still fussy, and Isabel had an idea. "Why don't you let Sullivan hold him? He has a way with kids."

Sullivan shot her a glare. "Kids, not babies."

"I think that's a great idea," Kit said. She shoved the baby into his arms, and immediately, the baby stopped crying.

"See?" Isabel said. "He's a natural."

Isabel almost laughed at Sullivan's deer-in-headlights look, but after a few moments, he seemed to relax. Then Sullivan wrinkled his nose. "He quit crying because he did his business. He stinks." He handed the baby back to his mother.

"I'll go change him," Kit said, then headed inside.

The men began discussing today's storm potential, and

Isabel felt left out. Non-talkative Sullivan was carrying on a conversation with her *tío* and best friend and had barely said two words to her. Did he feel awkward about their kiss Saturday night? Was this his way of avoiding the issue? Maybe when they were on the road and it was just the two of them, they'd talk about it.

By late morning, the western sky grew dark, threatening rain, and she and Sullivan took the LIV out. While they waited for the storms to percolate, Sullivan pulled into a McDonald's parking lot.

"Want anything?" he asked.

"I guess just some fries." She didn't have much of an appetite.

Sullivan nodded and got out of the vehicle.

As he was inside, Isabel pulled down the visor and checked her face in the mirror. She'd put on lipstick this morning, but Sullivan hadn't appeared to notice. Why was she making an effort to look beautiful when he was ignoring her?

He came back a few minutes later, and the smell of french fries filled the cab. Isabel found her appetite and dug into the bag he offered.

"Did you check the radar?" he asked.

She hadn't. She'd been too preoccupied with the way she looked. Hurriedly, she pulled it up. "We should head east. It'll pop up soon over the coast."

Sullivan took a fry out of the bag between them and backed out of the space.

They ate while driving, and it was quiet, save for some old Garth Brooks song playing in the background. It was all country music, all the time, but Isabel wasn't about to complain about it. Sullivan had kept up his end of the bet and hadn't smoked in a week.

It appeared that Sullivan would not bring it up, which

meant she had to. And she needed to know what he was thinking, otherwise, it would drive her crazy.

"So, are we going to talk about it?" she asked.

Sullivan bit off the tip of a chicken nugget. "Talk about what?"

Talk about what? Didn't he know?

"Our kiss Saturday night. You remember, right? I know you had a lot to drink."

"What's there to talk about? We were drinking. Alcohol makes you do things."

"Right." She pretended to agree, but it hadn't been the response Isabel wanted. Just as she figured, the kiss had meant nothing to him. All weekend, she thought of the way they moved together when they danced, their talk on the porch steps, and the way his stubble had rubbed her chin. Despite her chin being raw, the kiss had been nice.

But Sullivan said it was nothing, and for now, she'd have to hide her disappointment.

16

That night, after Miguel was tucked into bed, Isabel decided to soak in a warm bath with a glass of wine. It wouldn't help her forget Sullivan, but at least it would help her relax.

As she was deciding on a bath bomb, her sister called. Isabel thought about letting it go to voicemail, but she wouldn't be able to relax until she found out why her sister was calling.

She picked up the phone. "*Hola,* Paulie."

"Did you see Sullivan today?" Paulina asked, skipping the hello.

"Yes, I work with him."

"Well, did you talk?"

Isabel sighed and selected the lavender scented one. "He said it was the alcohol, so it's obvious he feels nothing. He's just a man with loose inhibitions when he drinks."

"Oh, I'm sorry, *hermanita*. I thought he felt something toward you."

"Yeah, me too. But I have to work with him, so it's probably for the best that we don't get involved, you know? It might make for awkward long drives."

"Are you sure there's no spark there?" Paulina asked. "Because I saw the way he was looking at you Saturday. And that was before he'd had anything to drink."

"Sorry to burst your and our mother's bubble, but I will not be dating Jase Holler's doppelgänger. I've got to go, Paulie. I want to take a soak in my tub and forget about this day."

"Okay, take care, *hermanita. Buenas noches.*"

"*Buenas noches.*" Isabel ended the call, then filled the tub with warm water. Somehow, though, she didn't think a warm bath would get her mind off of Sullivan.

SULLIVAN TOSSED and turned in his bed. He wanted a cigarette. He pushed the sheet off, grabbed his gum from the bedside table, and popped it into his mouth. The damn craving was keeping him awake.

The taste of cinnamon tingled his tongue, and for a moment, he was distracted. Sweet nicotine filled his body. Maybe he could relax a little.

His craving had subsided, but he still couldn't sleep. Wide awake, he now couldn't stop thinking about Isabel.

He'd made it seem like the kiss was nothing, that it was just the booze, but that wasn't the truth. He liked her, and when he told her about his past, she still saw good in him.

But he wasn't good enough for her, and it was best that Isabel think it was the alcohol that made him kiss her. Isabel shouldn't want to get involved with him. His fucked up childhood turned him into an adult that didn't play well with others, and Isabel deserved much better than him.

Sullivan cursed at the hour on the digital clock, then dragged himself out of bed. After a quick stop to the bathroom, he headed down the short hallway to the kitchen. The itch for a cigarette had returned, and the gum flavor was already wearing off. He opened the refrigerator and perused the contents. There was half of a pack of deli meat, and a sandwich seemed like a good midnight snack. He'd eaten little of his dinner anyway.

He ate at the kitchen table in the dim light under the microwave. It seemed pathetic; him sitting by himself at one in the morning eating a sandwich. Once, he thought it might be nice to get a dog for company, but pets were a lot of work, and he was away from home a lot.

When Sullivan was feeling this way, he'd usually go to a bar, find a willing woman to spend the night with, then go back to his daily life. But at the moment, the only woman he wanted to take to bed was Isabel.

That was a problem. For one, she was Torres's niece, and Torres was probably the closest thing Isabel had to a father since her own had died. Not to mention that Torres was sort of his boss.

Second, they worked together, and sleeping with your coworker was never a good idea. One time, he'd made the mistake of sleeping with a flight attendant he had regular contact with. When that relationship soured, things got awkward until she transferred to another airline. And he had to work with Isabel until mid-August.

Sullivan finished his sandwich, tossed the paper plate in the trash, then headed to the living room. If he couldn't stop thinking of Isabel, maybe he'd find something on television to distract him.

The first show that came up on his streaming service was *Bermuda Time Warp*.

"Fuck," Sullivan grumbled, then turned the television off.

Isabel was in a foul mood the next afternoon, and judging from Sullivan's road rage, perhaps he was as well. The LIV was stuck in the middle of lunch hour traffic, and Isabel wished she were driving.

"Move your ass," Sullivan said to the vehicle in front of them as they crept forward a few inches.

"You shouldn't go this way," Isabel said. "Take the alternate road."

"This is the fastest route."

"It's *not* the fastest route. You've got everyone and his brother going to lunch."

Sullivan didn't make a move to change lanes, and Isabel sighed. It was going to be a long drive. To make matters worse, she was still pissed at him for blowing off their kiss over the weekend. If he didn't feel any attraction toward her, he shouldn't have put his lips on hers. After all, *he* had been the one to make the first move. Well, her sister would argue that she had with her sexy dance moves, but if Sullivan didn't like what he saw, he shouldn't have let it get any further.

Sullivan pulled her out of her thoughts by honking the horn and slamming on breaks, jerking her forward. "Damn fool!"

Isabel looked up ahead and saw blue lights. "There's a wreck. Just go the way I told you to go."

Sullivan finally put on the blinker and switched lanes. But when it came time to turn, he missed it.

"Hey, you're supposed to turn back there."

"Let's go this way."

"You're going the wrong way!"

He glared at her. "I'm driving, Izzy. Your way looked just as busy. The navigation system will reroute us."

"This road leads to a neighborhood that comes to a dead end, so have fun with that."

"*Make a U-turn,*" squawked the GPS.

"Fuck," Sullivan cursed. They came upon the dead end, just as Isabel said they would.

"Told you."

He glared at her. "One more smart ass comment like that, and I'll stop at a gas station and buy cigarettes just to piss you off."

She sighed. "No, don't do that. You'll ruin all your good progress. And I'll play Ricky Martin on repeat. Chew your damn gum or something."

When they finally emerged from the traffic pileup, the storms they were chasing had fizzled out.

"Well, there goes our storm," Isabel said. "A fitting end to a shitty day."

Sullivan popped out a piece of gum from the blister pouch. "Damn traffic was to blame."

"I told you to go a different way. We could have avoided all of this, but no, you didn't want to listen."

"Your way wouldn't have been any better."

"Yes it would," Isabel countered. "I've lived here since I was eight. I know which areas are busy, so I told you to go the other way. And now, we missed our lightning."

"Just let it go, Izzy. Ain't like there's never going to be another thunderstorm again."

"I told you to stop calling me Izzy, *Elmer.*"

"I thought you said the name was growing on you."

"Not anymore. And I'm driving next time."

Sullivan glared at her. "Fine. I'm tired of you being a back-seat driver anyway."

The rest of the drive back had been quiet and blessedly short. As soon as they pulled into the parking lot, Sullivan hopped out of the vehicle, headed to his Jeep, and left without so much as a goodbye or see you later.

Fine by Isabel. One more minute with Mr. Grumpy and she would have lost her mind. Hard to believe she actually enjoyed kissing him last weekend. She'd never known someone to have so many mood swings, other than herself. Maybe that was why they fought so much.

They were too much alike.

THEY DECIDED NOT to work the next day on account of storm chances being too low. That was fine by Sullivan. At least he'd get a break from Isabel. He had a tendency to lose his temper when things didn't go his way, and not being able to act on his growing attraction to her was stressing him out.

But by Thursday, it was back to work. Not only was his break from Isabel ending, but he was also out of nicotine gum. Thank God the pharmacy was only a short drive from his home. Inside, Sullivan headed to the very back where the nicotine cessation products were sold. After Torres had given him the idea, he decided the patch was worth a try. Maybe that, in addition to the gum, would help manage his cravings a little better.

As he left the pharmacy counter, he took a shortcut to the exit and found himself on the condom aisle. He stopped and stared at them for a moment. He couldn't remember the last time he'd bought some, and he was pretty sure the ones he had in his duffel bag were expired.

On impulse, he grabbed his favorite box of Trojans and went to the self-checkout. He didn't know what possessed him, but he was certain a feisty Puerto Rican beauty had something to do with it.

When he arrived at work, Torres and Isabel were crowded around the computer. Isabel glanced up at Sullivan, didn't smile, then turned her attention back to the screen.

Torres looked up. "Good, you're here. You see the latest models this morning?"

He hadn't. He spent the morning yelling at his toaster for

burning his last slice of bread. That was after he discovered he was out of the nicotine gum. All around a bad start to the day. "No, I haven't looked at the computer yet."

Torres turned the laptop around so Sullivan could see the screen. A whole swath over Georgia and South Carolina was shaded in orange. "The SPC is calling for an enhanced risk of storms in central Georgia this Saturday. I know it's a drive, but there won't be that kind of thunderstorm activity here."

"So you want us to go to Georgia?"

"We'd have to get a hotel," Isabel said. "It'll be late in the afternoon when the storms develop, and it's about a six-hour drive. I don't know about you, but I'd prefer not to drive home late at night."

Sullivan shrugged. "Fine. I don't care. I'll pack an overnight bag."

"I'll plan for Miguel to have a sleepover," Isabel said.

"Well for now, storms are about to fire up in Lakeland," Torres said. "You two better hit the road if you want to catch them."

ISABEL WAS glad to be driving today. She didn't want a repeat of Tuesday's traffic disaster. Sullivan had a tendency to get mad behind the wheel, and it seemed like his road rage had only gotten worse since they kissed.

She had actually enjoyed that kiss, but what the hell had been wrong with her? She should have known that Sullivan felt nothing for her. He was simply a man, influenced by alcohol and his lower half.

Miguel had asked her to invite him to dinner again, but Isabel couldn't bring herself to do that. She had to spend enough time with Sullivan on the road. When work was over, she was glad to say goodbye to him.

"Some red popping up on the radar," Sullivan said.

Up ahead, Isabel could see dark storm clouds. "We'll be there soon." Moments later, droplets pelted the LIV's windshield.

"Drive out of this. The good storm is just on the other side."

What had been a light rain quickly turned into a downpour, and Isabel sped up the wipers to keep up. Suddenly, the LIV jolted, and Isabel knew the LIV had struck something.

"The fuck?" Sullivan snapped. "What'd you hit?"

"I'm pretty sure it was a pothole." Isabel eased the LIV to the shoulder. It was driving sort of wonky, and Isabel had a sinking feeling the vehicle had sustained some damage.

"You almost knocked the laptop off the stand," Sullivan complained.

"Well excuse me for not having control of the road conditions," Isabel shot back.

Sullivan grumbled as he reached for his raincoat. "I'll go look at it."

"Just wait until it stops pouring," Isabel said.

Sullivan ignored her suggestion and left the vehicle. He was outside for a long time, making Isabel worry about how bad the damage is. When he came back, he was dripping.

Isabel attempted to cover the laptop keyboard. "You're going to get the computer wet."

Sullivan just glared at her and flopped into the seat. "We're not going anywhere. You damaged the wheel and probably knocked it out of alignment. We're going to have to call for roadside assistance."

Isabel shook her head. "That's just great. We're going to miss the storm, and I'm stuck with your grumpy ass for a little longer."

"It's no picnic for me either," Sullivan said with a scowl. "Didn't you see the pothole?"

Isabel seethed. He was blaming her for this? "No, I

didn't see the pothole! It was pouring down rain! And even if it wasn't raining, that pothole would have been impossible to see until you're right up on it. I couldn't have avoided it."

Sullivan grunted. "I should have driven."

"*Gilipollas*," Isabel muttered.

Sullivan turned to her, nostrils flaring. "Now I *know* what that word means."

"That's what you're being right now," Isabel fired back. "An *asshole*. It's not my fucking fault that a pothole is in the road! It's not my fault that the Florida DOT doesn't keep up with the road repairs like they should."

Sullivan reached for his phone. "I'll call someone."

"What, you think I'm not capable of calling for help?"

Sullivan just glared at her and put his phone to his ear.

The damage was worse than they thought. The tire needed to be replaced along with damage to the wheel rim and steering repaired. The LIV would be out of commission for at least a day.

Sullivan threw his hands up in the auto shop's lobby. "We're going to miss Georgia this weekend."

"Relax, Mr. Grumpy," Isabel said. "He said he would try to get it fixed by the end of the day tomorrow." She followed him out the door into the parking lot. The rain had stopped now, leaving behind a few puddles and some muggy Florida humidity.

"That's what they always say, and then they need a part, which they have to order, or they get backed up in the shop, and it won't be until next week. And I was really looking forward to this weekend."

Isabel wanted to roll her eyes. "Chill already. You're acting like Miguel when he's having one of his temper tantrums. It's not like there won't be another storm."

"It's an enhanced risk, Izzy. Won't be another one like this for a while. We might as well call your uncle and have him pick us up."

Isabel already had her phone out. "I'm calling him now."

Sullivan just grunted and started walking away.

"Go chew your damn gum," she said. When he was out of sight, Isabel breathed a sigh of relief, then made the call.

"*Hola, princesa,*" Tío Fernando said.

Isabel gave Fernando the short version of what had happened and gave him their location. "Can you come pick us up? And hurry? If I have to spend one more minute with Mr. Grumpy, I'm going to lose it myself."

"I thought you two were getting along better."

"We were, but then–" Isabel stopped herself. She wasn't about to tell Tío Fernando that she and Sullivan had kissed. That was a conversation she'd much rather have with her sister. "Never mind. Can you just come pick us up?"

"I'm on my way."

"*Gracias.*" Isabel ended the call, then watched as Sullivan came around the building.

"He's on the way," she said to him. "I'll wait inside." The shop's waiting room smelled like motor oil and bad coffee, but it was preferable than staying out here in the heat with Sullivan's bad mood.

SULLIVAN SIGHED as he looked at the radar. It was Friday afternoon, and thunderstorms were firing up over southern Florida today. The LIV was still out of commission and he was missing it. He could, he realized, take his Jeep for a long drive, but he needed to stick around to pick up the LIV from the shop. Torres planned to give him a ride. If, in fact, the LIV got fixed today. Plus, without Isabel, chasing storms just didn't feel right.

He'd overreacted yesterday and regretted snapping at her.

The pothole hadn't been her fault. He'd just been in a grumpy mood and had needed a cigarette.

No, that wasn't it. That was his excuse. He did still have cravings, but they weren't as bad as they were in the beginning. No, the real problem was that he couldn't act on his attraction toward her. Sullivan knew he wasn't relationship material. Not that he was opposed to it, but Isabel deserved so much better than his worthless ass. And anyway, Torres would probably be upset if he knew he'd kissed his niece. The professor was counting on Sullivan to keep an eye on her from that creep Mateo, not entertain thoughts of taking her to bed.

"Hey, Sullivan!" Torres called from his office. "Come here!"

Sullivan poked his head into the room, and Torres swiveled around in his chair. He looked practically giddy. "Georgia and South Carolina are looking better."

"Moderate risk?"

"No, SPC hasn't upgraded the risk, but they fine-tuned the forecast. Check it out."

Sullivan peered over Torres's shoulder at the computer screen. The SPC had outlined a section all the way from central Georgia to the Carolinas in orange. Nasty weather was happening for sure.

"Hope that LIV gets fixed," Sullivan said.

"I just called the shop, and they're working on it now," Torres said. "It'll be ready in an hour."

"Good."

Torres's expression turned serious. "Hey, is everything okay between you and Isabel?"

Sullivan felt a knot in his stomach. Did Isabel say something to him about their kiss? "Why would you ask that?"

Torres shrugged. "There seemed to be some tension between you yesterday. I thought you two were getting along better."

Sullivan was saved from answering by the sound of

someone in the lobby. Footsteps sounded down the hall, and Isabel appeared in the doorway. She looked at Sullivan and seemed surprised to see him there. "What are you doing here?"

"Torres is giving me a ride to pick up the LIV," he said.

Isabel looked confused. "Oh. I just assumed I'd drive with you, Tío."

Torres stood and stuffed some papers into his briefcase. "Actually, now that you're here, why don't you two pick it up?" He smiled. "I've got some work to do, and it would really save me some time."

Isabel wasn't smiling, and if Sullivan had to guess, she wasn't looking forward to driving with him.

"That's fine, Tío," she eventually said.

"Great. Well, I guess I'll head to my office at the university. I'll catch you two later." Torres tucked his laptop under his arm and left the room. Isabel soon followed.

Sullivan sat in Torres's swivel chair and leaned his head back. He'd been looking forward to a drive without Izzy, but that wasn't happening.

ISABEL FELT a headache coming on as Sullivan's music blared out of his speakers. "Can you turn that down?" she complained. "I have a headache."

Sullivan turned off the radio.

"I didn't say you had to turn it off."

"Maybe I need some quiet time too. You know, you really didn't need to come. Torres said he'd ride with me to get it."

"He told me it would be ready this afternoon, so I thought he wanted me to ride with him."

"Figures," Sullivan muttered.

"I'm not happy about it either," Isabel shot back. "I could

have taken Miguel bowling today, but instead, I'm driving to Lakeland with your grumpy ass."

"Or we could be chasing in Fort Myers today if you hadn't run over that damn pothole."

"Oh, we're going there again? You know what, I hope and pray that you hit a pothole with this precious new Jeep of yours. And if you do, I'll be laughing. And I hope you get a flat tire."

"You won't be laughing if that happens right now, because that would mean you'd be stuck with my grumpy ass for even longer."

Isabel sighed. He made a good point. How the hell would she survive a drive to Georgia tomorrow?

Sullivan finally pulled up to the auto shop, and Isabel breathed a sigh of relief. "Thank God." She grabbed her purse and hopped out.

"See you tomorrow," Sullivan said through the open window, then rolled it back up. Seconds later, he peeled out of the parking lot.

"A gentleman would have waited, but whatever," she muttered as she headed inside. Hopefully the LIV was ready by now.

She was tempted to drive it down to Fort Myers just to spite Sullivan, but the storms would probably fizzle out by the time she made it there.

Maybe tomorrow's storm would make up for the one they'd lost today.

17

After breakfast on Saturday, Isabel dropped Miguel off at her mother's and headed to work. It was going to be a long drive to Georgia, made even longer because she'd be with Sullivan. She hoped he'd be in a better mood today, though that was a joke. He seemed to be perpetually grumpy. But this week, he'd been especially moody.

"It's like, ever since we kissed, he's easily angered by every little thing," Isabel had said to Paulina last night.

"I don't have any answers for you, *hermanita*. Maybe you should talk to him."

"If I can get him to talk," she muttered.

She wondered if he was mad at himself for telling her too much about his past. That was a possibility. He could have regrets.

Or maybe he was still going through cigarette withdrawals. She would be sure to smell him when she got to work. At the slightest hint that he had cheated and smoked a cigarette, she was prepared to play all the Spanish tunes she desired. Especially Ricky Martin.

But when she saw him, the only thing she smelled on him

was laundry detergent and cinnamon gum. At least he was still not smoking.

"Ready to go?" Sullivan asked, standing against the LIV with the keys in his hand.

"Yep, and glad you're driving. Wouldn't want to hit another pothole and piss you off." Isabel didn't wait for his response and headed to the passenger side with her overnight bag and camera equipment.

By the time she'd had her seatbelt fastened and the laptop booted up, the LIV was still in the parking lot. She glanced at Sullivan, who was taking his time fiddling with air controls.

"Are we going to leave today?"

He turned his head and held her gaze for a moment. "Look, I'm sorry about the other day. I shouldn't have lost my temper about the pothole. It wasn't your fault, and I'm sorry I yelled."

Isabel was surprised to hear those words from his mouth, and it was refreshing that he actually felt some remorse. "I accept your apology."

Sullivan nodded, then put the LIV into drive. "Let's go find a storm."

Once they hit the highway, Sullivan switched on the radio. With nothing on the radar yet, now would be a good time to talk to him, like her sister suggested. But Isabel didn't know what to say. She didn't need any reminders that Sullivan didn't feel a spark with her. The kiss had meant nothing to him.

Sullivan turned up the volume on the radio. Isabel put on her noise-canceling headphones and sighed.

By the time they made it to central Georgia, specks of green had popped up on the radar, a precursor to the coming storms. Sullivan glanced at the radar, then at the GPS. The rain would move east, and staying on the interstate would take them further west of it. He took the next exit.

"Where are you going?" Isabel asked.

"If we stay on the interstate, we won't get ahead of these storms."

"Yes we will. We're going fast enough. If we get stuck on some country road, we'll never make it."

Sullivan fought the urge to roll his eyes. "Just watch the radar."

"What do you think I'm doing? Playing solitaire over here?"

They came to a turn, and the GPS said to take a right and continue on the road… for twenty-six miles.

"Twenty-six miles?" Isabel said. "We better not break down, considering we're in the middle of nowhere."

"If you think this place is isolated, you haven't been to Kansas. And I've clocked more hours on the road than you. I know what I'm doing."

"What if I have to pee? There's probably no gas station around here. It's not like I can stop anywhere on the side of the road and pee. I'm not a man!"

"You yourself said this was the middle of nowhere. You could go behind a bush if it was an emergency. No one would see. I've got some leftover napkins you could use for toilet paper."

Sullivan heard her make an exasperated sigh. He turned up his music.

Several miles later, Isabel started mumbling complaints under her breath. He glanced at her and caught sight of her balled-up fist. "What now?"

"Our internet connection is spotty. I can't even get a signal on my phone. We must be in a dead zone, which means the GPS is down too. You should have stayed on the interstate like I told you to do."

"We're not lost."

"We're not?"

He pointed out the window. "You see those dark clouds up ahead? We're driving toward them, aren't we?"

"All the same, I think you should stop at the next gas station and ask for directions. If you can find a gas station."

"I'm not asking for directions because we're not lost."

"That's just like a man, not wanting to ask for directions."

Sullivan glared at her. "We're not lost."

"Well, without a working radar, we're in a shitload of trouble if a tornado comes up on us."

Isabel had a good point, but Sullivan had chased storms without a working radar before. "Don't worry. I'm sure we'll drive out of the dead zone soon."

When the radar and GPS came back to life ten minutes later, Sullivan grinned at her. "See, what did I tell you?"

He made a turn at the next intersection, and a rumble of thunder sounded.

"And we found our storm," Sullivan said, smirking.

"Why don't you pull over here?"

In the time that the radar had been down, it had grown from dots of green to blotches of red and yellow. A thunderstorm was definitely in progress.

Sullivan eased the LIV onto the side of the road next to a grassy field. A few trees dotted the landscape, but the view wasn't too obstructed. Isabel hurried to the back to get the camera equipment ready and in position.

"This storm is way too close. You're not getting out of this vehicle to make a time-lapse video, are you?"

She shot him an annoyed look. "Of course not. Do you think I'm crazy?"

"You don't want me to answer that."

Isabel huffed, then went back to operating the cameras.

Sullivan glanced at the radar. They were right on the edge of the red, the heaviest rain. There was already a flash flood warning in effect, and Sullivan wouldn't be surprised if there were a spin-up tornado or two. These storms were certainly capable of rotation. Right on cue, a sheet of rain enveloped them.

Isabel came back to the front and sat in the seat. "This is my favorite part," she said. "Just sit back and watch the show."

One tree suddenly lit up in a flash of light. A loud crack of thunder immediately followed, and Isabel screamed.

"*Dios mios*," she said, her hand over her heart. "Did you see that? Look at that tree!"

The strike had left a scorch mark on the bark, but otherwise, the tree was standing. "Yeah, I saw it. Your uncle will be pleased. We got that one on camera."

"And almost got struck ourselves. That thunder scared the crap out of me." She still had a tremble in her voice. The thunder had startled Sullivan too, but Isabel almost looked pale.

"You all right, Izzy?"

"I'm fine. It's pretty to watch, but it can be loud and frightening. I've never actually witnessed it strike a tree. In real life, I mean. On Youtube, sure."

"I saw lightning hit a tree once. I might have been five. It lit the whole thing up and split it in two. Most kids would be scared, but I thought it had been the coolest thing I'd ever seen."

Isabel laughed softly, and Sullivan loved the sound of it. It was certainly nicer than the curse words she spoke in Spanish. Sullivan looked them up on his phone one time. Isabel was feisty when she was pissed off.

"I used to watch lightning storms with Papá and Tío Fernando. I wasn't scared of it, but only because they weren't. I got my love of photography from Papá, and my love of meteorology from Tío Fernando. Papá would have loved this job."

"Texas has some good lightning storms too. It's beautiful when you see a storm over an empty field. Especially at night."

"Is that why you went into meteorology? Because you enjoyed lightning?"

"Yeah. Ryder will tell you that chasing tornadoes with him made me consider meteorology, but I've always been fascinated with storms."

"Me too. After Papá died, I'd watch them from my bedroom window and think of him."

"Emmy loved thunderstorms, too."

"She wasn't scared?"

"She was at first, like most kids. She'd come to my room when there was a thunderstorm. Mama and Dick always kept their door locked. If Emmy knocked, she'd tell her to go back to bed. So Emmy came to my room."

"That's nice that you could comfort your little sister. I used to snuggle up in Paulina's bed whenever I was scared in the night. Tell me more about your sister."

Sullivan was about ready to drop the subject. Talking about Emmy made him feel depressed. He wished things could have turned out differently, but that was life. Isabel stared at him, waiting for him to talk. Well, hell. He might as well tell her more.

"She'd find me at the window watching the storms. She'd be scared, of course, but I answered all her questions about what I knew caused thunder and lightning. By then, she was fascinated by it. After that, we always watched lightning together."

"That's a nice memory of your sister."

He nodded.

"Have you given any more thought to calling my cousin?"

"I don't know," Sullivan said, turning his attention back to the storm outside the window. "I'm still thinking about it."

Isabel reached for her phone. "I'll text you his contact. Just in case, you know, you decide you want to."

Sullivan's phone dinged with the text, but Sullivan didn't look at it. It would be there for him when—or if—he decided to track her down.

ISABEL REFRESHED the radar and examined the new scans. The storms were shifting east, as expected, so they followed them. There were plenty of opportunities to get lightning shots, just as Tío Fernando has predicted. The lightning had been spectacular.

At the wheel, Sullivan kept a steady speed. He, for once, was staying off the country roads, only getting off the main highway if they needed to follow a particular line of storms.

"Want to chase these storms all the way to the coast?" He gave her a teasing smile, as if it were a challenge.

"Do it," she said, and Sullivan kept on driving.

It was already dark when they reached a hotel at the shore that looked nice, and there was a drizzly rain shower still going on. Sullivan pulled up to the overhang near the entrance. "I'll let you get out here."

"I don't care about a little rain."

"Suit yourself," he said, pulling the LIV into a parking space. He had to get one that was far away as the truck was big and the parking lot was packed.

"Looks like everyone is here for summer vacation," Sullivan muttered.

Rain droplets collected on the windshield, and Isabel now wished she had let Sullivan drop her off at the door. Her camera bag would get wet, but there was no way she was leaving it in the truck. She gathered her things, tightened her raincoat hood, and hoped for the best. At least it was only a drizzle.

Once out of the truck, they sprinted across the parking lot to minimize getting soaked. Inside, her skin broke out into gooseflesh with the hotel's air conditioner on full blast. She felt bad that they were dripping water onto the tile floor, but it couldn't be helped.

At the front desk, a frazzled-looking blond looked up from her computer. "Checking in?"

"Yeah, we need two rooms," Sullivan said.

"Name?"

"Sullivan."

The lady clicked around on her computer and frowned. "I don't see a reservation for Sullivan."

"We don't have a reservation. Is that a problem?"

"We're mostly booked up. There's a conference in town, plus people are here on vacation. I only have one room left if you don't mind sharing."

Isabel sighed. "We should have made reservations. It was stupid to assume there would be two rooms available. This is a beach hotel at the height of summer."

"You want to go somewhere else?" Sullivan asked.

Isabel rubbed her eyes. She was tired, and the thought of going back outside in the rain didn't appeal to her. At this point, all she wanted was a hot shower and a warm bed. If she had to share a room with Sullivan, it wouldn't be the end of the world. She already spent the whole day with him on the road. What was a few more hours? "I guess not. Let's take the room. I'm exhausted. But I get the shower first."

"Fine." Sullivan handed his credit card to the lady. "We'll take the one room you have left."

As soon as the clerk handed over the key cards, Isabel reached for her bags and followed Sullivan to the elevator. "I get the bed by the window. I like a room with a view."

Sullivan pressed the button. "Fine. I like sleeping by the wall anyway. You don't snore, do you?"

The doors opened, and Isabel stepped inside. "No, of course not. Do *you?*"

"I guess you'll find out."

The elevator chimed as it opened to the second floor. Their room was at the end of the hall, which was a long walk.

"Looks like we'll have a room facing the ocean, at least," Isabel said. "That might be nice. It's been a long time since I've stayed at a hotel on the beach."

Sullivan inserted the key card. The lock beeped, and the door clicked open. He stood outside and motioned for Isabel to go inside. "Ladies first."

Isabel walked past him. "Well, no bad hotel smells, and…" She stopped as she looked at the room. It was roomy with a couch, table, and only one bed. "Oh."

"What?"

She indicated the bed. "It's a single room."

Sullivan shook his head. "Fuck. If I had known there was only one bed, we would have gone somewhere else."

It was a large bed, and Isabel didn't mind sharing it. But clearly, Sullivan was distraught over it. "It's a king. There's plenty of room. And I don't kick in the night, I promise."

"You take the bed. I'll sleep here." Sullivan tossed his duffel onto the couch.

The couch looked stiff and uncomfortable with a faded burgundy pattern. Isabel couldn't imagine Sullivan's tall form sleeping on that thing. Miguel maybe, but not a grown man. "Are you sure? It looks kind of small. Won't you be uncomfortable?"

"Don't worry about me, Izzy. I'll be fine. Now go take your shower."

"All right. I'll be quick." Isabel took her bag and headed into the bathroom.

THE SOUND of the shower was driving Sullivan crazy. For one, there was the fact that Isabel was just beyond that door, naked. And then, the scent of her flowery body wash made the whole room smell like a damn botanical garden.

When Isabel emerged, steam from the bathroom followed her. "Shower's all yours now."

She was wearing a long black t-shirt, the kind that was long enough to cover her underwear but short enough so that he could see her sexy legs in full view. She didn't look like she was wearing a bra underneath, and Sullivan tried not to stare.

He grabbed his bag and marched toward the steamy bathroom. The sooner he took a cold shower, the better.

But of course, the shower didn't help, and Sullivan came out of the bathroom still thinking about Isabel. And damn, he wanted a smoke. He reached for a piece of gum in the side pocket of his duffel.

"I found this in the closet," Isabel said. He turned around and saw a throw blanket and a pillow from the bed in her arms. "It's a thin blanket."

He grabbed the bedding. "It's fine."

"I'm exhausted, so I'm going to go to bed. If that's okay?"

"Yeah, me too."

Isabel turned off the lamp, sending the room into darkness. Sullivan waited a moment for his eyes to adjust, then spread the blanket out on the couch. It squeaked when he sat down, and it was hard as a rock. Isabel's sofa had been uncomfortable, but it had been way softer than this thing.

Despite what he said, he did mind sleeping on the couch. The bed looked damn comfy, and Isabel was already under the covers and halfway asleep.

The air conditioner clicked on, and Sullivan sighed in relief.

It was hot as hell in the room, and the blanket would not be needed.

He changed his position on the couch, found it uncomfortable, then changed position again. If he lay on his back, his legs hung over the side. If he lay on his side, he could raise his legs up, but then his neck was lying on the pillow at a weird angle.

"You can't sleep," Isabel said.

"Just trying to get comfortable."

"Are you sure you don't want to take the other side? It'll be a lot more comfortable than that hard couch."

"No. I'll be fine." Maybe what he needed was alcohol. When he'd slept on Isabel's couch, he'd been too drunk to care that it wasn't as nice as his own bed at home.

Isabel eventually fell asleep. Sullivan knew, because he could hear her breathing had evened out. Sullivan nodded off, but woke up again when his leg cramped. It was just after midnight, and Sullivan wasn't tired at all.

Outside, there was a flash. Lightning. Sullivan quietly got up and walked to the balcony door. He opened it slowly, being careful not to wake Isabel, and immediately heard the waves crashing to the shore. It was too dark to see the ocean, and there was no moonlight due to the cloud cover. But just over the ocean, a storm brewed. The sky lit up almost constantly with electricity.

He leaned against the railing and felt a cool ocean breeze hit his clammy skin. The salty air mixed with the scent of rain was calming, and the lightning was relaxing to watch.

"Can't sleep?"

Isabel stood at the door in her skimpy little night shirt. Immediately, Sullivan turned his attention back to the sky.

"Dangerous to be standing outside during an electrical storm," Isabel said. "You could get struck by lightning."

"It's far enough away. Look, you can't even hear the thunder from here. And you're one to talk. Ain't I always telling you to get back in the truck when it's thundering?"

She laughed softly. "You have me there."

She moved to stand beside him, and he caught a whiff of her scented body wash. Damn, she smelled good.

"It's beautiful," Isabel said. "This is my favorite kind of lightning. Where it lights up the sky almost constantly."

"I like this too, but my favorite are the zigzags you see across the sky. Some of those can get pretty long. Sorry I woke you."

"Don't be. I love a good lightning show. Were you able to sleep at all?"

Sullivan sighed. "No. That couch is hard as a rock."

"Worse than mine?"

"Much worse. Everything hurts. My legs cramp, my back aches. I've got a crick in my neck, for sure."

"Are you sure you don't want to share the bed? We have a long drive tomorrow and need to get a decent night's sleep. And it's actually quite big. Makes my queen at home look puny."

Sullivan kept his eyes on the sky. "I'm not sharing the bed with you." He wished the storm was close enough to hear the thunder. A good thunderstorm would put him to sleep. If he had to be in the same bed next to Isabel, he definitely wouldn't be able to sleep, nor would he want to.

They were quiet for a while, listening to the sounds of the waves crashing to the shore. The lightning lessened as the storm moved on.

"Was it really just the alcohol?" Isabel asked, her voice breaking the silence that had settled between them.

Her question confused him. "Alcohol? What are you talking about?"

"You said when we kissed, it was because of the alcohol. I thought maybe there was something between us, but ever since that night, you've been distant. If you're not attracted to me, that's fine. Just tell me. I don't want things to be awkward between us."

"You don't want to get involved with a guy like me." He couldn't look at her. She was right that there was some kind of spark between them, but Sullivan knew better than to let it get any further than that.

"You didn't answer my question. Was it just the beer, or are you attracted to me?"

"Of course I'm attracted to you," Sullivan said, his tone a little more forceful than he intended. "Look, that's why we can't share the bed, okay? If I have to sleep next to you and smell you and feel you against me all night, then I'm going to want to do more than just sleep."

She looked at him with a surprised expression. "You mean...?"

"Yeah, you heard me. I want to take you to bed."

Isabel smiled, which was unexpected. "So what's stopping you? I'm game if you are."

18

Isabel's stomach fluttered. Had she really just invited Sullivan to bed? Maybe it was her hormones. Seeing Sullivan standing out there on the balcony shirtless did things to her mind. And well, she had been thinking about it. She just hadn't expected him to reciprocate her feelings.

Sullivan grinned at her. "Well, aren't you full of surprises, Izzy?"

Isabel moved closer to him. "I've been waiting for you to make a move since that kiss last week, but you haven't so much as touched me."

Suddenly, Sullivan's lips were on hers. The stubble on his chin rubbed her face, and his tongue brushed against hers. His breath smelled like cinnamon.

He pulled away, his eyes locking with hers. "You really want to do this?"

"I've been trying to get you into bed all night," she said with a teasing laugh. Not that she planned this scenario, but in this moment, it felt right.

Her heart raced as Sullivan backed her into the room. They fell on the bed, lips touching and hands exploring. It was dim, but not so dark that they couldn't see each other. The light from under the microwave cast a soft glow in the room. Isabel would have preferred candles, but this light would have to do.

Sullivan was slow and deliberate, unlike other men who rushed her to the main event. She hadn't even undressed yet, and Sullivan seemed in no hurry to take off anything. Underneath his rough exterior, there really was a gentle soul inside. It was as if he were showing a part of himself that he rarely showed to others, and Isabel was touched that he felt like sharing that with her.

A warmth spread over her cheeks when Sullivan pulled her slim black shirt off. She'd only been with one other man intimately since she'd had Miguel, and felt self-conscious about the way her body looked post childbirth. But Sullivan looked at her as if she were the most beautiful woman he'd ever seen, and Isabel relaxed.

"You're gorgeous," he whispered.

"You're pretty sexy yourself."

Sullivan grinned. "You just like me because I look like that guy from the show."

Isabel laughed, and they shared another kiss. She hadn't expected Sullivan to be the kissing type, but he was good at it.

He slowly broke away. "I have condoms. Be right back."

She watched him cross the room to his bag and was relieved that one of them was being responsible. She'd been so caught up in the moment that protection had been an afterthought. That was how she'd gotten pregnant with Miguel.

Sullivan came back to the bed. "Now, where were we?" He hovered over her, and when his hands touched her again, they went lower.

Outside, thunder rumbled, and Sullivan grinned at her. "Sounds like another storm is coming. Ain't that perfect?"

"*Perfecto*," Isabel said.

SULLIVAN STARED AT THE CEILING, unable to sleep. He felt good, like the first drag of a cigarette when he was craving a smoke. It wasn't just the sex, though that had been pretty damn spectacular, but it was something else. It was Isabel. How did she go from being someone who annoyed him in the beginning to someone he actually liked?

Next to him, she stirred in her sleep, then changed her position until her head was under his neck with an arm draped around his chest. Her hair was soft and smelled nice. She wasn't like the women he'd been with before, who stank of cheap perfume and booze. He didn't know why he wasted his time with those kinds of women. Spending the night in a hotel with a woman he considered a friend had been a hell of a lot better than a drunken night with a stranger from a bar.

Out of habit, he reached for his phone and pulled up the radar app. The storms were long gone over the Atlantic now, and soon enough, the clouds would clear.

"You still can't sleep?"

He looked away from his phone and saw Isabel smiling at him.

"Wide awake, but it's not because I'm uncomfortable. Sorry if I woke you."

Isabel returned her head to his chest and sighed. "I forgot to call Miguel to say goodnight. And now, it's too late."

Sullivan touched her hair and ran his fingers through it. He had a thing for brunettes, and Isabel was the most beautiful one he'd seen. "I'm sure he was too busy playing with his drone to realize he missed your call. He'll be thrilled at all the videos we took."

"I know, but I always call him if I'm on the road. But when we got to the hotel, I was so tired. I feel like a bad mom."

"You're a good mother, and Miguel knows you love him. You

know what a bad mom is? A bad mom is someone who leaves her two kids home alone for five days with only a loaf of bread, stale crackers, and half a jar of pickles in the fridge. A bad mother is one who spends her paycheck on lottery tickets and beer and lets her children wear shoes with holes in them. You're not a bad mother."

"I'm sorry you had such a terrible childhood."

"Yeah, well, it's in the past, and it's over. What doesn't kill you makes you stronger."

Her hand brushed his shoulder, and her fingers ran across the front of his tattoo. It was dark, but a beam of moonlight illuminated the room. The clouds had finally cleared.

"Who does this tattoo remind you of? You said you got it to remind you of someone. Was it Emmy?"

"Yeah."

On the nightstand, Isabel's phone lit up and made a sound. "Oh, what time is it?" Isabel reached for the phone.

Sullivan caught a glimpse of the screen, seeing Mateo's name on the text notification before Isabel swiped it away. "Let me see that."

"It's nothing."

"Izzy, hand me the phone."

Isabel reluctantly handed it to him, and Sullivan pulled up her message app and read the text to himself.

> Mateo: I kno u dont wanna talk to me, but I saw a lightning storm tonight and thought of u. Remembr we used to watch the sky frm the deck at the station? I wish you'd give us a chance. Maybe it's for the best that we dont work together. Now theres no excuse for us not to see each other.

Sullivan fought the urge to throw the phone across the room. What he really wanted to do was to find this Mateo guy and tell him to leave Izzy the fuck alone. Hell, he wanted to do more than that. Some men needed to be taught a lesson that only a fist could teach. "This doesn't sound like a guy who is leaving you alone."

"He's probably just drunk," Isabel said. "Look at all the typos in his message."

"This guy is stalking you," Sullivan said, his voice raised. "Being drunk is no excuse. When we get back home, you need to report him."

"I can't," Isabel said, her voice cracking.

"Why? Are you scared of how he'll react? You said you didn't think he was violent, though any man who puts his hands on a woman without her consent is violent in my book."

"I'm scared of everything. I'm scared he'll retaliate. I'm scared no one will believe me. I'm scared that he'll humiliate me. He's a local celebrity, and once this gets out, it'll be a media circus."

"Izzy, he assaulted you. You don't think he's going to do this to some other woman? If you come forward, you'll put an end to this behavior."

She stared at him, biting her lower lip, and Sullivan felt he was getting through to her. "I guess I never thought of that. He seems so attached to me, but maybe he's done this before. Maybe that was why the last meteorologist left. That's how I got the job. She abruptly left, and there was an opening."

"If you come forward, others might come forward too. Perhaps they haven't for the same reason as you."

Isabel nodded. "Okay, first thing Monday morning, I'll go talk to someone. But will you come with me?"

"Yeah, Izzy, I'll come with you."

She touched his cheek, smiled, and kissed him softly on the lips. "Thank you." She then rested her head back on his chest.

Sullivan held her until she fell asleep, and finally, felt tired enough to close his own eyes.

ISABEL BLINKED AS the bright sunlight poured into the room. For a moment, she wondered if she had imagined last night, but the duvet cover was half-off the bed, and a condom wrapper was on the nightstand. No, she hadn't imagined it.

Sullivan, however, wasn't next to her. She thought he was in the bathroom, but the room was empty. Then, she noticed the balcony door wide open. Sullivan stood there looking at the ocean. He wore jeans, no shirt, and Isabel wished he'd turn around.

She grabbed her shirt from the floor, quietly got out of bed, and slipped into the bathroom. When she came out, Sullivan was still outside. She walked over to him, and when she made a sound, he turned around.

"Good morning," she said.

"Hey."

He turned his attention back to the view. The storms from last night had moved on, leaving behind clear blue skies. The ocean ahead looked beautiful.

She stood beside him and leaned over the rail. "You don't have any regrets about last night, do you?"

He turned, and a rare grin spread across Sullivan's face. "Hell no, I regret nothing. Do you?"

She smiled back. "No. Last night was good. I'm tired though."

"Yeah, me too. Wonder why." He smiled again, then turned to look back at the ocean. "That was some storm last night."

"The storm over the ocean, or the ones we chased?"

"Both. I guess your uncle will love the videos we took."

"And now it's all clear skies, not a cloud in sight. Think we'll get some rain tomorrow?"

"Probably."

Isabel laughed, making Sullivan give her a questioning look. "What?"

"We had sex last night, and the morning after, we're talking about the weather."

Sullivan gave a slight smile. "Well, not so boring when you're both meteorologists. But how about we go back inside and not talk?"

Isabel inched closer to him. "Check out isn't until eleven, and it's only seven-thirty."

Sullivan grinned and backed her into the room. "Then I guess we better make the most of the time we have."

They fell back onto the bed, and Sullivan reached for another one of his condoms.

ISABEL OPENED her eyes when she felt the vehicle stop. She'd driven most of the way home, but Sullivan had taken the wheel at the last gas stop. "Home already?" she asked with a yawn.

"Not exactly."

Her stomach clenched at the site of the building in front of them. They were at the sheriff's department. "What are we doing here?"

"Why don't we get this over with?"

"No, I'm not ready. I said I would go tomorrow."

Sullivan shook his head. "No, Izzy. You need to get this over with. The sooner, the better. By tomorrow, you'll lose your courage and find some other excuse to get out of it."

Isabel hated to admit it, but he was right. She dreaded making the report. Dreaded reliving what had happened. Dreaded the fallout. Monday was looking good for thunderstorms, and she'd secretly hoped that a trip to the sheriff's office could be avoided by work obligations.

Sullivan reached across the console and took her hand.

"Izzy, you mean a lot to me, and I don't want to see this guy continue to hurt you."

He squeezed her hand, and Isabel took a deep breath. "Okay, let's go."

Inside, she found a female deputy standing at the desk, and feeling more comfortable talking to a woman, Isabel approached her.

"Excuse me. I need to report an assault."

SULLIVAN SQUINTED his eyes at the late afternoon sun as he waited for Isabel. She'd just finished giving her report, but needed a moment to freshen up. She said she didn't want to go home with puffy eyes and have Miguel ask her what was wrong.

Out of habit, he reached for his pocket to pull out his cigarettes. Right, not there, because he had quit. Just thinking of that son of a bitch Mateo Ramirez made him want to go through an entire pack of Marlboro.

Isabel had asked him to stay in the room while she gave her report, which involved a lot of uncomfortable questions. While Isabel had told him the highlights, he didn't know about the picture he'd texted her, or the notes and gifts he left at her desk. This guy deserved to be locked up for putting Isabel through that misery. Thankfully, Isabel had saved pictures of it all, as well as documentation on her phone. She'd also had a note he'd left in her mailbox. The deputy said they would start an investigation, but the evidence Isabel had was enough to charge him with something.

The door opened, and Isabel stepped out into the sunshine.

"You okay?" Sullivan asked.

Isabel nodded. "*Sí*. I just needed a moment. Thanks for making me do this. I'm sorry you had to hear all of that."

Sullivan reached for her hand as they walked across the parking lot. "You don't have to apologize. I'm just sorry you had to go through all that. You didn't tell me everything that had happened."

They reached the car, and Isabel leaned against the passenger door. "I know. I just didn't want to relive it. But so much for putting it all in the past. Mateo is still obsessed with me."

"Even if he wasn't bothering you now, he committed a crime and needs to pay for what he did to you."

Isabel nodded. "Sí. Can we go now? I'd like to get home in time for dinner. I didn't think we'd be here so long. My mamá is probably wondering where I am."

Sullivan was ready to leave this place too. "Absolutely."

Fifteen minutes later, they pulled into the Lightning Institute's parking lot. A silence had settled upon them, and it felt strange coming back home after all that had happened between them. Sullivan cut off the engine and racked his brain for something to say.

Though he didn't want to admit it, he'd been dreading this moment. Now that they were home, and after what they had done this weekend, things felt different. It wasn't as if Isabel had been a one-night stand. He liked her. So what the hell was he supposed to do now? Kiss her? Hug her? Hang out with her?

"Minus the sheriff's department, I enjoyed this weekend," Isabel said, and Sullivan was grateful Isabel had broken the awkward silence.

"We should do it again sometime." When he said *it*, he definitely meant sex. He thought about inviting her over to his place before she headed home, but he knew she wanted to get home to Miguel. "I guess I'll see you tomorrow?"

"Or, if you want, you could come over for dinner tonight."

Sullivan thought of Isabel's mother and pictured her giving

them knowing glances across the table. "At your mother's or at your place?"

Isabel laughed. "My place. Mamá plays bingo every Sunday night with her friends. It would be just you, me, and Miguel. Not the whole family, don't worry. You want to come over around six-thirty?"

Sullivan nodded. "That's fine. I'd rather have your cooking than what I was planning to eat."

Isabel smiled. "Oh yeah? What's that?"

"Some frozen meal. I'm not so great in the kitchen. If I can't pick it up from somewhere or microwave it, I don't get it."

Isabel laughed. "My cooking is way better than that."

There was a moment of silence, and Sullivan panicked. He supposed they were at the point where they should part ways, but he still wasn't sure what to do. Fortunately, Isabel did. She clutched the front of his shirt, pulled him closer, and pressed her mouth against his.

"See you later, Sully," she whispered.

It was the first time she'd called him Sully. Not Elmer or Sullivan. Just Sully. He supposed she felt comfortable enough to call him by his nickname now that they'd seen each other naked. He liked hearing her say it. Hell, it was certainly better than when she called him Elmer.

Isabel got out of the car, and Sullivan watched as she made her way to her little white Honda. She was wearing her tight fitting jean shorts, and he regretted not inviting her over to his place now.

Sullivan put his vehicle into drive, making mental plans to rush through his shower and pack an overnight bag. He couldn't wait to see her again.

19

When Isabel arrived home, she saw her sister's car in the driveway. Paulina stood on their mother's porch with her three boys and Miguel. Once Miguel saw her car, he ran over to greet her.

Isabel threw her arms around her son. "Hi, *nene!* I missed you." She kissed his cheek.

"I missed you too, Mamá. Did you get some good lightning videos?"

"I did, and I'll show them to you later."

Paulina met her halfway. "Mamá already left for her Sunday night bingo, so I volunteered to watch Miguel. Thought you'd be back by now."

"I'm sorry I'm late."

When Miguel ran off to play with his cousins, Isabel followed her sister inside the house.

"You must be tired after your trip."

The long drive home and the trip to the sheriff's department had certainly drained her. That, and she'd gotten little sleep last night. "So tired." Right on cue, Isabel yawned.

Her sister fanned herself. "This heat will drain anyone's energy. Want some lemonade?"

"No thanks, but I'll take a caffeinated soda."

In the kitchen, Paulina poured Isabel a glass of Coke, which Isabel didn't drink often, but it gave her the extra pep that she needed.

"So, how was the drive with Mr. Grumpy?" Paulina joined her at the table.

Isabel took a sip of her cola, giving her time to gather her thoughts. "It was great, actually."

Paulina grinned. "Something happened. I can tell, because you seem different. Did you guys kiss again?"

Isabel felt a warmth spread across her cheeks. "We did more than kiss."

Paulina's jaw dropped. "You didn't! How did *that* happen?"

Isabel smiled and shrugged. "I don't know. We were in a hotel and they only had one room left. He took the couch, I took the bed, but somehow..."

"He ended up in the bed."

Isabel grinned. "He fought me on it, but I convinced him."

Paulina squealed. "I knew you liked him!"

"Believe me, I didn't have any intention of sleeping with him. But the couch was uncomfortable, and I told him we could share the bed. It was a king size, you know? Plenty of room. But he said if he was in the bed with me, he would have no intention of sleeping. And then, one thing led to another."

"So, how was it?"

Visions of Sullivan gently kissing and caressing her crossed her mind. "For a guy who's standoffish most of the time, he was surprisingly attentive in the bedroom."

Paulina laughed softly. "I see now why you were so late in getting back."

The smile on Isabel's face fell, and the lightness she felt was replaced by the dread in the pit of her stomach. "Actually, that's not why I was late getting back."

"What's wrong? Did something bad happen?"

Isabel shook her head. "No. Sullivan convinced me to report Mateo to the authorities."

"Oh, Isabel, I'm so relieved!"

"It was hard, but Sullivan pointed out that he may have done this to other women, and he may do it again. I'm still worried that he'll retaliate, but they're supposed to serve him with a restraining order."

"I'm proud of you, *hermanita*. That man is bad news, and you can't keep giving him this power over you."

Isabel nodded. "*Sí*. And if he tries to see me again, I'm sure Sullivan will scare him off."

A smile returned to Paulina's face. "Are you seeing him again?"

The screen door slammed shut, and four sweaty kids ran inside.

"Actually, yes, Sullivan is coming over for dinner."

Miguel's eyes lit up. "Mr. Sullivan's coming?"

"That's right, *nene*. Grab your things so we can go home and get ready for him."

"Yeah! We can play *restaurante!* And I want to show Mr. Sullivan how good I am at flying the drone now!" Miguel took off down the hallway.

As she placed her empty glass in the sink, her sister tapped her on the shoulder.

"Are you going to invite him to stay the night?" she whispered.

"I don't know. Did Miguel play hard?"

"He's been running around with my boys all afternoon. He'll fall asleep as soon as his head hits the pillow."

Isabel grinned and leaned forward to whisper. "Then I don't see why not."

As Sullivan walked into the house, his phone rang. Lately, he'd been getting so many robocalls that he silenced unknown callers in his settings. He wished he had found that feature sooner. Now his phone never rang unless it was a contact. Usually only Ryder called him.

"You know I prefer texting," Sullivan answered.

"Texting takes too long," Ryder said. "How was Georgia? Did you get your lightning storm?"

Sullivan tossed his keys on the table. "It's not like tracking down a tornado. Lightning is easier to find than twisters. And yes, Georgia was quite active yesterday."

"Did you see the outlook this morning? SPC has an enhanced risk for tornadoes in Nebraska on Wednesday. This might be the last good chase of the season, and the T-Rex is out of the shop. Kit and I are going to drive up there. Why don't you join us?

Sullivan reached into his refrigerator and pulled out a soda. "Shit, no. That's a long ass drive." He cracked open the soda and took a swig.

"You've got an airport nearby. Catch a flight to Oklahoma and ride with us in the T-Rex. I'll even ask Kit to let you drive. You know, for old time's sake. Come on, say you'll come. This might be your last chance to see tornadoes in the Plains."

Sullivan put his phone on speaker while he emptied the dirty clothes out of his duffel bag. "I've seen tornadoes this year."

Ryder laughed. "That little waterspout?"

"Ha ha. Sorry, but I'll pass. And anyway, there's going to be some decent thunderstorms here mid-week, so I'll be working."

"So let me get this straight. You'd pass up an opportunity to chase tornadoes in the T-Rex in favor of photographing lightning with Isabel?"

Sullivan opened his dresser drawer and pulled out a clean pair of jeans. "Yeah, I would."

"I would have thought after your long road trip that you'd need a break from her."

An image of Isabel naked flashed through his mind. A break from her? Hell, he wanted more of her.

"You're quiet," Ryder said. "Which isn't unusual for you, but I haven't heard you make one complaint about her yet."

Sullivan sighed. He was tired of this conversation. "I've got to go."

"Why?"

"Because. I'm having dinner with her."

Ryder laughed. "I knew you liked her. From the moment you said you quit smoking for her, I knew. Did something happen in Georgia? You stayed overnight in a hotel, right?"

"Goodbye, Ryder." Sullivan heard his friend laugh as he ended the connection.

His phone beeped with a text notification ten seconds later.

You hooked up!

Sullivan rolled his eyes. Yes, he and Isabel had enjoyed each other's company. So why did it feel like more than just a hook-up?

WHEN SULLIVAN PULLED into Isabel's driveway, he found Miguel waiting for him.

"Hi, Mr. Sullivan!"

"Hey, kid."

"I've been playing with the drone. I'm getting better at flying it."

Sullivan closed his car door. "Good. I'd like to see that sometime."

Miguel grabbed his hand, which wasn't something Sullivan was accustomed to, but he liked feeling needed by others.

"Mamá is cooking dinner," Miguel said as he led him up the stairs to the apartment. "Let me show you our home!"

He'd been inside already, though he hadn't seen Isabel's bedroom. Would he sleep in it tonight? He'd left the overnight bag in his car, just in case it was an option. He'd slept with a few women in the past who had children, but they always preferred him to stay over when the kids were with their father. That wouldn't be the case this time since Miguel's father was out of the picture.

"This is our living room," Miguel said, showing the couch and coffee table. "And over there is our TV and my video games. Do you like playing Nintendo games? It's not like Juan's video games. It's a really old system. Mamá got it for cheap at a yard sale."

"I remember Nintendo, but you might have to show me how to play." The only experience Sullivan had with video games was at a friend's house as a child. His mother said spending money on game consoles was foolish.

Sullivan caught a whiff of something cooking. Right on cue, his stomach growled. "What's your mom cooking?"

"Chicken and Puerto Rican *tostones*. You know what that is?"

"No."

Miguel grabbed his hand again. "Come on, I'll show you." The boy led him to the kitchen. "Mamá, Mr. Sullivan is here!"

Isabel turned around, and when her eyes connected with Sullivan's, she smiled. "Hey, hope you're hungry."

"Starving." Sullivan was hungry all right, but for more than just food.

"I've got chicken and *tostones* cooking."

"Mr. Sullivan doesn't know what that is."

"It's fried plantains. Ever had it?"

"Can't say that I have."

"You'll love it. Dinner will be ready soon. Miguel, why don't you show Mr. Sullivan your room?"

He wanted to say that he'd like to see *her* room, but kept the thought to himself.

Miguel showed him his bedroom. His twin bed had a baseball theme, and in the middle of it was the drone.

Miguel reached for it. "Let's go outside and I'll show you how good I am now."

"After we eat, *nene.* Go wash your hands."

Sullivan turned to see Isabel standing in the doorway. "Dinner's ready," she said to them both.

Miguel rushed to his closet and yanked open the door. "I'm going to get ready! Don't eat yet!"

Sullivan gave Isabel a questioning look. He wasn't sure what more the boy had to do to get ready other than wash his hands, but Isabel seemed to understand what Miguel meant.

She held out her hand to Sullivan. "Come on. We have to play a game."

Her soft, small hand fit perfectly into his. He followed her, still unsure of what was going on. "What kind of game are we playing?"

"Miguel wants to play *restaurante.*"

"Okay. What are we supposed to do?"

"We're the customers. Just follow Miguel's lead."

They sat on the couch, and shortly after, Miguel came into the room wearing an apron and holding a clipboard.

"Welcome to *Miguel's Restaurante*!" he said. "I'm Miguel, and I'll be your host and server. Will it just be the two of you?"

Sullivan smiled, understanding where this little game was going now.

"No, my son will join us later," Isabel said. "He's also named Miguel."

"Wonderful! Let me show you to a table. Right this way."

They followed Miguel to the small dining area where the

table had been set. "Please have a seat," Miguel said. "Our special tonight is chicken and *tostones*. Would you like the special?"

"*Sí*," Isabel said. "And my son will have the diabetic-friendly plate."

"And you, sir?" Miguel asked Sullivan.

Sullivan nodded. "Yeah, I'll try it."

He nodded. "Great. I'll be back shortly with your food."

Miguel disappeared into the kitchen, and Sullivan wondered if the kid was going to play waiter next.

"He's so excited to have you over for dinner," Isabel whispered.

"Do you play this game often?" He reached for the glass of water already on the table and took a sip.

"Sometimes, but it's always more fun when we have company."

Miguel came out carrying a plate of food, and Sullivan was impressed the boy didn't drop it as he placed it in front of Sullivan.

"Need some help, *nene*?" Isabel asked.

"The customers don't help the wait staff, Mamá," Miguel whispered.

"Oh, right. Of course. We're at a restaurant."

"I'll be back with your order, ma'am." Miguel went to the kitchen again.

Sullivan looked down at his plate, and on cue, his stomach growled. "This looks good."

"Thanks. My mother's recipe."

Miguel returned with two more plates. "Here is your order, ma'am. And here's a plate for your son when he comes."

"Thank you, Miguel."

"Enjoy your dinner!" Miguel turned and raced back to the kitchen.

"Is he going to join us?" Sullivan asked.

"Give him a minute. He has to get out of character."

Moments later, Miguel came back out. "Sorry I'm late!" He took his place at the table and smiled at his plate. "*Tostones*, oh boy! Try it, Mr. Sullivan!"

Sullivan forked one of them and took a tentative bite. Both Isabel and Miguel watched for his reaction, and he was relieved to discover that they were actually quite tasty. He nodded in approval. "Not bad. Not bad at all." He looked at Miguel. "Your mama is an excellent cook."

"I have many talents." Isabel held his gaze while underneath the table, her bare foot rubbed against his leg.

Sullivan cleared his throat and reached for his glass of water. "You sure do."

AFTER DINNER, Isabel cleaned up while Sullivan went outside with Miguel. She watched from the kitchen window as they played with the drone. The last guy she dated had been hesitant to have one-on-one time with Miguel. She figured at the time that he had little experience with kids. When she'd found out he was a father and chose not to have contact with his children, she showed him the door. Isabel didn't have time for anyone who didn't want to be around children.

A peal of laughter came from outside. Miguel pointed to the sky as Sullivan manned the drone, and Isabel smiled. She was glad her mother was not home now. Knowing her, she'd have questions.

Once Isabel finished the cleanup, she took some lemonade outside and joined them on her mother's back deck. Sullivan sat on the bench while Miguel flew the drone.

Isabel handed him a glass. "Thirsty?"

Sullivan nodded. "Yeah, thanks. This humidity is killing me."

Isabel laughed and joined him on the bench. "Welcome to Florida."

"Look, Mamá!" Miguel said as he flew the drone across the yard.

"I see! You're getting better at flying, *nene.*"

"He's obsessed with that drone," Sullivan said.

"Thank you again for being so nice to my son."

Sullivan shrugged. "Nothing to thank me for. He's a fun kid and I'm having a good time."

"Some men I've dated in the past weren't thrilled that I had a child."

Sullivan took a sip of the lemonade and pinched his lips together. "Sweet and sour. Just how I like it. You want to know something?"

"What's that?"

"When I found out you were a mother, and a caring one at that, it actually made me like you. I didn't have the best maternal influence, but I could tell that you weren't a mother like the one I had."

Isabel wanted to kiss him, but before she could react, Miguel raced up the steps. "Can I get some tape?"

"Why do you need tape, *nene?*"

Miguel held up one of his action figures. "General Hugo wants to fly! I'm going to tape him to the drone and he'll be a fighter pilot! Can I?"

Isabel laughed. "I suppose it won't hurt. Go get it."

Miguel took off for their apartment.

"Funny kid," Sullivan said, and Isabel saw it again. A hint of a smile.

"You should do that more often."

"Do what?"

"Smile. It looks good on you."

He smiled bigger. "This turn you on?"

"Oh yeah," Isabel said, leaning forward to meet his lips.

After a short while, Isabel felt eyes on her. She turned to see Miguel and wondered how long he'd been watching them.

Isabel cleared her throat and separated from Sullivan, acting as if kissing a man was an everyday occurrence. "Oh good, *nene*, you found the tape. Do you want Mr. Sullivan to help you attach General Hugo to your plane?"

"Are you and Mr. Sullivan boyfriend and girlfriend?"

She looked at Sullivan, who gave her a look as if to say it was up to her to explain. That was hard, because she didn't quite know the answer herself. They had kissed, and they'd had great sex, but were they in a relationship? Friends, maybe.

But Miguel didn't understand the complexities of love and romance. To him, everything was simple. If you were kissing on the lips, you were a couple. So Isabel smiled and reached for Sullivan's hand. "I guess you could call us that, *nene*. We're... together. What do you think about that?"

She held her breath. If Miguel didn't like it, what would she do? She wanted to explore this thing between her and Sullivan.

Miguel broke out in a grin. "I like it. Mr. Sullivan is cool!"

With that, Miguel ran back down the steps. He sat on the grass and began taping the action figure to the drone.

Isabel looked at Sullivan, wondering what his reaction would be. She couldn't tell by looking at him. "I didn't know what else to say. I hope that was okay."

"It's fine. Have to say... never had anyone call me 'cool' before. A 'grouch' or 'pain in the ass,' sure, but never 'cool.'"

Isabel laughed. "Well, you are kind of cool. You know, when you're not smoking. And I'm still very proud of you that you haven't had a cigarette yet. I would know if you cheated. I'd be able to taste it."

"I guess if I want you to keep on kissing me, I'll have to make sure I don't start back."

"You better not, because if you do, you ain't getting any more of this." She indicated herself.

"You think if I kissed you right now, Miguel would say anything about it?"

Isabel looked at Miguel as he prepared to send General Hugo on his first flight. "I don't think so. He seems pretty occupied at the moment."

"Good." Sullivan placed his hand on her chin and brought her lips to his.

BY THE TIME it got dark, Isabel announced it was time for Miguel's bath. Sullivan took that as his cue to leave. "I guess you're ready for me to go."

"No, stay," Isabel said. "I mean, if you want to. You can watch some television or something. I won't be long."

Sullivan nodded. "All right then."

He said goodnight to Miguel, then sat by himself in the living room, unsure of what to do or what would happen next. Was he spending the night? Was this what having a girlfriend was like?

He watched television only for a few minutes before turning it off. Nothing was on but those summer game shows. Miguel was done with his bath now, and from the bedroom, he could hear Isabel's soft voice reading a story in Spanish.

Sullivan looked at the pictures on Isabel's wall. There were about twenty of them, some in one of those frames that held multiple photos. Most of them were of Miguel at different ages. A few were of Isabel when she was younger. She'd been beautiful back then, and she was even more beautiful now.

He recognized Carlita in one picture and assumed the man standing next to her was Isabel's papá. It wasn't fair that Isabel had a loving father taken from her so soon. His old man had left as soon as the pregnancy stick showed two lines. It was nice that Isabel had such a big and loving family. Sometimes,

Sullivan wondered how different his life would have been if he had grown up experiencing that.

"He's out," Isabel said, coming back into the living room.

"Already?"

"Yeah. He'll sleep good tonight." Isabel wrapped her arms around him and leaned in closer. "And just so you know, Miguel is a deep sleeper."

"Are you asking me to stay over?"

Isabel grinned. "Up to you. But if you stay, we could have some fun."

"Glad I packed an overnight bag. I'll go grab it from the car."

Isabel stood on her tiptoes and kissed him on the lips. "Don't be too long," she said with a sexy smile.

Sullivan watched as she headed toward her bedroom. He hurried to his Jeep to get his bag.

20

Sullivan wasn't in bed when Isabel woke the next morning. At first, she wondered if he'd snuck out to go home, but then saw his shoes on the floor and relaxed. He couldn't have gotten far without those.

She heard sounds in the kitchen, and after a quick trip to the bathroom, went to investigate. She found Miguel and Sullivan standing over the stove, and it appeared Miguel was instructing him on how to make scrambled eggs.

"Good morning."

Both Miguel and Sullivan turned at the sound of her voice.

"I'm teaching Mr. Sullivan how to cook!" Miguel said.

"Oh yeah?" Isabel walked over to the stove to inspect the eggs. "It looks like he's a fast learner."

"Miguel's the one telling me what to do," Sullivan said.

"Are you making anything else?"

Miguel held up an avocado. "*Sí.* This and a corn tortilla."

Isabel nodded. "Sounds yummy."

Miguel turned his attention back to the frying pan. "Now you have to take it out."

Sullivan grabbed the spatula and scraped the eggs onto a plate. "Okay, now what?"

"Now you turn off the burner, and we eat!"

Isabel reached for three plates from the cabinets and handed them to Miguel. "Here, *nene*. Take these to the table and set it up. Grab some silverware and napkins too."

"Okay." Miguel grabbed three forks from the drawer and rushed to the dining area.

Once he was out of earshot, Isabel moved to stand next to Sullivan. "I'm sorry. I thought he'd sleep later. It would have given you a chance to leave."

"I didn't want to leave," he said, surprising Isabel.

"Really?"

"Sure." Sullivan leaned forward to whisper. "He caught me coming out of the bathroom. I told him I wanted to stay for breakfast since your cooking was so good, and Miguel decided we should cook together. When I told Miguel I didn't know how, he was determined to teach me. And anyway, corn tortillas with eggs and avocados sounded damn good."

"You said a swear word," Miguel said, coming back into the room. "Tío Ricardo has to put a nickel into a jar whenever he says that."

Sullivan laughed. "Dang good then," he corrected.

"The table is ready," Miguel said. "Can we eat now?"

"Yes, *nene*, let's eat."

They sat at the table with Miguel taking the center seat.

"I'm glad Mr. Sullivan stayed for breakfast," Miguel said. "Are you going to have dinner with us again? We could watch a movie next time."

Across the table, Isabel caught Sullivan smiling at her. "Well sure. I mean, you know, if your mom doesn't mind all that extra cooking again," he said.

Underneath the table, Isabel placed her bare foot on his ankle and ran her toe up his leg. "I don't mind at all."

Isabel was sure her mother had noticed Sullivan at her house last night. Nothing got past her mother. Though hopefully, she hadn't realized he stayed over. But when she dropped off Miguel, Carlita already seemed to know.

"I was up at four in the morning and saw his Jeep, *mija*," Carlita said with a grin.

"Why were you awake at four in the morning? No one needs to be up that early."

"I had to go to the bathroom," Carlita said. "So, are you two dating now?" A wide grin spread across Carlita's face.

Outside, Sullivan honked the horn, relieving Isabel from answering. "I have to go to work. Love you both! *Adiós!*" Isabel hurried out the door, knowing she'd have to answer her mother's questions later.

Sullivan nodded toward the porch when she climbed into the Jeep. "Your mom sure seems happy to see me." Sullivan waved at her. Carlita, with a grin, waved back.

"She knows about us. She saw your Jeep in the driveway earlier this morning. Don't worry, my mother likes you."

"Yeah, I figured. She still thinks I look like that guy from the show. I actually thought of watching it. Can you believe that?"

Isabel laughed. "It's a good show. We can binge it after Miguel goes to sleep."

"Or we can do other things."

Isabel smiled. "That too. Hey, thanks for staying with me last night. I was glad you were there. A part of me was worried that Mateo would show up."

"Do you think he's been arrested?"

Isabel shrugged. "I'm sure if he has, I'll hear about it later."

At the Lightning Institute, Tío Fernando was sitting at the front desk when they walked in. He looked up from the weather map. "Are you having car trouble again, *princesa?*"

She wondered why he would ask, then realized he must have seen her get out of Sullivan's Jeep. "No, Tío, he was just being nice and giving me a ride."

Her uncle gave her a weird grin, almost as if he were pleased they were carpooling. "Is that so?"

"*Sí.*" She wasn't about to tell her uncle they were having sex, and it was just convenient for them to ride in the same vehicle together. "So, what's the forecast?" she asked, hoping to steer the conversation away from her and Sullivan.

"Tampa Bay looks good," Fernando told them. "The southern coast looks good too, but it's a longer drive. I guess you'll have your pick of storms."

"We'll chase the best looking one," Sullivan said, smiling at Isabel.

FOR THE FIRST time in as long as he could remember, Sullivan didn't crave a cigarette. As he drove the LIV down I-75, the only thing on his mind was the woman next to him.

"Why do you think going south will be better?" Isabel asked. She wasn't asking it in a condescending tone like she used to. She seemed genuinely curious.

"It's not that I think it's better, Izzy. I'm sure both storms will be good lightning producers. I just wanted more time on the road with you."

A slow smile spread across her face. "Could you imagine yourself saying that the first day we met?"

Sullivan laughed. "Hell no. And you know what else I never thought I'd do?"

"What's that?"

Sullivan turned the radio dial to Isabel's favorite station. "It's growing on me."

Isabel squealed. "I knew it would!"

The song that played next was the one they had danced to at the party. The memory of it had been fuzzy earlier, so much so that he didn't believe it actually happened. But now, he recalled it in full detail. He hated dancing. He never liked to do anything to draw attention to himself and otherwise make himself look like a fool. But for Isabel and Miguel, he had.

It didn't bother him.

"You know what we should do?" Isabel said, breaking into his thoughts. "We should find an isolated road somewhere, park the LIV, and have a little fun. We can tell Tío Fernando we missed the lightning."

"Your plan has a flaw."

"No, I don't think so."

"Your uncle can track the LIV's location, right? He'll see we're close to the storms and wonder how we missed them."

Isabel sighed. "Well, in that case, we'll just have to find an isolated road when we're off the clock."

"A lot of those in Kansas."

"How'd you end up in Kansas when you grew up in Texas?"

Sullivan picked up his speed to get past a slow truck. "Got a job there. I wasn't picky about where I lived so long as I could chase storms. Speaking of which, have you checked the radar lately?"

"Oh, no. Distracted." Isabel laughed.

Sullivan heard her clicking around on the computer. "I think if we time it out just right, we might catch a storm rolling off the coast. Lightning over the ocean is my favorite."

He looked at her briefly before turning his eyes back to the road. "Becoming my favorite too."

They drove to the coast and found a spot with a good view. Most of the beach goers were leaving, as lightning and the ocean weren't a good combination. Though Sullivan noticed a few fools were still out there swimming.

"Not quite an isolated road, I'm afraid," Sullivan said. "But a nice view."

"I guess we'll have to wait until later tonight to be alone."

"If you're asking me to stay over, we'll have to run to my place first. I'll need a change of clothes."

"So I get to see where you live? The inside, I mean."

Sullivan glanced at her and smiled. "It's really not a great rental, but I have a comfortable bed."

Isabel grinned. "I like a comfy bed."

A loud crack of thunder brought their attention back to the storm.

"You better get your time-lapse video ready," Sullivan told her. "You know Miguel will ask."

"He will. Get the other cameras ready while I do that."

The storm had been spectacular with frequent lightning and gusty winds. It came on them fast though, and soon, a sheet of rain enveloped them.

"You got your camera back inside just in time," Sullivan said as she packed up her gear in the back.

"But I got some great footage. Oh, Miguel's going to love it."

Sullivan looked at his watch. "We should probably hit the road now. Unless you want to keep chasing."

Isabel came back to the passenger seat and reached for her seatbelt. "No, I think we're done for today. I want to see your place next. And your comfortable bed."

Sullivan grinned and put the LIV into reverse. He couldn't remember what sort of shape the house had been in when he left yesterday. Had it been messy? Probably. Were dirty clothes on the floor? He was sure of it. And hell, he never made the bed.

Sullivan decided he didn't care. If Isabel had a problem with his mess, then she didn't have to stay. But he didn't think she'd mind.

Her mother was sitting on the porch when they finally pulled into the driveway that night. They had missed dinner since their drive had been longer, and stopping at Sullivan's place had only delayed them further. Though food was the last thing on either of their minds.

Through the open window of Sullivan's car, her mother waved. "*Mija*, are you hungry? I can fix you and Sullivan a plate."

Isabel hoped for a quiet dinner at home, alone with Sullivan and Miguel, not an interrogation about her love life from her mother. "Sorry, I forgot my mother would probably invite us over," she whispered. "You want to?"

"Wouldn't mind. I am pretty hungry now."

In the kitchen, her mother shooed Isabel away. "You don't need to help me, *mija*. Go be with your boyfriend." Carlita wiggled her eyes.

"Mamá, I don't know if I'd call him that."

"That's what Miguel said you called him." Carlita stirred the soup in the pot. "And he's certainly someone you're having fun with."

Miguel's peal of laughter filled the room, and Isabel peered behind the wall. Miguel was showing Sullivan his latest slime creation. Sullivan had the sticky blue substance stretched out in his hands with a somewhat disgusted look on his face. "I think Sullivan is occupied at the moment. Let me help with that, Mamá."

"Oh, all right." She pointed to the counter. "You can slice that bread."

Isabel reached for a knife from the block. "Mamá, I went to the sheriff's department yesterday."

Carlita paused in her stirring. "You reported Mateo? Oh, *mija*, finally!"

"Sullivan drove me there after we came back to town yesterday and wouldn't let me back out. I'm glad I got it over with."

"*Mija*, I'm so proud of you. That *gilipollas* will finally get what's coming to him. Have they arrested him yet?"

Isabel imagined Mateo being dragged off the news set by the authorities, and the scandal that would likely ensue left a gnawing sensation in her stomach. "I don't know. They have to complete their investigation first, but they said I have enough evidence to get them started."

"I hope they throw the book at him," Carlita said with a fierce look on her face.

Isabel wasn't sure she'd be that lucky. He'd probably get his family lawyers to drop the charges, or if he went to jail, he'd easily get out on bail. After that, he'd be angry. Would he retaliate?

Sullivan came to the kitchen, distracting her from her thoughts. He held out his hands with bits of blue slime stuck to his palms.

"I enjoy science, but not these kinds of experiments," he said as he turned on the faucet.

Isabel laughed. "I see you got slimed."

When hands were clean and dinner was ready, Carlita and Miguel joined them at the table, though they had already eaten. While Miguel watched the videos on her camera, Carlita sat across from Sullivan and acted like a fan girl. Sometimes, she wondered if her mother really thought he was Jase Holler from *Bermuda Time Warp.*

Carlita leaned forward with her elbows on the table. "So, Sullivan, what are your plans after this lightning project wraps up?"

Isabel had been curious to know the answer to that too, but hadn't asked him yet. In the beginning, she would have been perfectly happy to have him pack up and move back to

Kansas. Now she was worried he might actually consider leaving.

Sullivan took a sip from his water glass, and Isabel waited with bated breath for his answer.

"I'm not sure yet. I have some money saved up, so I can live on that until I find a new job. Sometimes, I like to see where life takes me." He turned to look at Isabel. "Would be nice if I could storm chase all the time."

"Do you think you'll go back to your job in Kansas?" Isabel asked. She had to know, but what if the answer was yes?

Sullivan shrugged. "I don't know if I'll work for the same airline or not, but I'm probably not returning to Wichita, except maybe to pack up my rental house." He gave her a smile, and Isabel relaxed.

When Isabel and Sullivan finished their plates, Miguel was eager to go.

"Can we start our movie night now?"

Carlita cleared the dirty dishes from the table. "Movie night?"

"We're going to watch that one Miguel liked," Isabel said.

"Mr. Sullivan hasn't seen it yet," Miguel said.

Carlita raised her eyebrows. "Oh, so Mr. Sullivan is joining you?" Her mother gave Isabel a knowing smile.

Isabel felt her cheeks grow warm. "Miguel invited him. *Nene*, go get your things and we'll head to our place."

"*Sí*, Mamá," Miguel said, dashing off to the living room.

Her mother reached for a covered container in the refrigerator and handed it to her. "I made a special dessert for you, *mija*," she whispered. "Don't let Miguel see it."

"Thanks, Mamá."

"Enjoy the movie. Goodnight, Sullivan."

"Goodnight, Carlita."

Her mother smiled once more at them, then headed to the kitchen with the plates.

"Sorry about my mother," Isabel whispered. "I know she asks a lot of questions."

Sullivan just shrugged. "You say that like it's a bad thing."

"She can be nosy at times."

"You're missing the point, Izzy. Some parents don't care what their children are up to. It's nice that your mother does."

Isabel smiled. "I suppose you're right."

Miguel came back into the room. "I'm ready."

"Great. Let's go watch a movie," Isabel said.

SULLIVAN SQUINTED his eyes to read Isabel's tiny digital clock. One-thirty. Isabel wasn't in bed, but down the hall, he thought he saw a light on in the kitchen. Now that he was awake, he couldn't sleep. In the past, a craving for a cigarette would hit right about now, but Isabel had provided a pleasant distraction.

The sound of silverware clinking against a plate made Sullivan's mouth water. Isabel was eating something in the kitchen, and maybe a midnight snack was a good idea.

He reached for his boxers and jeans on the floor and hurriedly put them on. Since there was a kid in the next room, he figured he should be decent.

In the kitchen, Isabel stood by the stove eating something. Upon further inspection, he realized it was from the mysterious covered plate her mother had given to her just before they left.

Isabel must have sensed his presence, because she turned around and hurriedly covered her mouth. "Sorry, did I wake you?"

Sullivan shook his head and entered the kitchen. "No, I just woke up on my own and saw you weren't in bed. What is that?"

Isabel looked guilty. "Chocolate pudding cream pie. It's always been my favorite. Mamá makes it for me sometimes. But see, Miguel can't have anything sweet like this. Ever since his diagnosis, I try not to eat anything like this around him. If I did, he'd want a taste, and I can't risk him getting sick. So I have to sneak a bite whenever he's asleep."

"So I guess I finally found out what your bad habit is. You have a sweet tooth."

Isabel smiled. "Guilty as charged. Are you going to make me give it up like I made you give up smoking?"

"Not if you share some of that with me."

She pulled the drawer open and retrieved a second fork. "Help yourself."

Sullivan took the fork and dug into the pie. Upon tasting it, he nodded in approval. "That's good."

"It has an Oreo cookie pie crust."

"Want to know something?"

"What?"

"Oreos were always my favorite."

"Miguel's too, before we found out he had diabetes. Every now and then, I let Miguel have one, but I have to be very careful that it doesn't mess up his blood sugar levels."

"That must be hard."

She nodded. "It's getting easier to find things he can eat. And my mother and I enjoy cooking, so between the two of us, we can make something he likes."

"Halloween was always hard for our family," Sullivan said. "Emmy was allergic to peanuts."

"I remember you told me about someone you knew who was allergic. I figured it was you sister."

Sullivan nodded. "I never went trick-or-treating. Mama said she wasn't going to spend her money on a stupid costume. But when Emmy came along, I hated to see her miss out like I did. So I'd save money from cutting the neighbor's grass and buy her a princess dress or butterfly wings, whatever she was into at the time. But when we got home, half the stash of candy would be something that had peanuts in it."

"Oh, she must have been so disappointed."

"She was, but not for long. I'd trade the chocolate bars for candy she could eat. It wasn't hard. Kids would give up their Starburst in an instant for Snickers."

"Did you give any more thought to finding her?"

Sullivan had considered it, but didn't have an answer yet. "Still thinking about it."

"Why don't you just call Eddie? Look, he could find out the information you need, and then you'll know where she is. You can decide after that if you want to contact her."

Sullivan thought about it. "It would be nice to know what she's up to, like what kind of job she has or if she's married. I hope she's happy."

"Then it's settled. You contact my cousin tomorrow, and he'll find Emmy. I'll give him a heads up to expect your call."

Sullivan nodded, then forked another piece of pie. He let it melt in his mouth, and with a full stomach, decided he'd had enough. "Damn, that was good."

With the pie gone, Isabel rinsed the plate under the sink. "Got to hide the evidence. If you tell my mother how much you loved her chocolate pudding cream pie, I guarantee she'll make you a pie for you to have all to yourself. Anything, you know, for Jase Holler from *Bermuda Time Warp*."

Sullivan laughed. "I definitely could eat more pie later. But you know what I want right now?"

"What?"

Sullivan nodded toward the bedroom. "We're awake, and Miguel's asleep."

Isabel grinned and reached for his hand. "We should make good use of that time then."

She led him to the bedroom, and once there, Sullivan locked the door behind them.

21

After leaving Isabel's the next morning, Sullivan stopped by his house to catch up on some laundry. He emptied his pockets, pulling out loose change, pieces of nicotine gum, and his wallet. Once his clothes were tossing around in the washer, he settled on the couch and took out his phone.

It wouldn't hurt to call Isabel's cousin. And hey, if her cousin couldn't find Emmy, then he would know he tried all he could, and that would be that.

But if he found her... well, he'd decide what to do if that time came.

He found Isabel's text, selected Eddie's number, and tapped his foot as it rang. He'd been about to hang up, losing his courage to make the call in the first place, when a voice came onto the line.

"Eddie Garcia Investigations."

"Hey, my name is Sullivan. I work with your cousin Isabel and she said I should call you."

"Yeah, Isabel said you might be in touch. Who can I help you find?"

Sullivan relaxed a little. "My sister. The foster care system separated us, and I was hoping to reconnect. Or at the very least, find out what she's up to these days."

"Sure, I can help with that. I'm going to need some information from you to get me started."

Sullivan hesitated. "Look, I need to know something before we go any further. I've never hired a private investigator before. How confidential is this?"

"We don't share any of our client's information with anyone. Anything you tell me will be kept in strict confidence."

Satisfied with that answer, Sullivan told Eddie the entire story of his past, everything from Emmy's birth to their eventual separation.

"I mostly just want to make sure she's all right," Sullivan said. "I'm sorry I haven't given you much to go on."

"You've given me plenty. I have access to several databases. I'll run her name through my system and see what comes up. Can you give me until next week? I've got two cases I'm wrapping up and I'll be out of town for a few days. After that, I can give this my full attention."

"That'll be fine. I appreciate it."

"Say, on another note, Isabel says you've been driving around photographing lightning."

"Yeah, it's been an adventure."

"I'm in Miami, and we get quite a few storms here too. If you're ever this far south, you can stay at my place. I know it's a long drive."

Sullivan normally didn't like making casual conversation with strangers, but Eddie was easygoing. And hell, he'd just shared his life story with the guy. He didn't seem so bad. "I'll tell Izzy that."

"You better not call her Izzy. She hates that."

Sullivan laughed. "I know. I do it to tease her. But it's okay. She calls me by my first name when she's pissed at me."

Eddie laughed.

WHEN ISABEL ARRIVED at work later that afternoon, she found Sullivan leaning over the front desk counter. He was occupied with his phone and appeared not to hear her come in.

She tiptoed over and wrapped her arms around him from behind. "Hey."

Sullivan turned around, looked down at her and smiled. "Hey, yourself."

She stood on her tiptoes and placed a gentle kiss on his lips. Sullivan turned up the heat a notch and slipped her some tongue.

"Hey, no kissing at work," Fernando said.

Isabel immediately separated from Sullivan. Having her uncle walk in on them was like the time Papá caught her kissing Antonio Perez. She had been twelve and invited him to her treehouse. When Papá came up the ladder, she was mortified.

Next to her, Sullivan looked pale. She thought nothing could bother Sullivan, but maybe she'd been wrong.

"Torres, I can explain. Isabel and I..."

"Have gotten close," Isabel said, finishing Sullivan's sentence. She reached for Sullivan's hand and braced herself for a lecture.

But Fernando surprised her and instead, burst into laughter. "I'm teasing. You're grown adults, and I don't care what you do. I had a feeling something was going on between you two. I've had a few workplace romances myself."

Isabel wasn't sure if what she had with Sullivan qualified as a workplace romance, but she enjoyed their time together.

"So you're okay that I'm involved with your niece?" Sullivan asked.

"As long as you don't hurt her, I don't see why I would have a problem with it."

Isabel exhaled, and next to her, Sullivan visibly relaxed. It was crazy, but they were adults, not teenagers. There was no reason to sneak around.

"So, what are your plans today?" Fernando asked.

"Here looks good," Sullivan said, holding up his phone. On the screen was the latest forecast model. "We can stick close to home. Probably could operate the LIV from the parking lot."

"Why don't you two hang out here? I've got a group of students from the university coming over, and we're going to be doing some lightning experiments as the storm approaches. It's a sight to see."

"It's a lot of fun," Isabel said. "Fernando shoots up a rocket with a copper wire, and it creates a lightning bolt."

Sullivan nodded. "I'd like to see that."

"Great," Fernando said. "Well, I'll let you kids get back to... whatever you were doing." He smiled at them, then left.

Sullivan turned back to Isabel once they were alone again. "Well now, the moment is ruined. I don't think we'll get any time alone."

"There's always the storage closet," Isabel said into his ear.

Sullivan looked at her with raised eyebrows. "With your *uncle* here?"

Isabel frowned. "Right. Better not take that risk."

Her phone chimed with a notification, and Isabel remembered her phone blowing up with text messages on the drive over. She hadn't bothered to look at them yet, knowing if there had been an emergency, someone would have called.

Isabel glanced at the screen and gasped. She expected to find a family group text, but instead, there were several messages. Some from her family. Some from her former colleagues at the station. All of them were about Mateo. Isabel's heart raced as she scrolled through them.

Paulina: Just caught the noon news. They said Mateo was arrested!

Carlita: Mija, call me.

Tía Sofia: Isabel, please call me. That man who was bothering you was taken in by the police.

Jenna: Isabel, are you okay? Mateo was hauled off the set in handcuffs after this morning's news segment. They said he assaulted someone. Was it you who reported him?

Marisol: I know you were the one to make this accusation about Mateo. How could you do this to an innocent man?

Of course, Marisol would be the lone dissenter. Marisol was the bitchy news anchor who thought Mateo could do no wrong. She never liked Isabel.

"What's wrong?" Sullivan asked.

"Mateo was arrested."

"Good. About damn time."

Isabel returned to her phone, scrolling through about a dozen more messages. Her sister had sent a link to a video. Isabel clicked it, and she and Sullivan watched it. Though the report didn't reveal Isabel's name, somehow, people had known it had been her.

"This is a disaster," Isabel said, collapsing in the desk chair. She buried her face in her hands.

"Disaster? Hell no, it's not a disaster. That asshole is finally getting what's coming to him."

Isabel looked up. "I'm not upset that Mateo was arrested. I'm upset that this is becoming a media circus, just like I thought it would. Next thing that'll happen, reporters will knock on my door."

"You don't have to say a damn thing to them."

Fernando came out of his office holding up his phone. "Your mother just texted me that Mateo was arrested."

"We just heard," Sullivan said.

"It's not like he'll be in jail for long," Isabel said with a sigh. "You know what'll happen next, right? He'll get out on bail, and then he'll come after me."

"He'll have to come through me first," Sullivan said.

"And me," Fernando added. "Have you got those security cameras and motion lights yet?"

"No, I can't afford it."

"I'll pay for it. I'll call Javier and have him install something today. And if he can't do it, I'll do it myself tonight."

"*Gracias*, Tío."

The front door opened, and two university students walked in, providing a welcomed distraction from the conversation.

"I think I'll take a walk," Isabel said, standing. "I need to clear my head."

"Want some company?" Sullivan asked.

"*Gracias*, but I need some time to myself."

Sullivan nodded. "Understand."

She gave him a light kiss, but a phone notification interrupted the moment. "And I need to make some calls. I'll be back in time for the lightning show."

Outside, a wind whipped her hair into her face, and she reached for the hair tie around her wrist. The breeze felt good, signaling a storm was on the way. Unfortunately, it did nothing to lift her mood.

SULLIVAN COULD TELL that Isabel didn't wish to talk about Mateo anymore, so he left the matter alone. Privately, he was also worried about Mateo's reaction. What if he got out on bail? Would he come after Isabel? Hell, the man had the balls to show up at her home and work. Of course he'd come after her. He hoped the judge wouldn't be so lenient.

The approaching thunderstorm provided a much needed distraction, and he was glad to see a smile return to Isabel's face as they walked to the giant tower out front.

"You'll love this," she said.

Sullivan had been curious about it. He'd seen videos on YouTube where people sent a rocket up in the air to create lightning, but now, he'd get to see it in person.

They followed Torres and the students to the launch station, where Torres went into professor mode. He posed several questions, and for a moment, Sullivan was taken back to university days.

"With cloud to ground lightning, you can have a negative or a positive charge. Who can tell me which one is more common?"

None of the students answered. Sullivan couldn't believe it. That was an easy one.

"Anyone?" Torres repeated.

"Negative," Sullivan said.

Torres gave him a smile. "That's right. And which one is more dangerous, Sullivan?"

"Cloud to ground lightning with a positive charge is less common, but that one is more dangerous."

"Correct. And who can tell me where the lightning capital of North America is?"

Again, silence amongst the students. For crying out loud, did any of these students study, or were they too busy getting drunk?

"Come on, folks," Torres said. "You must know this."

"Got to be Florida, right?" one of them guessed.

Torres nodded. "It is. Where in Florida?"

The student shrugged. "Central Florida?"

"Tampa Bay," Sullivan shouted out, though he hadn't meant

to. He supposed he was eager to get on with the experiment, and they couldn't if these damn questions weren't answered.

"Right again, Sully," Torres said. "Remember that, folks. This is all going to be on the exam."

Torres resumed his lecture, and Isabel nudged him. "Were you this talkative in class?"

Sullivan gave her a small smile. "Hell no. I only talk when it's a subject I enjoy. And plus, I'm ready for this lecture to be over with."

Isabel laughed.

When it was time for the lightning experiment, everyone kept a safe distance as Torres launched the rocket. With a countdown, the rocket went up into the storm clouds with a copper wire attached. A sudden bolt of lightning appeared and followed the wire, which made it explode.

Everyone hollered in excitement. Lightning was always a spectacular thing to see.

ISABEL WATCHED as her cousin Javier came down the ladder. He had installed a security camera over the garage with a full view of the driveway. "There, you should be all set."

"*Gracias*, Javier."

"How does that work?" Sullivan asked. "It senses motion, and she gets a notification on her phone?"

Javier nodded. "*Sí*, and you adjust the sensitivity so that small animals aren't always setting it off. But the motion light I installed will come on regardless."

Isabel was grateful for the additional security, because by Wednesday afternoon, Mateo was released on bail, as expected. Though she worried about him coming over, it seemed the only people outside her door were the reporters camped out. Her name had somehow been leaked to the press, and now all of Florida knew she had made accusations against Mateo.

By morning, the pack of reporters remained camped outside on the sidewalk. Isabel peeked out of her blind and groaned at the crowd. They were constantly setting off the camera's motion sensor, but Isabel didn't want to turn it off in case Mateo made an appearance. On the bright side, if Mateo came after her, there would be witnesses.

Miguel peeked out with her. "Why are they out there, Mamá?"

"Because they want to ask me questions about Mr. Ramirez, but I don't want to talk to them." She had told Miguel that Mr. Ramirez had done something bad and had gone to jail, but had purposely been vague about the details of why. She didn't want Miguel to worry, and he was too young to understand anyway. "We're just going to stay inside today."

"You're not going to work?"

"No. I'm taking a day off."

"Will Mr. Sullivan have to drive the LIV by himself?"

"I don't know, *nene.*"

At the mention of Sullivan, she heard his Jeep rolling over the gravel driveway. He'd gone to pick up some eggs since she was all out and couldn't leave for the grocery store.

Isabel glanced down at Miguel and noticed his pajama pants were getting too short on him. Another thing she'd have to buy soon. "Go change out of your pajamas, *nene.* And get washed up for breakfast."

Javier had set up a monitor so she could easily see the camera without pulling up her phone. Sullivan headed up the stairs. Isabel hurried to the door to let him in, bracing herself for the onslaught of questions from the reporters.

"Ms. Torres, do you have a comment about Mateo Ramirez?"

"Did Mateo force you to leave your job?"

"Ms. Torres, why did you wait to go to the authorities?"

Sullivan rushed inside and slammed the door behind him. "Those reporters are relentless. Can't you call the cops and make them leave?"

"They're on the sidewalk, and that's considered public property. Not much the cops can do. But at least Mateo won't show up if they're here."

Sullivan rolled his eyes as he placed the grocery bag on the counter. "Some silver lining that is. Here are the eggs and a few more things."

"*Gracias.* Hopefully by tomorrow, things will die down. Are you going to work today? Maybe Fernando can drive the LIV."

"Hell no. You think I'm leaving you and Miguel by yourself with all those people out there? I say let's keep the blinds closed and hunker down until they go away. And I already spoke to your uncle. He said to stay with you. You're not disappointed about that, are you?"

Isabel took out the eggs from the plastic bag. "No. Are you? You've barely had a moment to yourself."

She saw him crack a smile. "I'll manage."

SULLIVAN CHECKED the camera Friday morning. Most of the reporters had given up, though one persistent son of a bitch remained. He sat in his car with the window down, probably hoping he'd be out of sight, but Sullivan saw him. Why the hell couldn't those weasels give Isabel some privacy?

"Are they still out there?" Isabel asked from behind him.

Sullivan turned, seeing Isabel wearing her long, faded nightshirt with tousled morning hair. He never thought such a thing could turn him on, but seeing her made him want to go back to bed, except Miguel was up. "Just one. We can probably dodge him and go to work today. Checked the weather report this morning. Going to be a stormy afternoon."

Isabel nodded. "I'll get Miguel ready to go to my mother's."

She turned, but Sullivan gently reached for her arm to pull her back. "Hey, how are you?"

"I'm fine."

He could see the worry lines on her face and knew she was lying. "No, you're not."

She blinked her eyes and inhaled, and Sullivan sensed she was trying to keep her composure. "I just wish this was all over."

"It will be. Bad times don't last forever." He kissed her on the forehead. Giving comfort wasn't something Sullivan was accustomed to, but with Isabel, it came easily.

"I better get Miguel ready."

She left, and Sullivan turned his attention back to the window. The weasel reporter was still out there, and Sullivan felt a nerve snap. He wrenched the door open, hollered he'd be right back, and stepped outside.

The reporter looked young. Probably some rookie looking to make his first break. It wouldn't be with Isabel. He needed to find some other story. He looked pale when Sullivan marched toward his small Nissan sedan.

Sullivan rested his arms on the open window. "You need to get the hell off this property."

"I'm not on private property."

"You really think it's appropriate to camp out all night in your car outside a woman's residence, waiting for the chance to harass her the moment she steps outside that door?" Sullivan had been told that he had the tendency to scare people when he got into their face. From the wide eyes and pale face of the boy in the car, Sullivan decided it was true.

"I–I don't intend to harass her," he stammered. "I just want to ask her a few questions for a news article."

"She doesn't have a comment, but I do. Get the fuck off this street. And if I see you again, I'll report you for stalking.

Sounds a lot like what Mr. Ramirez was arrested for, don't you think?"

The boy rolled up his window and started the engine.

When Sullivan came back into the house, he saw Isabel in the kitchen smiling at him.

"What?"

"What did you say to that guy in the car? I saw you on the camera."

"Told him to leave."

"Just like that? And he left? No argument?"

Sullivan grinned. "Yeah, just like that."

Isabel tilted her head. "What did you really say to him?"

"I might have used a bit more colorful language. You think Miguel will make me start a swear jar like Ricardo's?"

Isabel laughed and wrapped her arms around him. "I'll give you a pass this time."

ISABEL PLACED the laptop onto the tray in the LIV's passenger seat. Thank God it would be a stormy day, because Isabel needed the distraction. It was nice to leave the house without having reporters demanding answers. Unfortunately, her phone hadn't calmed down. She was still getting text and voicemails. Isabel put her phone on do not disturb and would allow only messages from family to come through.

The driver's side opened, and Sullivan appeared to be searching for something under the seat. "Have you seen my phone charger? I can't find it anywhere."

"No, you must have left it at my place. There's an extra charger inside. I think it's in the supply closet."

"Be right back." Sullivan closed the door and headed inside.

The heat was stifling inside the vehicle, and Isabel cranked up the engine to get the A/C going. Needing fresh air, she stepped out and inspected the vehicle. It was dirty and definitely needed a wash. The tires looked to be in good condition though, and hopefully they would avoid the potholes this time.

She heard Sullivan's shoes walking on the pavement behind her. "I'm just cooling the LIV off before we go. Did you find a charger?" When she turned around, it wasn't Sullivan.

"*Hola, cariño,*" Mateo said.

Isabel looked beyond Mateo, hoping to see Sullivan emerge from the building. No sign of him. In her peripheral vision, she didn't even see Mateo's car. Had he walked here?

"You're not supposed to be near me. Didn't they tell you to stay away from me?"

"Isabel, this has all been a terrible misunderstanding. I never meant for you to feel threatened. And I know I come on a little strong, but I can't help but be attracted to you. You're beautiful, and you're a very special lady. I apologize for getting carried away that night. It was my mistake, but I'll never do that again. Please talk to the police. You need to drop these charges."

"I'm not dropping the charges. You put your hand up my skirt and assaulted me." She tried to make her voice confident and angry. The last thing she wanted Mateo to know was that she was trembling inside.

"I didn't rape you."

"You assaulted me all the same."

"I didn't assault you. Everything we did was consensual. You followed me into the office."

Isabel rolled her eyes. "I didn't know you were going to close the door. And I recall I said 'no' and you didn't listen. That's not consent." She glanced toward the building, wondering what the hell was taking Sullivan so long. Surely it didn't take this long to find a phone charger.

"Isabel, please, I want to apologize. Listen, I promise to never bother you again if you'll drop the charges. I have a reputation in this community. Do you know how it looks to have the chief meteorologist of the local news accused of sexual assault?"

"I imagine that's very difficult for you, but it's not my problem. You need to leave now, Mateo. Did you even bring your car, or did you walk?"

"I parked down the road. I didn't want you to know I was here. I was waiting for an opportunity to talk to you."

"So you're still stalking me?"

"I wasn't stalking you. I just wanted a chance to talk. That's all."

From the corner of her eye, Isabel finally saw Sullivan come outside. His gaze connected to Isabel's as he hurried toward them.

"Thought I told you to stop bothering Isabel," Sullivan growled.

Mateo backed up slightly, which made Isabel smile. Mateo wasn't so tough when compared to Sullivan.

"I was just here to apologize. And to tell Isabel I'll never talk to her again. Please consider dropping the charges. I misread your signals and thought you were interested in me. For that, I apologize. I'll go now."

Sullivan moved to block Mateo's path. "No, by all means, stay. You see that deputy's vehicle across the street?"

Isabel looked to see where Sullivan pointed. Sure enough, there was a deputy, and it looked like they were headed their way.

"The judge ordered you to stay 500 feet away from Isabel, and it looks like you violated that. I already called 911. And as luck would have it, they said a deputy was in the area. That must be him or her now."

Mateo took off running. Moments later, his Mercedes emerged from the foliage he had parked it behind, and sped off. The deputy, blue lights on and siren squealing, took off after him.

Isabel placed her hand over her racing heart. "*¡Dios mios!* I can't believe that just happened."

"I can. He's a coward. Of course he'd run."

"I didn't hear him. He parked his vehicle out of sight. He's probably been watching me the whole time, waiting for an opportunity to get me alone." Isabel moved into Sullivan's waiting arms, wrapping her arms around his waist and placing her head on his chest. "I was so scared for a moment there."

"I'm sorry. I shouldn't have left. Just before I was about to come back out, I saw him talking to you. I made a quick call to 911 and hurried out here. I'm sorry you were alone with him for even a second."

Isabel raised her head. "It's okay. I was scared, but I handled him. He actually wanted me to drop the charges in return for him never speaking to me again. He doesn't believe he did anything wrong."

"Well he just gave himself more trouble. Running from the authorities is never a good idea."

A rumble of thunder sounded, and Isabel looked at the sky where a dark cloud in the east had formed. The afternoon storm they had been waiting for was about to arrive, but Isabel was so shaken up, she could barely concentrate on doing any work.

"Let's head inside," Sullivan said. "There will be another storm."

A GUST of wind sent rain sideways into the glass doors and windows. Sullivan kept watch. Surely Mateo wouldn't be stupid enough to show up here, but just in case, he wasn't leaving Isabel's side.

Her voice carried from Fernando's office, where she had been talking on the phone to her sister for twenty minutes now.

Isabel said she was fine, but Sullivan saw how rattled she'd been from Mateo's visit.

Headlights shined into the office as a car pulled into a parking space. Sullivan thought it was Torres, but the lights on top of the vehicle gave it away. A deputy.

The blond woman behind the wheel dashed out of her vehicle toward the entrance. Sullivan opened the door for her.

"That rain is coming down!" she said, wiping water drops from her face. "Are you Mr. Sullivan who called about Mateo Ramirez?"

"Yeah. Did you catch him?"

She nodded. "Yes. They caught him on a dead-end street, and he surrendered. I'd like to ask you and Ms. Torres some questions. Is she here?"

"*Sí*," Isabel said, coming out of the office. "Is Mateo in custody?"

"Yes, and he won't be bothering you anymore. I wanted to tell you in person that two other women he assaulted have come forward. They did so after you. We have more charges pending against Mr. Ramirez."

"Which I'm sure he'll eventually get dropped with help from his family lawyer," Isabel said with a hint of annoyance in her voice.

The deputy shook her head. "I'm not so sure. We have DNA in one case, and it's a match for Mr. Ramirez. He's looking at a long time behind bars, and I don't think a lawyer can get him off with these charges."

"DNA evidence?" Isabel asked. "You mean?"

The deputy nodded. "We had his DNA on profile from a sexual assault kit, but we didn't know it was his until now. The victim was afraid and didn't wish to pursue the charge. She changed her mind when you came forward."

Sullivan's eyes narrowed. "I knew he was dangerous."

The deputy stayed for about twenty minutes to ask them

questions for her report. When she left, the rain had cleared, and the sun peeked out from the clouds.

Sullivan watched as Isabel stared outside at the wet parking lot. He placed a hand on her shoulder. "It's over now."

"If it hadn't been for me, those other women may not have had the courage to come forward. And it sounds like what he did to at least one of them was way worse than what happened to me."

"And if you hadn't come forward, he may have done it to someone else."

Isabel turned to him and wrapped her arms around him. "Thank you for making me do this. I wish I hadn't waited."

"That *gilipollas* is getting what he deserves."

Isabel laughed. "My Spanish is rubbing off on you."

"Want to get out of here?" he asked her. "We could go to my place for a while."

Isabel nodded. "Please."

THE FOLLOWING WEEK FLEW BY. Between storms up and down the Florida coast, a spectacular fireworks display for the Fourth of July, and long nights in Isabel's bed, Sullivan had never felt so happy. He wondered if this was how normal people felt. Even Ryder picked up on his mood.

"Are you in love with Isabel?" Ryder asked on the phone.

Sullivan had never been in love. How the hell was he supposed to know what love felt like? But he certainly enjoyed her company. He couldn't, however, understand what the hell Isabel saw in him. He was rough around the edges and had a messed up childhood. His personality alone seemed to grate on most people's nerves. For some reason though, Isabel didn't seem to mind.

"I got to go," Sullivan said, not answering his friend's question. He hung up the phone and headed inside his rental. Sure, not answering the question was taking the coward's way out, but Sullivan was never one to talk about his feelings.

Inside the bathroom, Sullivan looked at himself in the mirror. Isabel complained the lighting in this room made her look terrible, but he disagreed. She always looked beautiful, though he didn't look so great at the moment. They'd had a long chase day, and something about being on the road for hours on end made him feel dirty. Not to mention the fact that he and Isabel did indeed find an isolated spot, and made good use of the truck's privacy.

His phone chimed with a message notification. Isabel.

Isabel: I'll text you when Miguel goes to sleep if you want to come over.

Sullivan responded with a thumbs up emoji, never one for words, and headed to the shower.

When he got out, his phone beeped, indicating a voicemail. Probably Isabel, but when he picked up the phone, he saw a missed call from Eddie Garcia.

Shit. The one time he was expecting a call, he'd been in the shower. Sullivan hurriedly pressed play on the message.

"*Hey, Sullivan. It's Eddie Garcia. Call me back when you get this message. I found the information you were looking for.*"

Sullivan's heart raced as the voicemail ended. He listened to the message again, hoping he'd heard him right.

Garcia had found his sister.

22

His hands trembled as he pushed the call back button. The phone rang a few times, then Garcia came to the line.

"You found my sister?" Sullivan asked impatiently.

"Yeah, but I'm afraid you won't like the news."

Sullivan felt his stomach clench as he gripped the phone tighter, his knuckles turning white. "Is she dead?"

"No, sorry," Garcia said quickly. "I didn't mean to imply that. I just wanted to prepare you for what I found."

Sullivan exhaled. Thank God she wasn't dead, but it was obvious he wasn't going to like what the PI had to say. He took a seat at the table and steeled himself for the bad news. "Tell me."

"She's working at a strip club in downtown St. Petersburg. Her stage name is 'Electra Sparks.'"

"Shit," Sullivan said. Out of all the things Garcia could have told him, that had not been what he expected. He could picture her as a waitress, or hell, even a bartender. But a stripper? Fuck no.

"What the hell happened?" Sullivan snapped, feeling the

anger in him rise. "How did she go from being adopted by a loving Christian family in Texas to working at a strip joint in Florida?"

"I don't have any details about that right now, but I can keep digging if you want. What I can tell you is that she didn't finish high school. Dropped out when she was eighteen and left home. Changed her surname back to Sullivan. Looks like she was in a relationship with a man seven years older than her, and they moved to Shreveport, Louisiana. She ended up in Florida a year later. Lived in a few places in the Tampa Bay area. Clearwater. Dunedin. St. Pete. Best I gather, she's been staying with friends."

"So she's in St. Pete now?"

"Yeah. I found a phone number for her, but unfortunately, it was disconnected when I tried it. But I can give you her current address and the address of the club she works at. It's called the Paradise Lounge Gentlemen's Club."

Sullivan grabbed a pen and the envelope from a piece of junk mail. "Give them to me."

When he got off the phone, he stared at the two addresses he had scribbled down. There it was, the answer he'd been waiting for.

Right away, he pulled up the Paradise Lounge's website. It looked like a sleazy joint trying to pass itself off as some up and coming hot spot. At the top of the web page, the logo had a silhouette of a naked woman dancing on a pole next to palm trees. Under the logo, it claimed to be St. Petersburg #1 Gentlemen's Club. Funny that it called itself a gentlemen's club, when the men who frequented the place were anything but gentlemen.

"*Fuck*," Sullivan cursed, throwing his phone across the room. He reached for the picture on his end table, the one of Emmy from Facebook. He'd printed it out and framed it, just so he could have a recent picture of her.

"What happened to you, Emmy?"

Because he knew in his heart that something bad had happened. No one grew up to work in a strip club if their childhood had been ideal. Granted, her life got off to a rocky start with their neglectful mother and abusive stepfather, but Sullivan had hoped a new family would be a fresh start for Emmy. Obviously, something had gone wrong. Why had she dropped out of school? Why was she taking off her clothes every night for sick and horny men?

He could not let this continue.

Isabel had just taken the chicken out of the oven when she heard Miguel say, "Mr. Sullivan's here!"

He pointed at the camera monitor. Sure enough, Sullivan's Jeep was parked in her driveway. "Let him in, *nene*. I'll go set an extra place at the table."

As she put the food on the table, Sullivan walked in.

"You're just in time for dinner, Mr. Sullivan!" Miguel said.

"*Nene*, go wash your hands." Once Miguel was out of the room, Isabel inched closer to Sullivan and gave him a light kiss. "Hey. I thought you weren't coming over until later."

"Just felt like coming over sooner."

The tone of his voice made Isabel wonder if something was wrong, but before she could ask, Miguel ran back into the room.

"I'm hungry!" the child said.

They ate the meal Isabel had prepared, and Sullivan still seemed off to Isabel. While he was never much of a talker to begin with, he usually attempted to make conversation at the dinner table. But tonight, he was quiet. Isabel had even asked if there was something wrong with his food, but he said he wasn't really hungry.

After dinner, she sent Miguel off to get ready for bed. Sullivan was occupied with his phone as she loaded the dishwasher. “Is everything okay? You seem like you have something on your mind.”

Sullivan put his phone down. “I heard from Eddie.”

“Oh. What did he say?”

Sullivan nodded toward the open bathroom door where Miguel was brushing his teeth. “I’ll tell you later.”

Judging from Sullivan’s mood, Isabel gathered the news wasn’t good. She closed the dishwasher door. “I’m going to check on Miguel, and then, you want to talk? Maybe have a drink? I make a mean margarita.”

She hoped to get at least a half smile from him, but he just gave her an emotionless nod. “Okay.”

Later when Isabel tucked Miguel in, the child had a look of concern on his face. “What’s wrong with Mr. Sullivan? He didn’t laugh at any of my jokes. Is he mad at me?”

“Oh, *nene*, of course not. I think Mr. Sullivan got some bad news earlier. He wasn’t really in the mood for anything funny.”

“But when I’m sad, jokes make me happy.”

“I guess Mr. Sullivan has a lot on his mind. But he wasn't mad at you.”

“He didn’t eat all his dinner. Do you think he didn’t like it?”

Isabel shook her head. “No, I think it’s just like he said. He wasn’t hungry. Sometimes I don’t feel like eating when I get bad news. Do you?”

Miguel seemed to think about it. “No.” The little boy yawned. “I’m tired.”

“You had a busy day playing. I heard you and Juan chased his dog down the street when he got loose.”

Miguel yawned again. “Yeah, but we caught him.”

“Get some rest, *nene*. I’ll see you in the morning.” She pulled his blanket up to his shoulders, kissed his forehead, then turned off the lamp. By the time she closed the door, she imagined Miguel was already half asleep.

Back in the kitchen, Sullivan was looking at his phone again.

"Miguel's in bed," she said. "I'll get started on those margaritas if you still want one."

He nodded. "Yeah, I sure as hell could use one."

"So, what did Eddie say?"

"Look at this." He handed his phone to her, and Isabel wasn't sure at first what she was seeing. "Paradise Lounge?" She scrolled further until it became obvious what this was. "This is a strip club. Why are you looking at this site?"

"Your cousin says this is where my sister works. She's a dancer there, and she goes by the name *Electra Sparks*. Can you believe that? My baby sister is taking her clothes off for strangers every night to make a few bucks."

Isabel scrolled through the images of scantily clad women in stilettos by a pole. She handed the phone back to Sullivan. "I've seen enough of that."

Sullivan put his phone face down. "I was just making sure her image wasn't on the site. I was afraid it was, but none of those women are her. Probably just some generic stock images."

Isabel took out two glasses and a bottle of tequila from her cabinet. "Did Eddie say how long she'd been working there?"

"No, but she's been in Florida for a while. She dropped out of high school when she was eighteen, moved to Shreveport with some guy, then somehow ended up in Florida a year after that. I can't believe she's working there. I mean, I guess I should be glad she's not a prostitute, though what the hell do I know? I know nothing about her."

"I'm sorry. It sounds like she's hit some hard times."

"This wasn't supposed to happen. She was supposed to go on and have a good life away from that hellhole trailer. Something bad happened. No young woman from a respectable home decides she wants to be a stripper when she grows up."

Isabel thought the same, but decided to put out a different perspective. "I had a friend in college who was an exotic dancer on the side. She said she made good tips. Maybe Emmy's doing it to pay for college."

Sullivan shook his head. "No. She didn't graduate. School doesn't seem to be a priority."

"Well, it's still good money."

Sullivan looked at her with dark eyes, though Isabel didn't think the anger was directed at her. "There are better ways to make money than to take your clothes off for strangers."

"I don't disagree with you." Isabel took some limes out of the refrigerator. "You want me to show you how to make margaritas?" Sullivan needed a distraction.

Sullivan stood. "No thanks," he said, then headed to the living room.

Isabel finished making the drinks in the quiet kitchen, definitely feeling like she needed some alcohol now. She carried the glasses to the living room and handed one to Sullivan.

"So, what are you going to do now?" Isabel asked, joining him on the couch.

Sullivan held his drink, but had yet to sample it. "I'm going to get her out of there. I won't stand for my baby sister to be working at some sleazy strip club."

"She's a grown woman. She gets to make her own decisions."

He put the drink down, untouched. "You don't get it, Izzy. It was my job as her brother to protect her. Something happened to Emmy to put her on this path. I wasn't there to stop it."

"Maybe she just has an outgoing personality and loves to dance. She's obviously beautiful. Some girls use that to their advantage." Isabel didn't believe working at the club was something Emmy enjoyed, but thought it would at least give Sullivan hope that her life hadn't been that bad.

Sullivan shook his head. "I have a bad feeling about this in the pit of my stomach. Something happened to her, and I got to find out." He pulled out a folded envelope from his wallet with his small writing on the back of it.

"What's that?"

"Some addresses. Eddie said her phone number was disconnected. When we get off work tomorrow, I'm going to go over to her place. And if she isn't there, I'll try her at work. Eddie seemed to think she's been living with friends, but I have a feeling she's in with the wrong crowd. I'll convince her to come live with me."

"Do you think she remembers you?"

Sullivan shrugged. "I guess I'll find out, but if she doesn't, I have pictures of us to prove it." He put the envelope back in his wallet, then leaned back on the couch.

Isabel placed her hand on his arm. "Do you want me to come with you? For moral support?"

"Thanks, but no. This is something I need to do alone."

Isabel nodded, then took a sip of her drink. She noticed Sullivan hadn't tried it yet, so she nudged him. "Hey, are you going to drink that? I want you to try it."

He leaned forward and picked up the margarita glass. He took a sip, and for the first time that evening, Isabel was pleased to see a smile on his face.

"You're right, Izzy. You make a damn good margarita."

THE PARADISE LOUNGE was packed when Sullivan arrived. It was the last place he wanted to be on a Friday night, but he needed to find Emmy.

He'd already tried the home address Garcia had given to

him, but that had been a dead end. Some stoned kid answered the door and said Emmy had left three weeks ago. He pressed the kid and the other twenty-somethings there for information on her whereabouts, but no one had an answer.

"She moved out and didn't say where she was going, man," the stoner said.

Which now brought Sullivan to the place he really didn't want to be.

He still didn't know if she would remember him, and maybe if she didn't, she'd wonder who in the hell this man was trying to take her away. All he wanted was to get Emmy out of this hellhole. If she needed the money, hell, he had plenty saved up.

A feisty looking redhead wearing a skimpy black dress stopped in front of him at the bar. "Hi, handsome. Can I get you something to drink?"

"No." What he needed was answers, not alcohol.

The redhead remained where she was. "Has anyone ever told you that you look exactly like Jase Holler from *Bermuda Time Warp?*"

Great, now she was flirting with him. "Yeah, but I'm not him. And I'm not interested in a drink."

The woman smiled. "You want a lap dance instead?"

Sullivan sighed. "No. I'm looking for someone."

"I don't know who you're looking for, but I guarantee I can give you a much better time than she could."

Sullivan was getting more annoyed by the minute with this lady. He wanted to come in and look around without drawing attention to himself, but he could tell that was going to be impossible. With a sigh, he sat down. "Actually, maybe you can help me."

The woman crawled into his lap, but Sullivan held his hands up in protest. "No, not that."

She removed herself, but was still in his personal space. "Are you sure about that? I could give you a good time."

"Look, I ain't here for entertainment. I need information about someone who works here. Can you help me with that?"

The redhead narrowed her eyes. "Maybe. It'll cost you though."

Sullivan cursed under his breath, reached for his wallet, and pulled out a crisp twenty dollar bill. "I'll give this to you if you can answer my questions. I'm looking for Emmy Sullivan."

"I don't know anyone named Emmy."

He rolled his eyes. "You know her as *Electra Sparks.*"

Her eyes lit up in recognition. "Oh, Electra. Why are you looking for Electra?"

"I'm her brother, but she might not remember me. She was young when we were separated. Can you tell me where she is?"

"She's not working tonight. She should be here tomorrow."

"I need to know where she's staying then, because she wasn't at the address I had for her."

"I don't know where she's staying."

"Then tell me if there's anyone who might know where I can find her." Sullivan hadn't meant to raise his voice, but he was getting pissed off that she couldn't, or wouldn't, give him the answers he was looking for.

A man cleared his throat, and Sullivan turned to see a stout bald man next to the redhead. "Is this man bothering you, Ember?" He glared at Sullivan.

"I wasn't harassing her," Sullivan told the man.

"He's looking for Electra," Ember said. "But I told him she wasn't on the schedule tonight."

"I need to find Emmy. I mean, Electra. Whatever name she's going by. Do you have a home address for her?"

The bald man narrowed his eyes. "I'm not at liberty to give out personal information about my employees. If you'd like to meet up with Electra after hours, you'll have to discuss that with her personally." The bald man stepped closer. "If you're looking for a good time, I'm sure one of these lovely ladies here can provide that for you."

"For the last time, I'm not here as a customer. She's my sister. Will she be here tomorrow?"

The man nodded. "Sure, Electra will be here. Now, why don't you have a seat, get a drink, and enjoy yourself? I'm sure Ember could show you a good time."

"No thanks," Sullivan said, glaring at both of them. He stood to walk away, but Ember jumped in front of him.

"Hey, what about my twenty dollars?"

"You didn't give me shit for that," Sullivan cursed, then stomped out without giving Ember the cash.

He thought of hanging around to see if anyone else could give him a clue, but honestly, he was tired of this place already. And if Emmy would be here tomorrow, he would have to try again.

When he arrived at Isabel's, she greeted him at the door wearing her long black shirt. And if Sullivan hadn't been so exhausted, he'd want to take her to bed.

"Did you find her?" she asked.

Sullivan tossed his keys on the table. "No. When I tried her apartment, there were a bunch of stoned college-aged students. Said she moved out three weeks ago. They didn't know where. And at the club, she wasn't working. I'll have to try again tomorrow."

"Maybe Eddie can find a more current address for her."

Sullivan shook his head. "I don't want to worry him about that. If I can't track her down at the club, then I'll have him look into it again."

"I'm sorry it didn't work out. You want something to eat? I could fix you some leftovers."

"No, not hungry. In fact, I'm exhausted. You mind if I just go to bed?"

"Not at all. Go ahead."

Sullivan stepped into the bathroom for a few minutes, then came out and stripped down to his boxers. He crawled in bed next to Isabel, and within moments, he felt himself dozing.

IT WAS STILL EARLY when Isabel woke the next morning. She reached for Sullivan, but found him gone. She blinked her eyes, saw something on his pillow, and reached for it. A note.

> Got stuff to do today. Don't know if I'll stay over or not. - S

Isabel sighed. She had hoped she and Sullivan could spend some time together. The storm chance was low today, and it would be the perfect beach day. But it felt like Sullivan was keeping his distance. She sensed he was depressed over the situation with his sister, and maybe he was trying to figure out what to do.

In the living room, she found Miguel in front of the television. He looked up expectantly.

"Mr. Sullivan's car isn't outside. Is he going to have breakfast with us?"

"No, *nene*. He had to go do some things. But we can make a big breakfast together. What do you like?"

Miguel looked disappointed. "I wanted to show Mr. Sullivan how to make black bean breakfast tacos."

"We can show him next time. In fact, we could make a list of things to teach Mr. Sullivan how to cook. Did you know he only cooks using his microwave? He could use a lot of help!"

This gave Miguel a laugh, and Isabel was glad to see that Miguel was cheering up.

She just wished that she could be in a better mood.

SULLIVAN TOLD Isabel he had some errands to catch up on, but that was a lie. Instead, he fell asleep as the exhaustion from the week caught up with him. He hadn't had an urge for a cigarette in a while, but out of habit, he wanted to run to the store and get a pack. But he'd been too lazy to go anywhere, so he didn't.

The only place he was going was Saint Petersburg. He was determined to find Emmy tonight. And if Emmy wasn't at the club, he'd question every damn person he saw until someone could give him answers. His baby sister would not continue to strip.

Later that night, Sullivan walked into the Paradise Lounge. He hoped to avoid Ember, and luckily, didn't see her. Instead, he saw a tall and leggy blond make her way over to him.

"Hi there. You look like you have a sweet tooth, and my name is Candy."

Sullivan wanted to roll his eyes. He thought men were bad at the cheesy pickup lines, but the women here were worse. And they flocked to him. He wasn't interested.

"I'm looking for someone," he said.

The blond smiled. "You found her."

"No. My sister. Electra." He hated calling her that. It wasn't her name. "Is she here?"

The blond frowned, obviously realizing Sullivan wasn't giving her any money. "Oh yeah, Ember said something about you coming last night. She's in the back. I'll go find her."

Thank God she was in the back. If his sister had been stripping on stage right now, he would have fought off security and carried her off.

He waited at a table and tried not to make eye contact with anyone. The last thing he needed was some woman coming over to offer him a lap dance. He wondered if Emmy gave customers that kind of treatment, and the thought made his stomach roil.

Loud music played over the speakers, to Sullivan's annoyance. A dark-haired girl, probably not much older than his sister, was gyrating on stage wearing stilettos and barely anything else. Some horny bastard leaned over the stage and tried to shove some bills in her underwear before security pulled him back. Sullivan grabbed a napkin on the table and balled it up. If that had been his sister on stage, he would have broken that man's neck.

After ten minutes of waiting, Sullivan grew impatient. Did Candy, if that was even her real name, even tell Emmy he was here? He hadn't seen his sister in twenty years, and he wasn't waiting any longer. He stood, determined to go find Emmy himself.

"Elmer? Is that you?"

Sullivan turned at the sound of a female voice. Standing before him was a face he would recognize anywhere. She was all grown up, of course, but the eyes were the same. The only thing that was different was that she'd lost that look of innocence about her. She looked as if she'd had a hard life.

What the hell had happened?

He walked over to her slowly. "Emmy. I wasn't sure if you would remember me. You're all grown up." He moved to hug her, something he didn't do often, but was surprised when Emmy backed up.

"Not here. Let's step outside. I'm on my break."

He followed her through the crowds of drunk men and barely covered women. Emmy at least had a dress on.

"Hey, Electra!" a man yelled out. "How's about you and I see if we have a spark together?"

Sullivan turned to see who the offending motherfucker was. He fought the urge to yank the man out of his seat and punch him in the face. Instead, he followed Emmy, who was already halfway to the door.

Outside, Sullivan felt as if he could breathe again. The inside of that club had been suffocating with all those drunkards ogling his baby sister.

Emmy came to a stop at the sidewalk. "I can't believe you had the nerve to come here."

It wasn't exactly the reaction Sullivan had expected, but he couldn't blame her. Emmy probably didn't want him to see her at a place like this. "Look, I'm sorry I had to track you down at the club, but you weren't at the address I had for you, and your coworkers wouldn't tell me where you were staying."

"No, I meant I can't believe you had the nerve to show up here after you abandoned me for all those years."

Emmy's words felt like a knife in his side. "Emmy, I thought I was doing what was best for you. Look, I'm here now, and I want to help you. You don't have to work at this filthy place anymore."

"I'm not a child anymore, Elmer, and I don't need your help. I can do whatever the fuck I want!"

Hearing profanities come out of her mouth was a shocker. When she was a child, she'd whisper to him whenever their mother or Dick said a curse word, as if that was the worst thing they could do.

Sullivan took a deep breath. "Can we start again? I haven't seen you in years. I missed you, Emmy." His eyes actually teared up, something he rarely allowed himself to do. Someone, probably one of his mother's boyfriends, told Sullivan that real men didn't cry. And he believed that. But suppressing the emotion only made it build up inside until the dam had no choice but to break.

"You missed me? Could have fooled me."

Her voice was laced with venom, and once again, Sullivan felt as if he had been struck. But he was here now, and even if

Emmy didn't want to see him, he had to see this through. "Of course I missed you. You're my sister, and I love you."

"Then why did you leave me?" Her voice cracked. "How did you go from being the most wonderful brother in the world to someone who leaves his baby sister to fend for herself?"

"I thought you were safe."

Tears streamed down her face. "I wasn't. If you had been for a visit, you would have known that."

Emmy moved to a bench by the curb. She buried her head in her hands and sobbed. Sullivan wanted to put his arms around her shoulders and hug her like he used to, but he felt as if his touch would annoy her. He settled for sitting next to her.

"Emmy, you listen to me. I wanted you to have a normal childhood, more than anything. No one should have to live like we did in that trailer. No one deserves a mother who's drunk or high all the time and an abusive stepdad. I thought when that couple wanted to adopt you that you'd be in good hands. That's what the social worker told me. She said they were nice people who would take care of you, provide for you."

Emmy looked up and snorted. "Oh sure, they gave me food and shelter and decent clothes for school." She looked Sullivan in the eye. "But they weren't nice. Far from it. What's that saying? Out of the frying pan and into the fire? It was worse. Way worse. And a good brother would have saved me. I waited for you. I thought maybe when you were old enough, you could come get me, and then I wouldn't have to live with the Johnson family again. But you never came."

Emmy wiped her cheek with the back of her hand, and Sullivan was at a loss for words. What the fuck had happened to his sister?

"Emmy, I thought you were okay. And you want to know why I didn't come back for you?"

She didn't respond, so Sullivan continued.

"The social worker thought you were young enough to not

remember what happened. I figured that if I remained in your life, I'd be a constant reminder of everything bad that happened, and I didn't want that for you. I wanted you to live your life happy and free from misery and pain. I wanted you to have the childhood that I never got to have. But don't you ever think for a second that I forgot about you or didn't love you. I wish things had been different."

Emmy wiped a stray tear from her cheek. She sniffled, and Sullivan wished he had a tissue to offer her. He knew his reunion with Emmy would be emotional, but he wasn't expecting this.

"Can't change the past, no matter how hard you try," she said.

They were quiet for a moment. Emmy sniffled again and wiped her nose with the back of her arm.

"Emmy, I'm sorry. If I had known you were unhappy, I would have come back for you."

"Well here we are, twenty years later. You finally came back for me. Too late."

"I'm working in Poquito Beach right now. I saw on Facebook that you were in Clearwater. I took that as a sign to track you down. I hired a private investigator to help me find you."

"I knew you were in Florida," Emmy said. "And Kansas before that. And you went to Texas A&M."

Sullivan felt confused. "You looked me up?"

She looked at Sullivan. "Don't be surprised. I'm on social media, but not under my real name. Except for that one Facebook account. I was curious what you were up to, what was more important to you than your own sister. I figured it was only a matter of time before our paths crossed again, though I didn't think you would intentionally seek me out."

"So you knew this whole time I was living only thirty minutes away from you?"

She nodded. "Mmm-hmm. And I didn't even need a PI for

that. The point is, big brother, if I wanted to see you, I would have reached out. Well guess what? I don't."

She stood, but Sullivan reached for her. "Emmy, please."

"Please what? Don't go? Give you another chance to explain why you abandoned your sister? Did your private investigator dig up any dirt on me? Did he or she tell you what happened to me after you left?"

"He said you dropped out of high school and left home. Why, Emmy?"

"Why the hell do you think? Once I was eighteen, I got the hell out of there. My adoptive father, the preacher, was worse than Dick."

Sullivan felt a gut punch. "Tell me he didn't..."

"Yes, he did. He did what Dick had done to me, and then he did more. The worst thing you can imagine. Yeah, *that*. For a man who said he was Christian, he was anything but. I ran away all the time, but it didn't matter. He'd always find me. He'd tell me not to tell. And for some stupid reason, I kept his secret. But I decided that as soon as I was of legal age, he wouldn't have control over me anymore."

Sullivan rose from the bench and kicked a soda can across the street. "Fuck!"

"Oh, you're upset? You realized how much you failed your little sister?"

"Emmy, I had no idea you were in that much pain. Please understand what was going through my mind. I was a messed up teenage kid. I thought I was doing what was best for you. I didn't... I didn't know."

"And who's fault is that?"

"Look, we can't change what happened, but I'm here now. I let you down before, but I won't again. You're my baby sister, and I'll take care of you. If you need help with money, you can stay with me, rent free. And you can find a better job. You should not be working in a fucking strip club."

"I don't need or want your help. I've done just fine without you. Now if you'll excuse me, I've got to get back. My break is over."

She turned to walk away, but Sullivan blocked her path. "Emmy, please. Do you have a new phone number? Let's talk later."

"I have nothing to say to you. I don't have a brother anymore. You mean nothing to me. Go home, Elmer."

She brushed past him and bumped his arm as she marched back toward the club. Sullivan watched as she opened the door and disappeared inside.

23

Sullivan slammed his front door behind him. Looking for his sister had been a mistake. No, the mistake was made twenty years ago when he cut Emmy out of his life. Emmy was right. Some loving big brother he was. How could he have been so stupid?

Sullivan grabbed the ceramic ashtray from the coffee table and hurled it across the room, causing it to shatter as it hit the tiled kitchen floor. The ashtray was broken now, just like he was.

"*You're worthless,*" said Dick's voice in his mind.

"*And when you're eighteen, you're gone. You hear me?*" said his mother. "*I should have given you up for adoption.*"

Sullivan sank into the couch cushion and regretted breaking his ashtray. He could use a smoke right about now. How did things get so fucked up? Florida had been a stupid move.

No, not stupid. If he hadn't come here, he would have never met Isabel or Miguel. For some reason, the very woman who annoyed him upon his arrival had wormed her way into his heart. And he was fond of the boy. He had little experience with kids, but Miguel was a good one.

But no, Isabel and Miguel deserved better than him. Isabel needed a man she could depend on, not someone as messed up as he was. And yeah, maybe people said he was good with children, but Sullivan knew the truth. If he was so good with kids, then how come he never checked on his little sister to make sure she was all right? He'd let her down, and Sullivan didn't deserve her forgiveness.

On impulse, Sullivan rose from his seat and headed to his bedroom closet. He dragged out his worn suitcase and tossed it on the bed. Maybe he should pack up and get the hell out of here. He knew Isabel would be hurt and Miguel would be disappointed, but in the long run, this decision was really for the best. Dick was right—he was a worthless son of a bitch.

He noticed a lump inside one of the interior side pockets when he unzipped it. Reaching inside, he felt an old pack of Marlboro with a lighter stuffed inside. And the pack was nearly full. Hot damn. At least something about this night was going right.

Sullivan shoved the suitcase onto the floor, sank onto the unmade bed, and lit up.

ISABEL SENT Sullivan a few texts on Saturday, but hadn't gotten a response. She knew he was upset about his sister and had a lot on his mind. But now, it seemed like he was shutting her out.

By Sunday morning, she knew Sullivan had probably gone to the strip club last night to look for his sister. She was eager for an update on if he found her or not. She sent him another text to check in.

As she and her family left church, Isabel glanced at her phone. Still no response.

"What's the matter, *hermanita?*" Paulina asked.

"I'm worried about Sullivan."

"What's wrong with Sullivan?" Carlita asked.

Isabel looked to see if Miguel was out of earshot. He was happily playing with his cousins on the church's playground equipment. "He's trying to track down his sister."

"Sullivan has a sister?" Carlita asked, surprised.

Isabel nodded. "They were separated when they were young. Eddie found her in Saint Petersburg, but I don't think his sister is doing so well."

"Let's sit down," Carlita said, leading them to a bench. "Now, what's wrong with his sister?"

Isabel didn't share the entire story, not wanting to break Sullivan's confidence. She felt it was okay to at least share what Eddie had told Sullivan, so she filled her mother and sister in.

"So she's working as an exotic dancer?" Paulina said. "I would be concerned about her too."

"I think Sullivan blames himself because he thought she was in good hands. Now maybe it's looking like her life wasn't so wonderful." She didn't know any of the details, but Sullivan had been right... no one from a well-adjusted home grew up to be a stripper.

"You should go to him, *mija,*" Carlita said. "If he's not answering his phone, you go see him in person."

Isabel thought that was a good idea. After dropping Miguel and her mother off at home, she made the trip to Sullivan's house.

At the door, she hesitated. If Sullivan wanted to see her, he would have texted her or come over. But something in her gut told her that Sullivan was not well, and she needed to find out if she was right.

Her knuckles tapped on the door gently. "Sullivan? It's Isabel."

No response.

Isabel tried the doorbell next. “Sullivan? Are you okay? You haven’t responded to any of my texts.”

His car was in the driveway, so unless he took a walk, he had to be home.

“Sullivan,” Isabel called out again. “Please answer the door. I’m worried about you. Don’t make me call 911 and have the police do a welfare check.”

At that, she finally heard footsteps inside. The door cracked open, and Sullivan squinted at the sunlight. “I’m fine.”

The stench of cigarette smoke hit her, and Isabel narrowed her eyes at him. “You’re smoking again.”

“Well, I had a good run. A few weeks? A month? I’ve never been able to quit. You should probably go. I know it bothers you.”

He closed the door, but Isabel pushed her way inside before it shut. Now that she could see him better, she was shocked at his appearance. It was almost noon, and Sullivan was dressed in only his boxer shorts. His eyes were bloodshot, and his hair hadn’t been combed. “You’re not dressed.”

Sullivan put out the cigarette in a cracked ashtray. “No need to be dressed when I’m at home. You didn’t need to come over.”

“I was worried about you.” Judging from the state of the living room, she had a right to be concerned. On the coffee table was an open pizza box, two slices left, and several empty beer bottles. A smell came from the trash bin in the kitchen, not to mention the stench from the ashtray. “Why are you smoking again? You were doing so well.”

“Found an old pack. Saved it for an emergency, which this is.”

“Why didn’t you answer my texts?”

“I just needed some time to myself.”

Isabel gathered the pizza box and tossed it in the garbage. It was the mother in her that couldn’t stand for last night’s food to still be sitting out. “This place is a mess.”

"I wasn't expecting company."

"I don't care about the mess. I care about you. Did you find your sister?"

Sullivan moved to sit on the couch. "Yeah."

He didn't elaborate on how the reunion went, but from his expression, he didn't look happy about it. She was going to have to pry it out of him. "Okay, so what happened?"

He stared off into space, not answering her question.

"Sullivan?"

"She's not a child anymore. She's a grown woman who takes her clothes off for those sick men in that club. You should have heard the way they were talking to her. Like she was a piece of ass for their enjoyment."

"How did she react when you showed up? Did she remember you?"

Sullivan reached for the beer can on the table, drank the last dregs of it, then tossed the can on the floor. "Oh yeah, she remembered me. And she hates me. Says I abandoned her, and she's right."

"Maybe she just needs some time. You were only doing what you thought was best for her. She'll come around."

"No, she won't. Remember I told you she went to live with a preacher and his wife? Well, that preacher did the same thing Dick did to her, and worse. And it's all my damn fault."

Her heart ached for the woman she never met, but before she could say anything, Sullivan grabbed the picture frame on the end table and threw it across the room. Isabel flinched when it hit the wall, shattering the glass.

"I should have checked on her!" Sullivan yelled.

"Hey, listen to me. What happened to your sister is not your fault."

He slowly turned to face her with flinty eyes and a bulging vein on his forehead. "Yes it is. I'm her brother. I should have made sure the family she was with was treating her right. If that preacher wasn't already dead, I'd be halfway to Texas right about now to kill him myself."

Isabel placed her hand on his arm in a comforting gesture. "But you were just a child yourself."

"I was old enough. She says I abandoned her, and she's right. What kind of sorry ass brother am I? Supposed to protect his baby sister, and then I threw her out of the lion's cage and into the wolves' den."

"It's the state's fault for letting that family adopt her. They should have never been considered."

Sullivan stared blankly at the wall. She wasn't sure he heard a word she said.

"I would have been better off not knowing," he said in a low voice. He rose from the couch and headed to the bedroom. "You should go, Izzy."

Isabel knew Sullivan was prone to bad moods, but this was different. He was depressed, if his disheveled appearance was any indication. She'd already lost Miguel's father, and she wasn't about to give up on another man she cared about. "No, I'm not leaving." Isabel followed him to the bedroom, which was just as bad as the rest of the place. His bed was unmade, and there was a pile of dirty laundry on the floor. Next to the dresser, Isabel spotted an open suitcase with folded clothes inside. "Are you going somewhere?"

Sullivan sat on the edge of the bed. "I'm sorry to do this to you, Izzy, but you and Miguel deserve someone a hell of a lot better than me. I was going to tell you later. Taking this job in Florida was an opportunity for me to find my sister. But after what happened last night, I don't deserve to have family or anyone in my life. I'm nothing but a worthless bastard, just like Dick said."

Isabel couldn't believe what he was saying. How could he think he meant nothing to her? She sat next to him and placed her hand on his shoulder. "Listen to me. You're not worthless.

Look how you protected me? If it weren't for you, I wouldn't have had the courage to come forward and report Mateo. And you're so good with Miguel."

"If I was so good with kids, I would have had the forethought to check on my baby sister. I shouldn't be allowed to take care of anyone. And like I said, you and Miguel would be better off without me."

"I don't agree."

Sullivan looked at her with pained eyes. "You might enjoy my company for a while, but hang around me long enough, you'll be unhappy. And you're really special, Izzy. I won't do that to you. I'll come over and tell Miguel goodbye before I leave."

She knew he didn't mean any of what he'd said. It was his depression talking. "Bad times don't last forever. Don't you remember saying that to me? This will pass. You're not going anywhere."

Sullivan raised the sheet and got under the covers. "At this moment, no. I need some sleep. Just go, Izzy. I have a splitting headache."

"You have a hangover. I wish you would have come over last night. You could have talked to me." But she knew Sullivan was never one for words. At that moment, he rolled over and turned his back to her.

Isabel slowly stood to her feet. He couldn't be serious about leaving, but how could she get through to him? Deciding to let him sleep, Isabel left the room and quietly closed the door behind her.

In the living room, she went about picking up the discarded beer cans, cigarette butts, and used napkins. An almost empty pack of Marlboro sat on the coffee table, and Isabel threw that away too. After taking out the trash, she loaded the dishwasher and wiped down the sink.

She checked on Sullivan when she was done. He was snoring, so at least he was getting some sleep. Isabel hoped when he woke up, he'd have some sense knocked into him, but Isabel's track record of helping troubled men wasn't very good. Miguel's father had a lot of problems, and she'd lost him too.

On the end table, Sullivan's phone lit up with a call. Isabel rushed to silence it, not wanting it to wake him up. It was Ryder calling, and on impulse, Isabel answered.

"Hi, Ryder, it's Isabel. Sullivan can't come to the phone."

"Hey, Isabel. How are you?"

Isabel sighed and sank into the couch cushions. "Not well, actually. I'm glad you called. I'm worried about Sullivan."

"What's wrong?" Ryder asked, his tone turning serious.

Isabel filled him in on how Sullivan found his sister and how their reunion had gone.

Isabel looked at the closed door. Behind it, all she heard was the sound of Sullivan's fan. "I've never seen him depressed like this. I'm really worried about him."

"Sully gets in these moods from time to time. I keep telling him he needs to see a therapist to work out all his childhood trauma, but he doesn't want to do that."

"Yeah, he's stubborn. Do you think he's serious about moving back to Kansas?"

"He pushes people away when he's feeling hurt or down, but I know he really cares about you. I mean, you've done the impossible. You made him give up cigarettes. He's never given up smoking for anyone but you."

Despite her own down mood, Isabel let out a small laugh. "Except he started back."

"And he'll regret that later. Did you throw away his cigarettes?"

"Already in the garbage."

"Listen, if he doesn't snap out of his mood by the end of the week, let me know. I can grab a flight and be there in a few hours."

"Oh, I couldn't ask you to do that."

"Sully's my friend. I'd do anything for him. You want to write down my number? You can call me anytime, day or night."

Isabel scribbled Ryder's number on a piece of junk mail, then said goodbye with a promise to keep him updated.

On the floor, she spotted the broken picture frame Sullivan had thrown earlier. In her cleaning, she had missed it. With a small broom and dustpan, Isabel swept up the shards of glass. The frame was useless now, but the picture was intact. Isabel tossed the broken frame and stuck the picture to the refrigerator with a magnet.

Emmy was a beautiful young woman. She could see a hint of Sullivan in her eyes. She tried to imagine growing up without her own sister, and how hurt she would feel if her sister didn't want to talk to her.

An idea formed in her mind. Isabel wasn't sure it would work, but she had to try. Maybe if she talked to Emmy, she could make her understand that Sullivan never meant to hurt her. If Emmy only knew how much he loved her, maybe it would be a start to mending their relationship.

She checked the time. Way too early for the strip club to be open. But hell, she supposed she would need a few hours to gather up the courage. The last place she wanted to be right now was somewhere full of men like Mateo.

But for Sullivan, she would do it.

SULLIVAN GROANED when he opened his eyes. The pain in his head had gone down to a dull roar, and it felt like he had a wad of cotton in his mouth.

Earlier, he'd heard the clanging of dishes—Isabel cleaning up his mess. He didn't know why she bothered to stay. As his hand touched the doorknob, he took a deep breath, prepared to see Isabel on the other side.

But when Sullivan peeked out, it was quiet.

On the table, he spotted a note written in Isabel's pretty handwriting.

> *I ordered some food for you. It's in the fridge. I would have cooked you something, but I couldn't find anything in your pantry. Eat, and don't smoke. Miguel and I need you.*
>
> *Love,*
>
> *Isabel*

Sullivan sat at the table and rubbed his forehead. His headache was worsening again. He didn't deserve Isabel. He knew she struggled with her finances, and wished she hadn't wasted the money. His appetite was gone.

He could use a cigarette, but when he searched for his pack of Marlboro, they were gone.

Isabel. She thought she needed him, but she didn't need a screwup like himself with all his baggage and problems.

Sullivan considered resuming his packing, but his energy was completely drained. Maybe he would just go back to bed.

It was the last place Isabel ever expected to find herself in, but here she was at the Paradise Lounge Gentlemen's Club. She felt embarrassed as she walked in, hoping no one would recognize her. Not that she really knew anyone in Saint Pete, but people might know her as the former meteorologist for the local news.

The light was dim except for the stage where a large-breasted woman was twerking. She watched as a heavyset man in a Hawaiian shirt tossed some bills her way.

"Hey there, sweetheart," said a male voice behind her. "Buy you a drink?"

Isabel cringed. She didn't come here to get hit on. Especially not from this guy, who looked sleazy as all get-out. Isabel thought the best approach was to ignore him. If she didn't give him attention, he would hopefully leave her alone. But when she walked away, he followed her.

"Are you new?" he asked. "Haven't seen you here before."

Apparently, this guy wasn't taking the hint. Isabel turned around and put on her best *I'm not interested* look. "Leave me alone."

The man had the nerve to grin. "That's a pretty accent you have. I love Latinas. I just want to buy you a drink and have a conversation."

"And I said leave me the fuck alone," Isabel snapped.

The man laughed. "Feisty one!"

A bald man in a suit came over. "Is Leon bothering you, miss? I'm Al, the owner. Sometimes Leon has a little too much to drink."

"Fuck you," Leon said, then stomped off.

"Sorry about that," Al said. "Leon's harmless, but he comes on a little too strong. Are you looking for a job? I have an opening."

Isabel must have looked horrified, for Al immediately backed off. "Or not. We don't get too many female customers here unless they're looking to dance."

"I'm actually looking for Emmy. I mean... Electra. Is she here?"

The man pointed somewhere behind her shoulder. "Right over there. Electra! Come here for a second."

The young woman walked over, and right away, Isabel

could see the resemblance to her brother. She had the same dark hair and brown eyes as Sullivan.

"This woman would like to speak to you," Al said.

Al walked away, distracted by someone calling for him, leaving her alone with Emmy.

"I don't normally perform for women, but I'm game if you are," Emmy said. "Do you want a lap dance?"

Isabel was taken aback. "What? No, I didn't come here for that. I need to speak to you. I'm Isabel, your brother's girlfriend."

Emmy shook her head. "I have nothing to say to Elmer. Did he send you?"

"No," Isabel quickly said. "He doesn't know I'm here."

"Well, it doesn't matter. If you came to get Elmer and I to reconnect, you can forget it. I need to get back to work." Emmy turned to walk away.

"Wait, please. I'm worried about him. He's very depressed, and I've never seen him like this. It's like he doesn't care about himself anymore."

Emmy's expression softened. "He's not suicidal, is he?"

Isabel honestly wasn't sure if he was suicidal. She didn't know Sullivan well enough to know how often he got in these moods. Could he hurt himself? "I don't know, but he's not in a good place mentally."

Emmy bit her lip and was quiet for a moment. "Okay, I'll talk to you, but not here. Hey, Al?"

Al looked her way. "Yeah?"

"I need to take my break now. Family emergency."

Al nodded. "That's fine, sweetheart. I'll get Daisy to take your spot if you're late."

"Thanks." Emmy nodded toward the exit. "Let's step outside."

Isabel was grateful to get out of there. Men kept staring at her like she was a piece of meat, and that Leon guy was still lurking. She couldn't imagine dancing and taking her clothes off for them every night.

Outside, it was humid, and the air smelled like fried food from a nearby restaurant. Emmy led them to a bench.

"Please tell me Elmer's not suicidal," Emmy said. "I didn't mean what I said to him. I was just angry."

"I don't know if he's thinking about that or not, but I know he's very upset about how you two left things last night."

"What's your name again? Isabel?"

"*Sí.*"

"Isabel, how would you feel if you were five years old, had a neglectful mother and an abusive stepfather, and the only person in the world who gave a damn about you was your big brother? Now, how would you feel if that same brother abandoned you after you were sent away to live in a foster home?"

"Sullivan wanted you to forget everything about your past. He hoped you were having a better life."

Emmy shook her head. "I wasn't. My adoptive father was worse than my stepfather. All I wanted was for Elmer to come rescue me, and he never showed. He just forgot about me."

"He didn't forget about you. Listen, it's terrible what happened to you, and Sullivan blames himself for not coming back for you. He thought he was doing the right thing."

"How is abandoning your baby sister doing the right thing?" she said, her voice rising. "I was probably a burden to him. He had to take care of me because our mother wouldn't lift a finger. He was probably glad to be rid of me."

"That's not true."

Emmy dabbed her eye with her fingertip. "I'm sure it is. He was probably glad Dick got himself killed and that Mama died. Then he got to wash his hands clean of me."

Something about what Emmy said didn't make sense. Did she know it was Sullivan who killed Dick? "You know what really happened to Dick, right?"

"I know he got shot. Good riddance. Probably pissed someone off at a bar. Not surprised. He had a temper. He was always hitting Elmer."

"You don't know."

Emmy's eyes narrowed. "Know what?"

She'd told Sullivan she wouldn't tell anyone, but if anyone had a right to know what happened, it was Emmy. "Your brother was the one who killed Dick. When he found out what Dick was doing to you, he decided to put an end to it. He didn't want him to hurt you anymore. And that's what really happened."

Isabel could see the realization sweep across Emmy's face. "The details of that night are fuzzy in my mind. I remember waking up to sirens and seeing red and blue lights flashing across my bedroom wall. And I remember the police putting Elmer in the back of their car in handcuffs. Mama wouldn't tell me why. I think Mama took me to stay at a neighbor's house. I don't remember much after that. All I was told was that Dick had got in a fight and someone shot him. Why would Elmer do that for me?"

"Why do you think? He loves you."

"So is that why he never came to see me? Because he went to jail for killing Dick?"

"He was arrested, but the detective believed him when he said it was self-defense. But your brother did not intend to hurt you. He was just a kid himself. He didn't make the best decision, but he's devastated about it now. Won't you please reach out to him? He's packing up his clothes and planning to leave Florida. He said he doesn't deserve anyone."

Emmy stared off into the distance. "He probably doesn't want to see me. I said some really hurtful things."

"He does want to see you. You're his baby sister, and he loves you. You're the main reason he came here in the first place. Please call him."

"I don't have his number."

"You have your phone on you? Or is it still disconnected?"

"I just got a new number today. My phone is in my locker."

Isabel pulled out her phone and a small notebook with a pen from her purse. "Here, I'll give you his number and address." She scribbled down the information from her contacts and tore the page. "Please reach out to him."

Emmy took the paper and folded it up. "I need to go back to work."

"Will you call him?"

Emmy stood up. "I don't know. I have a lot to think about."

"He loves you, Emmy. Never doubt that."

A tear fell down Emmy's cheek. "Thanks for coming."

With that, Emmy took off, leaving Isabel wondering if she'd gotten through to her or not.

SULLIVAN PEEKED out his front window the next day. Another afternoon shower was soaking western Florida, and his lawn was full of puddles. The yard had terrible drainage, and the driveway was full of muddy potholes. He should be out there, but not even a thunderstorm interested him now.

Isabel had already texted, and because he didn't want her to come over again, he told her he was taking a sick day. He sent Torres the same message. It wasn't exactly a lie. His head still hurt, and he didn't feel so great after smoking the rest of the cigarettes. He'd dug them out of the trash bin. Pathetic. Funny how it made him feel bad now.

Sullivan moved away from the window and sat on the couch. He wished Isabel hadn't seen him like this. She and Miguel deserved someone who had their shit together, someone who didn't have a tendency to fuck things up. Emmy too. He didn't blame her for not wanting him in her life.

The dryer buzzed, signaling his laundry was done. He should fold those clothes and put them in his suitcase, but somehow, he couldn't motivate himself to finish packing.

A knock on the door made his head pound. He winced at the pain, and there was a second knock. Probably Isabel with more takeout, but food couldn't put him in a better mood. He groaned as he got up from the sofa and trudged to the door.

He opened the door, prepared to tell Isabel to stop wasting her time on a loser like himself, but the figure under the pink umbrella and polka dot raincoat wasn't Isabel at all.

"Hi, Elmer," Emmy said.

24

Sullivan stared at her for a moment, shocked and confused at why Emmy was standing on his doorstep. How did she know where he lived? "Emmy?"

"I'm sorry for what I said. Can we talk?"

He nodded and moved aside to let her in. He hadn't felt embarrassed by the mess when Isabel came, but he hated for his sister to see it. "Sorry, my place is a disaster."

"I don't care. My new roommate is way messier." Emmy shook the rain from her umbrella and left it on the porch. Inside, she hung her wet coat next to Sullivan's rain coat. It was the only coat Sullivan wore in Florida.

"I didn't expect to see you. How did you know I was here?" Sullivan indicated the sofa, and Emmy took a seat.

"Your girlfriend came to see me last night."

Sullivan shook his head. "I'm sorry, what? At work?" The thought of Isabel tracking Emmy down at the Paradise Lounge gave him an unsettled feeling in the pit of his stomach.

Emmy nodded. "She said you were depressed, and I felt guilty for the things I said. She was worried about you. I thought you might... Elmer, please don't kill yourself."

Sullivan's mind was spinning. "Who said I was going to kill myself?"

"No one, but I was worried you were so upset that maybe you would. Mama did, you know." Emmy held up her arm, and for the first time, Sullivan saw the scars on her wrist. "See this? I used to cut. There was one time when I cut too deep, on purpose, and I almost died. I don't know how I survived, but I figured after that, maybe there was a reason for me to live."

Sullivan's heart lurched, and he felt his chin quiver. His sister had been in a world of pain, and where the hell had he been? On the road chasing tornadoes, that's where. Going to bars, drinking and smoking, and otherwise not caring about anyone except his own damn self. And all this time, Emmy had been out there in pain.

He felt his eyes water and wished he'd had a tissue other than the back of his hand. To his surprise, Emmy reached into her pocket and pulled out a Kleenex.

Sullivan dabbed his eye and balled up the tissue in his hand. He felt stupid showing emotion like this in front of his baby sister. He was supposed to be the strong one, so why was she the one comforting him? "I should have been there for you."

"I realized I said some things I didn't mean. You'll always be my brother, and I love you, Elmer. I was just mad at you, but being angry just makes me feel bad inside. Maybe it's time to let the past go. It's the only way we're going to move forward."

Sullivan looked at his kid sister, wondering how the dimple-cheeked child she used to be had grown into such a wise young woman. "I'd like to forget the past, except for the good memories. We had a few of those."

A smile came to her face. "Remember how we used to watch lightning from your bedroom window? That was my favorite memory."

Sullivan smiled back at her. "Mine too."

"Isabel told me what you did for me. About what happened with you and Dick. I had no idea you did that."

That surprised him. "You didn't know?"

Emmy shook her head. "No. I was told that Dick got shot, but no one ever told me you did it. I just assumed he'd gotten into a fight with someone at a bar."

"I could stand Dick hurting me, but not you. Once I found out what he was doing, that was it. He had to go."

"You could have gone to jail for murder."

Sullivan shrugged. "I didn't care. With Dick gone, he wouldn't be around to hurt you anymore. I didn't know things would get fucked up like they did. I thought when you went to live with that foster family, you were going to be all right. I'm sorry I was wrong."

"And I'm sorry I blamed you. I was angry that you never came back. You promised you'd come visit me, but you never did."

Sullivan looked her in the eyes. "That was my fault. I should have never promised you I would visit. You were so upset though, and I didn't think you'd go with the Johnsons unless I promised to come see you again." Sullivan dabbed his eyes with the balled-up tissue. "I truly am sorry I broke my promise. I believed that social worker when she said you would probably forget everything. Somehow, I got it stuck in my mind that it was best not to come back and remind you of it. I'm surprised you didn't forget me."

"I could never forget you, Elmer. You were the one good thing about my childhood."

"I missed you, Emmy. I can't believe how grown up you are."

"Oh, Elmer. I missed you too." Emmy slid over and threw her arms around him. Sullivan squeezed her back, even though he never considered himself a hugger. He made an exception for Emmy, and he didn't want to let her go.

They talked about the few good memories they shared and

caught each other up on where their lives had taken them. Sullivan, who had never been much of a talker, enjoyed every moment. The conversation only stopped when they realized they were hungry, and Sullivan heated the food Isabel had left for him in the refrigerator. His appetite had returned, and there was enough for both of them to eat.

"Please quit that job, Emmy," Sullivan said, placing the empty food container on the coffee table when he finished.

"It's good money. And as vain as it seems, I know I'm beautiful. I got to use my good looks to my advantage."

"Emmy, if it's money you're worried about, don't. I'll take care of you. You can stay here. There's a second bedroom down the hall, and I've got this Airbnb until the end of August. After that, I'll help you find a better place. You don't have to worry about anything now."

"I don't want to be a burden, or for you to feel like I'm taking advantage of you."

"You wouldn't be a burden, and you're not taking advantage of anything. I'm offering. That's my job as the big brother. I took care of you when you were a baby, and I'll take care of you now. You can't say you enjoy taking your clothes off for those filthy men, do you?"

Emmy shook her head. "No."

"So you'll quit?"

She considered it for a moment, then nodded. "I will, but under one condition."

"What's that?"

"You need to take care of yourself. Look at this place. This is no way to live either. I'm pretty good at cleaning. And I cook occasionally. You look like you could use some help with both of that."

Sullivan cracked a smile. "I could definitely use some help."

"You weren't planning on leaving Florida still, were you?

Because I like it here. Florida was a fresh start for me. I don't want to go back to Texas."

"I'm good with staying here."

"I'm sure your girlfriend would like that."

Sullivan's smile fell. Isabel. He thought of the things he'd said to her. Would she even want him back? "I guess I should tell her I'm not moving."

"Is something wrong?" Emmy asked.

"I told her I was moving. She probably thinks I'm a terrible person for breaking up with her."

"I don't believe she thinks that. She came all the way to Saint Petersburg to talk to me. I think she must love you."

"Love? Who would love some sorry fool like me?"

"Me. I love you. And if not love, then I know she really cares about you."

Sullivan groaned. He had acted impulsively, just like he always had. He didn't want to quit the job or leave Florida. And he certainly didn't want to cut Isabel and Miguel out of his life. Why had he said the things he said? "I need to talk to her."

"Why don't you go to her then?"

Outside, thunder rumbled. Another storm was rolling off the coast. Isabel would probably keep the LIV close to home today.

"I don't want to leave you."

"I'll be fine. I've been on my own for a long time. And if your offer still stands, I'd love to move in. I'm staying with a girl at work, and she's a nightmare to live with. I'd rather live with my brother and get to know him a little better. Nothing's more important than family."

"Nothing," Sullivan said, smiling at her.

"Now go find Isabel. Make things right with her. She'll want to see you."

Sullivan rose from the couch and reached for his raincoat. "Okay, I'll go. When did you get to be so wise and mature?"

Emmy shrugged. "I don't know. I guess you and I had to learn life's lessons the hard way."

He took a piece of paper and wrote down some numbers. "This is the key code to this place. Type these four numbers and the bottom button, and the door will unlock."

She walked to the front door and grabbed her purse. "I'll go pack up my things, and I'll be back later tonight. I'm glad we reconnected."

"Me too, Dimples."

Emmy laughed. "You haven't called me that in forever."

Sullivan smiled. "And it's still true. I knew when I saw the girl with dimples on that Facebook page, I had the right Emmy Sullivan."

"Come here, Elm." Emmy wrapped her arms around him, and for the first time in twenty years, he felt as if he had a family again.

TORRES WAS the only one at the Lightning Institute when Sullivan arrived.

"Hey, are you feeling better?" Torres asked.

Sullivan nodded. "Yeah, much. Where's Isabel?"

"You just missed her, but I can track down the LIV."

"Yeah, do that."

Torres clicked around on his computer until he pulled up the LIV's GPS location. "Looks like she's parked at the high school."

"Of course. She always likes to park near the ball field. Thanks."

Sullivan pulled his hood over his head, braced himself for the rain, and hopped into his Jeep parked by the curb.

The rain hadn't reached the school by the time Sullivan

arrived. The LIV was parked next to the soccer field, and there was Isabel on the grass setting up her tripod and camera.

Sullivan pulled up beside the LIV. He rolled down the window. "Izzy."

She turned to look at him, and just as Sullivan was getting out of the car, a bolt of lightning flashed, causing a deafening clap of thunder.

Sullivan watched in horror as Isabel collapsed to the ground.

25

"My girlfriend was struck by lightning!" Sullivan yelled into his phone as he ran to Isabel, heart racing. He tossed his phone on the ground and knelt down next to a motionless Isabel. When he gently tapped her, she didn't respond.

"What's your location?" asked the operator on speaker phone.

"Poquito Beach High. The parking lot near the soccer field."

"Is she breathing?"

He put his face next to her nose and mouth, but didn't feel her breath or hear any breathing sounds. "No, she's not breathing! Shit!"

"Do you know CPR?"

"Yeah, starting it now." He'd never given CPR to anyone before, but immediately flew into action and started chest compressions. For once, he was grateful that Ryder made him take a CPR course, even though he grumbled about it at the time.

"Come on, Izzy!" Sullivan yelled. "You can't die! Miguel needs you."

And so did he.

"Stay on the line, sir. We're sending an ambulance now. Perform CPR for two minutes and check again for signs of breathing."

As he pressed her chest, Isabel remained lifeless. She couldn't die, not when he'd just realized how much she meant to him. How in the world had this woman, who irritated him to no end when he first met her, become so important to him?

He checked for signs of breathing, detected nothing, and continued the life-saving measures. "Come on!"

The rain started now, followed by a rumble of thunder. Sullivan cursed. His raincoat hood had fallen down, and his hair was soaked. He didn't care that he was wet, but the rain would only increase Isabel's risk of hypothermia. Not to mention the threat of more lightning.

After a few terrifying moments, her chest began to rise and fall, and relief flooded Sullivan. He stopped the compressions. "She's breathing." Thank God, she was breathing again.

"That's good," said the operator. "Does she have any other injuries?"

Sullivan hadn't thought to look for injuries, his priority being to start her heart and lungs back. He now noticed that her shoe had been blown off, and she had burn marks on her leg. The earth was scorched where the impact was made. He described it all to the operator.

"Don't move her in case she has neck injuries from her fall. The ambulance will be there shortly."

He heard the sirens at that moment, and out of the corner of his eye, spotted the fire truck pulling into the school's parking lot. The station was thankfully just down the street, and though it had only taken five minutes for help to arrive, it had felt much longer than that.

Sullivan moved out of the way to let the professionals take over. As they checked her vitals, he stood off to the side, dripping wet with a pain developing behind his eye. The paramedics covered Isabel with a blanket to keep her warm. Sullivan was right to be worried about hypothermia. Or maybe she'd gone into shock.

"Is she going to be okay?" he asked.

One firefighter gave him a sympathetic look. "We'll do everything we can."

Sullivan was pretty sure that meant they didn't know if she would make it.

They loaded Isabel into the back of the vehicle on a stretcher. Sullivan ran to his Jeep, the door still wide open, and got behind the wheel to follow it.

IT HAD BEEN a frantic ten minute drive to the hospital. The whole time, all Sullivan could think about was Isabel on the ground and not breathing. Thank God he'd arrived when he had. What would have happened if he hadn't tracked her down? The parking lot had been empty, as school was out for the summer. By the time anyone else would have found her, it would have been too late.

He called Torres on the way, and by the time he reached the emergency room, most of Isabel's family was there.

"What happened, Sullivan?" a frantic Carlita asked, her eyes red from crying.

"She was outside setting up her camera. Next thing I knew, lightning struck, and she was on the ground unconscious. I did CPR and called 911."

Carlita threw her arms around him and sobbed into his chest. "Thank God you were there."

Sullivan held Carlita and let her cry. "She'll be fine," he said. "Isabel's a tough cookie. Nothing can bring her down."

Whatever he was saying, it seemed to comfort Carlita, for

she finally moved out of his arms and her tears reduced to sniffles. Sullivan just wished he could believe it all himself.

"You're right. My Isabel will be just fine. She's a fighter. I will pray now."

Someone tapped his hip, and Sullivan looked down to see a frightened Miguel. "Is Mamá going to be okay?"

Sullivan took the boy's hand and led him to the couch. "The doctors are treating her right now. We got her to the hospital in a hurry, so I'm sure they'll fix her right up."

If only he could be sure that what he was saying was true, he could relax. But no one could be sure. People died from lightning strikes all the time. He could not lose Isabel, not when he'd finally realized how much she and Miguel meant to him.

Miguel cuddled up next to Sullivan, and it felt natural to put his arms around the boy to comfort him. "She'll be fine."

He kissed the boy on top of his head, and all they could do now was wait.

IT FELT like hours had passed, but Sullivan couldn't be sure. A doctor came and spoke to the family. Miguel had fallen asleep, and Sullivan, not wanting to wake the boy, remained in his seat. He was desperate for answers as the family crowded around the doctor in scrubs.

After he left, Torres headed his way.

Sullivan felt his stomach clench as he tried to read the older man's expression. Was it good news? Bad news?

"How is she?" Sullivan asked.

Torres looked at Miguel, then at Sullivan. "She's in surgery to treat the burns on her body. The doctors are putting her into a medically induced coma. They say her body needs to heal, and this will be the best way for her to recover."

"And do they expect her to make a full recovery?" Sullivan had to know.

Torres had a cautious look about him, as if he wasn't sure. "The doctor seemed hopeful, but it's still touch and go."

Not exactly the answer Sullivan had been hoping for.

Miguel popped his head up and opened his eyes. "Is Mamá better?"

"The doctor says she needs to rest at the hospital for a few days. She's sleeping now."

Paulina tapped Sullivan on the shoulder. "Hey, Ricardo and I can take Miguel to our place."

"No, Tía!" Miguel said. "I want to stay with Mr. Sullivan." Miguel reached for a fistful of Sullivan's shirt and clamped on. Sullivan was surprised. Why did the kid want to stay with him? Surely, he'd rather be with his family.

Paulina knelt down. "Miguel, your mamá is going to be at the hospital for a while. We can't stay here in this waiting room all night. Let me and Tío Ricardo take you home."

Miguel looked across the room. "But Abuela is staying. And Mr. Sullivan is staying. Aren't you?" Miguel looked up at Sullivan with his big brown eyes.

"I don't want to go anywhere until your mom wakes up, but your aunt is right. It'll be best if you go home. How about I stay here, and the moment she wakes up, I'll let you know?"

Miguel rubbed his eyes and nodded. "You promise?"

"Cross my heart," Sullivan said. "Now go with your aunt. Get some rest. That's what your mama would want."

Miguel stood and threw his arms around him. "Bye, Mr. Sullivan. Tell Mamá I love her when she wakes up, okay?"

Sullivan gave Miguel a pat on the back. "I will. She'll be home before you know it."

He just hoped and prayed that she would.

~

HE WASN'T SMOKING ANYMORE, but the cigarettes from yesterday made his urges return. Sullivan excused himself to go pace and chew some nicotine gum. When he checked his phone, he realized he had a missed call from Emmy.

Shit. He'd forgotten she was coming back to his place tonight, and the message she left asked where he was. He hadn't expected to spend his evening in the emergency room.

He dialed her back, and when he got her voicemail, left a quick message to tell her what happened.

His next call was to Ryder, who had left a few voicemails and texts as well. Sullivan had ignored every one of them. But now, he had to admit, he could really use a friend.

Ryder picked up the phone right away. "Sully. Glad to finally hear from you. Are you okay?"

"Is-Isabel." His voice cracked, and right there outside the emergency room, Sullivan lost his composure. He used to be embarrassed to cry in front of anyone, but years of holding his emotions inside never did him any favors.

"What's going on?" Ryder asked.

Sullivan held it together long enough to explain what had happened.

"I'm an idiot. If I hadn't pushed her away, maybe we would have been somewhere else. She wouldn't have been out on that soccer field. And now I might lose her."

"She could have been struck anywhere. The important thing is that you were there, and you got her the help she needs. I have faith she'll pull through this."

The sliding glass doors opened, and Torres motioned for Sullivan to come inside.

Sullivan waved to Torres. "I got to go," he said to Ryder. "I think there's an update on Isabel."

"Call me later, and I'll be praying for her."

"Thanks, Ryder." Sullivan hung up, then followed Torres inside.

Back in the ER, the doctor in navy blue scrubs was back, and Carlita was talking to him. His stomach roiled as he hurried over, eager for an update.

Carlita turned to him and smiled. "She's in the ICU. We can go see her now."

"But one at a time," the doctor said. "And only for a few minutes."

Carlita gave Sullivan a weak smile. "Would you like to go first?"

Sullivan was eager to see her, but felt it wasn't his right to be first. Hell, he wasn't even family, so maybe they'd say he couldn't see her. Wasn't that the rule for hospitals? "No, you should go. I'll wait out here."

Carlita nodded, then followed the doctor behind the double doors.

Sullivan went back to the faded couch in the lobby and sank down on the cushion. Torres joined him.

"She's a fighter, our Isabel," Torres said. "She'll be just fine."

Sullivan thought there was a hint of doubt in his voice, but Sullivan didn't argue. He wanted to believe Isabel would be okay.

"Did she ever tell you about the time she fell out of the tree?"

"No."

"She was trying to get a picture of a bird. Her papá had given her a camera for her birthday. I think she was about eight or nine. We'd been inside while the children were playing, and unaware that Isabel had climbed the tree in the backyard. The next thing we knew, Paulina came running in saying Isabel had fallen. She was unconscious, and we were all terrified that she was seriously injured. Turned out to be just a concussion, thankfully. The next time, Miguel told her to use the camera's zoom feature." He ended the story with a smile, and Sullivan smiled back.

"She's always out there with that camera," Sullivan said. "I warned her it could be dangerous. That storm was too close."

"Isabel knows that, but she's a little headstrong. It's a risk us meteorologists take sometimes when we chase storms, isn't it?"

Sullivan nodded. "Yeah. I know I've gotten too close to a tornado a time or two."

They waited in silence, and a short while later, Carlita emerged from the back.

Sullivan nodded at Torres. "You go see her."

"Why don't you go next?"

"Nah, I know I'm not family." But he cared for Isabel like she was.

"I'll go in, and then you can go after."

Torres left, and Carlita took his place on the couch.

"How is she?" Sullivan asked.

"She's so pale," Carlita said. "And all those machines."

Sullivan saw her chin quiver. He wanted to say some words of comfort, but Carlita's lips moved, mouthing what Sullivan assumed must be a prayer. In her hand, she held a string of rosary beads. Sullivan remembered the crucifix hanging on Isabel's wall, and sometimes, he noticed the cross necklace she wore. Sullivan had never been a praying man, and the only time he attended church was when his mother was sober, which wasn't often. But if praying to God would somehow help Isabel recover, then Sullivan was willing to try it.

"How does that work?" he asked, pointing to the beads when she appeared to be finished praying.

Carlita seemed happy to explain it to him, and Sullivan felt it was a distraction for both of them while he waited to see Isabel.

Finally, Torres came back to the lobby. "You can see her now," he said. "It's the first room on the left, right through those doors."

As Sullivan stood, Carlita reached out and touched his arm.

"Talk to her. I think she can hear us, and I'm sure she would like to hear your voice."

He nodded, then headed to the back.

In the ICU, Isabel lay in bed, hooked up to various beeping monitors and machines. Her burns had been bandaged up, and a tube was shoved down her throat.

"Just a few minutes," said the nurse.

Sullivan nodded, then headed inside. He took the wheeled seat next to her bed and reached for her hand. There was an IV attached to her hand, so Sullivan was careful not to disturb anything.

Even though Carlita thought she could hear him, Sullivan doubted it. And even if she could hear him, she probably wouldn't remember once she awoke. If she woke up. God, he hoped she would. But just in case, he would say a few words.

"Do you know how scared I was?" he asked, though he knew she couldn't respond. "Izzy, when I saw you fall to the ground, I felt like it was over. I never met anyone quite like you, and damn it, I fell in love with you. So you can't die on me, okay? You better live. I want to find out what this thing is between us."

She didn't respond. The only sound was the beeping machine.

"You have to get better," he said to her. "Your family is out there waiting for you to wake up, but the doctor says you have to rest for a few days. I suppose it's for the best. Don't worry about Miguel. He's with your sister, and I'll help too if I'm needed. You just concentrate on getting better. Because that little boy needs you. And I need you, too."

Sullivan squeezed her hand and stared at her, playing in his mind the horrifying moment when the lightning struck and Isabel fell to the ground. He didn't want to think about that. He didn't want to think their last conversation was him saying he was leaving her.

"Emmy came to see me. Heard you were responsible for that."

He wanted Isabel to open her eyes. He wanted to tell her how happy he was to be reunited with his sister. But Isabel remained motionless.

"We talked all afternoon. She's going to quit that stripping job and move in with me. I told her I'd pay for whatever she needs, and she can get a decent job. I don't mind her living with me, though that probably means we'll have to be quiet if you stay over. Maybe I could spend the night in your comfortable bed a few nights a week."

He smiled, but Isabel didn't react.

The sliding glass door opened, and a nurse in aqua colored scrubs stepped in. "I'm sorry, sir, but your time is up."

Sullivan nodded. "Just one second." He raised Isabel's hand to his mouth, kissed it, then gently placed it back by her side. "I'll be waiting, and I'll come to the hospital every day and be right here, ready for you when you decide to wake up."

Isabel's eyes remained closed. It was doubtful she heard him, but Sullivan hoped she could at least sense his presence.

26

The next few days were agony. All they could do was wait. Isabel was still in the induced coma, though the doctors said her vitals were improving. It was possible that when she woke up, they could move her out of the ICU.

But until then, all they could do was wait.

Sullivan spent his days with the family in the waiting room. They decided that someone should be at the hospital at all times. That way, if there was a change in Isabel's condition, they would know right away.

Emmy came to the hospital and sat with him. Even though she'd only met Isabel once, she said it saddened her Isabel was injured.

"I keep replaying that afternoon," Sullivan said. "It was you, Emmy. You were the one who told me to go to her. If you hadn't encouraged me to go see her, I might not have been there the moment she got struck."

Emmy reached for his hand and squeezed it. "She'll be okay. The doctors are taking good care of her."

He felt his eyes water. He didn't want to cry. "I just wish she would wake up and be okay."

"She will. Her body needs time to heal. The coma is only medically induced, right?"

"Yeah," Sullivan said. "The doctors are reducing the drugs as her vitals improve. Maybe she'll be out of it soon."

Emmy looked at her watch and frowned. "I'm sorry, Elmer, but I have to go. I have a shift tonight, and I don't want to be late."

Sullivan narrowed his eyes. "I thought you were going to quit that stripping job."

Emmy smiled, bringing out those dimples he cherished. "I did. I meant to tell you, but with everything going on with Isabel, it slipped my mind. I got a job at a clothing store in the mall. It doesn't make as much, but I get to wear pretty clothes, and I get a discount on anything I buy."

Sullivan relaxed. "That sounds great, Dimples."

Emmy touched Sullivan gently on the shoulder. "Call me if Isabel's condition changes."

Sullivan nodded, then watched his little sister leave. If it hadn't been for Isabel, he might have never had this moment. Emmy would still be stripping at the club, and maybe Sullivan would be in Kansas by now.

The couch bounced, and Sullivan looked to see Torres next to him. The older man looked as if he had grown a few more gray hairs, and there were bags under his eyes.

"You look like hell, professor," Sullivan said. "Not that I'm judging. I feel the same."

"I have bad news."

His stomach lurched. "Isabel?"

Torres shook head. "No, not about Isabel, thankfully. It's about the lightning research project. After what happened, the university is shutting the program down."

Sullivan nodded. "I figured that was coming."

"I can't say I blame them. Hell, I blame myself. I shouldn't have let my niece do this kind of work."

"I don't think you could have stopped Isabel from taking the job."

A small smile spread across Torres's face. "You're right. Can't tell Isabel anything. She's headstrong, just like her father. In any case, this affects you too, and I'm sorry. You can put me down as a job reference, and I'll do whatever I can to get new employment lined up for you."

"Thanks, but I'm not concerned about the job right now. The only thing I care about is Isabel. I've had a lot of time to think these past few days, and I can't live without her. I'm in love with your niece. Can you believe that? Never in my life have I been in love."

Torres grinned. "I knew you two would get along. I didn't know it would work out that well, but damn, my matchmaking skills were on point."

Sullivan knitted his eyebrows. "You mean... you purposely wanted us to work together?"

Torres shrugged. "I didn't know you'd become a couple, though that was a happy coincidence. I just thought you'd form a friendship over your shared love of thunderstorms. You've always been a loner. I figured you could use another friend other than Ryder."

Sullivan smiled. "Well, you were right. We're a good match. I just wish I'd told her how I felt about her before..."

Isabel's doctor emerged from the back. Sullivan and the Torres family waited with bated breath for the doctor's update.

"Well?" Carlita asked. "How is she?"

The doctor smiled. "She's awake."

~

Sullivan paced outside the hall. After three days of being in a coma, Isabel was awake. Now, it was agony as he waited for his turn to see her.

Isabel had been moved to a private room, which was a relief. It meant the doctors felt like her condition was improving, and Sullivan hoped she'd be able to go home soon. According to what he read, she might have a long recovery ahead, but Sullivan would be there to help her.

Finally, the door to Isabel's room opened, and Carlita stepped out into the hall. "Paulina is bringing Miguel. In the meantime, she'd like to see you."

Carlita patted his arm as he walked through the door. There in the bed was Isabel. She smiled when she saw Sullivan. She looked tired, but beautiful.

"I'm so glad you didn't leave," Isabel said in a hoarse voice. "Ugh, sorry. That tube did a number on my throat." She reached for the water on the table, and Sullivan held the cup for her while she sipped through the straw.

Once she was done, Sullivan put the cup back, then settled into the chair next to her bed. "Izzy, I've told you not to get out of the vehicle," he said, trying to keep his tone light.

Isabel smiled. "I know, I know. I live on the edge, and I paid for it." She nodded toward her bandaged leg. "Trust me, I won't be doing that again."

"Do you know how scared I was? When I saw you go down, I thought... I thought I'd lost you for good." His voice cracked, but Sullivan didn't care. Let her see him cry. He was relieved to see her alive.

"What happened? I don't remember."

"You were at the high school. Emmy said I should make things right with you, and Torres told me where to find you."

"Emmy? You spoke to your sister?"

Sullivan smiled. "Yeah, thanks to you. She told me you stopped by to have a chat with her. Whatever you said, you convinced her to reconnect with me. So we talked, and when I told her how I'd left things with us, she urged me to make up with you. I'm so glad your uncle put a GPS on the LIV. I was there when it happened."

Isabel frowned. "A bolt from the blue."

"Well, the skies were kind of gray, but yeah, the storm must have been about three miles away. That lightning bolt found you."

"Mamá said you saved my life."

Sullivan shrugged. "The doctors did most of the work."

She reached out and touched his hand. "Don't be modest. You saved me, Sullivan. Thank you."

"I've been a fool. I'm sorry I told you I was going back to Kansas. Don't know where my head was. The truth is, I don't want to leave. I want to stay here with you. If, you know, you feel like putting up with me."

The corner of her lip turned upwards. "I do. As long as you give up the cigarettes."

Sullivan chuckled. "After that last pack, I quit again. Nothing but gum and the patch for me now. I want to be the kind of man you can be proud of."

"Don't doubt for a minute that you aren't. You're a good man, Elmer Sullivan."

"How can you not be upset with me? I was going to leave you."

"I wasn't upset. I was worried. You were depressed, and I knew you weren't thinking clearly. And I forgive you."

Isabel yawned then, and Sullivan realized she needed rest. "I should let you sleep."

"Sleep? No way. I slept for three days. Isn't that enough?" She laughed.

"I guess so. I just don't want you to overdo it. We almost lost you. You know your heart actually stopped."

Isabel's expression turned serious. "I know. You want to

know something? I think I heard my papá's voice. He said it wasn't my time to go. And he's right. Miguel needs his mother, and I think you need me too."

"I do."

"Good, I'm glad," she said, grinning.

"You're going to hurt your face with all that smiling," he said.

"I could say the same for you. I bet those face muscles have never gotten this much of a workout. I guess I can't call you Mr. Grumpy anymore. Or Elmer, for that matter, since you saved my life and all. I only called you by your first name because I knew you hated it."

"I called you Izzy for the same reason. I'm sorry, but sometimes, I slip up and still call you that."

"I'll tell you what—you, and only you, can call me Izzy."

Sullivan nodded. "All right. And you can call me Elmer. But you have to promise only to do that in private."

Isabel laughed. "I promise. Actually, I think I'll just call you Sully."

"I love you, Izzy." It was the first time he'd ever said those words to a woman, and it felt good to say them.

"I love you too, Sully. Now, aren't you going to kiss me?"

Sullivan grinned. "Damn straight I am."

EPILOGUE

CHRISTMAS EVE

Sullivan looked around Isabel's living room and saw the presents under the glowing tree. He still called it Isabel's place, even though technically he'd moved in with her a few months ago.

Sullivan never experienced a real Christmas with family. Growing up, they never had presents or a tree, and their mother spent her paycheck on the things she wanted. The only nice holidays he had were the ones he'd spent with Ryder and his family, but it was never the same. Sullivan always felt like an outsider looking in.

This year was different.

For the first time in twenty years, he was spending Christmas with his sister. Over the past few months, they'd gotten to know each other again, and were just as close as they'd ever been. Their relationship was different with Emmy all grown up, but they still enjoyed watching lightning together. He'd take her, Isabel, and Miguel out in his Jeep to chase storms. Emmy had even decided to go back to school to get her GED.

"Maybe I'll be a meteorologist like you one day and chase

storms," she had said.

"Afraid to disappoint you, Dimples, but most of the time, being a meteorologist is sitting in front of a desk looking at weather maps." He missed being out in the LIV, and the university had no plans to revive the lightning research program. But it was fine. Sullivan didn't mind his new job. He was working again as an aviation meteorologist, but he had better coworkers this time around. Or maybe he just got along better with people nowadays. In any case, he was happier.

Isabel had a new job too. Her uncle brought her on as his teaching assistant. So far, Isabel liked it, and it gave her a chance to see if teaching meteorology was something she would enjoy. Maybe when Torres finally decided to retire, Isabel would be a shoo-in for his position.

This year was also different in another way. He and Isabel had grown closer in the months after her accident. Not only was it the first time he'd ever lived with a woman, but it was the first time he'd entertained thoughts of marriage. His heart raced as he felt for the ring box in his pocket. All day long, he'd been working up the courage to give it to her. Maybe when Miguel went to bed, he would.

Isabel and Miguel came out of the kitchen holding a plate.

"Cookies for Santa?" Sullivan asked.

"Yep," Miguel said. "And sugar-free, because Santa is probably diabetic too."

Sullivan laughed. "Yep, probably."

Isabel sat next to him and offered him the plate. "They're actually really tasty. Want to try one?"

Sullivan had his doubts about a sugar-free cookie being any good, but Isabel had perfected the art of making sugarless food flavorful for Miguel. He reached for one of the smaller cookies and took a tentative bite. A burst of peanut butter touched his taste buds, and Sullivan wouldn't have known they were made with a sugar substitute if he hadn't been told. He nodded in approval. "Peanut butter cookies. These are good."

"We made a bunch," Miguel said. "We can save some for Emmy tomorrow."

Sullivan popped the rest of the cookie into his mouth. "No, Emmy can't have these. She's allergic to peanuts."

"Oh," Miguel said, his mouth full of cookies.

"Don't worry," Isabel said. "I can make different cookies. You can have one more, and then it's bedtime, *nene*. The sooner you fall asleep, the sooner it'll be Christmas."

Miguel looked at the tree. "Can I open a present now? Just one. Please?"

Isabel considered it, then finally relented. "Okay, just one. And I get to pick which present. Sully, will you hand me that small green package?"

Sullivan reached under the tree and pulled out the small box. He knew what was inside because he was with Isabel when she wrapped it. It was one of those squishy toys that cost almost ten dollars. In his day, he'd been excited about a bouncy ball from the quarter vending machine.

Miguel tore off the wrapping paper and squealed when he saw what it was. "A dog squishy!"

"Another one to add to your collection," Isabel said.

"And it looks like Juan's dog. I hope Santa will bring me a dog."

Isabel glanced at Sullivan and smiled, but only for a moment. They didn't want to let on to Miguel what Santa had planned for him.

Miguel yawned, and Isabel gathered the torn wrapping paper from the floor. "Well, *nene*, it's time for bed. Say good-night to Sully."

"Goodnight, Sully." The child wrapped his arms around Sullivan's neck, a gesture that Sullivan had grown used to.

"Goodnight, kid."

Miguel pulled away and looked into his eyes. "Don't eat all the cookies. Leave some for Santa."

Sullivan chuckled. "I'll do my best."

Isabel leaned into Sullivan, and he could feel her hot breath in his ear. "Be right back, and then we can go to bed." She grinned at him as she followed Miguel to his room.

Once alone, Sullivan rose from the couch and paced. He would not chicken out. Elmer Sullivan never chickened out. And it was just a ring, for crying out loud. Why was he so nervous?

From Miguel's bedroom, she could hear Isabel reading a book in Spanish. While she was occupied, Sullivan took the ring out of the box. If someone had told him last year he'd be holding an engagement ring, he wouldn't have believed them. Sullivan never intended to be a married man, but here he was, pacing in the living room with a diamond ring.

The light switched off in Miguel's room, and Sullivan shoved the ring box back into his pocket.

"You all right?" Isabel asked.

Sullivan put on a smile. "Yeah, I'm fine. Just waiting for you." He headed back to the couch. "Is he asleep?"

Isabel nodded. "Out like a light. Which is perfect, because Ricardo is going to bring over the puppy at ten. Do you think he'll be quiet until morning?"

Sullivan gave Isabel a pointed look. "Izzy, hell no. It's a dog. It'll bark. If the puppy wakes Miguel up, just tell him that Santa came early."

Isabel giggled. "Good idea. Miguel's going to love him."

Sullivan picked out the dog—an affectionate yellow lab. Having a pet was something he never got to experience as a child. "Every kid should have a pet. Have to admit, I'm almost as excited as Miguel to have a dog."

Isabel joined him on the couch. Her hand touched his neck, and her fingernails lightly scratched the skin under his scalp.

"It's eight, so, you know, we have some time before Ricardo gets here. If you want." Isabel smiled and wiggled her eyebrows.

He knew that look in her eyes. She wanted to go to bed. But if he didn't do this now, he'd miss his chance tonight. "Maybe later. I want to give you your Christmas present now. I'd rather do this when we're alone. It's sort of... private."

"Oh?" A grin spread across her face as she put her arms around him. "What did you get me? Some sexy piece of lingerie or something?"

"No, but I'll file that idea away for Valentine's Day."

"If it's not something sexy, what is it?"

Sullivan's heart raced, feeling himself on the brink of an anxiety attack. But he had to do this. He reached into his pocket and pulled out the black box. Isabel's eyes widened as he placed it into her palm. "Open it."

"Jewelry?" She opened the box and gasped at the diamond ring inside. "*Dios mio.*"

"It's, uh, you know. I was just thinking that if you wanted to, we could make this thing official."

Isabel looked up at him. "Are you asking me to marry you?"

Sullivan nodded. "I'm not being presumptuous, am I? I never thought I'd want to get married, but the thought of us not being together makes me miserable. So, what do you say? You gonna leave a guy hanging?"

Isabel handed him back the ring box, and Sullivan's stomach clenched. Was she rejecting him?

"Why don't you officially ask me?" she said with a teasing smile.

At least it didn't appear she would say no. But hell, no one ever called him a romantic. He sighed. "Jeez, you're going to make me get down on one knee?"

Isabel laughed. "Maybe."

With a grunt, Sullivan got off the couch and got on his knee. Another thing he never thought he'd do, but for Isabel, he'd do anything. He took the diamond ring out of the box and held it up for Isabel to see. "Isabel Torres Fuentes, will you marry me?"

Isabel nodded. "Yes, I'll marry you." She held out her hand for Sullivan to slip the ring on her finger.

"Can I get off the floor now?"

"Only if you kiss me." She reached for the collar of his shirt, pulled Sullivan closer, and pressed her lips against his.

WANT MORE?

The T-Rex is back! Get ready to join storm chaser Austin Jones as he joins his buddy Ryder for an exciting tornado chasing documentary.

INTO THE STORM, book four of the Storm Series, coming next!

AUTHOR'S NOTE

I'm a weather geek, but I'm by no means an expert in meteorology. If I made any errors in this novel, please forgive me.

The idea for this story came from the late storm chaser Tim Samaras. When he wasn't chasing tornadoes, he photographed lightning with a giant slow motion camera he hauled around in a truck, also called the Lightning Intercept Vehicle. Since his passing, I don't know if any lightning research like this is being done again, so I wrote about a couple of meteorologists chasing lightning storms, and in a fictional sense, continuing Tim's work.

I'd also like to add that I don't speak Spanish, and though I have researched for accuracy, I apologize if something got messed up in translation! I relied heavily on the internet to help me know some common terms of endearment, as well as common insults, in the Spanish language.

If you liked this story, please consider giving it a review or star rating, as it helps other readers find my books.

ACKNOWLEDGMENTS

Writing this book and getting it ready for publication has been a journey, and I couldn't have done it without the help of a few dear friends.

Jenifer, thank you for being my writing buddy and giving me your honest feedback when you read the first version of this story. You reminded me to give Sullivan a few "hero moments," and he is truly a better guy thanks to your advice!

Rochelle, thanks for your encouragement and for helping me make Sullivan less of a curmudgeon! Also, thanks for giving me a fun word to call him!

Vania, I can't thank you enough for all your help with the cover design of this book. I had the hardest time finding a face for Sullivan, and I think you sensed that! I didn't even need to ask—you just knew! I'm so grateful to have a friend who is good at these types of things.

To everyone else who helped me as I worked on this story, thank you for your support!

ALSO BY MELODY LOOMIS

Storm Series

Thrill of the Chase

When the Ice Melts

Young Adult Fiction

One Big Mess

Visit melodyloomis.com for updates on future books.

Made in the USA
Columbia, SC
05 August 2024

39636705R00205